Retu

This book may be kept

AYS

THREE NOVELS BY
RONALD FIRBANK

RONALD FIRBANK
from a pastel by Charles Shannon, R.A.

Ronald Firbank

THREE NOVELS

VAINGLORY

INCLINATIONS

CAPRICE

With an introduction by
ERNEST JONES

A New Directions Book

Published by James Laughlin, Norfolk, Connecticut,
by arrangement with Coward, McCann, Inc.

Printed in Great Britain

Contents

INTRODUCTION

BY ERNEST JONES

RONALD FIRBANK is a better and a more serious writer than it has ever been fashionable to suppose. The tiresome adulation of the claque which adores his *fin-de-siècle* wickedness and the grim incomprehension of the excessively serious have always obscured his real merits. The Firbank legend, for which Firbank himself was largely responsible, was constructed so carefully that even a quarter of a century after his death it is difficult to disentangle the artist from the delicate posturer who tried so hard—and with indifferent success—to astonish the bourgeoisie. Between 1915 and 1926, when his books were being published, the English novel seemed set for ever in the pattern of realism and a modified naturalism. Firbank's writing lacked the obvious purposefulness and the impressive documentation which Wells, Galsworthy, Bennett and Moore were bringing to the composition of seemingly indestructible fiction. If Forster, Conrad and Lawrence deviated from this pattern in ways unpopular or disturbing, still they were serious as Firbank, to judge by the surface of his writing, was not. To-day, when the formulas of realism-cum-naturalism which once seemed so inexhaustibly fruitful produce only apples of Sodom, Firbank is a green bay tree. His rococo palaces turn out to have been more solidly constructed than the sedate family mansions of the Georgians and their lower middle-class water-closets. The tradition of the contemporary novel now closest to our sensibility is that established by Joyce and Virginia Woolf. To this tradition, in his own eccentric fashion, Firbank belongs.

His style, his settings, and the themes which recur in his work can be accounted for, so far as such accounting is ever possible, by his background. Sociologically he belongs to the history of sensitive young men who escape from the materialism which has brought money into the family straight into the materialism of the æsthete and the social snob. It is a flight likely to end in dilettantism, or, worse, in alcoholism and nervous disorders. Firbank encountered these catastrophes and, as an artist, survived them. Every printed story about him, whether it appears in I. K. Fletcher's memoir, or in the recollections of Sir Osbert Sitwell or Vyvyan Holland or Lord Berners—all sympathetic observers— is like every other story, testimony of his charm, his affectation, and his private distress. But he did not succumb to the luxury, the ennui, and the neuroses which beset him.

His enterprising and illiterate north-of-England grandfather had made a fortune in contracting; his father married into the gentry, was created a baronet, and lost money; the son, spoiled by a mother whom he idolized, lived variously in the pre-1914 society of the Café Royal, in seclusion, during the War, at Oxford, and abroad. Until the last ten years of his life, when, for all his flittings-about, he settled himself earnestly to becoming a writer, he was engaged in a seemingly sterile pursuit of the amusing and the beautiful. His entire career recalls that of Proust: the spoiled mother's darling, the carefully-ordered *décor* which he carried about on his travels, the inflexible pursuit of rarefied pleasures, the early dabblings in authorship (Firbank published in 1905, when he was only nineteen, a mediocre little pamphlet). And then there is the mature work, impossible but for the kind of existence he had led, of his last decade. Out of sensuality, idleness, dissipation and buffoonery he created exquisite art.

Once he had really started to work, his books appeared in rapid succession: *Vainglory* (1915), *Inclinations* (1916), *Caprice* (1917), *Valmouth* (1918), *The Princess Zoubaroff* (1920), *Santal* (1921), *The Flower Beneath the Foot* (1923), *Prancing Nigger* (1924), *Concerning the Eccentricities of Cardinal Pirelli* (1926). *The Artificial Princess*, written shortly before 1915, was published posthumously in 1934.

The settings of the novels record his flight from the world of his father and grandfather into the refinements of a new-found-land—a Haiti in which the climate does not oppress, a glamorous Spain, " some imaginary Vienna " (his own term), populated by beautiful aristocrats upon whom, like Pater's Mona Lisa, all the ends of the world are come. Their weariness is part of their fascination. They all suffer from what, in the eighteenth century, the French designated as the specific English malady—ennui. Firbank is the first novelist to celebrate that fragmented, corrupt and anarchic milieu known to-day as café society. He adored the aristocracy, but the aristocracy he created is *parvenu*. It has no deeply-established roots in land or money or manners, but resembles that aristocracy of the circus described by Djuna Barnes in *Nightwood*. Its chief prerogative is eccentric behaviour; it is dominated by women, and they, in turn, are dominated by chic.

In transforming his bedazzlement into the permanence of fiction Firbank sometimes succeeded in spite of himself. He occasionally affected a fine carelessness about art. Often his prose is delightfully easy, but sometimes it sounds as if it were meant to be easy. The history of ennui among the English is the history of a fashionable pose which experience of the world is constantly transforming into the most painful reality. The ennui of *Vainglory* and *Inclinations* is, occasionally, simply fashionable; that of the later novels, particularly of *The Flower Beneath the Foot*, is realized artistically. Sex, for Firbank, was always a matter for comedy; but just as in life his infantilism betrayed him into preposterous affectation, in his novels the comedy of sex is too frequently marred by an almost obsessional bravado and schoolboy snickering. The world of his fiction, with its international élite and its splendid palaces, is a Nirvana in which homosexuals are the ultimate chic, and in which, as in *Le Temps Retrouvé*, almost everyone turns out to be at least bi-sexual. Even in his own time he was old-fashioned in his toyings with the ceremonial of Rome, his æsthetic interest in evil, " if for no other purpose, to add colour to life," and a dandyism which would have revolted Baudelaire.

But—and this fact saved him always—he was no more self-deceived or diverted, as an artist, by his predilections than he was by the world he chose to create. There is always a tough core of common sense to his dallyings with the trivial; the wit flicks even those enchanting and world-weary figures he most loves; he merely found the substance of his art in the fantastic behaviour of the inhabitants of a fantastic milieu. If, in *Caprice*, he shares some of his heroine's excitement over the London scene to which she has fled from the cathedral close, he can also see its pretensions:

" And how does Mrs. Smee? "
" So-so."
" One never sees her now."
" There she sits all day, reading Russian novels. Talk of gloom! "
" Really? "
" Oh, it is! "
" Well . . . I'm fond of thoughtful, theosophical reading, too, Mr. Smee," Mrs. Sixsmith said. " Madame Blavatsky and Mrs. Annie Besant are both favourites with me."

Or if, like several of his heroines, he was fascinated

with Rome, a sense of the incongruous was always calling him back to a point from which such fascination appeared slightly absurd. A conversation during a thunderstorm in *Valmouth* illustrates this gambit perfectly—a compound of religious trappings, artistic arrangement, and the masking of real concern in a giggle:

> "Let us go," Mrs. Thoroughfare said in a slightly unsteady voice, "shall we both, and confess?"
> "Confess!"
> "Father's in Nuestra now."
> "My dear, in my opinion, the lightning's so much more ghastly through the stained-glass windows!"

For all the occasional snickering, the deflating process is also apparent in his treatment of homosexuality. With the exception of Proust, Firbank is the one serious novelist of the twentieth century, overtly concerned with homosexuality, who avoids the bathos which mars even *Les Faux-Monnayeurs*. To him it is simply one more subject for comedy. Aside from the extensive account of the passion of Miss Geraldine O'Brookamore for Miss Mabel Collins in *Inclinations*, it appears chiefly in the form of omnipresent hints and jokes. In life he feared and disliked women, his mother excepted; in his fiction his entirely feminine sensibility concerned itself far more with women than with men. He is perfectly at home with their talk, their affairs, their clothes. Except for Cardinal Pirelli, half man, half woman, his heroes are perfunctorily drawn or deliberately muted. They are always beautiful, ruthless in the pursuit of pleasure, irresponsible and perverse. Because he feels more deeply about them, he never writes about men as freely as he writes about women.

He was afraid of feeling, a fear which seriously limited the range of his fiction, but which is directly responsible for his delightful ironies and flippancies. "His work," says a character in *Vainglory*, describing

xi

a novelist clearly meant to be Firbank, " calls to mind a frieze with figures of varying heights trotting all the same way. If one should by chance turn about it's usually merely to stare or to sneer or to make a grimace. Only occasionally his figures care to beckon. And they seldom really touch." They do not " touch " as does the passion which sometimes breaks so wonderfully through the comic mask in Molière or even in Congreve. Sex is amusing, but passion is at once a stimulant and a drug, always fatal to the addict. Those who reveal it are rejected, like Thetis Tooke in *Valmouth* or Laura in *The Flower Beneath the Foot.* Thetis, who is all feeling, becomes comic as she prepares to drown herself:

> " I shall remove my hat, I think," she cogitated. " It would be a sin indeed to spoil such expensive plumes. . . . It's not perhaps a headpiece that would become every one; —and I can't say I'm sorry! "

The famous twentieth chapter of *Inclinations*, in which Miss O'Brookamore laments the defection of the beloved, is comic and malicious:

> " Mabel! Mabel! Mabel! Mabel! Mabel! Mabel! Mabel! Mabel! "

And there is real venom in the picture, in *Valmouth*, of the ageing Lady Parvula de Panzoust in impassioned pursuit of the reluctant dairyman.

Occasionally in the later novels feeling is not resolved in comedy. Unlike most of his contemporaries, Firbank did not have any explicit messages. Life is sad, human beings suffer, the mask always conceals anguish. These are the conditions of life even in his luxurious world. There is nothing funny about Laura's anguish when she is forsaken by Yousef, or about the unhappiness of Miami Mouth. For all the scandal of his end, there is even a triumphant, if perverse, moral grandeur in the death of Cardinal Pirelli:

Now that the ache of life, with its fevers, passions, doubts, its routine, vulgarity, and boredom, was over, his serene, unclouded face was a marvelment to behold. Very great distinction and sweetness was visible there, together with much nobility, and love, all magnified and commingled.

Firbank's prose mirrors clearly the society with which he was preoccupied, his distrust of feeling, and the ironic habit of mind which replaced feeling. It has some obvious literary origins. As a young man he had read extensively in Gautier, Verlaine, and Huysmans, in Pater and in Wilde. I. K. Fletcher says that his first published piece, *Odette D'Antrevernes*, was influenced by his readings in Maeterlinck; in content it is a pastiche from Francis Jammes. He was " excessively well-read," says Sir Osbert Sitwell, in the eighteenth-century memoirs of every European country. But any account of the influences to which he so rapturously gave himself up must shift to the visual arts; there are, all through his novels, scenes which might be descriptions of Beardsley drawings or of the fragile beauties of Conder fans; there are numerous direct references to Italian painting. Here is Miss Compostella in *Vainglory*:

A lady whose face looked worn and withered through love, wearing a black gauze gown, looped like a figure from the Primavera, made her way mistilty into the room.

Again:

. . . Miss Compostella swept by them, in some jewelled hades of her own.

His careful selection and ordering of detail, his reliance on evocation and juxtaposition, are reminiscent of the methods of the Impressionists. Mrs. Hurstpierpoint's fête for the centenarians of Valmouth is described in such terms and recreates wonderfully that crowded, complex scene:

There uprose a jargon of voices:
" Heroin."
" Adorable simplicity."

"What could anyone find to admire in such a shelving profile?"

"We reckon a duck here of two or three and twenty not so old. And a spring chicken *anything to fourteen*."

"My husband had no amorous energy whatsoever; which just suited me, of course."

"I suppose when there's no more room for another crow's-foot, one attains a sort of peace?"

"I once said to Doctor Fothergill, a clergyman of Oxford and a great friend of mine, 'Doctor,' I said, 'oh, if only you could see my——'"

"*Elle était jolie! Mais jolie! . . . C'était une si belle brune . . .!*"

"Cruelly lonely."

"Leery. . . ."

"Calumny."

"People look like pearls, dear, beneath your wonderful trees."

This technique has been so widely imitated—by way of Joyce and Virginia Woolf and not of Firbank, who appears to have developed it independently—that it is difficult to remember how new it was in 1918.

But subject matter was even more important in shaping Firbank's prose than borrowings or influences. The world of his fiction is at once a realization of his private dream world and a re-creation of the real, if tiny world of pre-1914 English and continental chic. Dream and reality fuse in a milieu entirely material. The trappings of circumstance, fascinating in themselves, are indices to the most complex states of the soul. Landscape, architecture, clothes—these have never quite existed; they are the product of lifelong fantasy. Conduct and conversation are real, even if they belong to the limited world of his own society. The language of his characters is private, often that of aristocrats in luxurious exile who no longer trouble much to communicate with the outer world, but who can rely on one another (and, by inference, on the reader) for complete comprehension. But it is authentic speech. (Read Firbank aloud to comprehend fully the subtlety of his dialogue.) Their conduct may be bizarre, yet too much has been made of their artificiality. They stem in great part from the rich tradition of British eccentricity, which was at its height—since it could then best be financially afforded—in the world in which Firbank lived as a young man. A glance at the sober reporting of Sir Osbert Sitwell's memoirs should dissipate any notion that their goings-on are merely extravagant invention.

The pamphlet of 1905 which contains *Odette D'Antrevernes* and *A Study in Temperament* is of interest to-day only because in it may be discerned, in a state of suspension, the elements out of which Firbank constructed his novels. The first piece, a fairy tale, has an evanescent lavender-pink background composed of a dim forest, a misty river, and a romantic chateau. In the foreground are a cloyingly sweet girl-child and a sentimental concern with the Virgin. *A Study in Temperament*, which sketches an attempted seduction in the most elegant London society, is all interior decoration and faded smartness. A Pateresque madonna in whose " wearied eyelids " are gathered " the sins and sorrows of the whole world " adorns the drawing-room of the heroine. The lover talks like an imitation of a minor wit in a Wilde comedy; yet there is already a hint of something new in his speech, something which is to become the characteristic Firbank conversational tone, witty, private, entirely cognizant of the absurdities of which the speaker himself is a part. He wants to elope: " . . . let us be brave—and—and defy the evening papers."

Ten years later, in *The Artificial Princess*, the weariness of the madonna, the wit of the lover, and the pastelle landscape have been fused. Odd juxtapositions, references to the more or less *recherché* in literature and painting, and to the material chic have become the devices of this prose:

> To compose herself she thought of Carpaccio's St. Ursula
> in Venice, a woman without a trace of expression, with the
> veiled, crêpe-de-chine look of a Sphinx.

The " crêpe-de-chine look " is out of the private sensibility, a private witticism, typical of the fashionable
talk of a tiny set, and formulating the kind of percep-
tion on which Firbank came more and more to depend.
It is also responsible for much of one's pleasure in
reading him, for the sense of belonging, momentarily,
to the charmed circle and of sharing the intimate joke.
In *Valmouth* this joke has suffused the landscape:

> Through a belt of osier and alder Valmouth, with its
> ancient bridge and great stone church, that from the open
> country had the scheming look of an ex-cathedral, showed
> a few lit lamps.

In a world in which the artifact is of central importance,
landscape improves as it imitates art. A panorama from
palace windows becomes a " deceptive expanse ":

> So much, contained on so little, suggested a landscape
> painted delicately upon a porcelain cup or saucer, or upon
> the silken panel of a fan.

Hills are " quiet, modest hills, a model of restraint."
From *The Artificial Princess* to *The Eccentricities of
Cardinal Pirelli* there was no radical change in Firbank's
prose, although he modified and refined it as the occasional posturings of his early novels gave way to a real
ennui, to a sharper humour, and to a feeling, expressed
on occasion in elegiac terms, of the sadness and
mortality of all things human.

It is idle to seek conventionally-ordered narrative in
writing so absolutely dependent on the momentary
awareness of the beautiful, the comic, of the poignant
—the Firbank counterpart of the Joycean *epiphany*. He
habitually collected on cards those sentences which, in
the novels, illuminate so completely an individual
attitude or the mores of group, just as they occurred
to him, or as, overheard, they amused them. Later he

fitted them into a careful mosaic. His novels progress in a series of animated tableaux. It is no failure of his that the reader must fill up the gaps between the scenes; such a demand, indeed, has, since his time, become part of the economy of fiction. Plot or movement in themselves did not interest him—his play, *The Princess Zoubaroff*, is dismal reading—although it is possible to outline the actions of his books. They burlesque themes popular in nineteenth-century fiction. *Valmouth* is in part a parody of the Hardy and post-Hardy novel of rural life. In *Caprice*, Miss Sarah Sinquier, bored with life in a cathedral town, absconds with the family silver to the London stage and the Café Royal, the Firbank variation on the flight from the provinces. In *Prancing Nigger* a Negro family on some improbable tropic isle migrates to the local capital so that mother and the girls can get into society. Here, to some extent in *Valmouth*, and in *Santal*, the brief and unsuccessful Arabian tale which bored him in the writing " unutterably," Firbank achieved comedy by imposing English lower middle class values on a half-civilized society. The artificial princess imagines herself a Salome to a glamorous local evangelist, a *reductio ad absurdum* of all the highborn and imaginative maidens of romantic fiction. The heroines of *Valmouth*, *The Flower Beneath the Foot*, and *Prancing Nigger* take the veil, nourishing hopeless passions.

Nor was Firbank's interest in character that of most artistically successful novelists. For him the exterior always indicates an inner state which the imaginative reader must realize for himself. Interior monologues are frequent in his novels, but they are filled always with æsthetic judgments and self-deflating ironies which are contrived to evade the omnipresent anguish of the soul—an evasion endemic to a society devoted to the pursuit of fashion and the preservation of impeccable surfaces. The human countenance, even, is

xvii　　　　　　　　　　　　　　B

depicted rarely except as a mask of fashionable beauty, weary, passion-ridden, depraved. These novels are thronged with brilliant, entirely material grotesques.

Sometimes the Firbank dialectic spiritualizes the material, although it usually materializes the spiritual, processes most clearly illustrated in the closing and opening scenes of *Concerning the Eccentricities of Cardinal Pirelli*: the spiritually triumphant death of the corrupt priest and the baptism of the Duquesa DunEden's police dog. Irony, which must never approach the obvious, is the universal solvent, dissolving, itself, on occasion, into half-articulated phrases. Sir Osbert Sitwell has described how, while writing, Firbank would be so overcome with laughter at the absurdity of the situation he had created that he would have to abandon work for the day. Given his double view, the enchantment and disenchantment out of which he wrote, his humour, at its best, simultaneously affirms and denies. Consider the yearnings after the finer things of life of Mrs. Ahmadou Mouth, a jungle matron. " ' Lordey Lord; what is it den you want? ' " her husband queries. " ' I want a Villa with a water-closet—— ' Flinging wiles to the winds, it was a cry from the heart."

If the double view is responsible for many of Firbank's virtues as a novelist, it is also the reason why, for all his art, he is a minor figure in the history of English fiction. His writing is often explicitly concerned with Evil, but his sense of Evil is imperfect. It is really naughtiness that he portrays, just as those sinister figures in Beardsley drawings turn out on close examination to be merely naughty and perverse. What is Evil in the world he has created? Any behaviour, especially any sexual behaviour, which can be labelled Fun. Overtly he resolves in Catholic terms what he considers Evil; the real resolution is in terms of the moral atmosphere of the middle class into which he was born. Whenever the lovely ladies of his court circles, the Baroness Rudlieb or the Countess of Tolga, for example, embark on adventure they enjoy a sense of transgression against conventional mores. Their predestined end, associated, however, with none of the emotions usually attendant on conversion, is Rome. Certainly there are echoes here of the conduct of those great ladies of the eighteenth-century memoirs he knew so well and of those heroines of Balzac who forsake their paramours for convents. But the radical attitude is middle class watered-down Puritanism: material pleasure must be paid for with material chastisement. The last scene of *Prancing Nigger* shows this limitation clearly. The suffering and feeling Miami (whose lover has been eaten by a shark) joins a band of penitents; the unfeeling Edna, her sister, becomes the mistress of a dandy who will soon tire of her. Firbank's sympathies are with Miami; Edna, it is made clear, will come to a bad end. Evil resolved in these terms lacks stature. Not even Cardinal Pirelli is a great sinner. There are no Stavrogins in this fiction.

In an age which looked for the moral to be sharply indicated in literature, Charles Lamb excused a taste for Restoration comedy by explaining it as entertaining gossamer out of some cloud-cuckooland and totally alien to ordinary human concerns. Just as this pleading neglects the facts of life out of which that comedy arose and places it in a vacuum impossible to art, so is the judgment in error which finds in Firbank merely entertaining and delightfully wicked frippery, however inadequate his sense of Evil may have been. Essentially he is a comic writer; his chief device is a kind of romantic irony; on this level he is nearly always enormously successful. There is a consistent satiric intent in his novels, aimed at the usual objects of social satire. But there is more, more even than the joy of escaping into a perfectly realized world or of contemplating the perfect artifact. If his Evil is always turning into naughtiness, his sense of mortality is sharp and unfailing. One has only to read a page or so of Firbank at random to note his awareness of the transience of all the earthly beauty he loved so well, an awareness which makes these novels, with their curious materialism, their praises of the rich and the exotic, moving as well as comic.

ERNEST JONES.

VAINGLORY
1915

I

"And, then, oh yes! Atalanta is getting too pronounced." She spoke lightly, leaning back a little in her deep arm-chair. It was the end of a somewhat lively review.

On such a languid afternoon how hard it seemed to bear a cross! Pleasant to tilt it a little—lean it for an instant against somebody else. . . . Her listener waved her handkerchief expressively. She felt, just then, it was safer not to speak. Tactfully she rose.

On a dark canvas screen were grouped some inconceivably delicate Persian miniatures.

She bent towards them. " Oh, what gems! "

But Lady Georgia would not let her go.

" A mother's rôle," she said, " is apt to become a strain."

Mrs. Henedge turned towards her. " Well, what can you do, dear? " she inquired, and with a sigh she looked away sadly over the comparative country of the square.

Lady Georgia Blueharnis owned that house off Hill Street from whose curved iron balconies it would have seemed right for dames in staid silks to lean melodiously at certain moments of the day. In Grecian-Walpole times the house had been the scene of an embassy; but since then it had reflowered unexpectedly as a sympathetic background, suitable to shelter plain domesticity—or even more.

Not that Lady Georgia could be said to be domestic. . . . Her interests in life were far too scattered.

3

Known to the world as the Isabella d'Este of her day, her investigations of art had led her chiefly outside the family pale.

"It is better," Mrs. Henedge said, when she had admired the massive foliage in the square, and had sighed once or twice again, " to be pronounced than to be a bag of bones. And thank goodness Atalanta's not eccentric! Think of poor little Mr. Rienzi-Smith who lives in continual terror lest one day his wife may do something really strange—perhaps run down Piccadilly without a hat. . . . Take a shorter view of life, dear, don't look so far ahead! "

" I was thinking only of Monday."

" There will be eleven bridesmaids besides At'y! "

" They will look Satanic."

" Yes; it's perhaps too close to picture them! "

" I don't know, yet," Lady Georgia said, " what I shall wear. But I shall be very plain."

"The cake," Mrs. Henedge said, beginning to purr, "is to be an exact replica of the Victoria Memorial."

" Do you know where the honeymoon's to be spent? "

" They begin, I believe, by Brussels——"

" I can hardly imagine anyone," Lady Georgia observed, " setting out deliberately for Brussels."

" I suppose it does seem odd," Mrs. Henedge murmured, looking mysteriously about her.

The room in which she found herself was a somewhat *difficult* room. The woodwork by Pajou had been painted a dull, lustreless grey, whilst the curtains and the upholstery of the chairs were of a soft canary-coloured silk striped with blue. Here and there, in magnificent defiance, were set tubs of deep crimson and of brilliant pink azaleas. Above the mantelpiece was suspended a charming portrait of Lady Georgia by Renoir. No one ever warmed their hands there, or before the summer wilderness of plants, without

4

exclaiming "How wonderful it is!" In this portrait
she was seen promenading slowly in an economical
landscape, whilst a single meagre tree held above her
head its stiff branches lightly, screening her from the
sun by its just sufficient leaves. On the opposite side
of the room hung a second portrait of herself with
her husband and her children—a lovely Holy Family,
in the Venetian manner, and in between, all round
the room, at varying heights, in blotches of rose and
celestial blue, hung a sumptuous *Stations of the Cross*,
by Tiepolo. Upon the ceiling, if one cared to look so
high, some last few vestiges of the embassy might be
seen—quivers, torches, roses, and all the paraphernalia
of Love. . . . But the eyes, travelling over these
many obstacles, would invariably return to the Venetian
portrait, spoken of, as a rule, somewhat breathlessly
as the *Madonna in the Osprey*.

Glancing from it to her hostess, Mrs. Henedge had
not observed the remotest resemblance yet. She was
waiting. . . . Except, she considered, for dear Lord
Blueharnis, a fine, dashing St. Joseph, with blue,
slightly bloodshot eyes, and the darling children, and
the adorable Pekinese, it was decidedly a *Madeleine
Lisante*. Striking, as it most unquestionably was, of
Lady Georgia herself, it was not a satisfactory portrait.
But how, it might pardonably be asked, was it likely
to be? How was it possible for a painter to fix upon
canvas anyone so elusive? He must interpret. He must
paint her soul, taking care not to let her appear, as an
inferior artist *might*, an overdressed capital sin.

Lady Georgia's face, indeed, was as sensitive as a
calm sea to the passing clouds. She had variety. Often
she managed to be really beautiful, and even in her
plainest moments she was always interesting. Her
nature, too, was as inconsistent as her face. At first
sight, she was, perhaps, too individual to make any
very definite impression. . . . A single pink flower

5

on her black frock, this afternoon, made her look, somehow, very far away.

Who can she be angling for, Mrs. Henedge wondered, and for whom is At'y becoming too pronounced? Was it for poor Lord Susan, who was sick, so everyone said, of the world at three-and-twenty?

At this notion she caressed, with a finger of a creamy glove, a small bronze of a bird with a broken wing.

Mrs. Henedge, the widow of that injudicious man the Bishop of Ashringford, was considered, by those who knew her, to be Sympathy itself. His lordship, rumour reported, had fallen in love with her at first sight one morning while officiating at a friend's cathedral, when she had put him in mind of a startled deer. She was really only appropriating a hymn-book, as she had afterwards explained. Their marriage had been called a romance. Towards the end, however, the Bishop had become too fe-fi-fo-fum-Jack-in-the-Beanstalk altogether. She had had a horrid time; but still, she was able to speak of him always as "*poor dear Leslie*," now that he was gone. To-day, perhaps, it might be said of her that she had deserted this century for—she had hardly settled which. Wrapped in what looked to be a piece of Beauvais tapestry, she suggested a rumble of chariots, a sacking of Troy. As Lady Georgia observed, quite perceptibly, she was on the brink of . . . Rome.

But reflections were put to flight, as some of the angels, from the famous *Madonna*, and several of the Pekinese came whirling into the room.

" It ran away in Berkeley Square."

" She had been having ices."

" On her head were two very tall green feathers."

" The policeman went away with her parasol."

" She was on her way to see us."

The children were very much excited. " Hush, darlings! " Lady Georgia exclaimed. " And when

you're calmer, explain who it was that ran away from
Berkeley Square."

" Grandmamma did!"

" Who would have thought," said Fräulein, appearing, " that a one-horse cab could do *so much mischief!*"
They were returning from the large heart of Blooms-
bury, where the children were frequently taken to
learn deportment from the Tanagras in the British
Museum. After posing meaningly as a Corinthian, or
practising sinking upon a camp-stool like an Athenian,
they came home, as a rule, rampageous.

"This afternoon they are uncontrollable!" Fräulein
murmured, attempting to hurry them away. But Mrs.
Henedge, with an arm about a child, was beginning to
expand.

" Her complexion," she observed, " is as lovely as
ever; but she *begins to look older!*"

As a foreigner, Fräulein could fully savour the
remark. She had succeeded, only lately, to Mademoiselle
Saligny, who had been dismissed for calling Marie
Antoinette a doll. Unfortunately, as Lady Georgia
had since discovered, her Teutonic scepticism varied
scarcely at all, from the Almighty to a can of hot
water; but this was more pardonable, she considered,
than labelling Marie Antoinette a doll. Distinguished,
or harmless doubts were these!

" It's really rather an escape!" Lady Georgia
murmured, as soon as they were gone; " my mother-
in-law's dictatorialness is becoming so impossible,
and in this warm weather she's sure to be out of sorts."

She stretched out a hand, listlessly, towards a red,
colossal rose. So many talismans for happiness fettered
her arms! She could hardly move but the jingling of
some crystal ball, or the swaying of some malachite
pig, reminded her of the fact that she was unhappy.
" I can't bear," she said, " James to arrange the
flowers, he *packs* them down into the vases." She got

7

up and loosened some. "And when Charles does them," she murmured, "they're invariably swooning away! Come and see, though, all I've been doing; our lease, you know, doesn't expire until two thousand and one. And so it's quite worth while to make some little improvements!"

But Mrs. Henedge seemed disinclined to stir. Seated upon a sofa entirely without springs, that had, most likely, once been Juliet's bier, it appeared she had something to confide. Something was troubling her besides " *the poor Guards, in all this sun!* "

" My dear Georgia," she said, " now that you've told me your news, I want to tell you of a most exquisite discovery."

Lady Georgia opened wide-wide eyes. " Is it some new thing," she inquired, " about Mrs. Hanover? "

Mrs. Henedge looked about her. " It's rather a secret still," she continued, " and although in many ways I should have liked to have told Ada, she would probably immediately tell Robert, and he, in confidence, would, of course, tell Jack, and Jack would tell *everybody*, and so——"

" Better say nothing to Ada! "

Mrs. Henedge heaved a sigh.

"Do you remember Professor Inglepin?" she asked. "His mother was a Miss Chancellor . . . Fanny. Well, quite lately, whilst in Egypt, the Professor (he terrifies me! he's so thin, he's so fierce!) came upon an original fragment of Sappho. And I'm having a small party at my house, on Sunday, with his assistance, to make the line known."

Lady Georgia became immediately animated. The Isabella d'Este in her awoke.

" My dear, how heavenly! " she exclaimed.

" Exceptional people," Mrs. Henedge hinted nervously, " are coming."

" O—h? "

8

" Mrs. Asp, Miss Compostella, the Calvallys! "

" It will be delightful! "

" Well, you won't blame me, dear, will you, if you're bored? "

Lady Georgia closed her eyes. " Sappho! " she exclaimed. " I'm wondering what I shall wear. My instinct would dress me, I believe, in a crinoline, with a yellow cashmere shawl, and a tiny turquoise bonnet."

Mrs. Henedge became alarmed. " I hope we shall be all as *Ingres* as possible," she said, " since there's not much time to be Greek. And now that I've told you, I must fly! No, darling, I can't even stay to look at the improvements; since the house is yours for so long, I shall see them, perhaps, again. I'm going this evening with the Fitzlittles to the Russian dancers." And she added melodiously from the stairs: " I do so *adore* Nijinsky in *Le Spectre de la Rose.*"

II

MRS. HENEDGE lived in a small house with killing stairs just off Chesham Place.

"If I were to die here," she had often said, "they would never be able to twist the coffin outside my door; they would have to cremate me in my room." For such a cottage, the sitting-rooms, nevertheless, were astonishingly large. The drawing-room, for instance, was a complete surprise, in spite of its dimensions, being ocularly curtailed by a somewhat trying brocade of drooping lilac orchids on a yellow ground.

But to-day, to make as much space as possible to receive her guests, all the household heirlooms—a faded photograph of the Pope, a bust of *poor dear Leslie*, some most Oriental cushions, and a quantity of whimsies, had been carried away to the top of the house. Never before had she seen the room so bare, or so austere.

As her maid exclaimed: "It was like a church." If an entire Ode of Sappho's had been discovered instead of a single line she could have done no more.

In the centre of the room, a number of fragile gilt chairs had been waiting patiently all day to be placed, heedless, happily, of the lamentations of Thérèse, who, while rolling her eyes, kept exclaiming, "Such wild herds of chairs; such herds of wild chairs!"

In her arrangements Mrs. Henedge had disobeyed the Professor in everything.

Professor Inglepin had looked in during the week to ask that severity might be the key. "No flowers," he had begged, "or, at most, placed beside the fragment (which I shall bring), a handful, perhaps, of——"

" Of course," Mrs. Henedge had replied, " you can rely upon me." And now the house was full of rambler roses and of blue sweet-peas.

A buffet, too, had arisen altar-like in her own particular sanctum, an apology to those whom she was unable to dine; nor, for toothsome curiosities, had she scoured a pagan cookery-book in vain. . . .

Glancing over the dinner list whilst she dressed, it seemed to her that the names of her guests, in neat rotation, resembled the cast of a play. " A comedy, with possible dynamics! " she murmured as she went downstairs.

With a tiara well over her nose, and dressed in oyster satin and pearls, she wished that Sappho could have seen her then. . . . On entering the drawing-room she found her beautiful Mrs. Shamefoot as well as her radiant Lady Castleyard (pronounced Castleyud) had already arrived, and were entertaining lazily her Monsignor Parr.

" Cima's Madonnas are dull, dull, dull," Mrs. Shamefoot was saying, looking over the Monsignor's shoulder at her own reflection in the glass.

Mrs. Shamefoot, widely known as " Birdie," and labelled as politics, almost compels a tear. Over-shadowed by a clever husband, and by an exceedingly brilliant mother-in-law, all that was expected of her was to hold long branches of mimosa and eucalyptus leaves as though in a dream at meetings, and to be picturesque, and restful and mute. As might have been foreseen, she had developed into one of those decorative, self-entranced persons so valued by hostesses at dinner as an ideal full stop. Sufficiently self-centred, she could be relied upon to break up a line, or to divide, with grace, any awkward divergencies of thought. Her momentary caprice was to erect with Lady Castleyard, to whom she was devoted, a window in some cathedral to their memory, that should be a miracle of violet glass, after a design of Lanzini Niccolo.

It was therefore only natural that Lady Castleyard (whose hobby was watching sunlight through stained glass) should take the liveliest interest in the scheme —and through the mediation of Mrs. Henedge was hoping to kindle a window somewhere very soon.

A pretty woman, with magnificently bold shoulders and a tiny head, she was, as a rule, quite fearlessly made up. It was courageous of her, her hostess thought, to flaunt such carnationed cheeks. Only in a Reynolds or in a Romney did one expect to see *such a dab*.

" Tell me! Tell me! " she exclaimed airily, taking hold of Mrs. Henedge. " I feel I must hear the line before everyone else."

Mrs. Henedge, who did not know it, pressed to her lips her fan.

" Patience! " she murmured, with her subtlest smile.

Monsignor Parr gazed at her with heavy opaque eyes.

Something between a butterfly and a misanthrope, he was temperamental, when not otherwise . . . employed.

" I must confess," he observed, " that Sappho's love affairs fail to stir me."

" Ah, for shame! " Mrs. Henedge scolded, turning from him to welcome an elaborate young man, who, in some bewildering way of his own, seemed to find charming the fashions of 1860.

" Drecoll? " she inquired.

" Vienna," he nodded.

" This is Mr. Harvester," she said. She had nearly said " Poor Mr. Harvester," for she could not endure his wife.

Claud Harvester was usually considered charming. He had gone about here and there, tinting his person-

ality after the fashion of a Venetian glass. Certainly
he had wandered. . . . He had been into Arcadia,
even, a place where artificial temperaments so seldom
get—their nearest approach being, perhaps, a matinée
of *The Winter's Tale*. Many, indeed, thought him
interesting. He had groped so. . . . In the end he
began to suspect that what he had been seeking for
all along was the theatre. He had discovered the truth
in writing plays. In style—he was often called obscure,
although, in reality, he was as charming as the top of
an apple-tree above a wall. As a novelist he was almost
successful. His books were watched for . . . but
without impatience.

" Cleopatra," he said, " was so disappointed she
couldn't come."

" I thought I saw some straw——"

" Miss Compostella," the servant tunefully
announced.

"Ah, Julia ! "

A lady whose face looked worn and withered
through love, wearing a black gauze gown, looped
like a figure from the Primavera, made her way mistily
into the room.

Nobody would have guessed Miss Compostella
to be an actress; she was so private-looking. . . .
Excessively pale, without any regularity at all of
feature, her face was animated chiefly by her long
red lips; more startling even than those of Cecilia
Zen Tron, *cette adorable Aspasie de la décadence
Vénitienne*. But somehow one felt that all Miss Compostella's soul was in her nose. It was her one delicate
feature: it aspired.

" How was I? " she murmured, when she had
shaken hands. " I was *too nervous* for words ! "

" You were completely splendid."

" My dear, how beautifully you died ! "

Miss Compostella was experimenting, just then,

13   C

at her own theatre, with some tableaux inspired from Holbein's *Dance of Death*.

" Two persons only," she said, " were present at my matinée. Poor things! I asked them back to tea. . . . One of them is coming here to-night."

" Really! who can it be? "

" He plays the piano," she said, " composes, and he has the most bewitching hair. His name is Winsome Brookes."

Mrs. Shamefoot tittered.

" Oh, Winsome's wonderful," Mrs. Henedge exclaimed. " I enjoy his music so much. There's an unrest in it all that I like. Sometimes he reaches to a pitch of life. . . ."

" His tired ecstasy," Claud Harvester conceded, " decidedly is disquieting."

Miss Compostella looked at him. She admired terrifically his charming little leer; it was like a crack, she thought, across the face of an idol. Otherwise, she was afraid, his features were cut too clearly to make any very lasting appeal. . . .

Nevertheless, for her general calm she could have wished that it had been next year.

Each day she felt their position was becoming more strained and absurd. She had followed Claud Harvester closely in his work, until at length she stood beside him on a pinnacle at some distance from the ground. And there they were! And she was getting bored. It disgusted her, however, to be obliged to climb down, to have had her walk for nothing, as it were.

With a smile that might, perhaps, have been called pathetic, she turned towards her hostess, who, with a deeply religious eye upon Monsignor Parr, was defending her favourite Winsome Brookes from Mrs. Shamefoot's innuendoes.

" But why, why, *why*," she inquired, " do you think him dreadful? "

" Because I think he's odious," she replied.

" Children irritate you, dear, I know, but he will
do great things yet! "

" Can one ever say? "

" The most unexpected thing in my life," Monsignor
Parr broke in gently, " was when a certain cab-horse
from Euston ran away! "

" Thanks for your belief in us," Mrs. Henedge
exclaimed gratefully, rising to greet an indolent-look-
ing woman who brought with her, somehow, into the
room, the tranquillity of gardens.

Mrs. Calvally, the wife of that perfect painter, was
what her hostess called a complete woman. She was
fair, with dark Tzigane eyes, which, slightly dilated,
usually looked mildly amazed. Like some of Rubens'
women, you felt at once her affinity to pearls. Equa-
nimity radiated from her leisurely person. She never
became alarmed, as her friends well knew, even when
her husband spoke of going away and leaving her to
live alone in some small and exquisite Capitol.

She would just smile at him sensibly, pretending
not to hear. . . . Secretly, perhaps, his descriptions
of places interested her. She would have missed hear-
ing about the White Villa, with its cyprus-tree, between
the Opera House and the Cathedral, and she let him
talk about it like a child. She did not mind when the
town chosen was Athens, which was near Malta, where
she had a cousin, but she had a horror of Bucharest.

George Christian Calvally accompanied his wife,
unhappy, perhaps, at playing, if even for only a few
hours, an oboe to her violin. His face was delicate
and full of dreams. It was a perfect *grief face*.

" My dear Mary," Mrs. Henedge exclaimed
affectionately, leading the sympathetic woman to the
most sylvan seat she could find, a small settee, covered
with a chintz all Eve's apples, and a wonderful winding
snake, " had you to be very strategic? "

15

"Oh, not at all," Mrs. Calvally replied; "but what do you think followed us into the house?"

Mrs. Henedge looked alarmed.

"Oh, nothing so dreadful. . . . Only a butterfly!"

Mrs. Shamefoot, who was listening, became positively ecstatic.

How nice it was to escape, if even for a second, from the tiresome political doings of which she was so tired. Not that she could always catch everything that was said, now that she wore her hair imitated from a statue of the fifth century. . . .

But the inclusion to-night, however, of Winsome Brookes was something of a trial. Without any positive reason for disliking him, she found him, perhaps, too similar in temperament to herself to be altogether pleased.

He came into the room a few minutes later in his habitual dreamy way, as might one upon a beauty tour in Wales—a pleasant picture of health and . . . inexperience. From the over-elaboration of his dress he suggested sometimes, as he did to-night, a St. Sebastian with too many arrows.

A gentle buzz of voices filled the room.

Mrs. Henedge, admirable now, was orchestrating fearlessly her guests.

Mr. Sophax, a critic, who had lately lost his wife and was looking suitably subdued, was complimenting, just sufficiently, a lady with sallow cheeks and an amorous weary eye. This was Mrs. Steeple.

One burning afternoon in July, with the thermometer at 90, the ridiculous woman had played *Rosmersholm* in Camberwell. Nobody had seen her do it, but it was conceivable that she had been very fine.

"Tell me," she said to Mr. Sophax, "who is the Victorian man talking to that gorgeous thing—in the gold trailing skirts?"

" You mean Claud Harvester. His play the other night was a disaster. Did you see it? "

" It was delightfully slight, I thought."

" A disaster! "

" Somehow, I like his work, it's so lightly managed."

" Never mind, Mr. Harvester " Lady Georgia was saying to him, " I'm sure your play was exquisite; or it would have had a longer run."

He smiled.

" How satirical you are! "

She was looking tired, and not a bit wonderful; it was one of her lesser nights.

" I wish she would give her poor emeralds a rest," a lady like a very thin camel was observing to Monsignor Parr.

A flattering silence greeted the Professor.

" I'm afraid you must feel exhausted from your field day at the British Museum," Mrs. Henedge said to him half hysterically, as they went downstairs.

The success of the dinner-table, however, restored her nerve. To create a slight atmosphere she had made a circuit of the table earlier in the evening, scattering violets indiscriminately into the glasses and over the plates.

For a moment her guests forgot to chatter of themselves. They remembered Sappho.

The Lesbian wine (from Samos. Procured, perhaps, in Pall Mall) produced a hush.

Claud Harvester bethought him then that he had spent a Saturday-to-Monday once, in Mitylene, at " a funny little broken-down hotel upon the seashore."

It had been in the spring, he said.

" In the spring the violets in Athens are wonderful, are they not? " Mrs. Calvally inquired.

" Indeed, yes."

She spoke to him of Greece, but all he could

remember of Corinth, for instance, was the many
drowned lambs he had seen lying upon the beach.

"*Ah! Don't speak to me of Corinth!* "

"What a pity—and in Tanagra, tell me, what did
you see? "

"In Tanagra . . .? " he said, "there was a kitten
sunning himself in the Museum, beside a pile of broken
earthenware—handles of amphoræ, arms and legs of
figurines, and an old man seated in the doorway
mending a jar."

"How extraordinary! " she marvelled, removing
with extreme precaution an atom of cork that had
fallen into her glass. "Really! Is that all? "

"Really all," he murmured, looking with sudden
interest at Miss Compostella, whose face, *vis-à-vis*, he
thought, still bore traces of his comedy.

He could appreciate her subtle mask quite enormously just then: now that she recalled to him his
play. How very delightful she was!

"Surely," he reflected, "her hair must be wired? "

Probably, as his wife had hinted once, her secret
lay simply in her untidiness. She had made it a study.
Disorder, with her, had become a fine art. A loose
strand of hair . . . the helpless angle of a hat. . . .
And then, to add emphasis, there were always quantities
of tiny buttons in absurd places on her frocks that
cried aloud, or screamed, or gently prayed, to be
fastened, and which, somehow, gave her an air of
irresponsibility, which, for simple folk, was possibly
quite fascinating.

"She's such a messy woman," Cleopatra had said.
"And, my dear . . . so unnatural! I wonder you
write plays for her. If I were a man, I should want
only . . ."

And she had named the impossible.

"I feel I want to go away somewhere and be ugly
quietly for a week," Miss Compostella was confiding

to George Calvally, as she cut a little wild-duck with her luminous hands. "The effort of having to look more or less like one's photographs is becoming such a strain."

He sympathised with her. "But I suppose," he said, "you are terribly tied."

"Yes, but you know, I love it! Next month I'm hoping to get Eysoldt over to play with me in Maeterlinck. . . . It isn't settled, there's some incertitude still, but it's almost sure!"

"Her Joyzelle!" he began to rave.

"And my Selysette!" she reminded him.

"Now that Maeterlinck is getting like Claud Harvester," the Professor, without tact, put in, "I don't read him any more. But at all events," he added graciously, "I hope you'll make a hit."

"A hit! Oh, I've never done anything so dreadful," she answered, turning her attention towards her hostess who, beneath her well-tipped tiara, was comparing the prose of a professional saint to a blind alley.

"But what does it matter," Lady Georgia inquired, leaning towards her, "if he has a charming style?"

In the vivacious discussion that ensued Mrs. Steeple, imprudently, perhaps, disclosed to Winsome Brookes her opinion of Miss Compostella.

"Oh, Julia's so stiff," she said, "she will hold herself, even in the most rousing plays, as though she were Agrippina with the ashes of Germanicus, and in depicting agony she certainly relies too much upon the colour of her gown. Her Hamlet," and she began to laugh, "her Hamlet was irresistible!"

And Mrs. Steeple laughed and laughed.

Her laughter, indeed, was so hilarious that Winsome became embarrassed.

"Her H-H-Hamlet was irresistible!" she repeated.

"Do tell us what is amusing you!" Miss Compostella inquired.

But Mrs. Steeple appeared to be too convulsed.

"What has Winsome been saying?" her hostess wished to know.

In none of these disturbances did Mrs. Shamefoot care to join. Mentally, perhaps, she was already three parts glass. So intense was her desire to set up a commemorative window to herself that, when it was erected, she believed she must leave behind in it, for ever, a little ghost. And should this be so, then what joy to be pierced each morning with light; her body flooded through and through by the sun, or in the evening to glow with a harvest of dark colours, deepening into untold sadness with the night. . . . What ecstasy! It was the Egyptian sighing for his pyramid, of course.

As might be feared, she appeared this evening entirely self-entranced. Indeed, all that she vouchsafed to her neighbour, Mr. Sophax, during dinner, was that the King had once been "perfect to her" in Scotland, and that she was fond of Yeats.

"If you cannot sleep," she said to him, "you've only to repeat to yourself *Innisfree* several times. You might be glad to remember. . . ."

As Mrs. Henedge had explained, it was only a fragile little dinner. She was obliged to return to the drawing-room again as soon as possible to receive her later guests. It occurred to her as she trailed away with the ladies that after the Professor's Sapphic postscript they might, perhaps, arrange some music. It would bring the evening to a harmonious close.

There was Winsome, fortunately, to be relied upon, and Mrs. Shamefoot, who sang the song of Thaïs to her mirror very beautifully, and later, she hoped, there would be Mrs. Rienzi-Smith, who composed little things that were all nerves . . . and who, herself, was so very delightful. . . .

In the drawing-room she was glad to find that

wonderful woman, Mrs. Asp, the authoress of *The Home Life of Lucretia Borgia*, refreshing herself with coffee and biscuits while *talking servants* to Mrs. Thumbler, the wife of the architect, and the restorer of Ashringford Cathedral.

" She was four years with Lady Appledore," Mrs. Asp was telling her, taking a bite at her biscuit, " and *two* at the Italian Embassy, and although one wouldn't perhaps, think it, I must say she was always scrupulously clean."

" My dear Rose," Mrs. Henedge said, sailing up, " I do hope you haven't been here long? " She seemed concerned.

" I—I—I, oh no! " Mrs. Asp purred in her comfortable voice, using those same inflections which had startled, so shockingly, the Princess H. of B. when, by telephone, she had confessed: " Yes . . . I am Mrs. Asp. . . . We're getting up a little bazaar and we expect you royalties to help! "

" And there, I believe, is Mira? " Mrs. Henedge said, turning towards a young girl who, seated in a corner, seemed to be counting the veins in her arms.

" I admired your valsing, the other night," she said to her, "at the de Lerens'. It's so brave of you, I think, to like dancing best alone."

Mira Thumbler was a mediæval-looking little thing, with peculiar pale ways, like a creature escaped through the border of violets and wild strawberries of a tapestry panel.

As a rule nobody ever noticed her (in spite of a few eccentricities, such as dancing singly at parties, etc., sufficiently manifest, possibly, to have excited attention). She was waiting to be found. Some day, perhaps, a poet or a painter would come along, and lift her up, high up, into the sun like a beautiful figurine, and she would become the fashion for a while . . . set the New Beauty.

" These apparent icebergs," Mrs. Henedge thought, as she touched Mira's charming and sensitive hand, " one knows what they are! "

" My dear, what a witty frock! " Lady Georgia said to her, fingering it. " Is it that little Miss Finch? It's a perfect psalm! "

" The cupids are imitated from a church frieze," Mira explained, holding out the stiff Italian stuff of ruby and blue woven with gold.

" I have seldom seen anything so splendidly hard! " Lady Castleyard admired. " You're like an angel in a summer landscape, reposing by the side of a well! " And holding her coffee-cup at an angle, she surveyed the room, a bored magnificence.

" There's no plot," Mrs. Asp, who seemed utterly unable for continuity, was confiding to a charmed few, " no plot exactly. It's about two women who live all alone."

" You mean that they live just by themselves? "

Mrs. Thumbler was unable to imagine a novel without a plot, and two women who lived so quietly! . . . She was afraid that poor dear Rose was becoming dull.

" I wonder you don't collaborate! " she said.

" Oh no. . . . Unless I were in love with a man, and *just as a pretext*, I should never dream of collaborating with anybody."

" You would need a sort of male Beatrice, I suppose? "

" How amusing it would be to collaborate with Mr. Harvester," Mrs. Steeple murmured, glancing towards Miss Compostella, who just then was looking completely flattered, as she closed her eyes, smiled, and lifted, slightly, a hand.

" Certainly I adore his work," Mrs. Asp admitted. " He pounces down on those mysterious half-things . . . and sometimes he fixes them! "

" Do you know Mr. Harvester? " Mira asked.

" Of course I know Mr. Harvester. . . . He scoured Cairo for me once years ago, to find me a lotus. Why?"

" I should so much like to meet him."

" My dear, what an extraordinary caprice! " Mrs. Henedge exclaimed, disengaging herself to receive a dowager of probable consequence, who, in spite of a crucifix and some celestial lace, possessed a certain poetry of her own, as might, for instance, a faded bacchante. It needed scarcely any imagination at all to picture her issuing at night from her cave on Mount Parnassos to watch the stars, or, with greater convenience, perhaps, strutting like the most perfect peacock, before some country house, over the rose-pale gravel; as charming as the *little stones* in the foreground of the Parnassos of Mantegna.

Lady Listless, or Atossa, as her friends respectfully called her, had the look of a person who had discovered something she ought not to know. This was probably brought about by being aware of most people's family feuds, or by putting merely two and two together. In the year her mistakes came to thousands, but she never seemed to mind.

" I've just been dining with the Barrows," she said solemnly to Mrs. Henedge, keeping her by the hand. " Poor little Mrs. Barrow has heard the Raven. . . . She came up hurriedly last night from the country and has taken refuge at the Ritz Hotel."

" It's hardly likely to follow her, I suppose? " Mrs. Henedge inquired anxiously.

" I don't know, I'm sure. The hotel, it appears, already is particularly full. . . . The last time, you remember, they heard it croak, it was for old Sir Philidor." And looking exceedingly stately, she trailed away to repeat to Mrs. Shamefoot her news: " Violet has heard the Raven! "

" To be painted once and for all by my husband

is much better than to be always getting photographed!" Mrs. Calvally was saying to a Goddess as the Professor came in.

"I know," the Goddess answered; "some of his portraits are really *très Velasquez*, and they never remind you of Whistler."

"Oh, beware of Mr. Calvally!" murmured Mrs. Asp, flitting past to seize a chair. "He made poor Lady Georgia into a greyhound, and turned old General Montgomery into a ram—he twisted the hair into horns."

An unwarrantable rush for places, however, announced that the critical moment had come.

"Well, darling," Mrs. Thumbler, triumphant, explained to her daughter, excusing herself for a sharp little skirmish with Monsignor Parr, "I was scarcely going to have him on my knee!" And with emotion she fluttered a somewhat frantic fan.

"I think your *young musician* so handsome," Mrs. Asp whispered to Mrs. Henedge, giving a few deft touches to a bandeau and some audacious violet paste. "With a little trouble, really, he could look quite Greek."

"Is your serial in *The Star*, my dear Rose, ever to be discontinued?" Mr. Sophax, who stood close behind her, stooped to inquire.

"Don't question me," she replied, without turning round. "I make it a rule never to be interviewed at night."

Next her, Lady Listless, perched uncomfortably on Claud Harvester's *New Poems*, sat eyeing the Professor with her most complacent smile. She knew hardly anything of Sappho, except that her brother, she believed, had been a wine merchant—which, in those times, was probably even better than being a brewer.

"But if they had meant to murder me," the camel-lady was mysteriously murmuring to Monsignor Parr, " they would not have put chocolate in the luncheon-basket; my courage returned to me at that!" when a marvellous hiss from Mrs. Asp stimulated Miss Compostella to expand.

" My dear, *when an angel* like Sabine Watson . . ." she was heard to exclaim vaguely above everyone else.

Julia, just then, was in high feather. George Calvally had promised to design for her a beautiful poster, by the time that Eysoldt should arrive, with cyprus-trees and handfuls of stars. . . .

But the Professor was becoming impatient.

It would be utterly disgusting, Mrs. Henedge reflected, if he should get desperate and retire. It was *like* Julia to expatiate at such a time upon the heavenliness of Sabine Watson, who was only *one*, it seemed, of quite a troop of angels.

To conceal her misgivings she waved a sultry yellow fan. There was a forest painted upon it of Arden, in indigo, in violet, in sapphire, in turquoise, and in common blue. The fan, by Conder, was known perversely as *The Pink Woods.*

" I'm not going to inflict upon you a speech," the Professor said, breaking in like a piccolo to Miss Compostella's harp.

" Hear, hear! " Mr. Sophax approved.

" You have heard, of course, how, while surveying the ruins of Crocodileopolis Arsinoë, my donkey having——"

And then, after what may have become an anguishing obbligato, the Professor declaimed impressively the imperishable line.

" Oh, delicious! " Lady Listless exclaimed, looking quite perplexed. " Very charming indeed! "

" Will anyone tell me what it means,"Mrs.Thumbler queried, " in plain English? Unfortunately, my Greek——"

" In Plain English," the Professor said, with some reluctance, " it means: ' Could not ' [he wagged a finger] ' Could not, for the fury of her feet! ' "

" Do you mean she ran away? "

" Apparently! "

" O-h! " Mrs. Thumbler seemed inclined to faint. The Professor riveted her with his curious nut-coloured eyes.

" Could not . . ." she murmured helplessly, as though clinging to an alpenstock, and not quite sure of her guide. Below her, so to speak, were the roof-tops, pots and pans: Chamonix twinkling in the snow.

" But no doubt there is a *sous-entendu?* " Monsignor Parr suspiciously inquired.

" Indeed, no! " the Professor answered. " It is probable, indeed, that Sappho did not even mean to be caustic! Here is an adventurous line, separated (alas!) from its full context. Decorative, useless, as you will; a water-colour on silk!"

" Just such a Sapphic piece," Mrs. Asp observed, with authority, " just such a Sapphic piece as the *And down I set the cushion,* or the Γέλως παιδοφιλωτέρος, or again the *Foolish woman, pride not thyself on a ring.*"

" I don't know why," Lady Georgia confessed, " it thrills me, but it does! "

" Do you suppose she refers to——"

" Nothing of the kind! " the Professor interrupted. " As Mrs. Asp explains, we have, at most, a broken piece, a rarity of phrase . . . as the poet's *With Golden Ankles,* for instance, or *Vines trailed on lofty poles,* or *With water dripped the napkin,* or *Scythian Wood . . .* or the (I fear me, spurious) *Carrying long rods, capped with the Pods of Poppies.*"

" And isn't there just one little tiny wee word of hers which says: *A tortoise-shell?* " Mrs. Calvally murmured, fingering the huge winged pin in the back of her hair.

"I should say that Sappho's powers were decidedly in declension when she wrote the Professor's 'water-colour,'" Mrs. Steeple said disparagingly.

"I'm sure I don't see why!"

"Do you remember the divine Ode to Aphrodite?" she asked, and rapidly, occult, archaic, before anybody could stop her, she began to declaim:

"Zeus-begotten, weaver of arts deceitful,
From thy throne of various hues behold me,
Queen immortal, spare me relentless anguish;
      Spare, I beseech thee.

Hither haste, if ever of old my sighing
Moved thy soul, O Goddess, awhile to hear me,
From thy Father's house to repair with golden
      Chariot harnessed.

Lovely birds fleet-winged from Olympus holy
Fluttering multitudinous o'er the darksome
Breast of Earth their heavenly mistress hastened
      Through the mid ether;

Soon they brought the beautiful Aphrodite;
Softly beamed celestial eyes upon me;
And I heard her ask with a smile my trouble,
      Wherefore I called her.

What of all things most may appease thy frenzy?
Whom (she said) would Sappho beguile to love her?
Whom by suasion bring to heart adoring?
      Who hath aggrieved her?

Whoso flies thee, soon shall he turn to woo thee;
Who receives no gifts shall anon bestow them;
If he love not, soon shall he love, tho' Sappho
      Turneth against him!

—Lady now too come, to allay my torment;
All my soul desireth, I prithee grant me;
Be thyself my champion and my helper,
  Lovely Dione! "

" Exquisite, dear; thanks."

" Christianity, no doubt," the Professor observed, with some ferocity, to Monsignor Parr, " has invented many admirable things, but it has destroyed more than it has created! " The old pagan in him was moved.

" You have been stirring our antenatal memories, Mrs. Steeple," Claud Harvester said.

" Have I? " she laughed.

" Mr. Brookes has promised to play to us," Mrs. Henedge said hurriedly, with sufficient presence of mind.

" Can he play *Après Midi sous les Pins ?* " the camel-lady wondered.

" Certainly," Winsome snapped, lifting from the piano a photograph of two terrified-looking little boys, which somehow had been forgotten. " I can play anything when I have the music! "

" Poor Mr. Calvally . . . he looks always so atrociously sad! " Lady Listless murmured, staring about her.

" It's unfortunate," Mrs. Rienzi-Smith said to her, " that the Professor seems so displeased."

" Well, what more could he want? We were all on footstools before him."

" What am I to play to you? " Winsome asked of Mrs. Henedge. " A fanfare? A requiem? "

" Oh, play us something of your own. Play your ' Oakapple,' from *The Suite in Green*."

But, " to break the ice," as he put it, he preferred the exciting *Capriccio Espagnol* of Rimsky-Korsakoff to anything of his own.

"But didn't you hate waiting for Othello to press the pillow?" Lady Castleyard was questioning Miss Compostella. "I should have got up and screamed or rung the bell, I'm sure I should!"

"Really? I think it's almost the only moment in the play that gives an actress an opportunity to see where are her friends," Julia replied.

"Just as I've observed," Mira Thumbler murmured maliciously to Claud Harvester, "that a person who begins by playing the Prelude of Rachmaninoff seldom plays anything else——"

"Oh no," he said. "When Winsome plays like that, I want to live in a land where there'd be eternal summer."

Mira looked amused.

"All places, really," she said, "have glamour solely in essence, didn't you know, like a drop of scent!"

She paused a moment to listen to her neighbour. "So appallingly badly kept," the Goddess was describing Valhalla. "In the throne-room, for instance, the candles leaning in all directions . . . and everything else the same!"

"Tell me," Mira said, turning towards Claud Harvester abruptly, and speaking with sudden passion, "why are you so *genial* with everyone? Why? It's such—a pity!"

"Good heavens," he exclaimed, startled, "what is the matter?"

But she had moved away.

"No, something of your own." Mrs. Asp was begging Winsome, rather imprudently.

"I will play through the first act of my *Justinian*, if you think it wouldn't be too long."

"A few of the leading themes, perhaps," Mrs. Henedge suggested.

"Very well. I will begin with the folk-song of the Paralytics."

" That will be delightful."

" You must imagine them," Winsome explained
to Lady Listless, who was sitting next to the piano,
" grouped invalidishly about the great doorway of
Santa Sophia. The libretto directions will say that
there is a heavy violet moon, and that it is a warm
June night."

Whilst listening to music Lady Listless would allow
her aspirations to pass unrestrainedly across her face.
They passed now, like a flight of birds.

" And here," Winsome murmured airily, without
ceasing, and playing with delightful crispness of
touch, " is the *pas* of the Barefooted Nuns."

Lady Listless became rhapsodical. " It's almost as
delicious," she breathed, " as the Sugar-Plum Fairies'
Dance from *Casse Noisette*."

Mrs. Asp also nodded her approbation. " The finale
was distinctly curious," she exclaimed. " Just like the
falling of a silver tray! "

" And this," Winsome explained, folding his arms
and drooping back shyly, " is the motive for Theo-
dora."

" My dear young man," Lady Listless objected,
" but I hear nothing . . . nothing at all."

" The orchestra ceases. There's audible only the
movement of her dress———"

And, suddenly irresponsible, he began to play
" Summer Palace—Tea at Therapia," which seemed
to break away quite naturally into an exciting Czardas
of Liszt.

" But how amusing! "

Mrs. Henedge, slightly anxious now, judged that
the moment had come to ask Mrs. Shamefoot to sing.
Winsome was hardly serious. It was perhaps a pity,
she reflected, though it couldn't be helped, that her
dear Mrs. Shamefoot cared only for the extremely
exalted music of the modern French school. Just then,

a dose of Brahms, she felt, would have done them all more good, but doubtless Mrs. Rienzi might be relied upon to bring the evening to a calmer close with some of her drowsy gipsy dances.

"And when she died she left everything for the Capuchin Fathers," Mrs. Shamefoot was telling Monsignor Parr as Mrs. Henedge approached.

"Sing, dear . . .?" she said. "Oh, I don't really know if I can. . . . The room is so hot. And there are so many roses! I don't know which look the redder, ourselves or the roses. And I have been chatting all the evening. And my voice is just the least bit tired. But if you simply insist, and Dirce will play my accompaniment; and if——"

And ultimately, as was to be hoped, she rose and fluttered over the many prayer rugs to the piano.

Seldom, George Calvally thought, watching her, had he seen a more captivating creature.

"Do you think her as graceful as she passes for?" He could hear Winsome Brookes inquire.

"Graceful?" the camel-lady answered. "No, really! She's like a sack of coals."

"Ah! je suis fatiguée à mourir!" Mrs. Shamefoot sang. "Tous ces hommes ne sont qu'indifférence et brutalité. Les femmes sont méchantes et les heures pesantes! J'ai l'âme vide. . . . Où trouver le repos? . . . Et comment fixer le bonheur! O mon miroir fidèle, rassure-moi; dis-moi que je suis toujours belle, que je serai belle éternellement; que rien ne flétrira les roses de mes lèvres, que rien ne ternira l'or pur de mes cheveux; dis-moi que je suis belle, et que je serai belle éternellement! éternellement!

"Ah! tais-toi, voix impitoyable! voix qui me dis: 'Thaïs ne serai plus Thaïs! . . . Non, je n'y puis croire; et s'il n'est point pour garder la beauté de secrets souverains, de pratiques magiques, toi, Vénus, réponds-moi de son éternité! Vénus, invisible et

présente! ' . . . Vénus, enchantement de l'ombre!
réponds-moi! Dis-moi que je suis belle, et que je serai
belle éternellement! Que rien ne flétrira les roses de
mes lèvres, que rien ne ternira l'or pur de mes cheveux;
dis-moi que je suis belle et que je serai belle éternellement! éternellement! éternellement! "

"Exquisite, dear; thanks! "

"Oh, she's heavenly! "

"Edwina never sang so! "

"If she becomes invocatory again," Mrs. Asp
whispered, beating applause with a finger upon a fan,
"I shall have my doze—like Brunhilde."

"You would be most uncomf'y," Mr. Sophax
observed, "and then who would finish your serial
for *The Star*. . . . No one else could."

It was too true. . . . Nobody else could draw an
unadulterated villain with the same nicety as Mrs.
Asp. How she would dab on her colours, and then
with what relish would she unmask her man; her
high spirits during the process were remarked by all
her friends.

But there was to be another song, it seemed, for
with her back to the room and a glow of light flooding
her perfectly whitened shoulders, it was unlikely that
Lady Castleyard would yield immediately to Mrs.
Rienzi her chair. With her head slightly inclined, it
was permitted to admire the enchanting fold of her
neck and the luxuriant bundles of silvered hair wound
loosely about her head, from whence there flew an
aigrette like a puff of steam.

"An aigrette," Mrs. Asp calculated, "at least sixteen inches long! " No; there would be at least two
more songs, she felt sure.

"They tell me," she said to Mr. Sophax, shaking
long tearful earrings at him, "that the concert at
Jarlington House, the other night, was a complete
success, and that Lady Castleyard played so well that

someone in the audience climbed over a great many
poor toes and tried to kiss her hands. . . . Atossa
says that he received quite a large cheque to do it!"

But a troublesome valse, that smouldered and
smouldered, and flickered and smouldered, until it
broke into a flame, before leaping into something else,
and which was perhaps the French way of saying that
" still waters run deep," cast for an instant its spell,
and when it was over Mrs. Henedge decided that she
would ask Mira Thumbler to dance.

Not unlikely it would be giving an old maid her
chance. Indeed, at seventeen, the wicked mite was
far too retiring. Nobody ever noticed her. So many
people had said so! And her poor mother with nothing
but daughters; her only child a girl. . . .

She found Mira lolling beneath a capacious lamp-
shade looking inexpressibly bored. Her hostess gathered
by her silhouette that the temptation to poke a finger
through a Chinese vellum screen, painted with water-
lilies and fantastic swooping birds, was almost *more*
than she could endure.

" My dear, won't you dance for us? " she asked.

Mira looked up.

" Oh, forgive me, please," she exclaimed, " but I
should feel far too like . . . *you know!* "

She smiled charmingly. . . .

" The daughter of Herodias? " Mrs. Henedge said.
" Nonsense! Don't be shy."

" Anything you might ask for . . ." George
Calvally murmured kindly, who was standing near.

" Do you mean that? "

" Of course I mean it! "

She considered his offer.

" Then," she said, " I'm going to sit to you for
my portrait. Oh, it's stupid and dull of me, I suppose,
to have so few features—just a plain nose, two eyes,
and a mouth—still! " She flung a hand up into the

air to be admired. She smiled. She looked quite pretty.

" I shall be immensely flattered," the painter said.

And so—after what seemed almost incredible adjustments—Mira danced.

On their way home he spoke of her lovely Byzantine feet.

Mrs. Calvally yawned. " It's extraordinary that a little skimped thing like Miss Thumbler should fascinate you! " she said.

III

Just at the beginning of Sloane Street, under the name of Monna Vanna, Mrs. Shamefoot kept a shop.

It was her happiness to slap, delicately, at monotony by selling flowers.

Oh, the relief of running away, now and then, from her clever husband, or from the fatiguing brilliance of her mother-in-law, to sit in the mystery of her own back parlour, with the interesting Dina or with Jordan, her boy!

She found in this by-life a mode of expression, too, for which her nature craved. It amused her to arrange marvellous sheaves of flowers to perish in the window before a stolid public eye; and some of her discords in colour were extremely curious. Often she would signal to her friends by her flowers, and when, for some reason, at the last Birthday Mr. Shamefoot had been carefully overlooked, in a freakish mood she had decked the window entirely with black iris.

But notwithstanding politics, it was declared that in all England nobody could wire Neapolitan violets more skilfully than she.

It was her triumph.

In a whole loose bouquet she would allow a single violet, perhaps, to skim above the rest—so lightly!

On her walls hung charming flower studies by Fantin Latour, and by Nicholson, intermingled with some graceful efforts of her own—impressions, mostly, of roses; in which it might be observed that she made always a great point of the thorns. And when there was nobody much in town these furnished the shop.

This morning, however, Mrs. Shamefoot sat down

to make a wreath—she hardly knew for whom; but since to-day was only Monday, she had a presentiment that one might be needed. . . .

With her dark eyes full of soul she commanded Dina to fetch her one. She fancied she might make ready a lyre, with some orchids and pink lilies, and numberless streaming ribands; something suitable for a disappointed débutante, and hardly had she commenced her work when Mrs. Henedge came into the shop.

" My dear Birdie, who ever expected to see you! " she exclaimed. " I thought you fluttered in only now and then, to see how everything was getting on——"

She seemed embarrassed.

Mrs. Henedge had looked in early indeed solely to implore Dina to persuade her mistress to take back some of the rambler-roses from her last night's party, but now, as she put it, they were face-to-face her heart *failed* her.

" What is the cost of those catkins? " she inquired, pointing, in her agitation, at something very fabulous-looking indeed.

They might go, she reflected, to Winsome Brookes. Often she would thank him for music by a cake or a small shrub, and Rumpelmeyer's to-day was not in her direction.

Mrs. Shamefoot became vaguely flurried.

" I don't know, dear," she replied. " When I try to do arithmetic clouds come down upon me like they do in *Tannhäuser*."

With a gasp, Dina crossed over to a book—she seemed to be suffering still from lack of breath. The pretty creature lived in a settlement *William Morris*, some paradise on the confines of the Tube, from whence she would appear breathless each morning, and would stay so, usually, until the Guards went by. When this occurred she would commence her duties by flying to the window to sprinkle water from a Dresden can over the grateful flowers, admiring, meantime, the charms of the cavalcade through the handle of one of Mrs. Shamefoot's psychological baskets, or whatever else might be in stock.

After this, she would calm down slightly for the day. But unfortunately, even so, Dina lacked sense. Even in the afternoon she would say: " The roses this morning are two shillings each."

" I did so enjoy last night," Mrs. Shamefoot said to Mrs. Henedge, " though, when I got back, for no reason . . . Soco simply stormed at me; but I was splendidly cool. I said nothing. I just *looked* at him."

" You poor darling," Mrs. Henedge said sympathetically: " What an unhappy life! "

In silence Mrs. Shamefoot stuck a lily in her lyre.

"It is sometimes," she said, "rather unpleasant. . . ." She began suddenly to cry.

" They are not catkins at all," Dina observed, apparently herself somewhat surprised. " They're orchids."

But Mrs. Henedge ignored her. She was determined to have nothing to do with them.

" There," she exclaimed, " went poor little Scantilla stalking along. Did you notice her? She had on a black jacket and a vermilion-magenta skirt——"

" Half-mourning! "

" Exactly."

" I dare say she's off to the wedding," Mrs. Shamefoot said. " Lady Georgia and At'y are coming in, I believe, on their way. The wedding is at Holy Trinity."

Mrs. Henedge looked out at the stream of carriages through the flowers. The seldom coarse or unspiritual faces of the passing crowd . . . veiled by plum-blossom, had an effect, she thought, of Chinese embroidery.

" I can't quite forgive Nils for getting married,"

Mrs. Shamefoot murmured, twirling in the air a pale
rose with almost crimson leaves. "I used to like to
talk nonsense with him. He talked agreeable nonsense
better than anyone I ever knew."

"I'm more concerned for Isolde," Mrs. Henedge
said. "I pity her, poor child, married to a charming
little vain fickle thing like that!"

"Oh, what does it matter?" Mrs. Shamefoot
queried. "When I took Soco I married him for
certain qualities which now, alas! I see he can have
never had."

"That's just what's so sad! I mean, I'm afraid you
did something commonplace after all."

Mrs. Shamefoot became discomposed.

"Oh, well!" she said, "when I got engaged I was
unconscious, or very nearly. I had fallen sound asleep,
I remember, off an iron chair in the park. The next day
he had put it in the paper; and we none of us could
raise the guinea to contradict . . ."

"Have you sent Isolde the——?"

"No, . . ." Mrs. Shamefoot confessed.

To nine brides out of ten she would make the same
gift—a small piece of Italian gauze.

When the recipient, holding it to the light, would
catch a glimpse of her fiancé through it, she began to
realise something of its significance.

"What did you send?" Mrs. Henedge wondered.

A tenth bride invariably was interesting.

"I sent her," Mrs. Shamefoot said, "a Flemish
crucifix, with ruby nails for the hands and feet. . . ."

"Dear Biddy. . . . I ran only to a pack of cards;
supposed once to have belonged to Deirdre. I got
them in Chelsea."

But Dina at the telephone was becoming distressing.

"Hullo! Yes! No! To whom am I speaking?"

The "To whom am I speaking?" characterised,
as a rule, her manner.

"An order," she said, "for a shower of puff-puffs for Mrs. Hanover, to be at Curzon Street to-morrow morning by nine o'clock. If the flowers are not delivered by then she will expect them at the Law Courts."

"Poor thing!" Mrs. Shamefoot murmured; "send her a lovely spray, and tell Jordan to be there by eight."

Jordan lately had been imported from the country, only to exclaim, the first time it rained: "It's too-wet-for-to-go-far!"

It had been very disheartening.

Mrs. Shamefoot considered her lyre; in its way, it was going to be as wonderful as the anchor of peonies she had made for the late Lord Mayor.

"Do you remember it, dear?" she said, beginning to laugh. "It was so *huge*, so perfectly huge, that it had to be tilted sideways to get it out of the shop."

But Mrs. Henedge was considering an amazingly elegant landaulette—a landaulette that seemed to her to positively whistle with smartness.

"Here comes Lady Georgia, now," she exclaimed, "and Mrs. Mountjulian, 'Emily' is with her——"

"Oh, she's getting sinister and *passée*."

"Perhaps; but only sometimes! It's not so long ago that she was tinting her toes with blackberries to be a nymph! You'd never credit it, dear, but we were the same age once!"

"I shall hide behind the counter," Mrs. Shamefoot said, "if she comes in."

"For the love of heaven, mind the lyre!" Mrs. Henedge screamed as Mrs. Mountjulian entered.

Mrs. Mountjulian was long and slender, like an Imari vase, with a pretty, lingering manner which many thought tiresome.

As Miss Emma Harris the world had found her distinctly aloof. As the Duchess of Overcares, however, she had been very simple indeed; it had been a new form, perhaps, of pride. And now, as Mrs. Mount-julian, she was becoming "aloof" again. To add a dash of picturesqueness to her career, her husband, it was said, was doing his utmost to get rid of her; and although she had been in an aeroplane disaster, a fatal gala performance, two railway accidents and a ship-wreck, she always came back—smiling.

"We've come to rifle you of your nicest flowers," Mrs. Mountjulian said.

"Oh, I need nothing," Atalanta explained. "Only to smooth my hair."

In a muslin frock with a broad blue sash, and a bridesmaid's bouquet of honeysuckle and meadow-sweet, she was looking engagingly pronounced. She needed only a mop and a pail to be altogether delightful.

"Isn't she *voyou?*" Lady Georgia said nervously. "I'm really afraid to be seen with her."

"My dear, you look a dove!" Mrs. Henedge murmured.

"Properly managed, nothing need ever clash," Mrs. Mountjulian assured Dina, singling out for herself a savage, multicoloured leaf.

But Lady Georgia appeared transfixed.

"For whom," she asked, "is that heavenly lyre?"

"'For Time sleeps not, but ever passes like the wind . . .'" Mrs. Shamefoot replied vaguely.

"St. Catherine!"

"To the Queen of . . . Naples."

They smiled.

"Oh, do choose," Atalanta said, glueing down her hair inventively, with a perfect sense of style. "There's sure to be a struggle at the church. And Isolde will have a *crise des nerfs* or something if we aren't there soon. Besides, Victoria's getting impatient: I can see her dangling a long leg from the car into the street."

" It was too bad really of Mrs. Fox foisting her on to us," Lady Georgia said. " Prevent her, do, from getting out."

She was looking, perhaps, annoyed, in arsenic green with a hat full of wan white flowers.

" Blueharnis insists that you come to us for the Ashringford races," she said to Mrs. Shamefoot, as she said good-bye, " and stay at Stockingham for as long as you can."

" How sweet you are! If only to lie in the garden, I'll come."

" At present I'm revolving a Tragic Garden," Lady Georgia told her, " with cypress-trees, and flights of stairs."

" I'm admiring your pictures," Mrs. Mountjulian said, dawdling. " Those clouds—so stationary— surely are Cézanne? and the Monticelli . . .! And that alluring Nicholson. . . . Only last night I was talking to Sir Valerian Hanway; you know whom I mean? And he said: . . . ' It's an anxiety for a poor man to own beautiful things. Where would be the pleasure of possessing a Velasquez, and having to hold a pocket handkerchief all the time to the roof to keep out the rain? ' "

" If she thought to embarrass me," Mrs. Shamefoot said as soon as they were gone, " I'm afraid she failed!"

" Poor woman! " Mrs. Henedge considered it diplomatic to say. " Either she is growing old, or her maid is getting clumsy. . . ."

"I should imagine both," Mrs. Shamefoot observed, returning to her lyre.

" I'm delighted, at any rate, that we shall see some- thing of each other in Ashringford! We must contrive to conquer all difficulties to obtain the window."

" Otherwise," Mrs. Shamefoot said, " I shall try Overcares! "

" It's not so *obvious*, of course! "

"And the Bishop, I know, is not unfavourably disposed. . . . But somehow, dear, a manufacturing town is *not* the same."

"Indeed it isn't!"

"Besides, there were so many sickening stipulations——"

"The Bishop of Overcares is the most paralysing man I know," Mrs. Henedge said, "and she . . . Mrs. Whooper——"

"A terror!"

"A perfect terror!"

"Well, it's so nice of you to help me."

"And might a tiny nosegay be left for Mr. Brookes? Lilies he likes. . . . Just five or six; I'm making, unavoidably, in the opposite direction, or I'd drop them on his doorstep myself."

Mrs. Shamefoot stood a moment pensively watching Dina remove the dark hearts that stained from Winsome's lilies before continuing her wreath.

It would be quite too extravagant, she feared, when finished, for the penniless young man for whom her débutante had died. He could never afford to buy it.

What should be done?

Remove a few of the orchids? No!

Allow the father it? Certainly not.

Die and use it herself? Soco was so dilatory. . . .

She remained dreaming.

"Be so good," she called to Dina presently, "as to fetch me the scissors."

And, shaking her head sadly under her heavy hat, she cut a string to the lyre.

I V

13 SILVERY PLACE was the address of Mrs. Henedge's
latest genius.

" A young boy," it was her custom to describe
him.

With a few simple words she could usually create
an interest.

The young boy, gentle reader, was Winsome
Brookes.

Standing at his window, hairbrush in hand, we find
him humming some bars of *Cimarosa*, whilst staring
up at a far-off Fuji of clouds. The attitude was essentially characteristic. When not exercising those talents
of his, Winsome Brookes would spend whole hours
together grooming fitfully his hair.

" Don't mind me," his gracious lady often said to
him, " if you care to calm your hair. I know that with
you it takes the place of a cigarette." And at Chesham
Place, sometimes, she would supply the needful
weapons.

Just now, however, with two invitations for the
same afternoon, he was looking pestered. . . .

"Will you not make, Andrew, that appalling noise?"
he murmured distractedly, without turning round.
" You make me shudder."

" It's extraordinary," Andrew answered briskly,
waving, as he spoke, a file, " but ever since that
Arabian ball, the paint clings to my finger-tips, as if
to the cornice of a temple! "

Winsome removed an eye from the street.

" Well, need you point at me like a finger-post? "
he irritably inquired.

43

" I consider your friend to be half a minion, and half an intellectual," Mrs. Henedge, who had never taken to Andrew in the least, had said once to Winsome Brookes. " That violet muffler, and the no collar . . ." was the official reason, but in reality, a lurid sketch of herself leaning upon the arm of an Archbishop of Canterbury whilst smiling across her shoulder into the eyes of Monsignor Parr accounted for the antipathy. She had come upon the trifle altogether suddenly at the Grafton Gallery and had decided at first it must be a Forain.

" I wish your breakfast would come," Andrew exclaimed disinterestedly, stretching himself out upon the floor—a *nature morte*.

" And so do I," Winsome complained. " But what is one to do? I order an egg, I wait an hour for it, and in the end most probably they'll bring me some fearful thing that looks like an auk's."

" A hawk's? "

" Oh, my dear friend. . . . An auk's. The great auk! " Winsome rolled his eyes.

Let us follow these bright ornaments.

The rooms of their occupants are sometimes interesting.

Taking for granted the large, unwieldly furniture, the mournful carpet, the low-spirited draperies, the brown paper of the walls, the frieze, in which Windsor Castle appeared again, and again, and again, and which a patriotic landlady (a woman like a faded Giotto) would not consent to hide lest it might seem to be disloyal, let us confine our observations to the book, the candlestick, the hour-glass, or the skull.

In a litter upon the mantelpiece—some concert fixtures, a caricature of Owen Nares, an early photograph of Andrew in a surplice, a sketch of Mildenberg as Clytemnestra, an impression of Felia Litvinne in Tristan, might be seen, whilst immediately above, usually quite awry, was suspended a passionate engraving of two very thin figures wandering before a retreating sea.

Winsome, indeed, to Andrew's amusement, cared only for quite independent landscapes of disquieting colour. He found beauty in those long, straight roads bounded by telegraph poles, between which some market cart would trundle through the pale midday.

Upon the piano, swathed in a scintillating shawl, rose up a modern figurine with a weary gesture, which, upon examination, was not lacking in signs that the original must almost certainly have possessed the proverbial kind heart of a black sheep. Beside it, against a stack of music, was propped a mask of Beethoven in imitation bronze, which, during the more strenuous efforts of the player, would invariably slip, giving, often, the signal for applause.

While in a corner, intriguing the eye, reposed a quantity of boards: polished yellow planks, the planks of Winsome's coffin. These, in the event of a party, could be coaxed to extend the dinner-table. " If you're going to be ten for supper to-night," his landlady would say, " you'll need your coffin boards stretched out."

But as much as he was able Winsome sauntered out to dine.

In her cooking, he found his landlady scarcely solicitous enough about his figure. . . . So manifest, of course, at concerts. In her supremest flights the good woman would seldom get beyond suet. And even this was in her most Debussyish vein. . . . And the question of concerts was occupying largely his thoughts just now.

Continually he was turning over in his mind the advisability of being re-baptised, this time—Rose de Tivoli. For musical purposes it sounded so much more promising, he considered, than Winsome Brookes. . . .

Two persons would come to hear Rose, whereas only one, and perhaps not even one . . .

But if Winsome Brookes had talent, Rose de Tivoli had genius!

Could he possibly be Rose?

Mrs. Henedge was inclined to think so. She had been, indeed, most hopeful:

" I'll take the Aeolian Hall, one afternoon," she had said, " and you can give the concert——"

To be—or not to be Rose! It was one of the things that was troubling him most.

" Ah! here comes breakfast now," Andrew observed, as Mrs. Henedge's floral gift was ushered in upon a tray.

> " ' I offer ye these violets,
> Lilies and lesser pets,
> These roses here pell-mell—
> These red and splendid roses,
> Buds which to-day uncloses,
> These *orchids dear* as well.' "

" ' These opening pinks as well,' " Winsome corrected. And returning impassively to the window, he leaned out.

Everywhere, between the houses, those old and dingy houses, whose windows would catch the sunrise with untold splendour, showed plots of garden, like snatches of song. Sometimes of a summer morning, leaning from his window, it would not have astonished him greatly to have surprised the Simonetta of Boccaccio at the end of the shady place leaping lightly, with uplifted arms, between the trees, pursued by Guido degli Anastagi and his pack of hounds. . . . Nor were visions all. Across the street the Artistic Theatre, a brilliantly frescoed, Asian-looking affair, aspired publicly heavenwards every day. It was the adornment and the scandal of the place. Too late, now, to protest about the frescoes; they were there!

Winsome sighed. At that moment his gracious lady bored him badly.

For just as the bee has a finer nature than the wasp, so had Andrew the advantage of Winsome Brookes.

By nature mercenary, and, perhaps, a trifle mean, a handful of flowers suggested to him nothing very exactly. . . .

> " The courtyard clock had numbered seven
> When first I came; but when eleven
> Struck on my ears, as mute I sate,
> It sounded like the knell of Fate."

Winsome turned.

Nothing diverted Andrew more than to investigate Winsome's books.

With a *Beauty and the Beast* he was almost happy.

The entrance, fortunately, of breakfast put an end to the recitation.

Whilst Winsome breakfasted Andrew indulged himself by venting his indignation on Miss Compostella's poster for the *Dance of Death* at the theatre over the way.

" It's enough to make me cart the Magdalen back home! " he exclaimed.

" Perhaps some day," Winsome said, " I may go for curiosity to New York, but until then——! "

For Andrew frequently would model strange, unusual figures that were ostensibly Church pieces had they been more subdued . . . His Mary Magdalen, for instance, might be seen in the foyer of the Artistic Theatre, where, even there, it was usually abused. . . .

" The Eros looks at least sixty! " he observed, criticising the poster. " And Death in that small toque's absurd. Surely Death required a terrific Lewis and a Romney hoop to conceal the scythe."

" But Death isn't a woman! " Winsome objected, cracking the top of his egg.

" Indeed? Death is very often a bore."

" Only for Adonis," Winsome murmured absently.

" . . . Do I disturb you? "

"No, come in.   Not in the least! "

" I thought," Andrew said coldly to the intruder, " that you went to the Slade! "

" Certainly; but not to-day! I shall run round later on, I dare say, for lunch at the British Mu-z. . . ."

" How fascinating! "

" I want you to come upstairs," the young man said plaintively to Winsome, " and tell me what Titian would have done. . . ."

" Me? " Winsome said.

" Yes, do come."

" Knowing you," said Andrew, " I should say that most likely he would have given her a richer background, and a more expensive silk."

" How can I," the young man queried, as he withdrew, " when the model has only a glove? "

" Why will you appal him? " Winsome asked; " he has the soul of a shepherd."

" Impossible."

" What are you saying? "

" Nothing; but when I look at your landlady's frieze," Andrew said limply, " I've a sort of Dickensey feeling coming on. I get depressed, I——"

Winsome swallowed his coffee.

" Then let's go."

" Il tend à leurs baisers la plume de sa main," Andrew began to warble inconsequently as he escaped downstairs.

V

"I WONDER you aren't ashamed, Sumph," Miss Compostella said to her maid, "to draw the blind up every morning on such a grey sky."

"Shall I draw it down again, miss?"

"Yes, please do. No, please don't. Come back to me again when I ring."

"And the shampoo?"

After the final performance of any play it was the maid's duty to perform this office to precipitate from the mind a discarded part.

"Washing-out-Desdemona," Sumph called it, dating the ceremony from then.

"It's hardly necessary," Julia said, "after such a light part. And, candidly, I don't quite agree with this romance-exhorting haste. For five whole weeks now, I'm only myself."

"Lord, may it keep fine," prayed the maid, lowering an inch the blind.

She was as stolid a mortal, it is probable, as ever graced a bedside or breathed at heaven a prayer.

"A light part," she said, "becomes a load during fever. And none of us are so strong as my poor——"

"But after Hermione," Julia objected, "I remained a week. . . ."

"After Hermione," the woman replied, "you could have gone ten days. After Hermione," she repeated loftily, "you could do as you pleased."

Sumph, indeed, worshipped Shakespeare. . . . Stratford, it appeared, was her "old home." Consequently, she was scarcely able to endure her mistress to appear in those pieces—pamphlets, or plays of

49

domestic persecution—in which all that could be
done was to waft, with one's temperament, little puffs
of rarefied air, now and again, across the footlights.

And yet it must be said that Sumph was a bad critic.
It was just in these parts that her mistress most excelled.

Julia sat up and smiled.

Round the bed in which we surprise her hung a
severe blue veil suspended from oblong wooden rings.
Above it, a china angel upon a wire was suspended to
complete the picture.

At the sight of her tired mistress set in bolsters the
devoted woman was almost moved to tears.

"Oh, be quiet," Julia exclaimed. "I know exactly
. . . I remind you of Mrs. So-and-so in some death
scene. . . ."

Sumph straightened her cap, a voluminous affair
drawn together in front in a bewildering bow.

"You do," she said, "miss. Of Mrs. Paraguay, or
la Taxeira, as she was to become. She achieved fame
in *Agrippina at Baiae*, in a single night. Never will I
forget her pale face or her white crinoline. She was
marvellous. It was that first success, perhaps, that
drove her to play only invalid parts. Ah, miss, how
lovely she looked with the treasures of half the Indies
in her hair. . . ."

"Indeed?" Julia observed. "You're hurting my
feet."

The woman turned away from anything so brittle.

"Tell me truthfully," Julia queried, "how am I
looking?"

"Beautifully weary, miss."

Miss Compostella sank back.

Like some indignant Europa she saw herself being
carried away by the years.

"Sumph," she said feebly, "what do you think of
Mr. Harvester?"

"As a poet, miss, or as a man?"

" . . . As a poet."

" His poems are very cold and careful, miss; just what one would expect."

Julia turned her face to the wall.

Since her mother's death, caused, no doubt, by a flitting forth with an excursion ticket to Florence (Mrs. Compostella had succumbed almost immediately in the train), Julia had taken a charming house for herself in Sacred Gardens. The address alone, she hoped, would be a sufficient protection, and so spare her the irksomeness of a chaperon. And here, somewhat erratically, she lived with the invaluable Sumph, whom she ill-treated, and of whom, in her way, she was fond.

" Mr. Harvester came round last night, miss, just after you had gone," Sumph said; " and I'll confess to you I flew at him. At the totally unexpected, as they say, it's oneself that speaks."

" Indeed, it ought not to be."

" Surrounded as we are," said Sumph, " it's best to be discreet."

" I'm afraid you were very rude to him! "

" Oh, miss, why waste words on a married man? I'd sooner save my breath and live an extra day."

" Are you so *fond* of life? " Miss Compostella painfully inquired, her face turned still towards the wall.

" And an old gentleman, with the wickedest eye, called also, and asked if you was in."

" Did he give no name? "

" He left no card, but he called himself a saint," Sumph answered slyly.

Mr. Garsaint's political satire, *The Leg of Chicken*, which was to be played in Byzantine costume, was to be given at the Artistic Theatre in the autumn; unless, indeed, Miss Compostella changed her plans, and produced *Titus Andronicus*, or *Marino Faliero*, or a wildly imprudent version of the *Curious Impertinent* at the last moment, instead. For if there was one thing that she preferred to a complete success, it was a real fiasco. And Mr. Garsaint's comedy would probably be a success! What British audience would be able to withstand the middle act, in which a couple of chaises-longues, drawn up like passing carriages, silhouetted the footlights from whence the Empress Irene Doukas (a wonderful study of Mrs. A.) and Anna Comnena lay and smoked cigarettes and argued together—at ease? And even should Mr. Garsaint's dainty, fastidious prose pass unadmired, the world must bow to the costumes, foreshadowing as they did the modes of the next century.

" How tiresome to have missed him! " Miss Compostella exclaimed, sitting up, and blinking a little at the light.

In the window hung a wicker cage of uncertain shape that held a stuffed canary. It had had a note sweeter than Chenal's once. . . . And there it was! Poor, sad thing!

" Angel! Sweet! Pet! Pretty! " Julia would sometimes say to it by mistake.

Through the vigilant bars of the cage she could admire a distant view of a cold stone church by Vanbrugh. The austere and heavy tower, however, did not depress her. On the contrary, she approved its solidity. Flushed at sunset, it suggested quite forcibly a middle-aged bachelor with possessions at Coutts. At times she could almost think of it as *James*. . . .

" And there are several hundred more letters waiting for you in the next room, miss," Sumph said.

To Julia's inquiry for a man with ecstasy to stage-manage, she had received several thousand applications.

" Go to the next room," Miss Compostella directed, " and choose me two with your eyes shut."

It was in the " next room " that Miss Compostella sometimes studied her parts . . . though for modern comedy rôles she usually went " upstairs."

She sank back now and waited.

With five weeks at her disposal, with the exception of a complaisant visit to Stockingham for a race party, it was her intention to lie absolutely still, preferably at a short distance from London, and explore her heart.

For indeed the dread of Miss Compostella's life was that she had not got one. Unless that sorrowful, soft, vague, yearning, aching, melting, kite-like, soaring emotion was a heart?

Could that be a heart?

From the mantelpiece came a sudden " whirr " from an unconcerned Sèvres shepherdess, a coquettish silence, followed by the florid chiming of a clock.

Noon; or very nearly—for as an object submits meekly to its surroundings, Julia's timepiece, invariably, was a little in advance.

She held out long arms, driftingly.

It was noon! Sultry noon—somewhere in the world. In Cintra now . . .

She lay back impassively at the sound of Sumph's Olympian tread.

A gesture might revive a ghost.

It was irritating to discover that one recalled Polly Whatmore in *The Vicar's Vengeance*, or Mrs. Giltspur in *The Lady of the Lake*.

The indispensable woman, holding the testimonials of the men of ecstasy, approached the bed.

" And Mr. Harvester is here, miss," she said sedately, lifting up her eyes towards the quivering angel. " Should I show him into the next room, or shall I take him *upstairs?* "

Julia reflected.

" No," she murmured; " put him in the dining-room and shut the door."

"Yes, miss."

"And, Sumph . . . offer him a liqueur, and something to read—of his own."

"Yes, miss."

"And, Sumph . . . I shall be getting up now in about half an hour."

She waited—and recast her arms expressively.

"Claud . . .?"

But the worst of it was, she reflected, that with a chair upon Mount Parnassos (half-way up) he was somewhat inclined to *dictate*. . . .

VI

To Ashringford from Euston is really quite a journey.

Only an inconvenient morning train, or a dissipated evening one—described in time-tables as the Cathedral Express—ever attempt at concentration. Normal middle-day persons disliking these extremes must get out at Totterdown and wait.

As a stimulus to introspection, detention cannot be ignored.

Cardinal Pringle, in his Autobiography, confesses that the hour spent on Totterdown platform, seated in deep despondence upon his trunk, came as the turning-point in his career.

Introspection, however, is not to be enforced.

" It will hardly take us until five o'clock, Violet," Mrs. Shamefoot observed to her old crony, Mrs. Barrow of Dawn, fumbling, as she spoke, with a basket, " to drink a small bottle of champagne. Is there nothing particular here to see? "

She looked out at the world, through a veil open as a fishing-net, mysteriously.

Where were the *sunburned sicklemen of August weary!* The *ryestraw hats!* Surely not many yards off.

Mrs. Barrow put up her sunshade.

" Oh yes," she said, " a cousin of Oliver Cromwell is buried not far from here; and in the same graveyard there's also the vault of a Cabinet Minister who died only the other day."

Mrs. Shamefoot produced with perfect sympathy a microscopic affair.

" In this heat," she observed, " champagne is so much more refreshing than tea."

Mrs. Barrow accepted with gratitude.

It may be remembered from some exclamations of Lady Listless that just lately she had "heard the Raven." It was said, however, about Dawn, that whenever she wished to escape to town for a theatre or to shop she would manage to hear its croak.

"I do hope," she exclaimed, "that Sartorious won't be at Ashringford to meet me; it's perfectly possible that he may."

"Well, there's no good in singing a dirge over what can't be helped; the connection's gone."

"What tactless things trains are!"

Mrs. Shamefoot shook a panoply of feathers.

"What is that curious watch-tower," she asked diplomatically, "between the trees?"

Mrs. Barrow began to unbend.

Life, after all, seemed less raw after a glass of champagne.

"I don't know, dear," she said, "but I think the scenery's so perfectly French."

"Isn't there a hospital near here—for torn hearts, where love-sick persons can stay together in quarantine to enjoy their despair and help each other to forget?"

"I don't know, dear," Mrs. Barrow said again, "but I believe there's a sanatorium for nervous complaints. . . . All the country round Totterdown belongs to Lord Brassknocker."

"Oh, he's dreadful!"

"And she's such a thorough cat."

"And poor Lord Susan!"

"Poor, *poor* Lord Susan."

"I can almost feel Ashringford Cathedral here," Mrs. Shamefoot remarked. "Aren't the hedges like the little low curtains of a rood-screen?"

"Exactly!"

"And aren't the——"

"My dear, what a dreadful amount of etceteras you appear to bring," Mrs. Barrow replied with some aridity.

Mrs. Shamefoot's principal portmanteau was a rose-coloured chest, which, with its many foreign labels, exhaled an atmosphere of positive scandal. No nice maid would stand beside it.

A number of sagacious smaller cases clambered about it now into frantic streets, and sunny open piazzas, like a small town clustering about the walls of some lawless temple.

Mrs. Barrow was appalled at so much luggage. She had been to the ends of the earth, it seemed, with only a basket.

Mrs. Shamefoot re-helped herself to Clicquot.

She was looking to-day incomparably well, draped in a sort of sheet *a la* Puvis de Chavanne, with a large, lonely hat suggestive of *der Wanderer*.

"The relief," she exclaimed, "of getting somewhere where clothes don't matter!"

"But surely to obtain a window in the Cathedral *they will*. You'll need an old Ascot frock, shan't you, for the Bishop?"

"Violet, I'm shocked! Can such trifles count?"

"Well, I dare say, dear, they help to persuade."

"Bishop Pantry is quite unlike Bishop Henedge, isn't he?"

"Oh, quite. The present man's a scholar! Those round shoulders. He will probably die in his library by rolling off the final seat of his portable steps."

"But not just yet!"

"You have read his *Inner Garden!*"

"Oh yes. . . . And *Even-tide*, and *Night Thoughts*, and the sequel, *Beams*. But they're so hard. How can it be good for the soul to sleep upon the floor, although it mayn't be bad for the spine."

"Besides, to tread the spiral path means usually a

bother . . ." Mrs. Barrow observed. " There are the
servants! And to get a girl to stay in Ashringford——"

Mrs. Shamefoot fixed her eyes upon the hills that
slid back, she thought, with a fine monastic roll.

" And is he very plain? " she asked.

" I should never say so. It's a fine Neronian head."

" Lady Anne is charming, isn't she? "

Mrs. Barrow hesitated.

" Sartorious," she replied, " thinks her wily."

" But she is charming? "

" Oh, well," Mrs. Barrow said evasively, " she
doesn't shine perhaps at the Palace like dear Mrs.
Henedge. I suppose we shall never replace *her* again!
Fortunately, however, she's devoted to Ashringford
and comes there nearly every summer. Since she's
taken the Closed House she's thrown out fourteen
bow-windows."

Mrs. Shamefoot snapped the lid of her basket.

" Who are these condottieri? " she inquired, as an
imperious party drove up with considerable clatter.

Mrs. Barrow turned.

" Don't look more than you can help, dear," she
exclaimed, in a voice that would have piqued a stronger
character than Mrs. Lott, " it's the Pontypools."

" Ashringford people? "

" Theoretically."

Mrs. Shamefoot smiled.

" Sartorious——" Mrs. Barrow began.

" Thinks them? "

" Totally dreadful. They're probably reconnoitring.
Mrs. Pontypool is usually spinning a web for someone."

" The dowager's very handsome," Mrs. Shamefoot
remarked, " in a reckless sort of way, but the girl's a
fairy! "

" Oh, don't swear! Don't, don't swear! " Mrs.
Pontypool was adjuring a member of her family,

with brio, stepping, as she spoke, right into Mrs. Barrow's arms.

" Is it quite true," she asked, shaking hands, " that the connection's gone? "

" Quite! "

Mrs. Pontypool sat down. " It needs heroism in the country," she explained, " to keep sight of anybody."

" Certainly. Crusading, and without a car——"

" Crusading, dear Mrs. Barrow! Yet how did one's ancestors get along? "

" I don't know," Mrs. Barrow said. " It's so rare, isn't it? nowadays, to find anybody who had a grand-mother."

"In the times I mean," Mrs. Pontypool said, undismayed, " women went for miles in a sedan-chair, and crossed continents in their tilburies, and in their britschkas, and in their cabriolets! "

" Heroic! "

" Less heroic, surely, than those women one some-times sees who fasten their bath-chairs to their lovers' auto-bicycles."

" And where have you been—if it isn't indis-creet . . .? "

" We've been spending a few hours at Castle Barbarous."

" I hear Lord Brassknocker is going to open his pictures to the public," Mrs. Shamefoot said. " He has, of course, a very fine Ruisdael, an attractive Sisley and a charming Crome, but really the rest of the collection is only fit for the Sacristy scene in *Manon*."

" A Last Supper at *two tables*," Mrs. Pontypool said confidentially, " struck one as—scarcely——"

" Not if it was Veronese."

" It was Rubens."

" The busiest man who ever lived most certainly was Rubens."

" Was it a party? " Mrs. Barrow asked, less from

curiosity than because she would be glad to have something to say to Sartorious during dinner.

Oh, the trial of those dreary dinners at Dawn. . . . What wonder was it that Mrs. Barrow should sometimes become peevish or invent things that were untrue or, in her extremity, hear the Raven's croak? Had she been neurasthenic she would have probably sometimes screamed at the sight of her Lord enjoying an artichoke, slowly, leaf by leaf.

"Was it a party?" Mrs. Barrow asked again.

"Only old Mr. James and little Mrs. Kilmurry," Mrs. Pontypool replied. "Such a strange old man, who strolled once with the Tennysons in the Cascine in Florence."

There was a pause—just long enough for an angel to pass, flying slowly.

"Was Lord Susan there?" Mrs. Barrow inquired.

"He very seldom is," Miss Pontypool said.

"Unfortunate young man," Mrs. Pontypool exclaimed, playing with the tails of her stole; "perpetually he's on the verge of . . . and, although I'm told he's gun-shy, in my opinion . . . and I would willingly have sent a wreath, . . . only where's the use in sending one the day afterwards?"

"But you've heard nothing?"

"No. . . . Naturally the Brassknockers don't care to talk of it before they're quite obliged; but Lady Brassknocker did strike me as being so unusually distrait. Didn't you think so, Queenie?"

"I really didn't notice," Miss Pontypool said. "Where's Goosey?"

"To be sure! I thought if Lord Brassknocker could only see the boy he might take a fancy to him," Mrs. Pontypool said.

"Really, in what way?" Mrs. Barrow wondered.

"Who can tell? Lord Brassknocker's a very important man."

" He is a very rich one."

" Poor child! What is one to do with him? In any other age, of course, he could have ambled along in the retinue of some great lady."

" Oh, be thankful," Mrs. Barrow began.

" As it is, with a little influence, he's hoping to get into some garage."

" Poor young man," Mrs. Shamefoot said, with sympathy, " such a bending life! "

By the time the train reached Totterdown Mrs. Barrow congratulated herself that she would be artichoke-proof now, positively, for nearly a week.

In the railway carriage, Mrs. Shamefoot was sufficiently fortunate, too, to secure the seat opposite to herself for a magnificent image of the god Ptah.

The terrific immobility of Egyptian things enchanted her, particularly in the train.

Often the god had aroused her friendliest feelings by saving her from the strain of answering questions, or expressing hopes, or guessing whether the carriage would be there to meet them, or whether it would not, or from the alternative miseries of migraine brought on by feigning to read, for, as Mrs. Shamefoot was aware, she might be called upon to remove a dressing-case, but how seldom did it occur to anyone to deplace a god.

But Mrs. Pontypool was not to be suppressed.

" I once met a Mrs. Asp," she said, " who was writing the life of Hepshepset, wife and sister of Thothmes II, who, on becoming a widow, invented a hairwash and dressed as a man."

The beautiful summer's day had crumbled to dusk as the twin towers of the Cathedral and the short spire (which was, perhaps, an infelicity) came into view.

How desolate it appeared across the fields of wan white clover, now that the sun had gone! Saint Apollinaris in Classe never looked more alone.

"Ashringford is quite a healthy place, isn't it?" Mrs. Shamefoot inquired anxiously, turning towards Mrs. Barrow.

Mrs. Barrow opened her eyes.

"One wouldn't care to say so," she replied, "there's usually a good deal of sickness about; *of a kind.*"

"I consider it a regular doctors' town!" Mrs. Pontypool exclaimed; "the funeral horses are always on the go."

Mrs. Pontypool looked humane.

"Poor animals!" she said.

"You see the Ashringford houses are so old," Goosey explained, "and so stuffy, and the windows are so small. It's as if the Ashringford people had made them themselves by poking a finger through the brick."

"Which makes us all delicate, of course, and the climate doubly treacherous," Mrs. Pontypool said. "Although at one time I fancy it used not to be so bad. I date the change to Bishop Henedge. He was so High Church. His views were so extremely high! Quite unintentionally, perhaps, he attracted towards us the uncertain climate of Rome. I should advise anyone visiting Ashringford for the first time to do precisely as they would there."

"And what is that?" Mrs. Shamefoot demanded doubtfully.

"Wear an extra flannel petticoat."

Much to Mrs. Barrow's disappointment, there was no Sartorious to meet the train; only a footman— Lady Georgia's chauffeur attended to Mrs. Shamefoot and her maid.

"I wonder she keeps him," Mrs. Barrow observed, as she climbed into her brougham. "From the marks on his cheeks he looks as if he had been in more than one break up."

"My regards to Lady Georgia," Goosey called after Mrs. Shamefoot to say.

"My dear, at nineteen has one regards?" Mrs. Pontypool said. "Silly, affected boy!"

Mrs. Shamefoot was glad to be alone. How wonderful it was to breathe the evening air. As she sped towards Stockingham over a darkening plain, patched with clumps of heavy hyacinthine trees, almost she could catch the peculiar aroma of the Cathedral.

"As indefinable as piety!" she exclaimed, drawing on her glove.

VII

LADY ANNE PANTRY was sitting in the china-cupboard, a room fitted with long glass shelves, on which her fabled Dresden figures, monkey musicians, and sphinx marquises, made perfect blots of colour against the gold woodwork of the walls.

Heedless of her sister-in-law, she was reading her morning letters whilst massaging her nose.

" Such a dull post, Anne," that person exclaimed, lifting up an incomparable, tearful, spiritual and intellectual face from the perusal of a circular.

" Mine is not," said Lady Anne.

" Indeed? "

Lady Anne rustled her skirt.

" . . . Mrs. Henedge," she said, " it appears, has quite gone over to Rome."

" But is it settled? "

" Since she's to build in our midst a bijou church for Monsignor Parr. . . . Such scenes, I expect, there'll be."

" Certainly. If it's to be another Gothic fake."

" And Lady Georgia asks if she may lunch here to-morrow and bring a Mrs. Shamefoot. Mysteries with the Bishop. And there's been *almost* a murder at the workhouse again."

" How very disgraceful."

" And the Twyfords are coming—at least some of them. Less tiresome, perhaps, than if they all came at once."

" I love her postscripts——"

" To-day there isn't one. And that brocade, you remember, I liked, is seventy shillings a yard."

" Too dear."

" And I said *a spot*, Aurelia; I did not say a *cart-wheel* . . ." Lady Anne murmured, getting up to display her wares.

Lady Anne had turned all her troubles to beauty, and at forty-five she had an interesting face. She was short and robust, with calm, strong features, and in the evening she sometimes suggested Phèdre. Her voice was charming, full of warmth and colour, and although she did not sing, it might be said of her that she was a mute soprano.

Aurelia Pantry extended a forlorn and ravishing hand.

" Aren't they fools? " she exclaimed, spreading out the materials before her.

She spoke habitually rather absently, as though she were placing the last brick to some gorgeous castle in the air.

It was the custom at the Palace that the Bishop's eleven sisters should spend a month in rotation there each year.

Aurelia, who was the most popular (being the least majestical, the least like Eleanor), corresponded, as a rule, to August and September.

Of the Bishop's eleven sisters, indeed, she was the only one that Lady Anne could endure.

Eleanor, Ambrosia, Hypolita, Virginia, Prudence, Lettice, Chrissy, Patsy, Gussy and Grace were all shocking, hopeless and dreadful, according to Lady Anne.

But Aurelia, who was just a little mystic, added a finish, a distinction to the Palace; especially got up in muslin, when, like some sinuous spirit, she could appear so ethereal as to be almost a flame.

" I think, of course, it's perfect," Miss Pantry said, holding her head aslant *like smoke in the wind*, as she considered the stuff, " but the design limits it."

"I should call it hardly modest myself."

"There's something always so inconsecutive, isn't there, about a spot?"

"But a spot, Aurelia; in theory, what *could* be quieter?"

"Nothing, dear," Miss Pantry said.

"And yet," Lady Anne murmured, "when one's fastening one's mind on one's prayers, one requires a little something."

"I cannot see why it should be easier to sink into a brown study by staring at a splash."

"Often, I think it helps."

"Of course you may be right."

"Shall we take it down into the Cathedral, Anne, and try?"

"This morning I've so many things to do. There's always one's small share of mischief going on."

"I would never take part in the parish broils if ever I could avoid it."

"I cannot be so impersonal, I'm afraid."

"But surely a little neutral sympathy——"

"To be sympathetic without discrimination is so very debilitating."

"Do you never feel tired?"

"Oh yes, sometimes."

"I adore the country," Aurelia said, "but I should die of weariness if I stayed here long."

"No, really, I like Ashringford. I abuse it, of course, just as I do dear Walter, or anybody whom I see every day . . . but really I'm fond of the place."

"That's quite reasonable."

"And if sometimes I'm a wreck," Lady Anne explained, "I look forward to my St. Martin's summer later on."

"But Canterbury's so dreadful. It's such a groove."

"The proximity of our English Channel would be a joy."

66

" It's only seldom you'd get a whiff of the sea."

Lady Anne's eyes skimmed her lawn.

A conventional bird or two—a dull thrush, a glossy
crow—cowering for worms; what else had she, or
anyone else, the right to expect? Sun, wind and quivering leaves made a carpet of moving shadows.

" It's with Stockingham," she said, " at present,
that I've a bone. I shall scold Lady Georgia when she
comes. To tell a curate his profile is suggestive of
Savonarola is so like her. But it's really a mistake.
It makes a man firebrand, even when he's not. He
gets rude and makes pointed remarks, and offends
everybody. And I have to sit at home to talk to him."

Aurelia looked interested.

" Probably a creature with a whole gruesome
family? " she indirectly inquired.

" Unhappily he's only just left Oxford."

" Ah, handsome, then, I hope."

" On the contrary, he's like one of those cherubs
one sees on eighteenth-century fonts with their mouths
stuffed with cake."

" Not really? "

"*And he wears glasses.*"

" But he takes them off sometimes——? "

" That's just what I don't know."

" Then, as you will hardly need me," Aurelia said,
" I'll go over to the Cresswell Arms and see Chloe.
Poor dear, it's very dull for her all alone."

" How is Miss Valley getting on? "

" So well. She asks if she can come up one afternoon to examine the tapestries when Walter's out."

" By all means, but the tapestries are too fantastic,
I should imagine, to be of any service to her. His-
torically, they're quite . . . untrustworthy."

" Does it matter? Besides, the Archdeacon believes
that Mrs. Cresswell was an Ely anchoress and not an
Ashringford anchoress at all."

" That's nonsense," Lady Anne said; " she belongs to us."

" I don't know why you should be so keen on her," Miss Pantry said. " Of course, she *may* have been a saint, but from some of the little things I've heard, I fancy you might ransack heaven to find her——"

" I won't hear anything against Mrs. Cresswell. Her career here was an exquisite example to us all."

" Well, I'm sure I hope so, dear."

" And perhaps, Aurelia," Lady Anne said gently, " if you're going to the Cresswell Arms you'll call at the workhouse on your way, and find out what actually took place. I won't ask you to stop in Priest Street with a pudding. . . . And if you should see Miss Hospice in the garden, will you send her up to me? "

For some time after Aurelia had left her, Lady Anne stood in the window looking out upon the Cathedral. There was usually a little scaffolding about it. . . . If she had a voice in the matter it should never be allowed to come away. Her spirit shrank from the peculiar oppressiveness of perfection. And the Cathedral was very perfect indeed. How admirable, through the just sufficient drapery of the trees, were the great glazed windows that flashed like black diamonds in the sun. The glass, indeed, at Ashringford was so wonderful that sticks and umbrellas were left (by order) at the door. . . .

Lady Anne looked up at the large contented towers and fetched a sigh.

They were lovely.

Without veiling her eyes, they were as near perfection as she could conveniently bear. Placed at the end of the tennis lawn too, they had saved her from many a run.

Miss Missingham, in her *Sacerdotalism and Satanism*, has called the whole thing heavy, "*Very weighty indeed*," although she willingly admits that at twilight the towers, with their many pinnacles, become utterly fantastic, *like the helmets of eunuchs in carnival time*. But then, if there was not much spontaneity about them on the whole, they had taken so long to build. Stone towers cannot be dashed off like Fragonard's *Inspiration*.

At the Pilgrims' Depot in the busy High Street there is to be obtained an anthology of " Last Words," culled chiefly from the lips of the womenkind of the Episcopal set. If the sayings of these ladies were often salty and frequently pointed, the Palace, it should be said, faced a Gothic arch.

Built around two sides of a quadrangle, it was, according to local taste, an ugly, forlorn affair, its bricks having been masked by stucco in 1785. Here and there, where the stucco had chipped away, the brick peeped out as if some rare fresco lay smothered underneath. From a flagged courtyard a classic stair-case of divine proportions swept, exteriorly, to a broad balcony above the ground floor (spoken of sometimes as the loggia), which created, perhaps, something of a grand-opera effect.

It was here, recumbent upon a deck-chair, propped up by piles of brilliant cushions, that Mrs. Henedge, in her day, preferred to drink afternoon tea, surrounded by the most notable Church dignitaries that she could find.

It was told that at one of these courts she had had as many as three bishops simultaneously handing her toast.

What wonder was it that persons should linger in delighted amazement at the wrought-iron gates until they formed a substantial crowd?

Carts would draw up, motorists stop, pedestrians sit down.

Lady Anne, on the contrary, preferred to hold her receptions out of sight.

To many, unquestionably it was a blow.

She preferred, when not indoors, her tennis lawn, with its high clipped hedges, behind which the Cathedral rose inscrutably, a soft grey pile elongating itself above the trees, from whence would fall, fitfully, the saintly caw-cawing of the rooks.

Lady Anne's eyes fell from the wise old towers.

Framed in the expiring windows of the china-cupboard, the glimpse of Ashringford was entrancing quite. Across the meadows could be seen the struggling silver of the broad river, as it curled about Crawbery, invariably with some enthusiast, rod in hand, waiting quietly upon the bank. Nearer, hither and thither, appeared a few sleepy spires of churches, too sensible to compete with the Cathedral, but nevertheless possibly more personal; like the minor characters in repertoire that support the *star*.

She turned as her secretary, Miss Hospice, entered.

With a rather cruel yellow at her neck, waist and feet, and a poem of fifty sheets, on *Verlaine at Bourne-mouth*, at her back. What is there left to say——

Lady Anne was fond of her secretary because of her wild, beautiful handwriting, that seemed to fly, and because she really did enjoy to snub the Bishop's sisters. And others, too, liked her. Perpetually, she would make those pleasant little pampered remarks, such as, on a sultry August night, " B-r-r-r! it's cold enough to light a fire! " Now that Aurelia was at the Palace, she should have been away on holiday, but, somehow, this year, she wasn't.

Lady Anne had discovered Miss Hospice some years since, lost in the advertisements of *The Spectator* seeking, as she had explained, the position of guardian angel to some elderly literary man.

Intelligent and sympathetic, Nature had appeared to indicate the way. The short hair, the long wavy nose *à la* Luca Signorelli, that seemed scarcely willing to sustain the heavy gold glasses, the figure, as flat as

Lower Egypt, and the dazzling eyes like Mrs. Aphra
Behn—for a really ticklish post, all was right. With
complete clairvoyance Lady Anne had secured this
treasure for her own, whose secretarial uses had now
quite reached their zenith. Miss Madge Hospice was
Lady Anne's barbed wire.

" I was wondering what had become of you," Lady
Anne said to her as she came in. " Where on earth
have you been? "

" . . . Wading through fields of violet vetch. It's
so delicious out."

" Had you forgotten to-day? "

" I don't think so: I've told Gripper again to sponge
the stretchers, but he's so lazy, you know he never
will."

The bi-weekly Ambulance Classes at the Palace, so
popular socially, were, it must be owned, on a parallel
with the butter-making at Trianon.

" That's thoughtful," Lady Anne said. " And now,
here are so many letters to answer, I really don't know
where to begin."

When a few minutes later the Reverend Peter Pet
was announced they were entirely engrossed.

"Savonarola! " Lady Anne exclaimed. Miss Hospice
continued conscientiously to write.

" Is it possible that anybody cares a straw what he
says? " she queried.

" A curate should be quiescent; that's the first
thing."

" But tactlessness is such a common complaint."

" He has referred to the Bishop as *a Faun crowned
with roses*," Lady Anne said severely.

" I *heard* it was *Satyr*."

" And his encounter with Miss Wookie. . . . Well,
not since the last election have I heard anything so
scurrilous."

" And is he absolutely charming? "

Lady Anne arranged her descriptions; when the introductions came about there was often some confusion.

"He's fair," she said, "with bright green eyes. And such gay, attractive teeth."

"You make me curious to see him."

"I should hate to shake his faith in his vocation," Lady Anne murmured, "but——"

"Have you dropped anything?"

"Only my little bit of lace. . . ."

And although very likely Lady Anne was the most sensible woman alive, she would scarcely have had the claim had she not crossed first to the mirror and——

But oh, *Vanity!* is there any necessity to explain?

VIII

" How fond I am of this sleepy magic place! "

" In town," Mrs. Shamefoot said, " the trees so seldom forget themselves into expressive shapes."

" Well . . . You haven't answered my question yet."

" Because I don't know! "

Lord Blueharnis looked bored.

" Is it grey," Lady Castleyard wondered, chiming in, " or white; or would it be blue? "

She settled herself reposefully, as if for ever.

" That Sacharissa style," Atalanta remarked, bending forward, " of rolling your hair is so enslaving."

" I wish you would *not* look down my neck like an archer of Carpaccio."

" Tell me what you're guessing."

" The colour of the cuckoo's egg. . . ."

" If I recollect, it's a mystic medley of mauves."

Mrs. Shamefoot prepared to rise. " We shall get appendicitis," she exclaimed, " if we sit here long."

Lord Blueharnis prevented her. " Oh, what charming hands! . . . Don't move."

" If you admire them now," Mrs. Shamefoot said, sinking back, " you would worship them when I'm really worn out. My hands never look quite so marvellous as when I'm tired."

" But . . . fresh as you are; mayn't I see? "

" How perfectly idiotic you are."

" For years," Lady Georgia's voice came falling to them through the dusk, " she couldn't get rid of it. In the end, quite in despair, and simply prostrate, she exchanged it for a string of pearls."

"Might one learn what?" Lord Blueharnis inquired, half turning.

"Number 39. . . . Her great, comfortless house."

"Darling Georgia! Why will she always withdraw to the gladiators' seats?"

"Away, too, in all the dew."

"'Up in those tracts with her, it was the peace of utter light and silence.'"

"How fascinating your *cabochon* tips look, dear, against the night."

"Little horrid—owl—thing, I wonder you can see them at all."

"How astonishingly acoustic it is."

"These marble tiers are very cold."

"I don't suppose the Greeks wore any more than we do."

"Though, possibly, not less."

"Aren't you coming down to recite?"

"Oh no; when Miss Compostella comes, we'll get her to do it instead."

"I shall come up and fetch you," Mrs. Shamefoot said, "if Mr. Aston will lend me a hand."

And, with the indifference of Madame Valpy about to climb the scaffold, she rose.

She was wearing an imaginative plain white dress that made her appear like a broken statue.

"Good-bye," she murmured, "Dirce," her voice harking to the period of her heels—Louis XV.

"Be very careful. I've had Aase's Death Music running in my head all day. . . ."

And now beneath her lay the Greek theatre like an open fan. All around the glimmering sweeps of steps the sullen elms gave a piquant English touch.

"How perfectly fairy!" she exclaimed, falling breathless at the top.

Like some thin archangel, Lady Georgia stooped to help her rise.

" I adore the end of summer," she said, " when a new haystack appears on every hill."

Beyond the dark proscenium and the clustering chimneys of the house stretched the faint far fields. No lofty peaks, or Himalayas, but quiet, modest hills, a model of restraint.

" Isn't it soothing? " Mrs. Shamefoot said.

" I suppose so; but it quite makes me cry to think of you fastened up over there in Ashringford, with a stiff neck, till the day of doom."

" I always respond," Mrs. Shamefoot replied, " to the sun."

Lady Georgia opened wide, liquid eyes. " I shall hardly ever dare to come and look at you," she said.

" But I should be entirely flattering, dear, for you."

" Would you? Many people are so thoughtless about their lights."

Mrs. Shamefoot wound an arm about the neck of an architectural figure.

" Don't you agree," she said, " that there's something quite irresistible about stained-glass caught in a brutality of stone? "

Lady Georgia seated herself stiffly. " Caught," she exclaimed. " When I die, I should prefer to leave no trace."

" But you follow, darling, don't you, what I mean?"

" For anyone that needed a perpetual retreat," Lady Georgia said, " Ashringford, I should say, would be quite ideal. The choir's so good. Such peaceful voices. . . . And there's nothing about the Cathedral in any way forbidding! One could really hardly wish for anything *nicer*. The late Bishop often used to say it suggested to him *Siena*, with none of the sickening scent of hides."

Mrs. Shamefoot became ecstatic.

" We must make Dr. Pantry promise a two-tier window," she said, " and Dirce can take the top."

" Sharing a window," Lady Georgia said, " in my opinion, is such a mistake. One might just as well erect a Jesse-window and invite a whole multitude to join. It may be egotistical, but if I were going down the centuries at all, I should want to go alone."

" Unfortunately," Mrs. Shamefoot murmured, " it's too late to alter things, without behaving badly. . . ."

" That could be arranged. There's not the same rush now for monuments that there used to be."

" Just at present there's almost a revival. . . . There are so many Art Schools about, aren't there? Everybody one meets appears to be commemorating themselves in one way or another. It's become a craze. Only the other day my mother-in-law had designed for Soco a tiny triptych of herself as a kind of Madonna, with a napkin drawn far down over her eyes."

" Really? "

" Of course it's only a firescreen; it's *certain* to get scorched."

" But still——"

" And with some scraps of old Flemish glass Lady Faningay has set up a sort of tortoise-shell window to a friend; so pretty. . . . She would have it."

" Oh, that dreadful réchauffé of fragments. I've seen it."

" But you understand, don't you, dearest, my poor motives, what they mean. . . ."

" I should be disappointed," Lady Georgia said, " if you did not, with Mrs. Cresswell, become the glory of the town." And with a sorrowful, sidelong smile she turned towards Ashringford, admirable in a gay glitter of lights.

Faint as rubbed-out charcoal where it touched the sky, loomed the Cathedral, very wise and very old, and very vigilant and very detached—like a diplomat in disgrace—its towers, against the orange dusk, swelling saliently towards their base, inflated, so the

76

guide-books said, by the sweet music of Palestrina. Between them, an exquisite specimen of irony, careered the short spire, which was perhaps an infelicity that would grow all long and regretful-looking towards the night.

" Since you've climbed so far," Lady Georgia said, " I shall repeat to you a somewhat saturnine little song of Mrs. Cresswell."

And opening her fan, she said:

" I am disgusted with Love.
I find it exceedingly disappointing,
Mine is a nature that cries for more ethereal things,
Banal passions fail to stir me.
I am disgusted with Love."

" How heavenly she is! "
" Such an amusing rhythm——"
" I do so enjoy the bypaths," Mrs. Shamefoot said, " of poetry. Isn't there any more? "
" No. I believe that's all."
" Of course her words condemn her."
" But that she should have arrived at a state of repugnance, possibly, is something."
" Isn't it unkind," Lady Castleyard interrupted, advancing towards them, " to recite up here all alone?"
" Dearest Dirce, how silently you came!——"
" Like a cook we had on the Nile," Lady Georgia observed, " who once startled me more than I can ever say by breaking suddenly out of the moon-mist so noiselessly that he might have been treading on a cloud."
" Well, won't you come down? A stage and nobody on it is shockingly dull."
" This evening, I really don't feel equal to Euripides," Lady Georgia murmured, " although perhaps I might manage the *Hound*."

" *The Hound of Heaven?* My dear, what could be more divine? "

Mrs. Shamefoot looked away.

Star beyond star, the sky was covered. The clouds, she observed, too, appeared to be preparing for an Assumption.

IX

WHEN Aurelia left Lady Anne she set a straw hat harmlessly upon her head, powdered her neck at a tarnished mirror with crystal nails, selected a violet parasol, profoundly flounced, slipped a small volume of Yogi Philosophy into her wallet, took up, put down, and finally took up the cornflour pudding, gave a tearful final glance at her reflection, put out her tongue for no remarkable reason, and walked out into the street.

Oh, these little expeditions through the town! . . .

Hypolita habitually got over them by horse when, in a bewildering amazon, she would swoop away like a valkyrie late for a sabbat.

"One can only hope that heaven will wash," Aurelia murmured meekly, as she prepared to trudge. Which optimism, notwithstanding the perfect stillness of the day, fluttered her aside like a leaf.

It was disgraceful the way her linen came home —torn.

"Torn, torn, torn," she breathed, twirling her sunshade with short, sharp twirls that implied the click of a revolver.

But to reach the laundry she was obliged to pass the Asz—that river spoken of, by vulgar persons, often, as *the Ass*.

Between solemn stone embankments and an array of bridges spaced out with effigies of fluminal deities, a sadly spent river coiled reluctant through the town. Sensitive townsfolk felt intensely this absence of water, which, in many minds, amounted almost to a disgrace. Before the Cathedral, just where, artistically, it was needed most, there was scarcely a trickle.

As a rule Aurelia was too completely preoccupied with her own sensations to observe particularly her whereabouts, but instinctively, as her foot touched the bridge, she would assume the tiresome, supercilious smile of a visitor.

This morning, however, she paused to lean an arm upon the parapet to rest her pudding.

Has not Mrs. Cresswell (in a trance) described heaven as *another* grim reality? Aurelia stood, and remained to drum a tune.

" Oh, I could dance for ever," she exclaimed, " to the valse from *Love Fifteen!* " And she lingered to hum, by way of something more, Priscilla's air from *Th' Erechtheum Miss*. How giddy it was! What abandon there was in it. Happy Priscilla, hardworking little thing; from her part song with Bill, love, manifestly, was sometimes simple and satisfactory.

Aurelia peered down.

The creak of oarswhispered up to her with wizardry.

There was often a barge to be towed along. Here came one now, lifted over the sun-splashed water, with a mast, long and slightly bent, like the quill of an ostrich feather. The stubby willows, that mirrored their cloudy shadows from the bank, sobbed pathetically, though too well bred to weep.

" It gets emptier and emptier," she mused. " I suppose the weeds absorb the water! "

" Oh, beware of freckles! "

Aurelia turned.

" Who could have foreseen," she said, " that our intercession for fine weather would produce all this heat? "

" If two of the churches, in future, were to apply, I consider it should amply suffice." And Mrs. Henedge, leaning leisurely upon the arm of Winsome Brookes, and sharing the weight of half a mysterious basket with Monsignor Parr, nodded and was gone.

With her streaming strings and veils she suggested, from behind, the Goddess Hathor as a sacred cow.

" I'd rather go naked than wear some of the things she wears," Aurelia murmured critically, as she watched her out of sight.

But a ripple of laughter from some persons at the toll made Miss Pantry fix her eyes perseveringly into space.

The peals of laughter of the Miss Chalfonts were as much a part of Ashringford as the Cathedral bells. Constantly they were laughing. And nobody knew why. Along the crooked High Street they were often to be seen, almost speechless with merriment, peering in at the shop windows, a trio interlaced, or standing before the announcements of the Lilliputian Opera House, where came never anything more extraordinarily exhilarating than Moody-Manners or Mrs. D'Oyley Carte. Tourists avoided their collision. And even the delicate-looking policeman in the market-place, when he became aware of their approach, would invariably disappear.

Rossetti, long ago, had painted them, very pale, in bunched-up dresses, playing cats'-cradle in a grey primeval waste. And the reaction, it was politely supposed, had completely turned their brain.

" They will laugh themselves to death," Aurelia murmured, as she wandered on.

The scent of the bushes of sweetbrier from innumerable gardens followed her along the sentimental esplanade that faced the Asz as far as the gates of Miss Chimney's school for backward boys. Here Vane Street, with its model workhouse, began, the admiration of all. Debt, disaster, held few terrors, while gazing at this winter palace. . . . With a chequered pavement below, and an awning above, a man, trusting to philanthropy, might reasonably aspire to lounge away what remained to him of life, inhaling the suavest of cigarettes.

Deferring her errand there until her return, Aurelia wound up Looking-Glass Street towards the laundry. With its houses, that seemed to have been squeezed from tubes of multi-coloured paint, it was not unlike, she had often heard, a street in one of Goldoni's plays. Miss Hospice catches the peeping Brueghelness of it in her *Scroll from the Fingers of Ta-Hor*, in which, steeping herself in deception and mystery, she attempts to out-Chatterton Chatterton with:

" Poor pale pierrot through the dark boughs peering
  In the purple gloaming of a summer's evening,
  Oh his heart is breaking, can't you hear him sobbing,
  Or is it the wind that's passing among the yellow
     roses? . . ."

An imperfect scarab that owed its existence chiefly from loitering in Looking-Glass Street, or thereabouts.

Choosing her way along it, Aurelia perceived, midway, a lady with a pair of scissors, who, in an abstracted attitude, was inducing a yew-tree peacock to behave.

" Good-morning," the lady with the scissors cried, " I am so glad. . . . I was just coming round to inquire."

Miss Wookie was always *just going* somewhere. At all hours one would find her in a hat.

" To inquire? " Aurelia halted.

The lady leaned classically against her bird. In its rather dishevelled state, it resembled a degenerate swan.

" People are circulating such dreadful stories," she said.

" Indeed! "

" Such shocking stories. Poor mamma! This morning she seems quite pulled down."

" Some new nervousness, no doubt."

" She has sent me out to tidy this. As if I were in a condition for gardening! "

" To fulfil a ritual, if one isn't quite oneself, does often only harm."

Miss Wookie considered her work. " I clip the thing," she said, " in the wrong places. . . . In profile it has almost the look of a turkey. So unnatural! "

" Whatever happens, it could always be a blue bird."

" We hear you're going to pull down half of the Cathedral," Miss Wookie said tragically, " and put in a Russian ballet window. Is it *true?* "

Aurelia appeared astonished.

" It's the first I've heard of it! " she exclaimed.

" The Palace, of course, always is the last to hear of anything," Miss Wookie said, " but I assure you all Ashringford's talking. And, *oh, Miss Pantry,* Mr. Pet has been saying the most frightful things about us. About me, and about mamma."

" He's a horrid, conceited boy," Aurelia comforted her.

" Come in, won't you? I'd like you to hear the truth."

Aurelia blinked. " It's very kind," she said, " but with this nasty, sticky dish——"

" Never mind the dish," Miss Wookie murmured, unlatching the gate.

" Sycamores," the shelter of Mrs. Wookie, the widow of Brigadier Percy Wookie of the Ashringford Volunteers, to whom there was an explanatory tablet in St. Cyriac's which related, like a page torn from Achilles Tatius, how and where, and by whose manicured extremities he fell, was a bleak brick cottage, with " 1839 " scrawled above the door. A short path with a twist like a lizard's tail led up to the entrance, where an unremarkable tree with a long Latin name did its best to keep out the light.

" Poor, poor, poor, *poor* mamma ! " Miss Wookie repeated rhythmically, as she led the way in.

Mrs. Wookie was usually to be found reclining upon a sofa, agitating a phial of medicine, or embroidering martyrdoms imaginatively upon a stole. Interrupted in any way, she would become as flurried as a canary when a hand is thrust into its cage.

But to-day, because she was unwell, her daughter had given her, by way of distraction, a party frock to pull to pieces, and now the invalid was aggrandising perceptibly the aperture to an evening gown in a posture rather more at ease than that of Whistler's Mother.

The morning-room at the " Sycamores," mid-Victorian and in the Saracen style, would most likely have impressed a visitor as an act of faith throughout. Upon the mantelshelf, however, between much that was purely emigrant, stood two strange bottles.

Being in the City-of-Random-Kisses to receive a legacy, and by proxy (alas) a blessing; and caught in a shower of perhaps pre-determined rain, Miss Wookie and her guardian angels—handsome rural creatures— had sought shelter beneath the nearest arch.

It was noon. All three were completely wet.

" Christie's . . ." Miss Wookie observed the name, whilst the angels shook the water from their hair, and flapped the moisture sparkling from their wings. And reassured by the six first letters, she had gone inside.

" What else ? " she can recall remarking, prepared for a waiter to pounce out upon her from the top of the stairs.

And then, instead of the prosaic bone, as afterwards she explained, and the glass of lemonade, and the quiet rest, and the meditation on the unexpected behaviour of poor Aunt Nettle . . . Miss Wookie had found herself calling out in a sort of dream for the vases, until, for the life of her, it would have been impossible to stop. And when, ultimately, she reappeared in Ashringford, the legacy all gone, it never occurred to Mrs. Wookie to part with her *famille rose* again.

"Family Rose" the bottles had become to her—and accordingly as dear.

"I see that bodices are getting more and more scamped, Kate," Mrs. Wookie remarked, as her daughter came in, "and so, my dear, I hope I've done what's right."

Miss Wookie stood still. "Oh, Tatty," she said.

"With the scraps of stuff I've taken," Mrs. Wookie announced, "I can make four small pincushions; or two large ones."

"I didn't know how selfish you could be."

"Don't be absurd, Kate. You may be sure I'd not allow you to appear in anything unbecoming. And if you go out, my child, to-night, don't forget, like last time, to order yourself *a fly*."

"I'm so glad," Aurelia murmured, coming forward, "you're able to sew."

With her needle suspended in the air, Mrs. Wookie fluttered off to a favourite perch.

"I was very poorly first thing," she said. "Kate tried to persuade me to send for a physician. But I wouldn't let her."

"Luckily an attack is quickly gone."

Mrs. Wookie began to twitter. "And one of these days," she observed, "I'll go with it. I hardly expect to survive the fall of the leaf; I don't see how I can. . . . Shall you ever forget last year, Kate? Round Ashringford, there're so many trees."

"Possibly all you need's a change of scene. Scheveningen, or somewhere——"

Mrs. Wookie floated to the floor. "A few minutes more or less on earth," she said dejectedly, "what does it matter? And packing upsets me so. Besides, I wish to die here, beneath my own roof."

" But what pleasure would it give you? "

" None, Miss Pantry. But I wish to die there."

" You may be right," Aurelia assented; " the strained atmosphere of tuberose and trunks of a health resort in autumn is often a little sad."

" And Ashringford in autumn," Miss Wookie said, "isn't so bad. Of course the leaves come down. The worst of it is, one can get no grapes; I can get no grapes."

Mrs. Wookie looked pathetic. " If I could only see Kate married," she complained. " It comes, of course, of living in a cathedral town. Curates are such triflers."

" One little wedding, Mrs. Wookie, oughtn't to be so difficult. Consider, with five or six daughters to dispose of, how much more tiresome it would have been! "

At such a notion Mrs. Wookie's nose grew almost long.

" In the forties," she crooned, " we were always dropping our things, and we fainted more. Of course, in the country there are many ways still. One can send a girl out with a landscape figure, sketching. That always works. . . . Alice, Grace, Pamela and Teresa, my nieces, all went that way."

" Oh, Tatty, Teresa married a menial. She went away with a chauffeur."

" How very disgraceful! " Aurelia remarked.

" I suppose it was. Particularly as he wasn't their own."

" Be quiet, my dear; we live too near the laundry as it is."

" Besides," Miss Wookie said, striking her chord, " I don't intend to marry. I should be sorry to let myself in for so many miseries. . . . An habitual husband would, also, bore me to death."

" Hush, Kate! It's just those infantine reflections that circulate and get twisted, till they arrive, goodness knows how, to the ears of that dreadful Mr. Pet."

" I'm sorry you find him so troublesome," Aurelia said.

Mrs. Wookie glowered. " I wonder I'm alive," she exclaimed, " from the reports they bring. Not only am I affronted, but the Cathedral, it seems, itself, is in peril, and the name of our city also endangered. For a whim, if not from sheer madness, Dr. Pantry, it appears, has petitioned the Archbishop to contract the See of Ashringford into *Ashingford*. Merciful heaven, why can't he leave it alone? "

" I dare say if Mr. Pet had his way he would boil us down to *Ash*," Miss Wookie observed.

Her mother closed her eyes.

" If that happened," she said, " I should leave Ashringford."

Driven out with her Family Rose, and followed by her servant Quirker, and by Kate, she saw herself stumbling at sunset like the persecuted women on her stoles. And night would find them (who knew) where the cornflowers passed through the fields in a firm blue bar.

" That Mr. Pet is a disgrace to his cloth," she murmured, rallying. " Indeed, I'd rather we had Mr. Cunningham back again. He wasn't a great preacher, but he neither droned nor gabbled, and he could be wonderfully voluble when he liked."

" Oh, my dear, but he was so unbalanced. He would do his American conjuring tricks in the vestry before the choir boys. . . . Such a bad example."

" Still, it's an ill wind. . . . And Miss Wardle and her set seem quite satisfied with his successor."

" She would be. If you asked her for her hymn-book she'd imagine it was being borrowed for some felonious purpose. "

Aurelia looked interested. " I don't see what one could do with a hymn-book," she exclaimed.

Mrs. Wookie's nose grew long again.

" Don't you? " she answered. " Neither do I."

" Besides, fresh from a Cornish curacy, what can he know? " Miss Wookie wondered.

Aurelia corrected her.

" From Oxford, I fancy, isn't he . . .? "

" The man's a perfect scourge, wherever he's from," Miss Wookie declared. " Not half-an-hour ago he dashed down this street like a tornado. I was standing with Quirker at the door. You know I collect motor numbers, which obliges me frequently to run out into the road. . . . I have such a splendid collection. I hope I'm not so vulgar as to bang a door, still, when I saw him coming, I confess I shut it! "

Mrs. Wookie joined her hands.

" He must have discovered about Mrs. Henedge and Monsignor Parr," she said. " How shocking, should there be a struggle."

" What should make you think so? "

" They've gone to pace out the site of the new church. . . . Monsignor Parr has been hurrying to and fro all the morning, like St. Benedict at Monte Cassino. And his employees already are entrenched at the corner of Whip-me-Whop-me Street at Mrs. Cresswell's old Flagellites Club."

Aurelia raised her eyes.

" Surely in such a sweet old house it would feel almost vulgar to be alive! "

" I don't know," Mrs. Wookie replied. " I do not care for Mrs. Cresswell. She repels me."

"In any case, if anything should happen, Mrs. Henedge will be quite secure. That fair-haired pianist accompanied her. You remember him, don't you, mamma? "

" I remember him perfectly. Nobody in the world ever got over a stile like Mr. Brookes."

" To see her continually with that perverse musician or with that priest is enough to make poor good Bishop Henedge burst his coffin."

" Alas, Ashringford isn't what it used to be," Mrs. Wookie complained. " The late Bishop was, in many matters, perhaps not a very prudent man . . . but he had authority. And a shapelier leg, my dears, never trod the earth. He obtained his preferment, one may say, solely on their account. He had such long, long legs. Such beautiful long, long legs."

" And," Miss Wookie murmured, flinging her flower, " a really reassuring way of blowing his nose! To hear him do it was to realise immediately the exact meaning of *conviction.*"

" But in the official portrait," Aurelia objected, " he appears such a little gasp of a man! "

Mrs. Wookie became belligerent.

" That topsy-turvy thing in the Town Hall! I was fond of my husband, but I'd scorn to be painted in evening-mourning pointing at his dead miniature. His portrait indeed! His widow's rather, basking on a sofa, with a locket."

" Apparently Mrs. Henedge admires the baroque."

" Well, her new church will be dedicated to it," Miss Wookie assured.

" So ornate? "

" Mr. Thumbler has gone to Italy to make the drawings. . . . The exterior is to be an absolute replica of St. Thomas in Cremona, with stone saints in demonstrative poses on either side of the door."

" And the interior, no doubt, will be a dream."

" It is to be lit entirely by glass eighteenth-century chandeliers," Miss Wookie said, " and there will be a Pompeian frieze, and a good deal of art leather work from the hand of one of Lady Georgia's young men, who did some of the panelling at St. Anatasia's once, although, of course, he was rather *restricted.*"

" Art leather," Aurelia said, " sounds to me a mistake."

" If it's half as delicate as at St. Anatasia, it should be really rather lovely."

" Let us hope that it may——"

" And then there are to be some very nice pictures. In fact, the pictures will be a feast. Madame Gandarella, the wife of the Minister, has presented a *St. Cecilia Practising* and a more than usually theatrical Greuze. And Baroness Lützenschläger is to give a Griego. Nobody knows quite what it represents—long, spiritual women grouped about a cot. The Clalfonts, also, are offering a Guardi for the baptistery. But as there was never any mention of one, they ran no very terrible risk. And last, though hardly least, Lord Brassknocker is sending to Paris to be framed a mysterious pastelle entitled *Tired Eyelids on Tired Eyes* which, as Mrs. Pontypool truly says, is certainly the very last thing she looks."

" Kate hears everything," Mrs. Wookie said; " thread me a needle, Kate."

" And when everything is complete, the Grand Duchess Ximina will stay at Stockingham to unveil the leather. The Cardinal Pringle will appear to sprinkle the pictures and to bless it all."

" If the Grand Duchess stays at Stockingham," Mrs. Wookie said, " I suppose they will prepare the State bed."

" Poor woman," Aurelia murmured. " It's as hard as a board."

" Elizabeth——" Miss Wookie began, but Aurelia rose.

" How pretty the garden looks," she said.

Miss Wookie smiled.

" It's only charming," she observed, checked in her little tale, " on account of the trees."

" Tut, Kate. I'm sure in the spring, when the laburnums are out, and lilacs in bloom, the garden's hard to beat."

"It has been always summer," Aurelia said, as she took her leave, "when I've stayed here before."

Down an alley and through an arch led her straight to Washing-tub Square.

Notwithstanding the eloquence prepared, it was with relief that she perceived her laundress docilely pinning some purple flowers against a fence, while close by, in the dust, Miss Valley was kneeling, with her arms about a child.

At her approach the Biographer lifted loose blue eyes that did not seem quite firm in her head, and a literary face.

"I shall have to commence my life all over again," she said. "Six weeks wasted! This child—employed in the laundry here"—and she began to shake it—"this carrier of dirty linen . . . is Reggie . . . Cresswell—a descendant of the saint. . . ."

And because Miss Valley seemed in such distress, and because, after all, she was a friend, Aurelia let fall her dish and, with a glance right and left, first, to make sure that "nothing was coming," sank down upon the road, by her side.

"But can you not see," she murmured sympathetically, taking Miss Valley by the hand, "that an apologia is just what everyone most enjoys?" And then, drawing Reggie to her, she exclaimed: "Oh, you dear little boy!"

X

" And your own tomb, dear Doctor Pantry, what is it going to be? "

" My own tomb," the Bishop replied demurely, " will be composed entirely of encaustic tiles that come from Portugal—a very simple affair."

Mrs. Shamefoot sighed. " It sounds," she said, " almost agitating."

" Ah, these old cathedrals, my dear Mrs. Shamefoot, how many marriages and funerals they've seen!"

" I suppose——"

" Ashringford may not have the brave appearance of Overcares, or the rhythm of Perch, or the etherealness of Carnage, or the supremacy of Sintrap; but it has a character, a conspicuousness of its own."

" It stands with such authority."

" To be sure. You'd hardly believe there was a debt upon it."

" No; indeed one would not."

Lady Anne broke in. " There is often," she remarked, " a haze. Although I couldn't bear the Cathedral without a few sticks and props, I should miss them frightfully. It's curious the way the restorations hang fire, especially with the number of big houses there are about. Don't you agree with me, Mrs. Roggers? "

" Decidedly," the Archdeacon's wife exclaimed, beginning to docket them upon a glove. When revealing no small mishap, she quite omitted Stockingham from the list.

At this gust of tact Lady Anne appeared amazed.

"If Mrs. Shamefoot wishes to explore the Cathedral,"

the Bishop said, " it will be well to do so before the excursion train gets in from Perch."

" Then you had better take her across."

" But you'll come with us."

" I must remain here for Lady Georgia. Should Mrs. Henedge be out or telling her beads she'll be back directly."

" Very well, we will not be long."

" And be careful," Lady Anne adjured her husband, with fine frankness, " not to commit yourself. No rash promises! The Cathedral's all glass as it is. It will be like a conservatory before we've done."

" What are those wonderfully white roses? " Mrs. Shamefoot inquired of the Bishop, as she trailed with him away.

In a *costume de cathédrale*, at once massive and elusive, there was nostalgia in every line.

" They bear the same name as the Cathedral," the Bishop replied: " St. Dorothy."

Mrs. Shamefoot touched the episcopal sleeve.

" And that calm wee door? " she asked.

" It's the side way in."

" Tell me, Doctor Pantry, is there a ray of hope? "

" Without seeming uncharitable, or unsympathetic, or inhuman, what am I to say? With a little squeezing we might bury you in the precincts of the Cathedral."

" But I don't want to be trodden on."

" You might do a great deal worse than lay down a brass."

" With my head on a cushion and my feet upon flowers. Oh! "

" Or a nice shroud one. Nothing looks better. And they are quite simple to keep clean."

" But a brass," she said, " would lead to rubbings. I know so well! Persons on all fours, perpetually bending over me."

" I can see no objection in that."

" I don't think my husband would like it."

" Naturally; if Mr. Shamefoot would mind——"

" Mind? " She began to titter. " Poor Soco," she said; " poor, dear man. But a window's more respectable. Though I'd sooner I didn't borrow an old one."

And with an effort she manœuvred her hat through the narrow monastic door.

Darkness, and an aroma of fresh lilies, welcomed her, as though with cool, invisible hands.

Here, most likely, would she dwell until the last day surprised her. And, like twelve servants, the hours would bring her moods.

She sank impulsively to her knees. A window like a vast sapphire—a sumptuous sapphire, changing back —chilled her slightly.

Must colour change?

Here and there the glass had become incoherent a little, and begun to mumble.

" One could look for ever at the pretty windows! " she murmured, rising.

The Bishop seemed touched.

" We must try and find you a corner," he said, " somewhere."

She turned towards him.

" Oh, you make me happy."

" I said a corner," the Bishop replied. " Perhaps we can find you a lancet."

" A lancet! But I should be so congested, shouldn't I? I shall need some space. A wee wheel-window, or something of the kind."

The tones implied the colossal.

" A lancet would be rather limited, of course, but does that matter? "

" Wait till you see the designs."

With a sensation of uneasiness Doctor Pantry began to pivot about the font.

94

" In Cromwell's time," he explained, " it was used as a simple washtub."

" Oh, what a shame! "

" And from here," he said, " you get such a curious complication of arches."

Around the pillars drooped stone garlands that had been coloured once. From them a few torn and marvellous flags, that looked more as if they had waved triumphant over some field of scandal than anywhere else, reposed reminiscent.

" What shreds! "

" Certainly, they are very much riddled."

But she lingered apart a moment before the tomb of an Ashringford maiden, lying sleep-locked upon a pyre of roses, with supplicating angels at the head and feet.

" Do I," she whispered, " detect romance? "

The Bishop bent his head.

" Alas," he said, " the entire *bibliothèque rose.*"

" And how sweet something smells."

" Many persons have noticed it. Even when there has been barely a dry leaf within doors."

" Why, what? "

" It emanates from the Coronna Chapel, where Mrs. Cresswell is."

" Is it there always? "

" It varies. On some days it's as delicate as a single cowslip. On others it's quite strong, more like syringa."

Mrs. Shamefoot scanned the shadows.

" But Mrs. Cresswell," she inquired, " who was she—exactly? "

" Primarily," the Bishop replied, " she was a governess. And with some excellent people too. Apart from which, no doubt, she would have been canonised, but for an unfortunate remark. It comes in in *The Red Rose of Martyrdom*. ' If we are all a part of God,' she says, 'then God must *indeed* be horrible.' "

" Nerves are accountable for a lot. Possibly, her pupils were tiresome. . . . Or it was upon a hot day. In her *Autobiography* she confesses, doesn't she, to her sensibility to heat?"

Doctor Pantry smiled.

" What a charming book! "

" I love it too. It's a book that I adore."

" I have the 1540 edition."

" Have you? how rare! "

" Indeed, it's a possession that I prize."

" I should say so. I can repeat, almost by heart, the chapter that commences: ' What can be more melancholy than Stonehenge at sunset.' Her cry of astonishment on beholding it from the window of Lord Ismore's coach is the earliest impressionary criticism that we have. She was asleep, wasn't she, when a sudden jolt awoke her. ' The stones,' she said, to little Miss Ismore, whom she was piloting to Court, ' the stones are like immense sarcophagi suspended in the air. . . .' "

" Admirable! " the Bishop exclaimed.

" And Miss Ismore in her way was interesting too. Eventually she married Prince Schara, and retired to Russia with him. And kept a diary. Each night she would write down the common-places of the Czarina, with the intention of one day revealing them in a book; as if she hadn't sufficient incidents without! Before her death, in Moscow, where she was poisoned, one gathers that the influences of childhood, although most likely smothered, were not entirely put out. And she would wear her heavenly tiara at the opera as if it were a garland of thorns. Really, the Princess was one of the very first persons to get Russiaphobia."

" Russiaphobia; what is that? "

" Wearing one's rubies and emeralds at the same time," Mrs. Shamefoot said in a hushed voice.

The Bishop waved aside a hanging.

"There is usually," he explained, " a slight charge

asked for entrance to the Coronna Chapel. But to-day you're with me!"

She stood awed.

" How seductive she is; though, somehow, I should call her inclined to be too rotund for a saint! A saint should be slim and flexible as a bulrush. . . ."

" The effect, no doubt, of her fine gaiety! Her exuberance was wonderful. She was as gay as a patch of poppies to the last."

" I suppose, in her time, there were a few flower faces, but the majority of persons seem to have been quite appallingly coarse."

" It has often been remarked that she resembles Madame de Warens. . . ."

Mrs. Shamefoot became regretful.

" If only Rembrandt might have painted Madame de Warens!" she said.

" You have not yet been to our small gallery in the town?"

" I didn't know there was one."

" Oh, but you must go——"

" I will, but not before my own affair's arranged! Wait; a lancet, did you say? Or a wheel-window, or a chancel-light—I'll be confused."

" Before I can make any definite promises," the Bishop said, " an unworthy world is sure to demand a few credentials."

" Dear Doctor Pantry, were I to proclaim myself a saint you'd probably not believe it——"

" Indeed, I assure you I've no misgivings."

" I cannot conceive why, then, there should be any fuss."

" You have never yet come across our *Parish Magazine?* "

" I dare say if I stayed here long enough I'd get horrid too."

" No; I don't think you ever would."

" I might! "

" I assure you every time it appears I find myself wishing I were lying in the sanctity of my own sarcophagus."

"Dear Doctor Pantry, don't say such shocking things! I will not allow it. Besides, I could compose the notice myself."

" Indeed, I fear you'd have to."

" Behind a white mask and a dark cloak. Quite in the manner of Longhi. Thus: ' The beautiful Mrs. S., who (for the next few weeks) wishes to remain unknown, desires to remove from St. Dorothy one of those white windows (which resemble prose), and replace it by,' etc., etc., etc. Or, to slip away the west window altogether. . . ."

" But the west window . . . the pre-Raphaelite window. . . ."

" It's a blot to the Cathedral. I cannot make out what is written beneath; but isn't it to say that in the end the king marries the kitchenmaid and they lived happily ever after? "

" To remove the west window," the Bishop said, " when everyone is alive that subscribed for it, I fear would be impossible."

Mrs. Shamefoot peered about her. Once only, long ago, in the Pyrenees, could she recall a similar absence of accommodation.

" Perhaps," she said half shyly, " I might share the Coronna."

" Share the Coronna! "

Doctor Pantry turned pale at the impiety.

" Why not? Two triangles when they cut can make a star. . . ."

" I fear your Niccolo in Ashringford might be unapprehended."

" After all, what is the Dorothy window but a wonderful splash of colour? "

" Have you tried the Abbey? " Doctor Pantry asked.

" What, Westminster? "

" With a husband in the Cabinet. . . ."

Mrs. Shamefoot smiled sedately.

" But I'm not a public person," she said. " An actress. Although, of course, I do sell flowers."

" With such an object in view, Heaven forfend you should become one."

Mrs. Shamefoot closed her eyes.

" To be an actress," she said; " to ruin one's life before a room full of people. . . . What fun! "

" Every good preacher," Doctor Pantry observed, " has a dash of the comedian too."

" Do you go often to the play? "

" The last time I went," his lordship confessed, " was to see Mrs. Kendall in *The Elder Miss Blossom*."

" Oh, she's perfect."

" Although Lady Anne saw Yvette Guilbert only the other day."

Mrs. Shamefoot looked sympathetic.

" I can imagine nothing more sinister," she said, " than Yvette Guilbert singing ' Where-are-you-going-to-my-pretty-maid.' It will haunt me always." And she paused meditatively to admire a stone effigy of the first Lady Blueharnis, stretched out upon a pillow like a dead swan.

" How entirely charming the memorials are."

" I'm so glad that you like them."

" Somehow, some people are so utterly of this world," she mused, " that one cannot conceive of them being grafted into any other."

But a sound of unselfconscious respiration from behind the Blueharnis monument startled her.

" Macabre person! . . . Fiend! " she said.

Winsome looked up sleepily.

" I came," he explained, " to collect a few books for Mrs. Henedge."

99

Mrs. Shamefoot blinked.

" That looks," she observed, " like going."

" I don't want to be too hard on her," the Bishop said, " but I think she might have told me first."

" I cannot say," Winsome said. " In the country one is always grateful to find anything to do."

" Have you been here long? "

" Since yesterday. Already I could howl for staleness."

Mrs. Shamefoot glanced at the Bishop.

" Very likely," she said; " but to run away the moment you arrive, just because it's the most appealing place on earth . . . I should call it decadent! "

And, indeed, after a few hours nearer Nature, perpetually it was the same with him. A *nostalgie du pavé* began to set in. He would miss the confidential " Things is very bad, sir," of the newspaper boy at the corner; the lights, the twinkling advertisements of the Artistic Theatre . . . the crack of the revolver so audible those nights that the heroine killed herself, the suspense, the subsequent sickening silence; while the interest, on lighter evenings, would be varied by the " Call me my biplane," of Indignation as it flew hurriedly away.

Mrs. Shamefoot picked up a rich red-topped hymnbook.

" And so," she said, " the aloe, apparently, has bloomed! "

" No; not yet. But there's nothing like being ready."

" And when do you think it's to be? "

" I hardly care to say. Though, when the change is made, you can be certain it will be done quite quietly."

" In Ashringford," the Bishop said, " nothing is ever done quite quietly."

" But that's so silly of Ashringford! " Mrs. Shamefoot exclaimed. " When my sister 'verted, I assure

you nobody took the slightest notice. But then, of
course, she was always going backwards and forwards.
. . . She made excursions into three different re-
ligions. And she always came back dissatisfied and
grumbling."

" The world is disgracefully managed, one hardly
knows to whom to complain."

" Many people," the Bishop remarked, " are very
easily influenced. They have only to look at a peacock's
tail to think of Brahma."

Mrs. Shamefoot turned her eyes towards the entrancing glass.

How mysterious it was! Like the luminous carpets
that veil a dream.

She became abstracted a moment, lost in mental
measurements, unhappy and elaborate-looking, in
her mourning, as a wasted columbine.

" Well, since you're here, Mr. Brookes," she said,
" you must absolutely try the organ. And Doctor
Pantry has never heard me sing."

XI

From a choice of vivid cushions she placed the least likely behind her head.

" I'm ready! " And with a tired, distrustful smile she looked away towards the house as if it were a hospital.

At her feet crouched an animal who, hourly, was assuming an expression as becoming, and as interesting, she believed, as the wolf of St. Francis. Her hands full of dark clematis, clutched and crowned. . . .

" There'll be the funnel of the jam factory, and a few chimney-pots for background," Winsome said. " Do you mind? "

" My dear, what can I do? In the end, these horrid encroaching shapes will drive me out."

" One, two, three; do smile . . . less. I'd rather work a water-wheel than be a photographer."

Mrs. Henedge relaxed.

" I wish," she murmured, " instead, you'd decide about being Rose."

" I will. But in these wilds the very notion of a début makes one shiver."

" My dear Mr. Brookes, when you give your first concert I will lead you on to the platform and stay by you all the time! "

" Well, I'm vacillating. I only need a push."

" Oh, be careful of the tail."

And, indeed, an animal who had bitten a poet, worried a politician, amused a famous actress and harried a dancer was not to be ignored.

How was it possible, it may be asked, for anything in Ashringford to have come in contact with such celebrities? By what accident had these Illustrious crossed his path? Incidentally, St. Dorothy was responsible for all.

And now that Miss Compostella was awaited at Stockingham, and with a Rose de Tivoli within reach, there appeared every likelihood of lengthening the list—a poet, a politician, a pianist, *two* famous actresses, etc., in anticipation—he counted them over upon his paws, surveying, meanwhile, the newly planted scene; for his lady cared only for those airier sorts of trees, larches, poplars, willows, so that, in the spring, the garden looked extraordinarily inexperienced and green.

" I shall have to chloroform him," Mrs. Henedge said, " if he does it again."

" He might be grateful. One can never tell."

" Why, what's wrong? "

" I've so many moods. You cannot like 'em all. . . . I'm never characteristic! "

" Poor Mr. Vane! Never mind if you're bored. Relax! Recoup! The country's very good for you."

" That's what everyone says. Mrs. Shamefoot said the same to me this morning."

" Oh, have you seen her? "

" In the Cathedral. Do you know, if I stopped here long, I'd start a Satanic colony in your midst just to share the monotony."

" My dear, there's one already."

" Direct me—— "

" No; stay here and be good. I've something to tell you that will please you."

" Me? "

" Yes. Old Mrs. Felix said to my maid: ' I think Mr. Brookes so beautiful. He has such a young, romantic face! ' "

" What else did she say? "

" She said nothing more."

" Hooray! "

Mrs. Henedge raised a finger. " S-S-Sh! or you'll
disturb Monsignor Parr. He's half asleep in a rocking-
chair making his soul."

" According to Monsignor Parr, heaven will be a
perpetual concert. Do you think that true? "

" I believe he has been *favoured*. . . . In fact, in the
little powdering closet, before it became my oratory,
something picked him up, and danced him round. . . ."

" Oh! When? "

" Only the other day. My dear, yes! And *twice* in
the month of Mary! "

" Zoom—zoom! "

" Read to me."

" What shall I read? "

" Get the Lascelles Abercrombie, or the Francis
Jammes——"

" ' La maison serait pleine de roses et de guêpes '
—that's adorable."

" It makes one dormitive too."

" Let's talk of it."

She sighed shortly.

" With so many tiresome cats about, it ought to
be protected."

" Still, with a bronze-green door at night and a
violet curtain in the day——"

" I know! "

" And what is it to be? "

" I suppose we shall adhere to the original plan,
after all, and call it John the Baptist."

" Oh, don't! "

" And why not, pray? "

" For lack of humour," Winsome said, " I know
of nothing in the world to compare with the Prophet's
music in *Salomé*. It's the quintessence of villadom. It
suggests the Salvation Army, and General Booth.
It——"

" You don't like it? " she interrupted him.

" Not very much."

" If you're going to be childish, I propose you should take a walk."

" There is nowhere attractive to go."

" My dear, there are the walls. They are not Roman walls, but they are very nice walls."

" I find it rather boring, the merely picturesque."

" Then I'm sure I hardly know——"

" I've an irresistible inclination to attend Mrs. Featherstonehaugh's fête in the Close—*admittance a shilling.*"

" Keep your money, my dear boy, or look through the fence."

" Ah, Rome! . . ."

" Well, I'm going indoors. I've letters. . . . Perhaps you want to write to Andrew, too? I expect he must miss you."

" Poor Andrew! He goes stumbling along towards some ideal; it's difficult to say quite what."

" The more reason, then, to write to him."

" Oh, stay; another minute, please; and I'll be g-good——"

" Then put your tie straight, my dear Rose. . . . And, *mind Balthasar's tail!* "

XII

" Hail, angel! "

" Darling! "

" Dearest! "

" I've been thinking about you so much, dear, all day."

" Well, I find myself thinking of you too. . . . "

George Calvally had collided with Miss Thumbler, holding " a marvellous bargain," a score of music and a parasol.

" At the corner of Vigo Street," she confessed, " my *ear* began to burn, so frightfully."

" Are you going anywhere, dear? "

" I was in the act," she said, shivering, and growing strangely spiritual, " of paying a little bill."

" Then——"

He looked up. Overhead the sky was so pale that it appeared to have been powdered completely with *poudre-de-riz*.

" The proper place," he said, " to feel the first hint of autumn, I always think, is the angle of Regent Street, close to the Piccadilly Hotel."

" How splendidly sequestered, dear, it sounds! "

And already, quite perceptibly, there was a touch of autumn in the air.

In the shops the chrysanthemums mingled with the golden leaves of beech. Baskets of rough green pears lay smothered beneath blue heather.

" How sweet, child, you look! "

" I'm so glad. Have I changed since yesterday? Sunday in town leaves such scars. . . . Have I my profile still? "

" You've got it. Just! " he assured her.

For the dread of Miss Thumbler's life was that one day she should find herself without it.

" And do you like me, dearest, so? Mamma considers me quite ghastly in *crêpe;* she seems to fancy it may somehow cause an earthquake in Cremona, and bring down a doom upon papa. . . ."

" You're wonderful. You should never, never wear anything else."

" And it's scarcely a second since I commanded a muslin sprinkled with showers of tiny multi-coloured spots like handfuls of confetti flung all over it! "

" Darling! "

" Dearest! "

Now that George Calvally had lifted Mira up into the sun, she had become more melodious perhaps.

Continually she would be tying things round her forehead, to her mother's absolute astonishment, or perusing, diligently, the lives of such characters as Saskia, Heléne Fourment, Mrs. Blake. . . .

Sometimes, when the mood seized her, she would wander, for hours, through the slow, deep streets of the capital, in a stiff, shelving mantle, with long, unfashionable folds. At other times, too, she would meet George Calvally, swathed like an idol, and they would drive together in a taxi, full of twilight, holding each other's hands. Oh, the mad amusement of Piccadilly . . . the charm, unspeakable, of the Strand . . . the intoxication of the Embankment towards St. Paul's.

" Darling, what would you care to do? "

" At the Coliseum," she said, " they're giving *Georges Dandin*, with the music of Lully. Shall we go?"

He laughed.

" On such a glorious afternoon it would be ungrateful to stay indoors."

" But Professor Inglepin, dear, has designed the dresses, and his sense of costume is simply . . ."

" Angelic one, he's getting . . ."

" Though, certain busts of Bernini, George——"

" Oh, mind. . . . There's weariness! "

Holding a pink-purple flower to her nose, her eyes closed, Miss Compostella swept by them, in some jewelled hades of her own.

" How magnificent she looked! "

Mira turned, serpentine.

"Was that the first sign of autumn, do you suppose?"

" Listen. I've something to ask you, child."

With her scroll of music she caressed, sympathetically, his arm.

" It's about the church your father's setting up."

" Dearest, he says *it's the last he ever means to build.*" ·

" Mrs. Henedge has asked me to undertake the frescoes. . . ."

" That's joy! "

" But you must help."

" You mean . . . give me time, dear, I'll see."

" Darling! Decide."

" Wouldn't Rosamund——? "

" Impossible. Every five minutes she needs a rest! Besides——"

" Rubbish, besides! "

" But I need *you.*"

" What will Mary say? "

" What difference can it make to her? "

" I suppose not. She left, just now, the sweetest note, with tickets for the Queen's Hall."

" She's very fond of you, I know."

" Oh, George, it makes me miserable to think of her."

He hailed a taxi.

" How would the Wallace be? "

" The Collection? " he exclaimed. " Isn't it indoors . . . dear! And surely it's the most *stagnant* place on earth? "

XIII

" Wierus, Furiel, Charpon, Charmias! "

The very air seemed charged with tragic thoughts. The play of colour from her aura was so bright it lit the room.

" Charmias! " she called compellingly.

Stretched out upon an Anne settle, watching her, Lady Castleyard lày, in a rather beautiful heap.

" Can you see anything? " she inquired. With a bottle of pact-ink overturned upon the dressing-table, she had retreated to the background, to be " out of the way."

" Selah! . . ."

Lady Castleyard took up a mirror.

" If the devil won't come," she said, " we can't force him."

Mrs. Shamefoot seemed piqued.

" Not come? Why, he's taken all the wave out of my hair."

" It certainly *is* less successful, from the side."

" What would you advise? "

" I should take what the Bishop offers you. Don't break adrift again."

" You'd accept Ashringford? "

" Well. . . . One may as well as not! "

She collapsed, disheartened.

" I'm like a loose leaf," she moaned, " tossed about the world."

" Don't be so foolish; probably it's more amusing for the loose leaf than for the rooted tree."

" And you no longer care to join? "

" Birdie, when I've squared my card losses, and

my race losses, and my dressmaker, and redecorated
our new house a little, I'll have nothing over."

" There's Lionel! . . ."

" Oh, he's so prodigal; I know I'll die in a ditch."

" Then it's clear, of course, you mustn't."

" Besides, Biddy, you couldn't expect me to climb
away into the tracery lights; it would be like singing
Souzouki in *Butterfly*."

" And you forgive me? "

" I bear no bitterness."

Mrs. Shamefoot moved towards the window.

The gardens looked almost heroic in the evening
light. If the statues, that lit the sombre evergreens of
the walks, did *not* suggest Phidias, they did, at least,
their duty.

" When the birds fly low, and the insects turn, and
turn," she said, " there's rain! "

Lady Castleyard closed her eyes.

" I like a storm," she murmured, " particularly at
night. Sometimes one can catch a face in it—somebody
one's been wondering about, perhaps, or who's been
wondering of you. And one meets in the explosion."

With a string of pearls Mrs. Shamefoot flicked at a
passing bat.

" We should dress," she observed, " for dinner."

" Sir Isaac is strolling about outside still, isn't he? "

Mrs. Shamefoot peered out.

Already the sun had dipped below the hills, using,
above Ashringford, the golds and purples of Poussin
that suggested Rome. In the twilight the old, partly
disused, stables looked strangely mysterious and
aloof.

" And Sir Isaac? "

" Yes, he's there still; like a tourist without a guide-
book. But he's not going to be stitched into a Poiret
model by eight; nor has his head been ruffled recently
by the devil."

" Is that a Poiret shimmering across the bed? . . .
What does Soco say? "

" My dear, he never looks. In the spring he goes
striding past the first violet; and it's always the same."

" I wish he'd take up Lionel until my ball-room's
done. His idea of decoration never varies, and it's
becoming so wearisome. Horns at intervals! . . ."

" How appalling! "

" We shall be all spears and antlers when you come."

" Have you that same artistic footman still? "

" Oh, heavens; yes! "

" I adored him. He would clap his hand to his forehead whenever he forgot the . . . potatoes in an
attitude altogether *Age d'Airain.*"

" Biddy, see who it is; there's somebody at the
door."

" It's me! "

" Who's me? "

" It's Sumph."

" Who's Sumph? "

" It's me."

" I know."

" I'm Miss Compostella's maid."

" So Julia's *here.*"

" Opst! "

" And when did she arrive? "

Sumph smiled. " I've been buzzing about the
house," she said, " this last *half*-hour."

" Indeed! "

" Miss Compostella sent me downstairs after a
cucumber. Travelling disorients her so. And I must
have missed my way."

" I believe she's in the Round Tower."

" The housekeeper did say. But had she been the
mother of Roxolana, Duchess of Dublin, she could
hardly have been more brief."

Mrs. Shamefoot became concerned.

" When you find your way again," she said, " give your mistress these, with my love; they're certain to cure her."

" The poor soul was stretched out like some dead thing that breathes," Sumph murmured, " as I came away."

Nevertheless, at dinner, nobody could have guessed Miss Compostella's recent critical condition. Had she returned that moment from a month at Mürren one would have wondered still what she had employed.

" It's only now and then," she informed Lord Blueharnis, inclining towards him, " that I ever venture; wine has to be utterly exquisite, or I make a face! "

Falling between Dean Manly and Mr. Guy Fox, she resembled a piece of Venice glass between two strong schoolroom mugs.

" I expect he'll fall in love some day with some-body," Lady Georgia exclaimed, injuring a silence, " and marry; or don't you think he will? "

" Marry; who? "

" Claud Harvester."

" Why should he? If Claud can be the Gaby Deslys of literature now, he doesn't seem to mind."

" But would he be literature? "

" Why, of course! "

" *Love's Arrears*," Dean Manly said, " was an amazing piece of work."

Miss Compostella turned upon him.

" I'm Maggie! " she said.

But Mrs. Shamefoot took compassion upon the Dean's surprise.

" He's become almost *too* doll-like and *Dorothy* latterly," she inquired, " hasn't he? "

" Of course, Claud's considered a cult, but every-body reads him! "

" And Mr. Garsaint's comedy? "

"With the exception of Maria Random, Anna's maid, the cast is quite complete."

"I suppose Anna Comnena had a maid?" Mr. Guy Fox remarked.

Lady Georgia stiffened a candle that had begun to bend.

"I want you to tell me, presently," she said, "about young Chalmers. I used to know his mother long ago. She was a great hypocrite, poor dear, but I was very fond of her, all the same!"

But Miss Compostella never put off anything.

"Oh, well," she said, "of course he's wonderfully good-looking and gifted, and rather a draw; but I dislike playing with him. Directly he comes on to the stage he begins to perspire."

"And that nice little Mr. Williams?"

"*He* joined the Persian Ballet."

Mrs. Guy Fox put up her lorgnon. Her examination of the purple Sèvres dessert service and the James I spoons, she intended, should last at least two minutes; her aversion to the word *perspire* was only equalled by her horror of the word *flea*. . . .

And indeed Mrs. Guy Fox was continually upon the alert.

Ever since her sisters-in-law had been carried off by peers, she had looked upon her husband as a confirmed stick-in-the-mud. It was unreasonable of her, Mr. Guy Fox complained, when it was hardly to be hoped that Fortune would repeat herself with him.

"No, really, I ask for nothing better," Mrs. Shamefoot said to the Dean, "than to waste my sweetness on the desert air. . . ."

"And I see no reason why you should not," he replied. "The Bishop, I'm confident, doesn't intend to be disobliging."

"Yes; but you know he is!"

"I wish it were in my power to be of service to

you. But you're negotiating, I believe, with five or six cathedrals, at the present time? "

" Not so many. I've Overcares in view, though to be surrounded by that unpleasant Gala glass would be a continual strain. And then, there's Carnage. But somehow the East Coast never appealed to me. It's so stringy."

" Even Ely? " he inquired.

" Oh, Ely's beautiful. But how sad! "

" Ashringford, also, is sad. Sometimes, in winter, the clouds fall right down upon us. And the towers of St. Dorothy remain lost in them for days."

" A *mariage mystique* would be just what I'd enjoy."

" Has it occurred to you to become identified with some small, some charming church, the surprisal of which, in an obscure alley, would amount almost to an adventure? "

" But I'm so tired," she said, " of playing Bo-Peep."

" Still, some cosy gem! "

" A cosy gem? "

" St. Lazarus, for instance——"

" I'm told it leaks. There are forty-two holes in the roof."

" Or St. Anastasia."

" St. Anastasia is quite unsafe. Besides, I can't endure a spire. It's such a slope."

" St. Mary Magdalen? " he ventured.

" I have her life upstairs! Did you know she was actually engaged to John the Baptist? Until Salome *broke it off*. It was only after the sad affair at the palace that Mary really buckled to and became what she afterwards became. But her church here is so pitch dark, and it's built, throughout, with flints. I couldn't bear it."

" Or Great St. Helen's! "

She shuddered.

" There's the graveyard," she said. " I'd never like

it. I don't understand the tombs. And I hope I never shall! Those urns with towels thrown over them cast shades like thirteenth-century women."

"It's unaccountable to me," the Dean said, "that you should care to tie yourself to consecrated ground, when you might be an Independent. A Theodoric!"

"I hope you'll make it plain to Doctor Pantry," Lady Georgia said to him, as the ladies left the room, "that she's fading fast away. She has scarcely tumbled a crumb between her lips now for weeks. It almost breaks my heart to look at her."

Miss Compostella twined an arm about her friend.

"If *I* worship anything," she confessed, "it's trees. . . ."

"Come outside; the flowers smell so sweet in the dark."

The tired cedars in the park had turned to blackened emerald, the air seemed smeared with bloom. Here and there, upon the incomparably soft grey hills, a light shone like a very clear star.

"How admirable. ' Orgy,' it is!"

"Though to my idea," Lady Georgia said, "the hills would undoubtedly gain if some sorrowful creature could be induced to take to them. I often long for a bent, slim figure, to trail slowly along the ridge, at sundown, in an agony of regret."

Mrs. Guy Fox drew on a glove.

"I'm quite certain," she remarked, "that Lord Blueharnis would not require much pressing."

Lady Georgia made her gentlest grimace.

"I wish," she said, "he would, for his figure's sake. He is getting exactly like that awkward effigy of the late Earl in the Public Gardens."

"Mrs. Barrow of Dawn vows she can fall in love with it a mile away."

"Poor Violet! Cooped up half the year with an old man and seven staid servants, it cannot be very gay."

" They say if she's absent, even an hour together," Mrs. Guy Fox said, " he sends a search party after her. And he's so miserably mean. Why, the collar of pearls he gave his first wife strangled her! "

" I heard she died in torment; but I didn't know from what."

Mrs. Shamefoot held the filmy feathers of her fan slantwise across the night. It pleased her to watch whole planets gleam between the fragile sticks.

"Nobody," she exclaimed, "would do for me the things that I would do for them! "

". . . One can never be sure *what* a person will do unless one has tried."

Lady Georgia drew a scarf devotionally about her head.

" Julia has offered to speak some scenes from tragedies to us," she said.

" Gladly, Georgia, I will, when we're full numbers."

" Here come our husbands now! "

" At the risk of seeming sentimental," Sir Isaac declared, " I want to tell you how good your dinner was; it was excellent."

" All millionaires love a baked apple," Lady Georgia murmured, as she led the way with him towards the Greek theatre.

" ' Que ton âme est bien née Fille d'Agamemnon,' " Miss Compostella declaimed dispassionately, by way of tuning up.

In sympathetic silence Mrs. Shamefoot followed with the Dean.

The statues stood like towers above the low dwarf trees, dark, now, against the night. Across the gardens, from the town, the Cathedral bells chimed ten. Ten silver strokes, like the petals falling from a rose.

She sighed. She sought support. She swayed. . . .

XIV

ALAS, that conviviality should need excuse!

While Miss Compostella, somewhat tardily, raised
the Keen for Iphigenia, Lady Anne conducted a dinner
conference, for women alone.

A less hospitable nature, no doubt, would have
managed (quite charmingly) upon tea. But Lady
Anne scorned the trickle.

Nor was it before the invitations were consigned
to the pillar-box in the Palace wall that she decided,
in deference to the Bishop, who was in Sintrap, to add
the disarming nuance. To append which, with a hair-
pin, she had forced the postman's lock.

For indeed excess is usually the grandparent to
deceit. And now, with a calm mind beneath a small
tiara, she leaned an elbow, conferentially, upon a table
decorated altogether recklessly by Aurelia, with
acacia-leaves and apostle spoons.

She had scarcely set her spark.

" No, really! . . . I can't think *why* she should have
it," Miss Wardle exclaimed, leaping instantly into a
blaze.

" She's very handsome, isn't she? And that's always
something. And when you're next in Sloane Street
you'll observe she has a certain wayward taste for
arranging flowers."

" If those are her chief credentials, I shall not
interfere. . . ."

" Nobody denies her her taste for flowers," Mrs.
Pontypool exclaimed. " Though, from her manner
of dress, one wouldn't perhaps take her to be a Christian. But handsome! I must say, I don't think so. Such

a little pinched, hard, cold, shrivelled face. With a profile like the shadow of a doubt. And with a phantom husband too, whom nobody has ever seen."

" To be fair to her, one has read his ridiculous speeches."

" If a window is allowed at all, surely Miss Brice should have it? "

" But why should the Cathedral be touched? It's far too light as it is. Often, I assure you, we all of us look quite old. . . . The sun streams in on one in such a manner."

" Besides, when she has already nibbled at Perch, why must she come to us? "

" Nibbled! One fancies her to have stormed Overcares, Carnage, Sintrap, Whetstone, Cowby, Mawling, Marrow and Marrowby, besides beseeching Perch."

" If she could only bring herself to wait," Mrs. Wookie wailed, " Mrs. Henedge might cater for her at St. John's. . . ."

" St. John's! From what one hears, it will be a perfect Mosque."

Lady Anne refused a peach.

" I've begged the Dean to propose something smaller to her," she said, "than St. Dorothy, where she can put up a window and be as whimsical as she likes."

" That's common-sense. It wouldn't matter much what she did at Crawbery."

" Or even in the town. So many of the smaller churches are falling into dilapidation. It's quite sad. Only this evening Miss Critchett was complaining bitterly of the draught at St. Mary's. Her life, she says, is one ceaseless cold. A window there, that would shut, would be such a blessing."

" And the building, I believe, is distinctly Norman."

" Call it Byzantine to her. . . ."

" It's a pity she won't do something useful with her money. Repair a clock that wanders, for instance, or pension off some bells. Whenever those bells near us begin to ring they sound such bargains."

" Or fence in St. Cyriac, where my poor Percy is," Mrs. Wookie said pathetically. " It really isn't nice the way the cows get in and loll among the tombs. If it's only for the milk——"

" What is your vote, Mrs. Pontypool? "

" Oh, my dear, don't ask me! I mean to be passive. I mean to be neutral. I shan't interfere."

" But isn't it one's duty? "

" Well, I'm always glad of any change," Mrs. Barrow said. " Any little brightness. Nothing ever happens here."

Miss Wookie became clairvoyant. " If I'm not much mistaken," she said, " it's an expiatory window she intends us to admire."

" That's perfectly possible."

" Indeed, it's more than likely."

" For some imprudence, perhaps. Some foolish step. . . ."

" Ah, poor thing . . .! "

" And in any case the window, for her, will be a kind of osprey! "

" One could understand a window in moderation, but apparently she's quite insatiable."

" When my hour comes," Mrs. Wookie said, " I shall hope to lie in the dear kitchen-garden."

Miss Wardle groped about her, and shivered slightly.

" I'd like my cloak," she murmured, " please, if you don't mind."

And indeed it was a matter of surprise, and a sign of success, that she had not sent for it before.

For any gathering that might detain her beyond her own gate after dark it was her plan to assume a cloak of gold galloon that had hidden, once, the shoulders of the Infanta Maria Isabella.

119

How the garment had reached Miss Wardle's wardrobe was unknown; but that she did not disown it was clear, since frequently she would send a footman for it midway during dinner. It was like the whistle that sounded half-time at a football match, bucolic neighbours said.

"What is the feeling about it in the town?" Lady Anne inquired.

"Until the decision is final, people hardly know which way to object. But Mr. Dyce says if she has the window, he'll show up the Cathedral."

"Really! Horrid old man! What can he mean?"

"Insolency!"

"And Mr. Pet. . . . But, my dear, fortunately he's such a rapid preacher. One misses half he says."

"The text he took on Sunday was Self-Idolatry, the Golden Calf. . . ."

"I thought it was to be green!"

"What, the calf?"

"No, the window."

"Perhaps he'll go before it's all arranged."

"Very likely. I hear he finds Ashringford so expensive. . . ."

Mrs. Pontypool scratched her smooth fair fringe.

"I suppose," she said, "poor young man, with exactly twopence a year, he'd find everywhere ruinous."

"And then, I wonder, who will take his place?"

"Oh, surely Mr. Olney will."

"He's such a boy. . . ."

"My dear, age is no obstacle. And his maiden sermon came as a complete surprise! Of course, he was a trifle nervous. He shook in his shoes till his teeth rattled. And his hair stood on end. But, all the same, he was very brilliant."

"Oh, don't!" Miss Pontypool murmured.

And indeed, notwithstanding a certain analogy between her home circle with that of the Cenci, she was almost an Ingenious. She would say " Don't! " " Oh, don't! " " My dear, don't! " apropos of nothing at all.

" Oh, don't! " she murmured.

" I recall a song of his about a kangaroo," Mrs. Wookie said, " once. At a hunt ball."

" Garoo-garoo-garoo, wasn't it? " Aurelia asked. " Disgraceful."

" My dear, *don't.* . . ."

" How fortunate for that little Miss Farthing if he should come. Although she'd have to change her ways. As I've so often tried to tell her, one should wear tailor-mades in the country, instead of going about like a manicure on her holiday."

" I don't believe there is anything in that," Miss Hospice said.

" I'm not at all sure. Whenever they meet he gives such funny little gasps. . . ."

" Mr. Olney needs a wife who could pay *at least* her own expenses."

" What has he a year? "

" He owns to a thousand. But he has quite fifteen hundred."

" Besides, he's too pale, and his face lacks purpose." Lady Anne rapped her fan with pathos.

" Any side issues," she said, " might be settled later."

" Well, I don't see why she should have it," Miss Wardle repeated. " To the glory of Mrs. Shamefoot, *and* of the Almighty. . . . No, really I can't see why! "

" Had she been a saint," Mrs. Wookie observed, " it would have been another matter."

" There's not much, my dear, to choose between women. Things are done on a different scale. That's all."

" Hush, Aurelia! How can you be such a cynic! "

" All the same," Miss Pantry said, " trotting to the Cathedral solely of a Sunday, and caring about oneself, solely, all the week, is like crawling into heaven by weekly instalments. . . ."

" Indeed, that's charitable," Miss Chimney, who was dining at the Palace as a " silent protest," was constrained to say.

" But it's such a commonplace thing to do, to condemn a person one knows next to nothing of! "

" Mrs. Shamefoot was at St. Dorothy, for the Thanksgiving, wasn't she? "

" I believe so. But Miss Middling sat immediately before me. And with all that yellow wheat in her hat I couldn't see a thing."

" I remarked her rouging her lips very busily during a long Amen."

" Well, I couldn't quite make out what she had on. But she looked very foreign from behind."

" That was Lady Castleyard. Mrs. Shamefoot's little jacket was plainer than any cerecloth. And on her head there was the saddest slouch. . . ."

" Then she shall have my vote. For counting the pin-holes in it made me positively dizzy."

" And you may add mine."

" And mine. . . ."

" I forbid anything of the kind, Kate," her mother said. " Lady Anne will return it me, I'm sure." And extending a withered hand in the direction of the vote she slipped some salted almonds into her bosom.

" Oh, Tatty! "

" I shall put your vote with mine, Kate," she said, " for it grieves me to see you are such an arrant fool."

" *Don't!* "

" Where's the good of stirring up Karma for nothing? " Aurelia wondered.

Mrs. Barrow shook her head sceptically.

" I've too little confidence," she said, " in straws

and smoke, as it is, to credit the pin-marks of a bonnet. It was her maid's."

" How agnostic, Violet, you are! I shall have you going over to Mrs. Henedge before you've done."

" Why, she wears the Cathedral even now."

" I thought she had dropped it. She is getting so tawdry."

" There's a powder-puff and a bottle of Jordan water, or Eau Jeunesse, of hers here still," Aurelia said. "*Besides* a blotting-book."

" I'm not surprised. She appears to have entirely lost her head. The last time I called upon her, the cards *In* and *Out*, on the hall table, were both equally in evidence."

" It's safer to keep away from her," Mrs. Wookie murmured. " I've maintained it all along."

" No doubt, in our time, most of us have flirted with Rome," Mrs. Pontypool remarked, " but, poor dear, she never knew where to stop."

Lady Anne accepted a conferential cigarette from Mrs. Barrow of Dawn.

" Since the affair appears a decided deadlock," she pronounced, " I move that we adjourn."

Miss Valley manœuvred, slightly, her chair.

" I'm so eager to examine those Mortlake tapestries of Mrs. Cresswell," she said, " if they're not away on loan."

" They're on the Ponte di Sospiri," Lady Anne replied, " that connects us to the cloisters. But at night, I fear, it's usually rather dark."

" Impressions I adore. And there's quite a useful little moon."

Aurelia appeared amused.

" Even with a young moon," she said, " like a broken banana, and Lady Anne's crown, and my carved celluloid combs, and all the phosphorescent beetles there may be (and there are), trooping in

beastly battalions through the corridors of the Palace,
and the fireflies in the garden, and the flickerings in
the cemetery, and, indeed, the entire infinity of stars
besides, without a little artificial light of our own, one
might just as well stop here."

Lady Anne looked at her.

" Don't be so ridiculous, my dear, but lead the
way! "

" If the electric isn't in repair I refuse to stir."

" I'm taking the Historian to inspect some curtains,"
Lady Anne announced, " if anyone would care to
come."

" Historian? . . ."

Mrs. Pontypool revealed her Orders.

Quite perceptibly she became the patroness of
seven hospitals, two convalescent homes, with shares
in a *maison de santé.*

" We must have a little chat," she exclaimed, " together, you and I! All my own family had talent.
Only, money, alas, came between them and it."

" My dear, don't! "

" Indeed, it was getting on for genius. And even
still my brother (her uncle) will sometimes sit down
and write the most unwinking lies. Of course,
novels——"

Miss Wardle fastened her cape.

" I should hate to prostitute myself," she remarked,
" for *six* shillings."

" Or for four and sixpence cash. . . ."

" Some people publish their works at a guinea,"
Miss Valley murmured, as she followed Lady Anne
towards the door.

The Ponte di Sospiri, whither Lady Anne advanced
—built by a previous bishop, to symbolise a perpetual
rainbow—broke, quite unexpectedly, from the stairs
with all the freedom of a polonaise.

Behind their hostess the ladies trooped, as if Miss

Pantry's timely warning had made it imperative to wade. The concern, indeed, of Mrs. Barrow was such that it caused a blushing butler to retreat.

" My dear Violet! " Lady Anne began, " the only time, I believe, I ever——"

But Mrs. Wookie intervened.

" There is somebody," she remarked, " thumping at the gate."

" It is probably only the post."

And turning to the tapestries Lady Anne commenced the inspection, starting instinctively at the end. And the end, as she pointed out, was simply frantic Bacchanals. After (*à rebours*) came the Martyrdom, spoken often of as " I've had such a busy morning!", the saints' final word. A model, in every particular, of what a martyrdom should be. And indeed nothing could have been simpler, quieter, or better done. There was no squeezing, fainting, crushing or tramping. No prodding. . . . The spectators, provided, each, with a couch and a cup of chocolate, were there by invitation alone. Although, in the market-place (as one might see), tickets were being disposed of at a price. And in the centre of all stood Mrs. Cresswell, leaning with indifference upon a crosier, inset with a humorous and a somewhat scathing eye.

And so, in the dim light, the fourteen panels ran: growing, as they receded, less and less serene, until, at the opening scene, the atmosphere was one of positive gloom.

" It was the ' Marriage.' "

" What do people marry for? " Miss Wardle said. " I've sometimes wondered."

" My dear, don't ask me."

" One marries for latitude, I suppose."

" Or to become a widow."

" I'd give such *worlds* to be a widow," Miss Pontypool declared.

" It's a difficult thing to be," Mrs. Barrow assured her.

" I'm that disgusted with Love," Miss Valley volunteered in her chastest Cockney voice.

" I find it dreadfully disappointin'," Lady Anne supported her.

Mrs. Wookie sighed.

" Mine," she said, " is a nature that cries for more ethereal things."

" Banal passions," Miss Wardle whispered faintly, " fail to stir me."

" ' I'm that disgusted with love,' " the ladies chanted charmingly all together.

" If that is Mr. Cresswell," Mrs. Barrow remarked, " I'm certainly not surprised."

" He's so worn," Miss Chimney observed critically, " and she's so *passée*."

Aurelia touched the tapestries with her thumb. " It's probably only the stuff."

" And who would this be? " Miss Valley queried, trailing towards an easel with a little quick glide.

" That! " Lady Anne said. " I suppose it was Walter once."

" If I were getting painted," Mrs. Pontypool announced, " again I'd try Mr. White. He doesn't reject beauty. And he reveals the sitter's soul."

Miss Chimney showed some sensitiveness.

" Anything nude, anything undressed, anything without a *frill*," she said, " revolts me somehow so. I'm sure in the winter, when the trees show their branches—well, I go, when I can, to the South."

But the appearance of the Miss Chalfonts upon the stairs, closely entwined, their eyes astream, their bodies racked by laughter, a single superb boa shared more or less between them, caused a commotion.

" We rang and we rang," Miss Clara said.

" I'm so sorry. But, at all events, you've dined? "

Miss Blanche quite collapsed. " Why, no! " she said.

" Do you abominate almonds? " Mrs. Wookie asked.

Miss Constantia placed a hand before her eyes. " If there's anything on this earth," she said, " I've a horror of, or an aversion for, it's that."

And her gesture seemed to make vibrate all those other objections latent in her too. All those other antipathies, *less* than almonds, that were hereditary, perhaps. She began suddenly to droop. She stood there, dreaming.

" Unwind, can't you," her sister said, " and let me out."

Miss Chalfont commenced to turn.

" It's not from coquetry," she confessed gaily, " that we're last. But the nearer one lives, somehow, the later one's sure to be."

" To be frank," Lady Anne said absently, " you might be stopping in the house."

They were free. . . .

Their garments, the ladies noted, were white and sparkling streaked with green.

Never, Miss Valley affirmed, had she encountered so many charming Ideas. Even at a Poet's dinner.

" Now I know," she said, " exactly where to tie a necklace. On my arm."

" We were getting rather nervous about the vote," Miss Clara said, " so we decided to bring it ourselves. It's the first engagement we've kept for I don't know how long! "

" And which way is it? "

Miss Clara indicated the Cathedral.

" I would read them my essay on Self-Control," Miss Hospice murmured, " if you thought it would have any effect."

" It would probably make them infinitely worse.

It might even kill them outright. And then it would be murder," Miss Valley said.

Miss Hospice smiled sedately.

" My publisher, at any rate, could be found," she said. " I've had the same man always. Byron had him. And Coleridge had him. And Keats. I should be really ashamed to flutter from *firm to firm* like some of those things one sees. . . . I simply couldn't do it. And God looks after me! He has never abandoned me yet to sit up night after night in a public-house to libel His saints by Christmas."

" My dear, I congratulate you! To compose an essay on Self-Control when one is so strangely devoid of it oneself was an admirable *tour de force*."

But the Miss Chalfonts were becoming increasingly unstrung.

" Oh, hold me!" Miss Blanche sighed, sinking, slowly, like the Sienese Santa of the frescoes, to the floor. Miss Clara and Miss Constantia made a movement, which, although a miracle of rhythm, was ineffectual upon the whole.

With quiet complacence Mrs. Wookie took a chair.

" They're off!" she said.

" If Lord Chesterfield could only see them now!"

" Don't!"

" By birth they may be County," Mrs. Pontypool murmured. " But by manners——"

" Indeed, by manners——"

" By manners! . . ."

" Crazy creatures," Mrs. Wookie crooned, " crazy-crazies!"

Mrs. Barrow agreed.

" That a certain Signor Calixfontus," she said, " followed St. Augustine over here and married a savage—and ran through his life before most people would have cared to be seen about at all, is no excuse for his descendants to behave like perfect idiots."

" Or to drape themselves in those loose misfits."

" Lampshades! "

" It's Vienna! "

" Teheran!! "

" Vienna or Teheran," Mrs. Pontypool said, " or the Edgware Road, I've never seen such a riddle! "

But Lady Anne was looking bewildered. " When Saul was troubled," she said, " David played to him. Didn't he? "

Miss Valley nodded.

" There's a Rembrandt," she said, " about it at the Hague. I remember it so well. Chiefly because of David, who is tucked away in a remote corner of the canvas, almost as if he were the signature."

" And has he got a golden September-skin like Hendrickje Stoffels? " Aurelia asked.

" Yes; and a smile like sad music."

" Oh, but I know it! "

" Well, won't somebody go to the piano? "

" Miss Wookie will," her mother said. " Won't you, Kate? And, perhaps, sing some little song besides. She knows such shoals. What was that one, my dear, that despairing, dismal one about the heliotrope? *When Heliotropes Turn Black.* It's the true story of a sailor. Or he might have been a coastguard. And he goes away. And he comes back. And, of course, he finds her dead."

" A fugue and a breath of air," Lady Anne said, " should be quite enough. Come into the drawing-room and the Miss Chalfonts can have some supper there while we play cards. A little fruit, a little wine. . . . Poor Miss Blanche is simply sinking."

Miss Wardle disappeared altogether into her *point d'espagne.*

" O heavens! " she said.

Lady Anne's drawing-room, that had belonged, upon a time, to Mrs. Henedge, who had " rescued "

it from Mrs. Goodfellow, who had come by it from
Mrs. Archer, who had whipped it from Lady Lawrence,
who had seized it from Mrs. Jones, of whose various
" improvements " (even to distant pretty little Saxon
Ethel) it bore some faint chronological trace, was
picking up, as well as might be expected, to be a trifle
Lady Anne's. Although there were moments even
still in the grey glint of morning when the room had
the agitated, stricken appearance of a person who had
changed his creed a thousand times, sighed, stretched
himself, turned a complete somersault, sat up, smiled,
lay down, turned up his toes and died of doubts. But
this aspect was reserved exclusively for the housemaids and the translucent threads of dawn.

It appeared quite otherwise now.

Upon an oval table that gleamed beneath a substantial chandelier a solitary specimen of Lady Anne's
fabled Dresden was set out, equivalent, in intention,
to an Oriental's iris, or blossoming branch of plum.

It was her most cherished *Rape*.

With as many variations of the theme in her cabinets
as the keys in which a virtuoso will fiddle a gipsy
dance, it revealed the asceticism of her mind in re-
fraining from exhibiting them all. So situated, it is
certain Mrs. Henedge would have exposed the lot.

Eyes beseeching, arms imploring, fingers straining,
raiment blowing, an abduction, of necessity, must be
as orthodox as a wedding with a Bishop to babble it
off.

Mrs. Wookie wished.

" That's precisely my fear for Kate," she said,
" when she runs out to take a motor number. Somebody, some impulsive foreigner, perhaps, visiting the
Cathedral, might stop the car and capture her, and
carry her away, possibly as far as Ringsea-Ashes,
before she could resist. And there, I should hope, Mr.
Walsh would marry them before they went on."

"She'll have many a million, I dare say, before that occurs," Miss Wardle observed. "People aren't handcuffed, seized, gagged and pinioned. Are they?"

"Still, foreigners visit the Cathedral—even blacks. While I was watering my garden to-night I saw a Moor looking at me through the fence."

Mrs. Pontypool sighed.

"Ashringford's getting *too* discovered," she said. "It's becoming spoilt. Mrs. Fulleylove was telling me at the Dean's that Lolla's to finish abroad. 'And what will she gain by it?' I said. She could pick up quite enough languages from the tourists in the Close."

"All that would be good for her."

Miss Chimney looked fiendish. "I detest all foreigners," she said.

But, from a withdrawing-room, Miss Wookie was being borne rapidly away upon the wings of a perfectly hysterical song.

"Can nobody stop her?" Mrs. Barrow asked. The human voice, in music, she considered far too explanatory. And what did it matter *what* the heliotropes did, so long as they were suppressed.

"Her *coloratura*," Mrs. Wookie observed, "most surely improves. Although, to vibrate like Fräulein Schuster isn't done in a day."

Notwithstanding, upon the verandah, Miss Valley and Aurelia were sketching out a valse. Gently, with gowns grasped, through the moonlit spaces they twirled, the Historian gazing up abstractedly at the Cathedral towers.

"I lay you ten to one she gets it!" she cried.

"Of course, if she persists she'll prevail."

"I wish she were dead."

"Surely the world is large enough for us all."

"But I need a *Life*."

Aurelia glanced about her timidly. The solemnity of their shadows startled her.

" Though, indeed, when my investigations are over in these parts, I hope never to set foot in Ashringford again. Never, Never, Never, Never, Never, Never! "

" Some of the Spanish saints were so splendid, weren't they? "

" Oh, Aurelia—not another. "

" But try a man this time. "

" Man, or woman! " Miss Valley said.

" Or edit letters. Those of King Bomba to the Queen of Snowland require revision badly. "

" And drown the text in the notes! "

" Make an anthology. "

" *Euh*, that's so messy! "

Aurelia reversed. " Mrs. Shamefoot won't die, " she said, " unless we kill her. "

" Luckily, there's the climate. The air here has been called a moist caress. "

" It's a poor prospect anyway. "

" How I wish she were dead! "

" She's like some heavy incense, don't you think? " Miss Valley became visionary.

" At the back of her mind, " she said, " in some strange way, she's convinced her spirit will be caught in colour, and remain merged in it, as long as the glass endures. "

" Has she said so? "

" Certainly not. But in our profession naturally one knows. . . . And my intuition tells me that if an atom of her, a teeny-weeny particle, *isn't* woven into the window, she'll be very cruelly chagrined. "

Aurelia blinked, uncertain.

" And when would one know? " she inquired.

" Not, of course, until after she were dead. "

" I call it really rather disgraceful. "

" Why . . .? "

" Because, by the time she'll have done, St. Dorothy will be too disturbed to be nice. Nobody would go into it unless they were obliged. All the tranquillity would be gone. I'd never enjoy a quiet minute there again."

" My dear, that's selfish. Besides, you're scarcely two months in the year here ever, are you? "

" I should still think it horrid."

" Nonsense. Beyond a little vanity, it's hard to explain exactly what the idea indicates. But I'm sure it points to something."

" Earthiness. The extremes of it. Earth spirit! "

" Oh, more. And even if it did *not*, Mrs. Shamefoot can furnish an opera-box as very few others can. And if one can furnish an opera-box one should be able to fill in a window."

" I can imagine her asleep in a rather boring Louis the Sixteenth bedroom with a window on Sloane Square."

" Why not in Sloane Street? Over the shop. Though if you troubled to get a directory, you'd see she doesn't live that end of town at all."

But Miss Pontypool was singing now.

" Paris! Paris! Paris! Paris! O Paris! Cité de joie! Cité d'amour. . . ."

" It's the arietta of *Louise*."

" I knew it couldn't be David."

Like a riband flung in carnival the voice trailed away across the night.

" Poor girl! If her lines are cast in Ashringford. . . . For an instant she brought almost into this ghastly garden the glamour of the Rue de la Paix."

" Is it policy? The Miss Chalfonts will be on the floor."

" What does it matter, if they are? "

But, peeping through the window, Aurelia was unprepared to find the Miss Chalfonts listening intently while the tears were streaming from their eyes.

XV

The municipal museum in Ghost Street was rarely, if ever, thronged, especially after noon.

"You can have the key," the wife of the custodian said, "if you want it. But there's nothing whatever inside."

And the assertion, sometimes, would spare her husband the weariness of struggling into a pair of black and silver trousers and vague historic tunic that was practically a tea. For in Ashringford, the Corporation, like a diver in a tank, was continually plunging back into the past.

"Since it pleases visitors to catch a last glimpse of this vanishing England," the Mayor had said, "*and if Stratford can*; why . . .!"

And after the customary skirmishing of the Board, and reconciliatory garden-party, a theatrical tailor had been beckoned to, from Covent Garden, who had measured half the town.

And now, beneath the grey horse-chestnut trees, where stood "the Fountain," round which, of a summer morning, the "native" women clustered, chatting charmingly, as they sold each other flowers, or posing, whenever they should be invited, to anxious artists for a shilling an hour, an enchanted American, leaning, observant, from a window of the Cresswell Arms, might almost fancy that, what with the determined duennas thronging to the Cathedral, and darting chambermaids holding long obtrusive envelopes, and tripping shepherdesses and dainty goosegirls, and occasionally, even, some pale, ring-eyed-powdered-nervous Margaret, with empty pitcher and

134

white-stockinged feet, it was still the threshold of the thirteenth century.

" There's nothing in the museum, whatever," the woman repeated. "Nothing at all." And she added almost desperately: " It's where they keep the rubbish."

But Mrs. Shamefoot was not accustomed to be baulked.

" There're the sepulchral urns, and the tear-bottles, at any rate," she said, " and there's a good skeleton, I believe? "

" Yes, marm. There is that."

" Well, then . . ." And pushing apart the light gilt gates, she swept inside. And even if it were only for the fascinating fanlight on the stairs, she was glad that she had come.

And there was also a mirror! The unexpected shock of the thing brought a flush of pleasure to her cheek She had hardly hoped to find so much.

" Marvellous woman," she exclaimed, going up to it, with an amicable nod, " where've you been? "

She was looking bewitching beyond measure, she believed, bound in black ribands, with a knot like a pure white butterfly under her chin.

And, to her astonishment, there were mirrors, or their equivalents, upon most of the walls.

" That habit of putting glass over an oil painting," she murmured, " makes always such a good reflection, particularly when the picture's *dark*. Many's the time I've run into the National Gallery on my way to the Savoy and tidied myself before the Virgin of the Rocks. . . ."

And selecting a somewhat spindle-legged settee she glanced yearningly around.

It was the room of the Blueharnis Bequest.

In a place of prominence, unmistakable, was the Dehell portrait of the donor, leaning against a door, in full uniform, the arms folded, the eyes fixed, dangling a sword.

What could have happened?

Anxiously, for a clue, she scanned the pendant of his wife, a billowy, balloon-like creature, leading by a chain of frail convolvulus a prancing war-horse. But the mystery still remained.

Near by, upon a screen (being stored for her), was the *Miss Millicent Mutton* of Maclise. Here, in a party pinafore, *Mrs. Henedge* was seen riding recklessly upon a goat clasping a pannier of peaches and roses while smiling down at an angelic little boy who, with a thistle and a tambourine, was urging the nanny on.

Eventually, authorities affirmed, the canvas would find its way to the South Kensington Museum, where (besides being near to dear Father . . . and to old Father . . . and the Oratory) there was a room ready waiting to receive it where it would be perfectly happy and at home.

And as one work will beget another, Mrs. Pontypool, not to be outdone, had contributed an ancestral portrait of a lady, reclining upon a canopy, plainly prostrate, beneath the hot furnaces, and the fiery skies, of Manchester. . . .

But, for the most part, as was but fitting for a Cathedral town, the mildly Satanic school of Heironymus Bosch was chiefly to the fore.

Yet, whimsically wistful, an elderly frame in curtains was waiting to be found. Leisurely, Mrs. Shamefoot rose.

That something singularly wicked was concealed beneath the hangings she had no doubt.

And indeed it was " *Le thé à l'Anglaise*, chez Lucrezia Borgia," in which an elegant and radiant Lucrezia, tea-pot in hand, was seen admiring the indisposition of her guests like a naughty child.

A glass of flowers by Fantin brought her to herself.

"If I could feel it were all arranged!" she murmured. "Unless this window-quibbling ceases, I'll soon be in my grave. And Soco, I'm confident, could not be counted upon, even for the simplest cross. He'd marry again. The brute!"

She looked out across a half-wild garden to the Asz. Beyond the broad bridges, the peaked hayricks, sprinkling the hills, stood sharp, like pyramids, against the sky. There was something monstrous and disquieting in their shapes that thrilled her. To be an Independent upon some promontory, she mused, above the sea; a landmark; perhaps a shrine! . . .

White birds, like drifting pearls, would weave their way about her, examining her with their desolate empty eyes.

Or to be a lighthouse; looped in lights!

Although to search out some poor face when it the least expected it would be carrying ill-nature, perhaps, to a rather far extreme. Better some idle tower. But in England towers so seldom mellowed rightly. They were too rain-washed, weather-beaten, wind-kissed, rugged; they turned tragic and outlived themselves; they became such hags of things; they grew dowdy and wore snapdragons; objects for picnics; rendezvous of lovers, haunts of vice . . .; they were made a convenience of by owls; they were scarred by names; choked by refuse, and in the end they got ghoulish and took to too much ivy, and came toppling down.

She stood oppressed.

Over the darkly gleaming water of the Asz a boat passed by with cordings like the strings of some melancholy instrument. From the deserted garden below an odour of burning leaves loitered up to her. The long pink Infidels flared stiffly from the shade.

"Heigh-ho," she yawned, "one can't play fast and loose for ever. . . ." And she turned away, dolefully, through the damp deserted rooms.

A piece of tessellated pavement, a sandled foot, detained her. " Street! " she murmured, stooping down, enthralled.

The frou-frou of the custodian's skirts disturbed her.

" Such a mixture of everything as there is; a country Cluny! "

" I dare say, marm. I've never been round the worruld; I've lived in Ashringford, man and boy, these sixty years."

" Indeed; that's why you look so young! "

" I beg your pardon, marm? "

" I say, that's why you look so *young!* "

And startled by his historic attire, she trailed slowly towards the door, gazing back at him across her shoulder, with one arm stretched before, the other lingering behind, in the attitude of a nymph evading a satyr upon a Kylix.

It was a relief to hear voices! Chatting beneath an immaterial study of the sunset breeze, she beheld the ample form of Sumph.

" And in Act IV," she was saying, " the husband *pretends* to go away. But, of course, he doesn't! He goes only a little distance. . . . And the ' curtain ' should be beautiful! Lovely it ought to be. The birds all singing as if their last hour had come. And Miss Compostella and Mr. Chalmers——"

" Is your mistress anywhere about? " Mrs. Shamefoot interrupted her.

Sumph smiled.

" Why, no," she said, " she's not. I'm here with Mrs. Henedge's maid, just taking a look round."

" Really? . . ."

" Whenever I'm able I like to encourage anything that's Art."

" And how do you like Ashringford? "

" I like it. It puts me in mind of the town Dick Whittington came to when all the bells were ringing."

"You've been up the tower!"

"It didn't seem worth while. They told us before-hand we could never see *back there*. . . . But we watched them pull the bells. Quite a receipt of their own they seemed to have. Such swingings and pausings and noddings and rushings. You should have seen the dowdies run! And in such bonnets. As Thérèse remarked, it was an education in botany."

"Oh-h-h!"

There came a cry.

Mrs. Henedge's maid was before the Borgia *thé*.

Nodding sympathetically to Sumph, Mrs. Shame-foot disappeared.

XVI

" EVER since the accident," Lady Georgia said, " she has been going about in such heavens of joy. I've seldom seen anyone so happy."

Mrs. Guy Fox passed a hand across her eyes.

" It fell," she remarked, " so suddenly; I was in my bath."

Miss Compostella helped herself to honey.

" I fear St. Dorothy's badly damaged."

" Half of it is down."

" Oh no, dear; not half."

" It's as if the gods granted it to her," Lady Georgia declared; " she's been so brave."

" Such gusts of wind! The way they pulled the bushes——"

" How did it happen, exactly? "

" A pair of scissors, it appears, was left upon the scaffolding, and caught the lightning's eye."

" What a dreadful thing! "

Mrs. Fox shuddered.

" That the Cathedral should submit to be struck," she said, " strikes me as being so strange. It never has before."

" Lady Anne has twice 'phoned."

" . . . Surely not already? "

" Before breakfast, too! "

" Polite. . . ."

Lady Georgia rolled her eyes.

" What is one to do with a person," she demanded, " who cannot feel the spell of a beautiful supreme thing like Tintoretto's *Crucifixion?* "

" And where is she now? "

" Oh, my dear, she's wandering exultant about the house. She's been doing it since six."

" Leave her," Mr. Guy Fox advised. " Perhaps presently she'll come down and have a good cry."

" Darling Biddy, she's been divinely patient. But the strain was becoming too much for her. It was undermining her health."

" Holding ten cathedrals at arm's-length must have been terribly tiring."

" I had an idea it was quite the other way. In any case, thank Heaven, the wrangling's over. Done."

" I wouldn't say that. But clearly a difficulty is removed. They're sure to secure her for the Restorations."

" My maid has asked if she may go over and see the ruins," Miss Compostella said.

" She should take the bridle-path through the fields," Lady Georgia murmured, rising to welcome Mrs. Shamefoot as she came in.

Over a rug that suggested a summer morning Mrs. Shamefoot skimmed, pale in cloud-white laces, her hands buried beneath the flimsy plumage of a muff, like some soul who (after a tirade or two) would evaporate and take flight.

" You may kiss me," she murmured wistfully, " but kiss me carefully."

" I heard you at the telephone as I crossed the hall."

" Lady Anne re-rang."

" I hope she was pleasant."

" No. She was only half-charming, if you know; she was nice, without being nicer. . . . But one feels she's climbing down. Of course, I told her, without the approbation of all Ashringford, I wouldn't for the world . . . and, on her side, she spoke of making a ragoût with the remains."

" She's so tasteless," Lady Georgia exclaimed. " But there it is, many people seem to imagine that a stained-glass window is nothing of the kind unless some over-good-looking young saint is depicted in bathing drawers and half-an-inch of water."

Mrs. Shamefoot raised her muff beneath her chin.

" Soco's so silly," she said. " He'd fire at anything like that with his revolver. And, oh, Mr. Guy Fox . . . I've got to scold you. Standing beneath my window and calling me by my name millions and millions of times was fearfully indiscreet. . . ."

" I thought you'd be interested to know."

" ' It's down,' you said, ' it's down.' The servants must have wondered what you meant! Though it's really rather odd; when your voice disturbed me, I was having such a curious-funny dream. People were digging me up for reliques. . . ."

" Here's your coffee, dear."

" All I need, darling, is a Railway Guide. I must return at once to town; I'm so busy! "

" Remain until to-morrow," Miss Compostella said, " and travel back with me."

" But, Julia, you're not leaving us so soon! "

" I must. You know I'm in despair with my helmet for the Garsaint piece. I do not care about myself in it at all: it's too *stiff*. And the crown; I'm sure the crown's too timid."

But Mrs. Guy Fox was reading aloud some extracts of a letter from her son, a dutiful diplomat who, even when fast asleep, it was said, suggested the Court of St. James.

" Just now," she read, " the Judas trees along the banks of the Bosphorus are coming into flower. The colour of these trees is extraordinary. They are neither red nor violet, and at evening they turn a sort of agony of rose."

" Delicious! " Lady Georgia said, staring at Atalanta in dismay. There were moments, especially in the early morning, when she alarmed her mother. Moments when she looked remotely Japanese. . . .

" No; there's nothing in the paper at all, except that the Wirewells have arrived," Lady Castleyard said, stepping out upon the lawn.

Mrs. Shamefoot joined her.

After the gale a yellow branch lay loose beneath each tree, making the park appear to be carpeted by some quite formal silk. The morning was fine with courageous crazy clouds.

" You're tired? "

" A little," Lady Castleyard confessed. " All this death makes me melancholy."

" I expect it's merely Lionel! "

" Lionel? But I'm not tired of Lionel. Only, now and then, I long rather for a new aspect. . . ."

" Do you suppose, if there were no men in the world, that women would frightfully mind? "

" I don't know, really. . . . What a pity to leave that gloriously bound book out all night! "

They turned aside through a wicket-gate into an incidental garden.

At periods, upon the enclosing walls, stood worn lead figures of cupid gardeners, in cavalier hats and high loose boots and cunning gloves, leaning languidly upon their rakes, smiling seraphically over the gay rings of flowers that broke the grass.

" Age holds no horrors for me," Mrs. Shamefoot said, " now, any more. Some day I'll have a house here and I'll grow old quite gracefully."

" Surely with age one's attractions should increase. One should be irresistible at ninety."

"A few of us, perhaps, may. You, dear Dirce, will——"

" But in Ashringford! You used always to say it would be at Versailles, or Vallombrosa, or Verona, or Venice; a palladio palace on the Grand Canal. Somewhere with a *V!* "

" I remember . . .; although I was tempted too rather, wasn't I, towards Arcachon. And that's an *A!*"

" Poor Soco. He'll be so surprised. . . ."

" It's a pity, whenever he speaks, he's so very disappointing."

" Still, there'll be the bill. . . ."

" Well, he could scarcely have seriously supposed I'd throw myself away upon a lancet! Besides, I believe I'll be desired somehow more when I'm gone. What good am I here? "

" My dear, you compose in flowers. You adorn life. You have not lived in vain."

They were in the dogs' cemetery.

Lady Castleyard tapped a little crooked cross.

" One fears," she said, " that Georgia must have poisoned them all for the sake of their epitaphs."

" Here come the children! "

" And remember, Frank," Fräulein was warning Master Fox, in her own wonderful Hanoverian way, " not to pursue Mirabel too much towards the end. It makes her hot."

They were preparing to play at Pelléas.

Lady Georgia insisted that her children should practise only purely poetic games. She desired to develop their souls and bodies harmoniously at the same time.

" Remember the chill she caught as Nora! " Fräulein said. " And, Dawna, must I re-implore you not to pick up the sun-money with your hands? Misericordia! One might think your father was a banker."

" I do so love the sun! "

" Do you, dear? "

Obviously, it was an occasion to kiss and form a group.

XVII

"CERTAINLY I should object to milk a cow," Miss Compostella said. "Why?"

Sumph smiled.

"I see so many," she said. "One, the prettiest possible thing, the very living, breathing image of the Alderney that you engaged, miss, to walk on in *The Princess of Syracuse*."

"It would be the signal," Miss Compostella said, "often for a scuffle."

"And don't I know it!" said Sumph.

"Although to me it was always extraordinary that Miss Elcock, who almost fainted whenever she encountered it in the wings, would become indifferent to the point of being tossed the instant the curtain rose. She was too preoccupied about appearing young, I suppose, to care about anything else, her own part included."

"Oh no, miss. She was a great, great actress. Watching her in certain scenes, how cold my hands would grow! The blood would fly to my heart!"

The invaluable woman grew nostalgic.

"I fear you don't delight in the country, somehow, as you should."

"I don't know, miss. Ashringford amuses me. I find myself dying with laughter here several times a day."

"Indeed——"

"Naturally not in the house. It's too much like a sanatorium for that. Every time I come to you along the corridors I feel just as if I was going to visit some poor sick soul and had forgotten my flowers."

Miss Compostella gave an arranging touch to a bouquet of blue berries above her ear.

"I hope you passed a pleasant afternoon," she said, "among the ruins."

"It was lovely. I sat on a piece of crumbled richness in the long grass for over an hour. Afterwards I took tea at the Closed House with Thérèse. She was so busy with her needle. 'I shall need a frock for my conversion,' Mrs. Henedge told her the other day, 'and another for my reconversion, in case that's necessary.' 'But fashions change so quickly, madame,' Thérèse said to her. 'And so do I,' she said; 'I can travel a long way in a week.' Chopping and changing! But it's to be quite a decided little frock for all that. Very plain. With some nice French buttons. The *other* is one of those curious colour contrasts. . . . So sickly. But rather smart. A discord of lemon, pink, and orange. And I came back, miss, to Stockingham, by way of the Asz, in spite of Signora Spaghetti. 'Never walk by the water-side,' she said to me, when I was a child. That's why we left Stratford. Because of the Avon."

"But surely the Thames——"

"Bless you, no!"

"And you saw nothing of the Bishop?"

"His pinched white face frightened me. It gave me such a turn. . . .

Weep, willow, weep,
Willow, willow, weep,
For the cross that's mine is difficult to bear."

Miss Compostella interposed.

"You needn't pack up everything," she remarked.

"It's my impatience! I could sing when I think we're returning home to-morrow. If it's only to escape the housekeeper here. For we had quite a quarrel just now. . . . 'Where's your wedding ring?' she says. 'I never wear it,' I replied. 'It makes one's hand look

146

so bourgeoise. And don't you go flinging your nasty aspersions over me,' I said, ' for I won't have it.' "

" Quite right."

" My word. I was very carefully brought up. My mother was most tyrannical, especially with us girls. Why I wasn't even allowed to read *The Vicar of Wakefield* until after I was married. . . . Not that I didn't belong to a Rabelais—lovers—Society by the time I was twelve."

" What, in Stratford? " Miss Compostella wondered, taking up with lassitude the manuscript of a play left with her by Mrs. Shamefoot (before the accident), in the expectation of obtaining an interest at the Palace by overwhelming Miss Hospice by an eternal and delicate debt of thanks.

It was a *Tristram and Isolde*.

" *Brangane and Isolde*," she read. " *Deck chairs. Isolde making lace. Soft music.*

Br. But what makes you think he's so fond of you, my dear?

Is. He presses my hand so beautifully.

Br. You know he does that to *everybody*.

Is. O-h?

Br. Take my advice. *I* should never marry him.

Is. Really? Why not?

Br. He would leave you.

Is. Nonsense!

Br. He has ears like wings. . . .

Is. Is that all?

" Not such a bad beginning," Miss Compostella commented. " But why must Isolde be so impatient to confide to the waves her age? ' I'm exactly nine-and-twenty.' I cannot see that it helps. And why, oh, why," she murmured, rising to her feet, " when Tristram inquires for her, should Brangane lose her head so, and say ' She's out, she's not at home, she isn't there '? Were she to reply quite calmly, almost like a butler, ' The family's away,' or, ' I expect them home in about a fortnight,' it should be amply sufficient."

A lazy ripple of strings surprised her.

" What is that——? "

" I don't know, miss, I'm sure. It sounds like *Pippa Passes.*"

" Well, go and see."

" It brings back to me the reading Mrs. Steeple gave at the Caxton Hall when I, Miss Falconhall and her fiancé received Press tickets. . . . Coming away, foolish fellow, he slipped on a piece of cabbage-stalk and snapped his coledge bone."

" Can you make out who is serenading us? "

" It's the Honourable Mrs. Shamefoot," Sumph informed. Pacing beneath a magnificence of autumnal trees, Mrs. Shamefoot was strolling slowly up and down with a guitar.

" She's been on stilts all day," Sumph said.

Miss Compostella coiled an arm across her head.

" Give me a phenacetin powder," she exclaimed, " at once. For what with the crash the Cathedral made in falling, and your silly jabber, and her guitar . . .!"

XVIII

"THE little turquoise flower you admired, my beloved, on Wednesday, is known as *Fragment of Happiness*. You will find it again in some of *Dürer's* drawings. Oh, George! . . . On my desk there is an orange-tree. How it makes me yearn, dear, for the South! I count my oranges. Eight poor, pale, crabbed oranges. Like slum cripples. I think of Seville now. Yes. To-morrow. Absolutely. But, dearest, *downstairs*, Rosalba Roggers sometimes sallies up. She saw us together last time and begged so to be told who my wonderful big child was with the tragic face. Five o'clock, dear. And don't be late as you usually are.　　　M.

"*P.S.*—I will carry some of your troubles, if you will send them to me with your thoughts.

"*P.P.S.*—You say I blush! When, I wonder, shall I learn to have a mask of my own?"

"Minx!" Mrs. Calvally exclaimed. "The snake. . . ."
She seemed stupefied, stunned.
"I merely opened his paint-box," she began, stammering to herself.
"Mamma! . . ."
And, as if to demonstrate that domestic drama is not entirely tired of its rather limited tricks, her little son Raphael entered the room at that minute and rushed right into her arms.
He came. . . .
She stooped. . . .
"My dear!"
And now she was calm again, complacent, with all her old tranquillity of gardens.

" Oh, how ugly! . . ."

" Where, my precious? "

" And is it a present, too? "

For the artist's anniversary Miss Thumbler had despatched a door-knocker, wrought in bronze, that represented a woebegone, wan Amour.

" By all means," Mrs. Calvally had said, " let us put it up. I will call a carpenter. And some of the mirrors, as well, need glueing. . . ."

And the gift decidedly had eclipsed her own humble offering of the Hundred Best Pictures, in photogravure, that did not appear to have aroused in him all the interest that they might.

" Mrs. Asp and Mrs. Thumbler are in the drawing-room."

" Are they, my pet? "

" And Mrs. Asp is concealing such a lovely-looking thing. All wrapped up. It must be something for papa."

" Come along and let us see."

" Don't sigh, mamma. It bores me to hear you sigh."

" I'm so sorry George isn't in," Mrs. Calvally said, as she lounged leisurely round the huge Ming screen that began her drawing-room. " But he went out, quite early, almost before it was light, to make a Canaletto of the space before White Hall."

" I believe he's unusually busy. . . . So I hear! " Mrs. Asp announced.

" No. Not so very. . . . He's making Mrs. Jeffreys at present in all her jewels? or, at any rate, more than he usually likes. And the old Duke of Spitalfields. And the cartoons of a country church. . . ."

Mrs. Thumbler began to purr.

" And he obliges Mira," she said, " nearly every day. And in such varieties of poses! Even as Absalom, swinging from a tree."

" I know. He raves about her. He told me he looked

upon her almost as an inspiration," Mrs. Calvally replied, confident that the " almost " would be repeated to haunt Miss Thumbler for days.

" All the same, quite between ourselves, I confess, I wish he didn't. It's making her so vain! Lately (I'm ashamed to tell you) she's taken to wear *a patch*. A crescent-moon-shaped affair above the lip that gives her such an o-ri-gi-nal expression. Really, sometimes in the street . . . Well, I won't go out with her again. I let her take the dog."

Mrs. Asp untied an ermine stole.

" My dear," she exclaimed, " do be careful. When it comes to dragging a dumb animal about as a chaperon one gets generally misunderstood."

" But what am I to do? Mira's so sensitive. I dare hardly say a word. Although those pen-and-ink embroideries Mr. Calvally made for her, charming as they are, are only fit for the house."

" I wasn't aware he had ever made her any," Mrs. Calvally said. " I'm sure he never made pen-and-ink embroideries for me! "

" Occupation," Mrs. Asp reflected airily, " is an admirable thing, especially for a man. It restricts restlessness as a rule."

" How you comfort me! He talks of a farm-house now near Rome."

Mrs. Thumbler shuddered.

" I should hate to keep an Italian cow," she said. " I should be afraid of it! "

" But *we* should be Byzantine. Just peacocks, stags and sheep. . . ."

" The danger of Italy," Mrs. Asp observed, " is, it tends to make one florid. One expands there so. . . . Personally, I go all to poppy-seed directly. I cannot keep pace with my ideas. And then I fall ill, and have to have a nurse. Shall I ever forget the creature I had last year! My dear Mrs. Calvally, she looked just about as stable as the young woman on the cover of a valse. Unfortunately, I was too exhausted to object. But I simply couldn't endure her. She made me so uneasy. A habit of staring vaguely into space whenever she spoke to me would make me shiver; I began to believe she must be in league with the doctor; that she was hiding something, keeping something back. . . . At last, one day I collected all my strength together and sat up in my bed and pointed towards the door. After that, I took a nun, who was quite rapacious for martyrdom. But all that was ever allowed to her was, sometimes, to get cold feet."

" And what are you doing now? "

Mrs. Asp relaxed.

" At present," she said, " I'm preparing a *Women Queens of England.*"

" Isn't it idle—to insist? "

" Not as euphony. *The Queens* of England, somehow, sound so bleak. And, really, rather a brigade. . . . More like history! "

At the portentous word Master Raphael rolled down upon the floor.

Mrs. Asp considered him. She was old-fashioned enough to believe it necessary for a young thing, when it gaped, to know exactly where to place its hand.

" Does he take after his papa? " she asked.

" I hardly know. He loves to flick his tongue up and down the rough paint of a picture, and to cool his cheek along the shrubberies on my fans."

" He promises! " Mrs. Asp declared.

" But so wicked. Yesterday Princess Schara came to show George a fan. You know her husband used to paint the most wonderful fans. Poor man, in the end he became so decorative that he died! His last fan—would you care to see it?—is such a muddle that very few people can discover what it means. And now Raphael has made it utterly impossible."

"Most modern fans are so ill and sickly," Mrs.
Thumbler observed, "I hope nothing will happen to
your courageous little boy."

Mrs. Calvally lit—one of those . . .

It was a caprice of hers that could still charm, thrill
and fascinate a wayward husband.

He had studied her too, thus, at three different
angles on a single canvas. More vagabond, possibly,
than the Charles, or the Richelieu, or the Lady Alice
Gordon of Reynolds, but, nevertheless, with not one
whit less style.

"How stately the studio is," Mrs. Asp said, a little
confused. "A perfect paradise!"

"I regret I've nothing to show you much that's
new. You've seen his joy-child for the top of a fountain, I expect, before?"

But Mrs. Thumbler did not seem cast down.

"I admire your plain black curtains," she said,
"and, oh, where did you get these?"

Continually, Mrs. Calvally would design an eccentric frame for her husband's pictures. It was a pathetic
attempt, perhaps, on her side, to identify herself in
his career.

For, indeed, she was notoriously indifferent to art.

She was one of those destined to get mixed over
Monet and Manet all their life.

The exhibition of some "lost" masterpiece, in
Bond Street, was what she most enjoyed, when, if
not too crowded, she could recline upon a sofa and
turn out the lining to her purse.

"I'm such a wretched, wicked housekeeper," she
would say. "And were it not for an occasional missing
Gainsborough, George, I should never know what I
had."

"Bristling with intellect," Mrs. Asp pronounced,
laying down the fan, "and I seem to catch a face in it,
too. Little Mrs. Steeple's! . . ."

" Oh, quite——"

" Poor thing! She says Sir Samuel has become so vigorous lately. It nearly kills her every evening waiting for his slap."

" We were at Smith Square on Sunday," Mrs. Calvally said, " and sitting at her feet found Julia's new man—Charley Chalmers! "

" And I suppose a god? " Mrs. Asp inquired.

" Not at all. It's a doll-like, child-like, Adamy sort of face, and very healthy."

" Dear Julia, I've seen nothing of her since the Sappho supper-party Mrs. Henedge gave in the spring."

" I hear she's been safely landed now about a week."

" One can hardly credit it! "

" She sent us a jar of Ashringford honey," Mrs. Thumbler said, " recently. Perfectly packed, in half-a-field of hay."

" She takes a kind of passionate pleasure in her bees. And Mr. Brookes helps her in them, muffled up in all the newest veils."

" He's been away now so long. He might be almost learning to be a priest," Mrs. Asp remarked, as Lady Listless came in.

" I heard a thrush singing in the park," she said. " It was so attractive. I don't know what came over me! Are my eyes wet still with tears? I held back one to bring your husband (I saw the many-happy-returns in The World), but I lost it. It rolled, unluckily, under the wheels of a miserable motor bus. But I managed to get another! So I carried myself as if I were Lily, Lady Ismore, and got nearly safe with it, when it fell down as the lift stopped."

" You should have warned the boy! "

" I did. . . ."

" The incredible thrush! " Mrs. Asp exclaimed.

" Very likely it wasn't totally the thrush. I won't

be positive. It may have been merely the reaction
after Mr. Hurreycomer's Private View. His *Susanna!* ...
Have you seen it? ... A young woman (my dear, his
wife) splashing herself in some perfectly lilac water.
... And the Elders. ... Oh, they are all portraits. ..."

" Tell me about the Elders," Mrs. Calvally begged.

" Your husband. *Most* prominent."

" But George isn't forty! "

" Are you sure? "

" It's incredible, in any case, that an insignificant
stupid thing like Carla could interest even Elders,"
Mrs. Asp remarked, getting up. " Moreover," she
continued, drawing on a glove, " she revels in making
herself needlessly hideous; it appeals to her sense of
truth. Added to which," she rambled on, " his candid
studies of women are simply hateful. ..."

" Brutal! " Mrs. Thumbler opined.

" Has anybody seen my stole? "

" And, remember, Rose," Mrs. Calvally said, returning it to her, " for Friday, it's *you* who've got the
tickets! "

" I shan't forget. But since it's likely to be a debate,
don't expect to see me smart. I shall simply wear my
old, soiled, peach-charmeuse. ..."

" My dear, don't bother to dress! "

Mrs. Asp hesitated.

" I trust that nobody of yours," she said, " is ill or
stricken, for there's a strange old man seated on the
stairs, with such a terrific bag of tools! "

Mrs. Calvally chuckled.

" I conclude it's only the carpenter," she explained,
" who has come to pass a screw through Miss Mira's
charming consumptive Amour! "

XIX

"Don't the hills look soaked through and through with water?"

"My dear, I don't know!"

"If you don't object, I'll go back, I think, to bed."

"What can you expect at the fall of the leaf?"

"But, except for the evergreens, all the leaves are down."

"Well, last winter, it rained so, and it rained so, that the drawing-room became a lake. All my beautiful blue silk chairs . . .; and a few gold fish I'm attached to were floated right out of their bowl, and swam upstairs into Thérèse's room."

"Ashringford's becoming dreadfully disagreeable."

"Patience. The sun will come up presently. Even now it's doing something behind the Cathedral. It usually takes its time to pick a path across St. Dorothea."

Now that she had actually abandoned it, St. Dorothy, for Mrs. Henedge, had become St. Dorothea.

"Hannah was telling us the night it fell she noticed devils sort-of-hobble-stepping beneath the trees."

"My dear, she tells such lies. One never can believe her. Only the other day she broke the child's halo off my plaster Anthony and then declared she didn't."

"The most wonderful name in all the world for any child," Winsome said, "is Diana. Don't you agree? Your gardener intended to call his daughter Winifred, but I was just in time!"

"There now, there's a pretty motive for a walk. Save Mrs. Drax's baby. It's to be christened Sobriety, to-day, at half-past-two. Such a shame!"

" But I should miss Goosey."

" Winsome, lately, had taken quite a fancy to
Goosey, while risking their necks together upon the
scaffolding of St. John's."

" You see so much of him. The Miss Chalfonts, in
comparison, aren't to be compared."

" Don't ever speak of them! "

" Why not? "

" I've such a shock in store."

" Yes; what is it? "

" The Miss Chalfonts have scratched."

" Scratched! . . ."

" Their Guardi."

" What does it matter if they have? I've really no
need for any *more* pictures. People seem to think that
St. John's is going to be a Gallery, or something of the
kind."

" And I've something else to tell you."

" Sit down and tell me here."

" While we were leaning from the campanile an
idea occurred to me. Another opera."

" Bravo! You shall kiss my hand."

" I start *fortissimo!* The effect of the Overture will
be the steam whistle that summons the factory hands.
Such a hoot! . . ."

" But you'll finish what you're doing? "

Since his arrival in Ashringford he had been at
work on a *Gilles de Raie*, an act of which already was
complete. The sextet between Gilles and his youthful
victims bid fair, Mrs. Henedge declared, to become
the most moving thing in all opera. While the lofty
theme for Anne de Bretagne and the piteous *Prière* of
the little Marcelle seemed destined, also, to be popular.

" I'm so glad, for, naturally, while the building's
in progress I have to be on the spot. And I do so hate
to be alone. . . . I cannot bear it. I like to have you
with me! "

" Still, you've got Monsignor Parr. . . ."

" Dear, charming, delightful Monsignor Parr! "

" Are there any more new designs? "

" No. But Mr. Calvally is constructing some confessionals for us utterly unlike the usual *cabines-de-bains*. . . . And apropos of them, I've something serious to say to you. I'm sorry to have to say it . . . for I'd really much rather not! "

" I'm listening."

" It's about *Andrew*. Those Dégas danseuses he sends to you . . . on letter cards. . . . I know, I know, *I know!* And, perhaps, if he didn't scribble over them . . . But—how very often have I said it?—I never liked him. That violet muffler. And the no-collar. . . ."

" Why, what? "

" Here is a card that came for you. When I saw it I assure you it made me feel quite quaint and queer. *I thought it was for me!* "

" Oh, but you couldn't! "

" ' My dear old Sin, do ask me not to write to you again. Or answer my letters properly.' "

" I wish Andrew wouldn't correspond with you in that coarse way. Ever! At least not while you're at the Closed House. What must the postman think? "

" That's nerves! You mustn't begin to worry like Lady Brassknocker. Her apprehension of the servants is a disease."

" But a postman isn't a simple servant. One doesn't dismiss him. I like my letters. Here is one from Atossa Listless. She says Lady Castleyard and Mrs. Shamefoot are going to Cannes. And there's another difficulty apparently: whether the window shall open, or *not*."

" How capricious the Palace is."

" Mrs. Shamefoot is ill with strain. Lady Listless says she speaks of nothing now but death. She says it's almost shocking to hear her. Nothing else amuses her at all. . . . And it gets so gloomy and so monotonous."

" Probably the casino——"

" That's what they try to hope. At present she's continually cabling to India about her pall. After the coffin she says she'll have violins—four: Kubelik, Zimbalist, Kreisler, and Melsa. . . . And no doubt Dina will send a splendid sheaf of something from the shop."

Winsome tossed back his hair and half clouded his eyes. He glazed them.

" Wait! " he murmured, moving to the piano.

Mrs. Henedge obeyed, expectant, upright, upon the tip of her chair. She knew the signs. . . . Her finger-tips hovering at her heart caged an Enchantress Satin Rose.

> " Lillilly-là, lillilly-là,
> Là, là, là.
> Lillilly, lillilly, lillilly-là,
> Lillilly-là, lillilly-là,
> Lillilly, lillilly, lillilly-là,
> L-à-à-à. . . ."

" Well; really! . . ."

" I couldn't help it. It just broke from me. It's *The Song of the Embalmers*. . . ."

" . . . I call it lovely! Poor Mrs. Shamefoot. That lillilly, lillilly, lillilly. One feels they really are doing something to the corpse. It's sitting up! And the long final l-à-à-à It's dreadful. Don't they fling it down? " And with finger rigid she pointed towards the floor.

" It's good of you to like it," Winsome said, with some emotion. " And here's Goosey? "

" Never lend your name, or your money, or your books, or your umbrella, or anything, to anybody— if you're wise," Goosey Pontypool remarked over his shoulder to Winsome as he pressed Mrs. Henedge's hand.

" But it isn't raining? "

" It doesn't matter. Here, they pour down dust upon you as you go by."

" It's a sign," Mrs. Henedge said, " that the houses are tenanted. Thérèse will sometimes say to me that that melancholy Miss Wintermoon must have gone away *at last* when suddenly up flies her window and a hand shakes a duster into the street."

" In Ashringford there's chatter enough indoors. You'd be surprised? "

" Well, I never know what goes on, except when the sow gets into the Dean's garden. And then I hear the screams."

" I hear everything."

" Which, invariably, you exaggerate! "

" It's no crime to exaggerate. It's a sign of vitality rather. Health . . ."

" Whisper what you've heard."

" That Mr. Pet is to marry Miss Wardle and Mr. Barrow's to be made a peer."

" Upon what grounds? "

" For doctoring the Asz. You know it used always to ooze away; he's just discovered where. While she was watering her rhododendrons he noticed. . . . Anyway, he's going to Egypt officially soon to do something to the Nile."

" How delightful for her! "

" She's advertising for a cottage at Bubastis, a bungalow, a villa. . . ."

Mrs. Henedge became staid.

" I suppose she'll get like Salabaccha now," she said. " Ah well! "

" Even so, it's much more wonderful for Jane. . . ."

" I'm at a loss to conceive anyone . . ."

" I don't know. Miss Wardle isn't, perhaps, what

you'd expect. When I called at Wormwood she said:
'I was so sure we should find plenty in common. *I could
feel it through the window.* I've often watched you pass.'"

" Those complicated curls of hers remind me of
the codicils to my poor dear Leslie's will."

" Who arranged the match? "

" St. Dorothy. She was expatiating on her escape
. . . ' I heard a noise,' she said, ' a sound. But country
servants are so rough. Aren't they? Breaking, dropping,
chipping things. . . . I haven't a dish that isn't
cracked. . . . So, if I didn't hurry immediately to
look out, it was because . . . because . . . because . . .
because . . . Because I was in the middle of my prayers.'

" ' Had it fallen a *leetle* more your way,' he said,
' there would have been an end of them.'

" ' Oh, Mr. Pet,' she said, ' What difference could
that have made to you? ' "

" So simple! "

" Well, if it's true, it's the best thing possible. Now,
perhaps, we shall get rid of them *both.*"

" I believe it's not at all unlikely. Wormwood's to
be let; not noisily. But, at the land agent's, nobody
could mistake the exaggerated description of the con-
servatories and the kiosk by the lake."

" Mrs. Shamefoot's searching for a house here-
abouts, isn't she? "

" Oh, Wormwood's hardly what she wants. It isn't
rustic enough. It doesn't thrill."

" Besides, she's already made an offer for the Old
Flagellites Club."

" It should suit her. That long flaying room would
make an exquisite drawing-room. And there's a
sheltered pretty garden at the back."

Winsome began twisting across his eyes a heavy,
heliotrope veil.

" Don't let me interrupt you," he murmured, " I'm
merely going to peep at the bees."

XX

LADY BARROW lolled languidly in her mouse-eaten library, a volume of mediæval Tortures (with plates) propped up against her knee. In fancy, her husband was well pinned down and imploring for mercy at Figure 3.

How eagerly, now, he proffered her the moon! How he decked her out with the stars! How he overdressed her!

Coldly she considered his case.

" Release you? Certainly not! Why should I? " she murmured comfortably, transferring him to the acuter pangs of 9.

And morally she could have started as her maid came in.

" Yes, what is it? "

" Sir S'torious is looking everywhere for your ladyship."

The difficulty the servants seemed to find in saying " Sir Sartorious," without a slovenly contraction, was frequently distressing.

Grigger, his man, would quite break down, while the housemaids tripped, and the chauffeur literally sneezed.

" Say that I'm busy."

Lady Barrow closed her book.

Something would have to be done.

" Had it been a peerage, was elocution compulsory, there need have been none of this fuss," she exclaimed.

And with her finger-ends pressed to her eyes she began to conjure up his latent baptismal names:

" Sartorious, Hugh, Wilful, Anne, Barrow. S,H,W,A,B. *Schwab!* " she murmured.

And loosening a pencil from her wrist, she put them sharply to the test.

" Sir Sartorious regrets——"

" Sir Hugh and Lady Barrow regret——"

" Sir Wilful and Lady Barrow much regret——" Or even " deeply——"

" Sir Anne—— *San*——" She shuddered. Lady Barrow walked towards the door.

" Wilful! " she called, in what her maid later described as a light silvery voice, " I'm here! . . ."

But the silence oppressed her. " Presently," she reflected, " perhaps, will do. It'll be something to discuss during dinner. Although, indeed, after what's occurred, I hadn't intended to say very much to him to-night."

And apathetically she looked away across the cloud-shaded hills.

How well she knew the roads round Dawn! Here and there a tree would lift itself above the rest. . . .

The forlornness of it!

Up to the very house crept the churchyard yews, whose clipped wide windows never held a face.

And, somewhere, in the dark, dipping branches of a cedar, lurked the Raven. . . .

" I'm *all* romantic feelings," Lady Barrow murmured. " I always was. I always will be."

And from a lavender cardboard box she slipped a smart sombrero piled up with wings and wings and wings.

" What is the good? " she murmured, dispirited, as she tried it on. Still, in every shadow, of every room, Lady Barrow would store a hat.

" I never intend to lose sight of town clothes," was the explanation that she gave.

But to-day it was not essentially in vain. Scarcely had she poised it than she saw Lady Georgia's car coming up the drive.

" I'm perfectly ashamed," Lady Georgia began,
" not to have been over before."

" Say nothing of it! "

" And so, thanks to Sir Sartorious, one may curtail
one's domestic troubles. Like poor Mrs. Frobisher——."

" Who is Mrs. Frobisher? "

" She was our nearest neighbour with a soul."

" The Asz is in arrears. A short while ago even
my cook went down. (Sartorious, if anything goes
wrong . . .) And there were we! All of us upon our
knees to her, flattering her, from the bank."

" And a Mrs. Luther Gay—such a shocking thing
—sprang quite suddenly off her lawn——"

" And one of the Olneys, too, was driven home
from the Dean's dance, drenched. And with her heavy
head, and her thin neck, and her poinsettia-pink
arms——"

" So long as it isn't bathing."

" And then there was Captain Hoey."

" Cards! "

" And Azeza Williams."

" Love! "

" And little Miss Chimney."

" Despair! "

" And Admiral van Boome."

" I heard——"

" It makes one long to get away. The responsibility
is beginning to tell."

" And so you're positively off? "

" Yes. We've got rid of Dawn to such a very pretty
widow—a Mrs. Lily Carteret Brown. . . ."

" Who, at all, is she? "

" I couldn't be sure. But after a career of dissipation
she seems delighted to settle down."

" And where *is* the great man? "

" Sartorious? He's packing."

" Packing! "

" All great men are prosaic at close quarters. Didn't you know? "

" Dear Violet——"

" Not since we were married have we been away together once."

" It should rekindle happy memories."

Lady Barrow shook the dancing, whispering things upon her hat.

" When we were first married," she said, " I was very, very wretched. I would weep, weep, weep at night! And in the morning, often, my maid would have to put my pillow-case out upon the window-ledge to dry. Fortunately, it was in Sicily, so it never took long."

" And later, what are your plans? "

" I had the project of Paris."

" Mrs. Henedge goes there too, in connection with the festas at St. John's."

" My dear, she's always covered in embroideries; one never sees her in anything else."

" She was superintending her building just now very busily as I came through the town."

" How is it getting on? "

" Fairly fast. . . . It will have a very fine front. And, of course, nothing at all behind."

" I believe it's only going to be very large——"

" Exactly! "

" When once they're gone she'll almost regret her workmen's blue sleeves."

" It must be a little lonely for her sometimes."

" I can't conceive when! She's for ever dancing round her yclept geniuses. . . . Making their death-masks, or measuring their hands. She never leaves them alone one minute."

" Of all the discoveries, Mr. Brookes appears to be the best."

" The least anxiety, perhaps——"

" That requiem he sent Biddy showed ſtyle."

" Where is she now? "

" At Cannes. Lady Ismore caught sight of her in the casino the other day, in magnificence, brilliance, beauty. . . ."

" One either admires her extremely or not at all."

" Of course, she's continually criticised."

" Sartorious thinks her colourless! "

" How?. . ."

" Pale. I don't know. He believes she makes up with chalk."

" What an idea."

" I suppose we shall receive cards for her vitrification before very long."

" Not until the spring. She wants the sun."

" She used to hate it."

" Poor Mrs. Frobisher's girl was to have taken part in the cortège."

" Cortège! "

" She's to be supported. Children singing; scattering flowers."

" What does Dr. Pantry say? "

" For the moment he objects. The *panther skins* upset him. . . ."

" Lady Anne would never hear of it! "

" On the contrary, she adores processions. They are quite her weakness."

" Depravity! "

" Biddy will be charming. I shall persuade her, if I can, to wear a crinoline."

Lady Barrow beamed.

" Take her to Madame Marathon," she said.

" I've never heard of her."

" Of course, she's rather expensive. You pay her ninety guineas for a flicker of a gown. . . ."

Lady Georgia's geſture was sublime. " Look. *All that for a shilling!* " she murmured as she rose.

XXI

HAIL, hyacinth! Harbinger of spring . . ." Miss Hospice hesitated.

Before being whirled away, before descending deeper, it would be well to decide in what situation it was to be.

Should it be growing or cut. Should it be lying severed. Besmirched. Should it be placed in some poor weary hand, withering upon a quilt. Should it wave upon a hill-top, or break between the slabs of crumbling marble of the theatre tiers beneath the Acropolis; the soul of a spectator. Should it be well wired, writhing in a wreath. Or, should it be a Roman hyacinth, in which case, should she trace Christianity to its sources, musing on many a mummery by the way?

She raised a delicate witty face.

" Or . . . should she seek another flower instead? Above her the branches of the chestnut-trees rocked rhythmically. A warm wind rippling round St. Dorothy stirred the dark violet of the Bougainvillæa along the wall.

" What have you found? " Lady Anne inquired.

She was seated before the Palace, a panther skin upon her knee.

" Only——"

" Then come and help me, do. To make it less schismatical, I believe I'm going to take off the tail."

" Oh no. Give it a careless twist."

Lady Anne snapped her scissors.

" It's such an infamy! " she declared.

" Mrs. Shamefoot will say you tried to slight her if you harm a hair."

" I begin to think we've made a mistake. . . ."

" Well, she's in the saddle now. The window's up."

" I fear it'll cause a good deal of horror, scandal and surprise."

" I don't see why it should."

" It must be altogether impossible or why aren't we allowed to go near? Why must it be concealed behind a thousand towel-horses, and a million screens? Oh, Madge, you haven't a conception what I shall endure when the curtains come away. My dear, I shall probably have to sit down. All my amusement in the procession's *gone*."

And Lady Anne buried her face in her panther skin because of the sun.

" No doubt it's better than we expect. Kitty Wookie got a glimpse from the organ loft."

" She's such a cunning creature. What does she say? "

" She says it's a thing quite by itself. Apart."

" What does she mean by that? "

" She says, of course, it's entirely without reticence. . . ."

" For instance! "

" Apparently, the features are most carefully modelled. The ennui of half the world is in her eyes— almost, as always. And she is perched upon a rather bewildering throne, in a short silver tunic, showing her ankles up to her knees."

" Aurelia always said it would jar."

" It depends. Miss Wookie's easily scared. Very likely it's exquisitely lovely."

" I wouldn't willingly offend the Segry-Constables or the Nythisdenes or the Doneburning'ems or the Duke."

" I should tack a pocket to my libbard skin and let it make very little difference. . . ."

" Walter has told her she shall sleep a night in the Cathedral whenever she likes."

" He might have offered her the pink room here for the matter of that."

" It wouldn't do. She wishes to watch the colour roll back into the glass again."

" What a curious caprice! "

" I call it simply shallow."

" I'd die of terror. Mrs. Cresswell—they say, constantly . . ."

" Oh, nonsense! At most she'll confront the dark."

" For a nervous soul what could be more appalling?"

" You forget she isn't timid."

" It's hard to tell. She gave me the saddest, the whiptest, look last night as I passed her in the lane."

" Those tristful glances of hers are so irritating. Especially when everyone tries to kill her with kindness."

" That's probably why she does it."

" Well, I'd be so glad if you'd leave a book for her at the ' Four Fans ' whenever you go for a walk."

" Such an address almost makes one flurried."

" Still, poor thing, one understands intuitively, she wouldn't choose the Cresswell Arms. . . . And to stop, on the contrary, at Stockingham, where Lord Blueharnis I believe . . . And the Flagellites, of course, is overrun still by a firm from . . . And, frankly, I'm not altogether sorry. For, if there's anything I dislike, it's a house-warming."

" In Ashringford what egotists we are."

" Are we? "

" Tell me where the book is I'm to bear."

" It's here; Harvester's *Vaindreams!* "

" Not exactly the kind of book, is it, to take to her? "

" Why not? He has such a strange, peculiar style. His work calls to mind a frieze with figures of varying heights trotting all the same way. If one should by chance turn about it's usually merely to stare or to sneer or to make a grimace. Only occasionally his figures care to beckon. And they seldom really touch."

" He's too cold. Too classic, I suppose."

" Classic! In the *Encyclopædia Britannica* his style is described as *odd spelling, brilliant and vicious.*"

" All the same, dear, if you wouldn't mind carrying it across."

" Shall I allude to the tail at all while I'm there? "

" Too late! I fear it's already off."

Lady Anne turned.

She was sufficiently alert to feel the vibration from a persistent pair of eyes.

" May I come in? "

With her weight entirely on one foot and an arm raised towards a gilt rosette Miss Wardle was leaning against the wrought-iron gate.

" By all means do."

" Might I have a word with the Bishop? "

" Unhappily, he's gone round to Miss Spruce."

" Something serious? "

" I trust not. She has sent to him so often *in extremis* that really——"

" Then perhaps I'd better confess to you."

Lady Anne glanced away.

Clouds, like scattered cities, dashed the blue.

" You needn't," she said. " I guess. I sympathise. Or will try to. You mean to leave us for St. John's! "

" St. John's is still without a roof."

" But ultimately, I understand, it will have one."

Miss Wardle drew a deep breath.

" No," she said, slightly shocked, " it's not that— I'm married! "

" Already! "

" I can scarcely credit it either."

" To Mr. Pet? "

" *Lippo Lippi* man! He's too sweet to be true."

" I'm delighted. I 'm glad you seem so happy."

" . . . He's twenty-three. . . . Five for elegance. Four for luck. Three for fate! "

" Of course, now, he'll need a little change? "

" A change! But Peter raves about Ashringford. He says there's nowhere like it."

" No honeymoon? "

Mrs. Pet opened a black parasol.

" Oh no," she said. " A honeymoon must always end in a certain amount of curiosity. So we've decided not to have one, but just stop here."

" It's really refreshing to find anyone nowadays who tries to avoid a fuss! "

" Peter, you see, insisted that the wedding should be quite—quite—quiet. For although you mightn't think it, he's as sensitive, in his way, as anybody in the town. And so I simply walked from Wormwood to Violet Villas with a travelling-clock and a bag."

" How dull. And surely a trifle dusty? "

" It was my first small sacrifice," Mrs. Pet said, sitting down. " As a girl I used always to say I would be married in my *point d'espagne*."

" You must make up for it at the unveiling. A dot of gold . . . against those old monks' stalls. . . ."

" I'm very uncertain yet whether I shall go."

" Indeed, I don't feel up to it myself."

" After all, one isn't always inclined for church! "

Lady Anne fetched a sigh.

" I've a tiny favour to ask," she said.

Mrs. Pet twirled, quite slightly, her parasol.

" If you wish to be really charming exert your influence! Keep your husband at home."

" I'm afraid I don't understand."

" During the little masque amuse your husband indoors."

" But I've no influence with him at all! "

" Have you none . . .? "

" Hardly any."

" At any rate promise to do what you can."

Mrs. Pet stared, reflective, across the *mors-in-vita* of the Cathedral green.

" I realise my limitations," she said.

" But you mustn't! "

" According to *The Ashringford Chronicle* there'll be almost a procession."

" Oh, nothing half so formal. . . ."

" And one of the Olneys, it appears, as the curtains fall away, will break from behind a pillar with a basket of orchids, and say: '*Accept these poor flowers.*' "

" Not in the Cathedral: only in the porch."

" And those foolish, silly Scouts are to fire off minute-guns from the walls."

" I haven't seen the *Chronicle*."

" Sometimes," Mrs. Pet protested, " I have no loftier wish than to look upon the world with Kate Greenaway's eyes! "

Lady Anne shivered.

"I'm all nerves," she explained, " to-day, and here's Hypolita and the Bishop! "

It was Hypolita's turn.

Aurelia had gone away to a pale silver palace in Bath, where she was casting into purest English the *Poemetti* of Pascoli.

" We looked in for a moment at the Four Fans," Dr. Pantry said.

" Well! . . ."

" Mrs. Shamefoot wasn't quite up, but I spoke to her under the door."

" Anything new? "

" She sent her love! . . . She will make her vigil on the eve of the day."

" Surely if she spends a night in the Cathedral somebody should be within call? "

" Things change so, don't they," Hypolita said,

"when the daylight goes? Frequently, even the shadow of a feather boa . . ."

" Who would look after her? "

" One of the students, perhaps——"

" Ah, no flirtations! "

" It should be an old, or *quite* an elderly man."

" What elderly person is there? "

" In this neighbourhood there're so many. There's such a choice! "

The Bishop was affected.

" I don't mind being ninety."

" You, Walter? Certainly not."

" Mr. Poyntz, perhaps. . . ."

" He'd need to raise a bed."

" Still, on Sunday he manages wonderfully well without."

" I'm down in the garden every morning by five . . ."

" My dear, what ever for? "

" Besides, she refuses! She desires to be alone."

Lady Anne gazed at her sister-in-law in dismay.

How was it possible that one did nothing to such a terribly shiny nose?

She considered it etched against the effortless chain of hills, designed, apparently, to explain that the world was once made in a week.

The morning was so clear the distances seemed to shrink away—one could even trace the racecourse, to its frail pavilion, by the artificial fence.

" It will be so nice when it's all over," she exclaimed.

" All over, Anne? "

" The unveiling——"

" Life was never meant to be quite easy! "

When Hypolita began upon *Life* she simply never stopped.

Dr. Pantry raised his wife's wrist and examined the watch.

" Are you coming, my dear, to——? "

" Oh, my dear, very likely! "

" Then make haste: the bells will begin directly. . . ."

But to-day she invented an entirely new excuse.

" I must run indoors *first* to wave my white hairs,"
she said.

XXII

A SMART, plain sky stretched starless above St. Dorothy. The night was sultry, sweet and scented.

Miss Thumbler shrugged her pretty, crippled shoulders and pressed volcanically her hands.

" Beautiful! " she murmured. " But how walled in! "

" Answer me! " he said.

" Oh, George . . . haven't I enough already? Of course I cannot recall all the trifling ins and outs. Although, I believe, he kissed me, once, in the Vermeer Room at the National Gallery! "

She turned away.

These continual jealous scenes. . . .

Only a few hours back there had been an aria from *Tosca*, in St. John's.

There came a babel of voices.

On the lawn and in the lighted loggia the total town was waiting for Mrs. Shamefoot to pass. And as usual everyone was turning on the hose.

" . . . Vanna! Mrs. Nythesedene got a palm there . . . ages ago. She said . . she could see her . . . plainly . . . in the little room behind the shop . . . tearing the white lilac out of a wreath . . . and wiring it up for . . ."

" Her dull white face seems to have no connection with her chestnut hair! "

" . . . with *him* to Palestine last spring. Oh, dear me, I thought I should have died at Joppa! "

" You mix them with olives and a drop of cognac."

" What could be more tiresome than a wife that bleats? "

" His denunciations of the Government nearly brought the lustres down."

" I can't get him to come with me. He doesn't like the pendant lamps."

" . . . above-board, when one can! "

" . . . Half the profits."

" Ce gros Monsignor Parr! "

" . . . A day together."

" . . . Rabbits."

" . . . As tall as Iss'y."

" . . . Precedence! "

" . . . A regular peruke."

" . . . An interesting trio! "

" A tiara swamps her."

" She will become florid in time. Just like her mother."

" Don't! "

" For him a *tête-à-tête* would be a *viva voce*. . . ."

" . . . glare."

" . . . lonely! "

" . . . no sympathy for——"

" . . . Idolatry."

" . . . a top! "

" I heard a noise. A sound. But country servants are so rough. Aren't they? Breaking, dropping, chipping things. I've scarcely a dish that isn't cracked. . . ."

" . . . escape! "

" . . . *is* such a duck in his . . ."

" The only genuine one was Jane."

" . . . poison."

" . . . fuss. . . . "

" My husband was always shy. He is shy of everybody. He even runs away from me! "

" Let us sell the house, dear," she said, " but keep the car! We can drive round and round the park in it at night. And it looks so charming for the day."

Lady Anne trailed slowly up and down. She seemed worn-out.

" I'll go on," Hypolita said. " Life's too short to walk so slow."

" As you please. But there's no escape from Eternity," Mr. Pet's voice came, unexpectedly booming out.

At which vision, of continual middle age, the younger Miss Flowerman fainted.

On a litter, in the garden, where the stairs streamed up towards the house, Miss Spruce surveyed the scene with watchful, wondering eyes. It was cruel to be an invalid with her energetic mind. . . .

Still, a good deal came her way.

" Come now, and meet him, and get it over! " Mrs. Henedge was exhorting Winsome Brookes.

It was her first appearance anywhere since the change.

Attended by George Calvally, Mira Thumbler, Winsome and Monsignor Parr, she would have responded willingly to an attack.

From beneath a black bandeau sparkling with brilliants and an aigrette breaking several ways she seemed to Miss Spruce like some radiant Queen of Night.

" Anybody born in 1855 I've no desire to meet," Winsome declared.

" Hush! Remember your *future!* " the relentless woman murmured, dragging him towards Lord Brassknocker to be introduced.

" . . . Belongs to the Junior Carlton, the Arts, and to several night *cabarets*."

" Sir Caper Frisk was explaining to me that cocktails——"

By the great gold gates that closed at dusk the choir· was waiting to give three cheers.

" Poor mites! I hear they've been told to give four," Mrs. Wookie said.

" What are we waiting for? "

" I haven't a notion."

" The moon——"

" It must have been the year that Drowsy-Dreamy-Dora won the Derby. . . ."

" The old Duke begins to look a bit hipped."

" One tooth missing. And only half rouged. On one side only. I'd not call her pretty."

" Pan? "

" . . . descended from *a waiter*."

" If anything takes him to town it's the cattle-show."

" I loathe London."

" ' Sable, sable, indeed! ' I said. There's no depth to the skin. Nothing to fathom. It might be crocodiles."

Monsignor Parr drew in his feet. He had been so very nearly asleep. All his life he had waited for something attractive to happen. Usually, now, he would sit huddled up like a Canopic jar saying nothing at all.

" . . . too tired to make converts. . . ."

" . . . totter from party to party. . . ."

" How do you do? "

" . . . sorry."

" If my father marries again it will be to some sweet soul to stir the fire."

" . . . does enjoy a rubber! "

" The lanes round Dawn are so narrow. And Sir Sirly and Lady James. . . . Well, there's hardly room for us all. . . . "

" Only Miss Knowle and Mrs. Lloyd! "

" . . . sheet-lightning? "

" Naturally, for the moment," Mrs. Shamefoot was confessing, " it's the least bit gorgeous, perhaps. But one has to look ahead. Posterity? "

" Such a pity not to have gone halves. You and Lady Castleyard together. A Beaumont-and-Fletcher ——"

" So, actually, you've come! "

" What a wonderful wrap. My dear, what skins ! "

" In case you should feel faint at all in the night you'll find a lobster mayonnaise and some champagne in the vestry ! "

" Dear Lady Anne, how could you dream of such a thing ? "

" In the grey of dawn, when a thousand grinning fiends peer down on you, you may be very glad of a little something. . . ."

Above the toppling timber, and the long low vineries, towered St. Dorothy. Urging each quivering leaf, and every blade of grass, to strain higher, *higher*.

" I hope you've a nice warm pair of stockings? " Mrs. Wookie wailed.

Mrs. Shamefoot stretched wearily above her head some starry spangled stuff.

" The mornings," she observed, " are still quite chilly ! "

" I'm looking everywhere for Kate. It's like search-ing for a needle in a bundle of hay."

" It ought not to be ! "

" You'll find Miss Wookie in the drawing-room, playing Siegfried's Journey."

" I must make sure she's ordered our *fly*."

" A representative of the *Chronicle* would so much like to know——"

" Not now. Just when my spirit cries to be alone everything that's earthly seems to pass between ! "

" He merely desires to ask you how you are."

" How I am? "

" How you feel."

" I feel such a strange sadness. You might tell him." She moved away.

Miss Thumbler had apparently consented to dance.

Stiffening her fingers and thrusting out her chin, she began slightly to sway, as though pursuing an invisible ideal.

" Sartorious always said she had a horrid mind! "

" I'm delighted she's so busy."

" Really——"

" She's been doing her utmost to *will* the tower down upon us this last half-hour."

" You mean——"

" I'm afraid so."

"·Could anyone be so rough? "

"No, I haven't yet finished," Miss Valley was saying. "Alas, a little fame! One buys it at such a price. . . ."

Beneath the big blue Persia-tree, the Miss Chalfonts lay quite still. They had attained their calm.

" It might be almost the Hesperides! " Lady Georgia declared.

" . . . foot's on the wane! "

" In a gloomy corner she is still quite pretty."

Mrs. Shamefoot held up her fan.

" . . . the crops! "

" Ah, here comes our dreadsome friend! "

" Leave him to me," Miss Valley said. " I'll undertake to tame him."

" Use some of your long writing words to him, my dear! "

" Shall I? Would you like me to? "

" Few people are worth untidying one's hair for," Winsome Brookes observed.

" Mrs. Shamefoot! "

" Yes, my angel."

Master Guy Fox was staring at her with great googoo eyes like a morning in May.

" Mr. Pet says you've done something to be ashamed of."

" I? . . Oh, good heavens! " Mrs. Shamefoot began to laugh.

" We've such trouble," his mother said, " to get him to close his mouth. He gapes. But at Eton, probably, there are instructors who will attend to *that*."

" There are certain to be classes——"

" Perhaps even oftener than any other! "

And the Dean smiled sheepishly and tried to look less like a wolf. It was a favourite expression of his when addressing youth.

" What would you like to do eventually if you live to be a man? "

Almost nervously St. Dorothy chimed the hour.

" I would like to hang in a large gold bird-cage in the window."

" Is that all? "

" And be a bird! "

" And not a wild one? "

" Supported? "

" Kept! "

" Oh, you lazy little thing."

" I wish my boy had his quiet tastes," the Duchess said. " A child in the Life Guards runs away with so much money! "

" O-o-o-h. . . . When that Miss Thumbler bends so far it makes me quite afraid."

" I long to see La Taxeira in a new set of attitudes."

" Has she fresh ones? "

" Oh, she's unearthly! "

" They say she never dances without her Pompeian pavement! "

" Dear Lady Barrow, I've had no opportunity before! . . . We seem, now, surrounded by water as we are . . . quite to be floating. The Castle is my *yacht*."

" I do so love a wreck."

" From our upper stories, I must tell you, the Asz has almost a look of the sea! One has an impression of chestnut-trees and swans, and perfectly pink roses."

" Some day, perhaps——"

" Unfortunately from my room, sir, there is really nothing to admire. . . . A view over tiresome chimney pots. And that is all."

" I adore tiresome chimney pots."

" Where is everybody going? "

" Indoors. There's such an absorbing . . ."

Through the wide windows of the drawing-room someone could be heard to say:

" Town Eclogues! . . . Epistle from Arthur Grey the Footman. Words by Lady Mary Wortley. Music by Chab-bon-nière."

" Delightful! "

" So suitable! "

" Ingenious! "

" Ingeniousness *is* so rare! "

" And so enchanting! "

" Prevent the Pets——"

" Dear Peter," Mrs. Pet murmured, tapping her husband lightly, " he is everything I admire, and like and love."

" I wonder I'm not in strong hysterics," Lady Anne confessed.

" Before the Monsignor wakes wouldn't it be well to uncover the piano? "

" Uncover it? . . ."

" Remove that cope! "

" How can I, while——"

A. G. declared:

" ' Though bid to go, I quite forgot to move;
    You know not that stupidity was love! ' "

" Afterwards, then! . . ."

" You have the sweetest heart! "

" Should you hear the organ sounding in the night," Mrs. Shamefoot remarked, " you'll realise it's *me*."

" How piqued! "

" An over-sensitive person in the country is always a strain."

" Try."

" Oh, I'm sure I never could——"

" I should never, never, no never, have believed it to be so difficult to enlist a *prima donna*."

" Flatterer! "

" You wouldn't fail us! "

" My poor repertoire," Mrs. Henedge explained. " If I sing anything now it's *Divinités du Styx*."

" Gluck! "

" Jeanne Grannier *en vacances* couldn't equal her! " Lady Georgia affirmed.

Up the steps, from the garden, clitter-clatter, with the agility of an antelope, came Mrs. Budd, whose claim to being the oldest woman in Ashringford nobody seemed likely to dispute.

The piano had lured her from beneath the shadow of the trees. She stood mumbling and blinking in the light, leaning on the arm of Reggie Cresswell of the choir.

" Her son is sexton here! "

Mrs. Shamefoot held out a hand.

" I'm so happy—— "

" Here, Reggie," Winsome said.

" Oh, what a darling! "

" We want him to sing."

" Sing? "

" *Come away Death*, or something."

" Shakespeare is all very well in his way—and in his place."

Reggie looked shy.

" He's been crying! "

" Tears! "

" What is the matter? "

" Mr. Pet—— "

" What did he do, dear? "

" I aroused his provocation."

" You aroused his . . . that surely was very indiscreet."

" Yes, miss."

" Reggie's all feelings. Aren't you, Reggie? "

" Yes, miss. "

" Reggie will do anything for sixpence," Mrs. Budd said. " He is a true Cresswell."

" She introduced the parlour or salon," Miss Valley observed. " She helped, too, to give afternoon-tea its vogue: the French five o'clock. She was also one of our original vegetarians. Oh, my dear, she took the silliest things. Her adoration for apricots is well known. She would tin them. And sometimes she would sleep for days on days together——"

" So sensible."

" And her love for animals! Even as a girl she would say: ' And I shall have a doll and a bird and talk to it.' "

" Why not them? "

" Because she prefers a solecism! And then, her fondness for flowers. . . . ' How beautiful violets are,' she says, ' in a room, just as the day is closing. I know of no other flower *quite* so intense.' "

" There's a sensuousness, a concreteness in her ideas. Isn't there? "

" She was so human. So practical. An artist in the finest sense."

" You'll quite miss her when you've done."

" I dare say I shall."

" And afterwards who will take her place? "

" I've scarcely settled yet. I never care to arrange anything at all ahead. I dislike a definite programme. Perhaps, a Judas Iscariot——"

" ' Vapours of Vanity and strong champagne,' " Arthur was beginning to drawl.

Mrs. Shamefoot glanced about her.

The moon shone out now high above the trees. In smoke-like, dreamy spirals streamed the elms, breaking towards their zeniths into incredible *ich diens*.

" Between us all," the Bishop said, " I was afraid we should lose the key! "

She took it, seizing it slightly.

There were ribands attached, countless streaming strings.

" How charming! "

" It has been circulating about like one of those romances of Mrs.——"

" Am I to lead the way? "

" A coterie of ladies, first, expect a little prayer."

" A prayer! "

" Lady Victoria Webster Smith insists on something of the kind."

" You know she has never really got over her *mésalliance*. . . ."

" What am I to do? "

Mrs. Shamefoot raised her face.

Above her, silver-white, a rose dangled deep asleep.

" There's one thing I've done," she said, " I've sent to the Inn for a hat."

" Indeed! "

" One feels securer, somehow, beneath a few fierce feathers."

" You're not afraid."

" Certainly not."

" Permit me to say you look bewitching."

" This unfinished rag——"

" Has teased——"

" When she comes it will be as if a Doge espoused the Adriatic! "

" Hark . . . to your soulless flock! . . ."

" In Ashringford, if souls are rare, we've at least some healthy spirits."

" Dear Dr. Pantry, everybody's wondering where you are! "

" You seem upset."

" Lady Anne is over-tired, I fear. These warm airless nights. . . . Just as Miss Pontypool was commencing her second encore——"

Mrs. Shamefoot slipped away.

In the garden all was dim.

Along a walk laced with weeping violet fuchsias she skimmed, glancing apprehensively from side to side.

There appeared to be a good deal going on.

In the chiaroscuro of the shrubberies marriages were being arranged. . . .

On a garden bench in a shower of moonlight an Ashringford matron was comparing shadows with her child.

" And why *not*, pray? " she seemed to ask.

" Marry. . . . Have a substantial husband? Oh no, I couldn't, I couldn't, I really couldn't."

" Well, dear, there's no need to get so agitated. It wouldn't be—just yet."

Round and round a great gloomy bush of thorn Miss Thumbler was circling in the oblivion of a dance, while, threading here and there, Lady Barrow annulled a thousand awkward calls. . . . " Your poor husband." " Your interesting son." " Your gifted girl." " Your delightful wife."

Observing her the Miss Chalfonts were assailed again. Monsignor Parr, revealing his mind, moved a finger from forehead to chin, and from ear to ear. And through the gilded gates that closed at dusk Mrs. Henedge's dog had found a way and was questing inscrutably about. . . .

" He ought to be muzzled! " Mrs. Wookie declared.

" Come now. Just once more! " Mrs. Henedge was entreating still.

" But I'm so tired," Winsome said, " of meeting other people. I want other people to meet me."

" Really, and what should you say to them? "

" Nothing; I don't know."

Mrs. Shamefoot hurried on.

A dark cloud like an immense wild bird had drifted across the moon.

Were the gods, she wondered, taking any interest in her affair?

" Oh, don't spoil it," someone she did not recognise implored. " *I think Alice and Dick are holy.* They're each eighteen. And they're in love! . . ."

Mrs. Shamefoot turned aside.

Before her, serene, soared St. Dorothy.

It was a joy to admire such beautifully balanced towers.

" No, I never once lost hope! " she informed a grimacing, ghoulish gargoyle of a sprite.

Those demons, imps, fiends and fairies with horns like stalactites and indignant, scurrying angels and virgins trampling horrors beneath their firm, mysterious feet, and the winged lion of Mark and the winged ox of Luke and the rows and tiers of things enskied above the cavernous deep doors were *part of her escort now!*

And within, elusive, brittle, responsive to every mood, in every minute, and every year improving. . . .

" Shall we go? "

" Certainly. Let's."

Figures flitted by.

She bolted in.

The utter void unnerved her.

" A collier," she reflected, " would laugh at me. He would say . . . He would *call it light!* . . ."

She sank across a chair.

In the dark nothingness the flags drooped fearfully. . . .

Imaginatively, she strove to hold her man.

" Bill? "

" She admired his full lips, his tip-tilted, inquisitive nose. She thought he had a soft Italian face. . . ."

Marble quarries!

Dirty, disgusting coal!

She recalled visiting marble quarries. Soco and she together. "Oh dear! . . . That slow sad drive. Up, and up, and up! And when the road turned, such a surprising view. . . . Then the coachman invited somebody on to the box . . . I remember I said nothing!"

" A footstool! "

She lay back on her chair . . . relieved.

How still it was. . . . She could almost hear the worms nibbling the carved images of the saints!

" My poor maid must be searching everywhere for me in vain. . . ."

Which little hat would she bring? Lately, she had become so revoltingly stupid. . . . What had come over her at all? She was so changed. . . .

She could make out the Ashringford Juliet now borne as though a leaf on a misty-shadow sea. And, more massive, the Blueharnis monument of course! Over the canopy crouched an occult, outrageous thing, phosphorescent in places. Beyond, an old statesman was reclining, his head resting upon a confused heap of facts.

He had a look of Soco.

Where would he be while she was vigiling here?

The club. . . . Savoy. . . .

Never in her life had she thought so much about him before. Twice in two minutes!

That pretty Miss Chance. . . .

Oh, well! . . .

And in future, this was to be her home!

Had she chosen wisely? . . . By waiting, perhaps——

Cupolas and minarets whizzed and whirled.

After all, Overcares had its points. . . . It rose with brilliance from its hill. It made a deep impression from the train. One dropped one's paper, one changed

one's place, chatter hung suspended in the air. . . .
Dear Dorothy was in a hollow rather. The trees
shaded it so. Sintrap, too, had style. And Mawling.
. . . But, there, there was nothing to regret. Placed
in the midst of the town. Stifled! All about it stood
such fussy, frightful shops. Post-cards, bibelots, toys
for tourists. . . . And a cab-stand and a horse-trough
and a pension. And, besides, the stone was changing
yellow—almost as if it had jaundice. And Mrs.
Whooper had said . . .

Did such trifles matter now?

To be irrelevant at such a minute. . . .

At the Inn to-night she had thought ten thousand
thrilling things were taking place about her.

How long ago that seemed!

She had spent the day at the Flagellites in a corner
of the orchard listening to the ecstasy of the bees.
And then Pacca had come to rouse her. And she had
returned to the Inn through the cornfields by the Asz.
How clear the river ran! Every few yards she had
paused to stand entranced. And a young man with a
fishing-rod and in faint mourning had entreated her
earnestly not. " I could not watch you do it," he had
said. " Not that you would spoil my . . . At least! "
And his hands were quite hot and clammy. " What
is a flaw more or less in an imperfect world? " he had
asked. And he had accompanied her back to the Inn.
And she had wept a little while she dressed. . . .
And a white-winged moth had fluttered into the lamp.
And she had gone to close the window. And everywhere the stars had sprung out like castanets and then
gone in again. And the sunset had been heroic.

And she had waited so anxiously for to-night!

Mortifications had paved the way to it.

Was it only to suffer aridity and disappointment?

Such emotions were experienced best at home.

And would vignettes give way to visions?

Bill again.

" No, no! "

Or Satan. . . .

With dismay she waved her fan.

She was aware once more of leering lips. A tip-tilted, inquisitive nose. . . .

" Then the coachman," she began, speaking in her agony aloud, " invited somebody on to the box. I remember I said nothing——"

XXIII

EVER since Mr. Calvally had taken a total adieu of his wife the building operations in Ashringford had practically ceased.

"It is certainly unfortunate," Mrs. Henedge complained, "that the daughter of my architect should run away with my painter—the husband, too, of my most valued friend!"

She was in town again, for someone, of course, must be brought to finish the frescoes at St. John's.

"If only I were able," she declared, "I would finish them myself!"

For, after all, what was there, when one came to consider?

A torso . . . an arm of a centurion . . . a bit of breast-plate . . . a lady—*if any lady* . . . a few haloes . . . and a page.

Carefully she arranged the items in a list while waiting for the *School of Calvally*, Andrew who had failed to come.

From her writing-table, whenever she looked up, she caught the reflection of her car in the downstairs windows of the house opposite.

"When I invited him to my fireside," she reflected, "no doubt he thought it was to roast him. But I was in such a tremor, I hardly remember what I said. I might have been bespeaking paste pearls——"

And she recalled the casual words of the master.

"Andrew can't draw," he had often said; "he gets into difficulties and he begins to trill!"

And on another occasion he had remarked: "All his work is so pitch dark—that little master of the

pitch dark. . . ." And had not she too foolishly
mistaken his *Ecce Homo* loaned about at pre-impres-
sionist shows for an outing of Charles I?

And here was she sitting waiting for him?

" Poor Mary," she reflected. " I ought to have gone
round to her before. Though, when I do . . . she
is sure to set upon me! She will say I threw them
together."

And, perplexed, she picked up a pen, a paper-knife,
a letter-weight——

A postscript from Lady Twyford peeped at her.

" In recommending to you Martin as chauffeur,"
she read, " I feel I should say that his corners are
terribly *tout juste*."

What could be better in her present mood? She
would have preferred to fly.

" I adore an aeroplane," she breathed; " it gives
one such a tint——"

She rang.

" Thérèse? *My things!* "

" Oh, London. Native place! Oh, second string to
my bow! Oh, London dear! " she prayed.

Whose uplifting was it?

As Martin sped along she was moved.

" The way the trees lean . . . the way the branches
grow——" she addressed the park.

How often, as a child, had she sat beneath them,
when, with hands joined primly across her solar
plexus, the capital, according to nurse, was just a big
wood—with some houses in it.

She found Mrs. Calvally propped up by a pink
pillow shelling peas.

It brought to mind her husband's disgraceful
defence.

" How could I ever have been happy with her,"
he had asked, " when her favourite colour is crushed
strawberry? "

"I had no idea," Mrs. Calvally said, "that you were in town."

"I felt I could not pass——"

"Everyone has been so good to us."

"Yesterday," Raphael said, who was lying upon the floor, "a cat, a peacock-person, an old lion and a butterfly all came to inquire. And to-day, such an enormous, big, large, huge, terrific——"

"Yesterday, dear, will do."

Mrs. Henedge raised an eyebrow.

"I was afraid," she said, "I should find you in one of Lucile's black dreams——"

"Tell me all your news!"

"In the country what news is there ever? This year we fear an epidemic of yellow flowers will spoil the hay. . . ."

"I am sure the country must be quite a sight."

". . . I prefer my garden to everything in the world."

"There is a rumour that it has inspired an opera!"

"I fancy only a consecration. Mr. Brookes is certainly to be Rose. A Christmas one! He makes his début this winter."

"And *the other*, when is that to be?"

"One can only conjecture. . . . It occurred to me that very likely Andrew——"

"Oh, Andrew! An-drew can't draw. He never drew anything yet."

"Run away, dear; do."

"Besides, he's going to Deauville to decorate *a Bar*. . . . Scenes of English Life——"

"My dear, all Europe is very much alike!"

"And all the world, for the matter of that."

"I heard from George this morning."

"Really, what does he say?"

"Oh, it's only a line. So formal, with the *date*, and everything. And there is a tiny message, too, from her."

" Poor demoniac——"

" Of course I haven't seen you since! "

" No——"

Mrs. Calvally settled her pillows.

" She came round like a whirlwind," she began.

" . . . Manner means so much."

" A tornado. I was just putting on my *shawl*. You know how he loved anything strange——"

" Well! "

Mrs. Calvally paused.

" I think there must be thunder about," she said. " I've been at the point of death all day."

" And where are they now? "

" In Italy. Trailing about. And he went away with such an overweight of luggage. . . ."

" I expect he took his easels! "

" This morning the letter was from Rimini. It appears it reminds them of Bexhill. . . . And the hotel, it seems, so noisy."

" How painfully dull it sounds."

" Quite uninteresting! "

" I think it sounds jolly."

" Shall we evoke Morocco with a rose and lilac shoe? "

" What would be the good of that? "

" No good at all, my treasure, only it might be fun."

Mrs. Henedge struggled to her feet.

" Evoke Morocco! " she said. " I fear I haven't time. I've a dentist and a palmist, and——"

She surveyed half nervously the shoe.

There was hardly any rose and scarcely any lilac. It was *a crushed strawberry*.

XXIV

" To-day I'll have threepennyworth! "

In a flowing gown tinged with melancholy and a soupçon rouged Mrs. Shamefoot stood ethereal at her gate.

She laughed lightly.

" And, perhaps, I'll have some cream. . . ."

With the movement of a priestess she handed him a jar.

" That jar," she said, " belonged, once, to . . . So mind it doesn't break."

And while the lad ladled she studied with insouciance the tops of the chimneys across the way.

The sky was full of little birds. Just at her gate a sycamore-tree seemed to have an occult fascination of its own.

Whole troops of birds would congregate there, flattening down each twig and spray, perpetually outpouring.

" Before I came here," she inquired, " were the birds so many? "

He shook his head.

" There was only an owl."

" It's extraordinary."

" Shall I book the cream? "

" What is the matter with the bells? "

" They're sounding for the Sisters."

" Are they ill? Again? "

" They died last night—of laughter."

" What amused them, do you know? "

" They were on the golf links. . . ."

" Death, sometimes, is really a remedy."

195

" Soon there'll be no call for a dairy. What with the river——"

" Indeed it's more like somewhere in *Norway* now ! "

" Not that, in milk——"

" Crazes change so, don't they? "

" A nice deep pail of——"

" Since yesterday, has anyone else? . . . "

" It's a pretty jar," he said in a subdued voice. " What is it? "

" That's Saxe," she said, as she carefully closed the door.

The long flaying room was flooded by the evening sun.

" One needs an awning," she murmured, setting down the cream.

Before the house stretched a strip of faint blue sand. There were times when it brought to mind the Asz.

Only last night she had trailed towards the window, and with the tip of her toe . . .

She turned, half charmed, away. There could still be seen the trace . . .

" I think the house will be the greatest success! "

Of course, the walls were rather carpeted with pictures——

There was the *Primitive*, that made the room, somehow, seem so calm. And a *Blessed Damozel*—that fat white thing. And a Giorgione, so silky and sweet. And a Parma angel. And the " study-of-me-which-is-*such*-an-infamy ! "

" I must have blinds," she exclaimed.

It was tiresome there were none now since Georgia was coming in to tea.

How prim the cups were upon their china tray !

She had placed them there herself. . . .

In a bowl beside them floated a few green daisies with heavy citron hearts.

And if they chose to make eyes at the cherries, what did it matter, since the background was so plain?

She glanced at her reflection.

" O mon miroir, rassure-moi; dis moi que je suis belle, qui je serai belle éternellement! "

She paused, causelessly sad.

Even here, the world, why . . . one was still in it——

" We should pray for those who do not comprehend us! " she murmured. And, of course, that would end in having a chaplain. Or begin by having one.

A camera study of her sister, Mrs. Roy Richards, a woman whose whims would have made the theme of a book, or a comedy *en famille*, with her seven children standing round her nearly naked, had arrived, only lately, as if to recall her to herself.

" Not since the last famine . . . " she murmured, tucking it into a drawer.

" Ah, there! " One could hardly mistake that horn.

. . .

She lifted the wooden pin in the door and peered through the grill.

" Who knocks? "

" A sinner."

" A couple," Lady Castleyard corrected, " of the very worst. Regular devils."

" Come in. Unfortunately, my Gretchen has gone out."

" I hear you are achieving sainthood by leaps and bounds! "

Mrs. Shamefoot embraced her guests.

" I fear . . . it's far more gradual."

" It must be so desolate for you, dear, here all alone, cut off from everybody."

" I love my solitude."

" What ever do you find to do, in the long evenings? "

" I'm studying Dante——"

Lady Georgia rolled her eyes.

" I imagine you keep a parakeet," she said. " Where is it? "

Mrs. Shamefoot busied herself with the tea.

" Have you noticed the birds? " she asked. " Such battalions. . . . And before I came there was only an owl! "

" I admire your garden. Those tragic thickets of thorns——"

" I think the autumn here should be simply sublime."

" I will witness it, I hope, from my roof-top! I'm like an Oriental when I get up there. I'm sure I was one, once."

" How, dear? "

" Oh, don't expect me to explain."

" Jack would insist still that you had saved the country."

" Locally, of course."

" He's so enchanted with the window. He has got me to change our pew. ' Poor Biddy,' he said to me, ' she looks really royal. A kind of grandeur——' "

" Several young men in town seem struck by it too. They like to sit before it. I believe they even kneel. . . . So annoying! Often, just when I want to be there myself——"

" I'm glad you go somewhere. It's wrong to withdraw yourself too completely. Without a servant even! "

" My servant, Gretchen, ran, silly child, to the post office about a week ago."

" I wonder you let her. . . ."

" I needed stamps."

" Stamps! "

" Soco had scribbled. . . ."

" What are his views? "

" He speaks of a visit. He has never seen St. Dorothy. I received such a volume from him this morning, quires and quires and quires, all about nothing."

" You must bring him to Stockingham when he comes. We're giving *The Playboy of the Western World* in the Greek Theatre. . . . I don't know how it will be! "

" Julia's Pegeen——"

" I see she's reviving *Magda.*"

" So she is. But you know nothing lasts her long."

" And her strange maid, apparently, is going on the stage. She is to take a part of a duchess."

Lady Castleyard yawned.

" I love your room," she said. " It's so uncommon."

" I want to show you my mourner's lamps."

" Where are they? "

" In my bedroom."

" Your bedroom, Biddy. I expect it's only a cell."

" It overlooks the grave-ground."

" Oh, how unpleasant! "

" I don't mind it. I like to sit in the window and watch the moon rise until the brass weather-cock on the belfry turns slowly silver above the trees . . . or, in the early dawn, perhaps, when it rains, and the whole world seems so melancholy and desolate and personal and quite intensely sad—and life an utter hoax——"

Lady Georgia rubbed away a tear.

" I don't know! " she said.

" A hoax! You wonder I can isolate myself so completely. Dear Georgia, just because I want so much, it's extraordinary how little I require."

" Don't the neighbours tire you? "

" I hardly ever see them! I am afraid I frighten Lady Anne. . . . Old Mrs. Wookie made me some advances with a *face-cloth* she had worked me for my demise. . . . And I've become quite friendly with the Pets. He has such character. Force. I am leaving him a lock of my hair."

" S-s-sh! How morbid! Shall we explore the cell? I've never seen one yet."

" I'd sooner not be over-chastened," Lady Castle-yard confessed. " It might spoil me for the antiquarians. . . . And the last time I was here I unearthed such a sweet old chair with hoofs."

" Poor Mrs. Frobisher found four Boucher panels there once."

" I'm quite sure it was once! "

Mrs. Shamefoot slid aside some folding doors.

Ashringford, all towers, turrets, walls, spires, steeples and slanting silver slates, stretched before her in the evening sun.

" I'll come as far as St. Dorothy with you," she murmured, " if you like. It's just the time I go for my quiet half-hour."

INCLINATIONS
1916

PART I

"*Besides, I never ventured once to carry you with me to any conference I had with the Pope for fear you should be trying some of your coquettish airs upon him.*"—Lady Kitty Crockodile to Miss Lydell.

I

" ' Hair almost silver—incredibly fair: a startling pallor.' " Otherwise, unmistakably, there was a close resemblance.

It is true, whenever she began a new work she said the same.

There were the Ducquelin, the Pizzi, the Queen Quickly periods . . . and that curious autumn evening when she had experienced the impulse of an old and wicked Cæsar. . . .

" And here am I rusting in Yorkshire! " she exclaimed.

In the twilight her face showed vague and indistinct: an earring gleamed.

" I adore your patience! "

" She seems to have had eleven children."

" Who, dear? "

" Mrs. Kettler. Catherine. Kitty."

" I wonder you don't get tired of going just on and on."

" My dear, you're always wondering."

" But now that Effie has begun her Tuesdays——"

" So often the mood only takes me as the gong sounds for dinner."

Viola Neffal moved her lips as if she were counting.

" Well, that Mortlake tapestry," she said, " pierced with nails and overhung by mirrors, is enough to make one weep! "

The Biographer clasped nervously her long, expressive hands.

" I sometimes think," she ventured, " that Modern things, rightly chosen, accentuate the past."

Through the open windows, a line of trees, leaning all one way, receded across the garden like figures escaping from a ball.

"Who was that woman, dear, who put her lover's head into a pot of basil?"

"You mean Isabel. But nothing shall ever dissuade me! Besides, after Princess Orvi I need a change. Two Italian women . . ."

Miss Neffal sprayed herself liberally with "Lethe Incarnate."

". . . Here's luck!" she wished.

"Somehow I feel it may be a failure. I saw the new moon with my left eye."

"You never told me quite what there is to admire in Mrs. Kettler. Why she attracts you."

"It's hard to explain. . . . As a man of rare weight once remarked, she was like some radiant milkmaid."

"Are milkmaids so radiant as a rule?"

"She was. And then she was so English! Even from her earliest utterance: 'I would worship,' she said, 'to spend a summer in a hut in a hollow of Old Sarum.' She was then barely two."

"She appears to have been a gipsy."

"After all, very little about her is known! There's not much material. Hers was one of those flickering shadow-lives. . . . You catch her in flashes. In her hey-day she is said to have grown weary of her world and gone to Ceylon."

"*Ceylon?*"

"Well, if it wasn't Ceylon—— With these constant changes one is bound to get mixed. I'm not sure if it wasn't Greece. I've an idea it was Athens!"

"At any rate she was insular."

"Soul is as rare as radium."

Miss Neffal revealed her mind.

"The persons whom I should most have cared to meet were Walpole and Sappho," she said.

"If you aren't contented now you never will be!"

"That's vain."

"I was referring only to Hugh."

"Hugh! I am marrying him, Geraldine, as you know, mainly for his conversation. And of course I shall be very glad to be married. . . ."

"My dear Viola."

"When one is nearing the *end* of the twenties——"

"Nonsense!"

"Tell me more about the little milkmaid."

"Oh, well, very soon, now, I hope to be setting out again on my travels. I intend making a fairly extensive trip in *her* footsteps."

"You're off to Greece?"

"I'm going wherever she went."

"Perhaps you'll wander round by Cannes!"

Geraldine O'Brookomore, the authoress of *Six Strange Sisters*, *Those Gonzagas*, etc., unlocked a sombre lacquer case: a work of art, in its way, with its many painted labels all on tinted pearl.

"Reminiscences. Anecdotes. Apologias. Crimes. Follies. Fabrications. Nostalgia. Mysticism. Trivia. Human Documents. Love Letters. His to Me: Mine to Him," she read.

"It's Nostalgia you need. . . ."

Miss O'Brookomore raised her eyes.

"I'm sure I'm willing to hope so."

"Isn't it difficult often to be impartial?"

"It depends so much upon one's health. When one is tired a little or below par——"

"How I wish you were more sensible. *Is* it wise when the gong goes——"

"I know. But Effie spoils me. . . . Only a moment ago she sent me a peach that tasted like a dark carnation. . . ."

"Effie overdoes her hospitality I somehow think.

Placing rouge in all the bedrooms. Even in Mr. Fair-mile's room, poor boy! "

" Who is there downstairs? "

" Such gold-wigged Botticellis—playing bridge. They've sent me up to look for you."

" For me? "

" To watch them."

" I won't. Because where would be the good? "

" Then they'll come trooping here instead. After dinner it's usually Effie's way to take a candle and drag everybody to gaze at the children in bed and asleep."

" Here comes someone now! "

" Were I to look in should I bother, weary, worry you? "

" It's Miss Collins."

" Mabel! "

" I've been waiting for you ever so long. This is quite the dullest house——"

" You poor little dreary cat! "

Miss Collins, who had never gone out before, seemed to believe a soirée to be a succession of bons-mots, songs and bursts of laughter.

" One should try to be happy always! "

" I suppose you'll say it's silly, but I want so much to l-i-v-e! I want to go flitting about the world like you."

Miss O'Brookomore became pensive.

" My work," she said, " lies largely among the dead."

" Is it imperative? "

" The worst of modern biography, you understand, is, one is never quite sure to what one is entitled——"

" If only to avoid the pitiful consequences," Miss Neffal theorised, " we should go through the world neatly and compact."

Miss Collins turned from her, oppressed.

" Effie sends a fresh supply of fruit. She is coming up very soon to look at the children."

" Raspberries! "

" Are there raspberries in Chaldea? "

" You astonish me! Why do you ask? "

" For information. Naturally, living continually in the same place——"

" Do you never go away? "

" From home? Oh yes . . . Sometimes, in winter, we go to Scotland."

" Surely Scotland in winter would be a desolation! Stone, and slate, and asphalt, and the wrong red hair. . . ."

" You see, we cannot get rid of our house."

" Indeed. And why not? "

" Because it stands in a valley. Although, of course, at times one gets some surprising effects of mist. . . ."

Miss Neffal leaned back in her chair with listless arms and fingers interlaced.

" Why attack the scenery? " she inquired.

Miss Collins shuddered.

" All that waving green," she said, " before the windows. . . . Why, the Chase looks haunted even in the sun."

" Poor child! "

" You've no conception. . . . I assure you there isn't a creature in all the countryside to interest one except, perhaps, Madame La Chose, who's an actress, although she has nothing to do with the stage."

" How can one be an actress without anything to do with the stage? " the Biographer wondered, drawing Miss Collins to her.

But Miss Collins did not seem to know.

" I love that ripple in your throat," she said. " It isn't a second chin. It's just a . . . ripple! "

" Mrs. Kettler had the same."

" Are you perpetually pondering your great men? "

" Naturally, those in hand."

" Often they must haunt you."

Miss O'Brookomore smiled.

" Occasionally," she said, " they do. In my dream last night I seemed to hear all those whose lives I've lately written moaning and imploring me not. Let the editions die, one good woman said to me. Let them be cancelled! "

" Ingratitude! "

" Dreams, have you never heard, go by *contraries*."

" Still, I'm sure you must need a change."

" Am I getting cloddish? "

" Quite otherwise."

" Once again in a *wagon-lit*——"

Miss Collins slipped to her knees.

" What would I not give," she said, " to go with you ! "

Slightly startled, Miss O'Brookomore took from a cardboard box a cigarette.

" Supposing . . ."

" . . . supposing? "

" Supposing—I only say ' supposing '—supposing you were to accompany me to Greece. . . ."

Sparkling, Miss Collins rose.

" Only at the thought," she cried, " I could clap my feet in the air."

The Biographer considered her. Dark against the brilliance.

" My chief amusement," she explained, " has always been to exchange ideas with someone. And to receive new ones in return."

" At Corinth! . . ."

" At Aulis! "

" At Athens! "

" At Epidauros! "

" At Mycenæ! "

" In Arcadia! "

" It would be like a fairy dream."

" So long as you're good-humoured and sunny! "

" They say I'm rather silly sometimes at home."

Miss O'Brookomore dropped a sigh.

" Few of us are born mellow," she declared.

Miss Collins sank again to the floor.

" I suppose we should stifle all our emotions," she said. " And hide things. . . . But I never do. I just let my heart speak. And so——"

" I'm reading Lady Cray's *Travels*," Miss Neffal broke in. " ' In the desert,' she says, ' once, I tried to cook a partridge with a string, but the fire burnt the string and the partridge——' "

" Better to be foolish at home than——"

" Here's Effie! "

Candlestick in hand, and quite alone, their hostess appeared at the door.

" I knocked, but could get no answer! "

" I never heard you."

" Wild, interesting woman! Have you been doing *much*? "

" Not a great deal. One's best work is always unwritten."

" What she needs most," Miss Neffal reflected, " is the forsaken wing of a palace."

" Are you coming, Viola, to look at the children? "

" Dare I, I wonder, in these shoes. . . ."

" Is there anything wrong with them? "

" They might wake little Phillis. . . ."

" In any case, Mrs. Orangeman, I fancy, is destined to do that."

" . . . You hear her sad mind when she sings! "

Miss Collins looked shrewd.

" Her worries aren't enough," she prophesied, " to keep her going. . . ."

" Unless you are more careful," Miss Neffal threatened, " I will write you down in my *Book of Cats*."

" Have you kept it long? "

" Since I became engaged."

Their hostess tittered.

" Even we! . . ." she said. " Usually now on a dull day Jack likes to touch up his will."

" Doesn't it make you *nervous?* "

" Why should it? "

" I'd be afraid of his painting me out."

" That's because you're over highly strung. When people are pale and tired like you they need a rest."

" Well, I've finished almost for to-night. Perhaps I may come down presently when the curate's gone. The last time we met he referred to poor Kettler as a Hospital Case. . . ."

" Have you no sketch of her at all that we could see? "

" Only a replica. The original, if I recollect, is in the Liechtenstein Gallery."

And with her long and psychic fingers Miss O'Brookomore smoothed out a scroll.

" As a portrait," she said, " of course, it's a miracle of badness. But I think her face is so amusing and so alight."

Miss Collins gazed at the likeness sadly.

"I've seen so few good pictures," she lamented; " although an artist did come one autumn to Bovonorsip. He took a room at the Wheat Sheaf and trespassed all day at the Chase."

" Some artists can be very insinuating."

" So was he! It was impossible not to share this man's joy when he said he had captured a whole mood with a little grey paint. . . . 'Do not be too anxious to be like Corot, young ladies,' he would say when we went sketching too. And before he left he gave me a little wood scene with naked peasants."

Her hostess took up her torch.

" Poor Mr. Fairmile seems so miserable, Mabel, since you've disappeared! "

" How is he to show what he feels when——"

" When? "

" Oh, Effie, why did you tempt him? . . ." Miss Collins asked as she darted out.

" I wonder at anyone sitting down to pen the life of a woman so baggy about the eyes! " Miss Neffal exclaimed, returning the engraving.

" . . . Hark to Mrs. Orangeman. Well, Viola, will you come? "

Alone, Miss O'Brookomore wandered leisurely to the window and leaned out.

Beneath her a landscape all humming with little trees stretched away towards such delicate, merest hills.

" Was it solely Vampirism that made me ask her," she queried, " or is it that I'm simply bored? "

She looked up.

There was a suggestion of azalea in the afterglow that recalled to her the East.

" Either way," she murmured, " her mother most likely would never consent."

And seating herself before her mirror she began an examination of her raspberries for fear of little worms.

" When people are pale and tired like you . . ." had not Effie said?

She paused to dream.

How it tallied with Kate Kettler's description:

" Hair almost silver—incredibly fair: a startling pallor. . . ."

A BEEHIVE in Brompton, a tray of gleaming fish, the way the wind blew—everything that morning seemed extraordinarily Greek.

As Miss O'Brookomore made her way towards Harrods she rejoiced.

Miss Collins actually was in town!

" Take her and keep her," Mrs. Collins somewhat unexpectedly wrote. " Who better than Miss O'Brookomore could break my child of her tomboy habits? Athens, I imagine, must be a sweet spot. Those glorious noses! Fancies fade, but a portrait of Byron on horseback," etc.

And now, as Miss O'Brookomore strolled along, for some reason or other she screwed up her eyes and smiled.

All about her in heroic strips of green showed pastoral plots. Dark shrubberies. . . .

" Of course she will need a few new frocks," she mused, pausing before a—" Robes—Artistic Equipments "—at the corner of Ygdrasil Street, from whose folding doors at that same moment stepped the famous Mrs. Asp.

The veteran Biographer held out a hand.

" Your extensive acquaintance," she said, " I fear, has almost destroyed you for myself! They told me you had gone."

" I shall be leaving town now in about a week."

" Are you to be alone? "

" I shall have a maid—and a little Miss Collins, who is not yet fifteen."

Mrs. Asp began to purr.

" Should you need a really reliable maid," she said,
" I could tell you of an excellent woman. Nine weeks
with a Mrs. Des Pond and two . . . A treasure! Or,
should you be requiring a becoming blouse, or an
eerie hat, or anything . . . Mrs. Manwood in there
. . . It would be a charity! Silly thing . . . She
put all her money on Quiet Queenie, or was it Shy
Captain, and lost. . . ."

" For my journey," Miss O'Brookomore said, with
a glance of concern, " I shall take with me only what
is most serviceable and neat, and absolutely austere."

" My dear, you will allow me, I hope, to know as
much about travelling as you do. I expect I have been
abroad as many times as you have."

" Rumours, no doubt, have reached you of my
present choice? "

Mrs. Asp became faintly asthmatic.

" How hugely, purely, curiously and *entirely* reckless
one's disciples are. . . ."

" Naturally, I shall suggest poor Kitty's cynicisms
with fairy lightness . . . in fact——"

" To me," Mrs. Asp said, " Mrs. Kettler has always
made her appeal. . . . And when you're in Athens
you should go to Tanagra—not that there's very
much there to see."

Miss O'Brookomore held up an arm.

" If I'm late at all," she observed, " I shall miss
Miss Collins . . . or keep her waiting, perhaps, about
the street. One can hardly credit it, but she has never
been away from home before! "

" Well, even when I was still seventeen I would
take my skipping-rope into the Park. . . ."

" I should like to have seen you."

" We have a wee box in the third tier at the opera
for to-night if you would care to come! "

" This evening we are going to the Dream Theatre,
and can't. . . . Besides, I've an aversion for Covent

Garden, I fear. One sits in a blaze of light, looking eighty, or ninety, or a hundred—as the case may be.'

Mrs. Asp nodded.

" I shall expect to hear from you," she said, " at any rate, quite soon. An Athenian husband for you both . . . a villa each in Thrace. . . . I could wish for nothing more! And now, as the Oratory is so near, I feel tempted almost to run in. Although, as a rule, I never care to go to Confession in anything that's *tight*."

And there, in front of Harrods, teasing a leashed dog with a requirements-list, stood Miss Collins.

" Let us make haste," Miss O'Brookomore said, saluting her somewhat nervously, " to do our shopping. And afterwards, just to break the ice, I intend to take you to an Oriental restaurant in Soho. . . ."

III

"IT's funny," Miss Collins said, "but even the most trivial things amuse me now I'm away from home!"

"Your strong *joie de vivre*," Miss O'Brookomore informed her, "your youthfulness, already have done me good."

"Tell me whom you see."

"Hardly one's ideal. On the couch, half asleep, are Guarini and Ozinda. Pirouetting round them, making their survey, is Lord Horn and the Misses Cornhill, and on the dais there's January, Duchess of Dublin, and her Doxy."

"Which is Doxy?"

"In tears. At galleries she's quite dreadful. She will begin to weep almost for the Spinario's 'poor foot.'"

"Once while beagling, accidentally——"

There came a murmur of voices.

". . . terrifying nightmare women."

". . . One of his wild oats."

". . . fascinating, fiendish colours."

"It's unmistakably *his*."

"Pish!"

"Take me away!"

"And behind us," Miss O'Brookomore chimed in, "Lady Betty Benson is being escorted by a tenth son and a real murderer, and in ambush by the door, chatting to Miss Neffal's fiancé, is Mrs. Elstree, the actress."

"O-o-o-o-h!"

"You have the catalogue."

"What should you say it was?"

215

" Dear old Mr. Winthrop! He's so vague always—
' Sunrise India.' And I know for a fact it was painted
in his street. Those trees are in Portman Square."

" Is not that Miss O'Brookomore? We heard that
you had gone."

Miss O'Brookomore turned slightly.

" We are in Ospovat's hands," she murmured,
" still."

" Have you chosen yet your route? "

" We go from Marseilles to the Piræus, and from
there we take the tram."

" O-o-o-o-h! "

" You have the catalogue."

" . . . know Mr. Hicky? " Mrs. Elstree was beginning to scream. " Why, when I was playing in the
Widow of Wells I died in his arms every night for over
a year."

" Hugh, where's Viola? "

" I'm afraid I must decline to tell you."

" Indeed! . . ."

" I left her burning *Zampironi* before a Guardi and
invoking Venice."

" Anything later than the eighteenth century I
know how she dislikes."

Mrs. Elstree addressed the Historian.

" Daring one," she murmured, " I admire you
more than you're aware of! You're simply never
trite."

" You mean my Mrs. Kitty? . . ."

" And even should you not discover much, failure
makes one subtler! "

" All I hope to get's a little glamour."

" Once—did I ever tell you?—I rented a house in
Lower Thames Street, where the Oyster Merchants
are."

Miss O'Brookomore closed her eyes.

" When I was quite a child," she said, " I did not

care for sweets . . . but I liked Oysters. Bring me
Oysters, I would say. I want Oysters."

"Poet."

Miss Collins folded herself together as though for
a game of hide-and-seek.

"Really, Mabel! Noting you with dismay is Mrs.
Felicity Carrot of *Style*."

"A reporter!"

"One should be the spectator of oneself always,
dear, a little."

"Don't move—I am not sure but I see my aunt!"

"Your aunt?"

"Mrs. Hamilton-of-Hole."

". . . My husband's horizons are solely political
ones," Mrs. Hamilton was explaining as she elbowed
by.

"And there is Mr. Winthrop, whose landscape——"
Mrs. Elstree moved away.

"Ozinda has fallen sound asleep in Guarini's
arms! . . ."

There came a confusion of voices.

"Babes-in-the-Wood."

"We think of crossing over to witness the autumn
at Versailles."

". . . goes to auctions."

"The slim, crouching figure of the Magdalen is
me."

"Those break-neck brilliant purples."

"Pish!"

"A scarlet song."

"'Order what you please from Tanguay,' he said
—'a tiara, what you please.'"

"——You'd think they'd been set by Bœhmer!"

"O-o-o-h!"

"You have the catalogue."

"Mrs. Elstree took it with her."

IV

" LET us all cling together! "

Miss O'Brookomore blinked her eyes.

" Is it a station? "

" To-morrow," Miss Collins announced from behind her chronicle, ignoring the sleep-murmurings
of the Historian's maid, " six Cornish girls are to dance
at the Lune Grise. What a pity to have missed them.
Although I believe I mind more about Mona. When
she discovers I've been in Paris without even trying
to find her——"

" Who is that, dear? "

" Napier's sister—Mr. Fairmile's. Oh, Gerald! "

" What is it? "

" Mr. Fairmile and I once . . . Yes, dear! We're
engaged. . . . And when he said good-bye he didn't
kiss me. He just crushed me to his heart. . . ."

" Crushed you? "

" My frock a little. One of Miss Johnson's jokes."

" That white one? "

" Of course Mona I've known always. She's just
a dear. Tall, with a tiny head. And such beautiful,
mystic hands. . . . She and I were at school together."

" I didn't know you had ever been at school."

" . . . a Term. She was quite my bosom-chum at
York Hill. Once we exchanged a few drops of each
other's blood. Oh, Gerald! "

" Really! "

" It was on a certain Sunday in June."

Miss O'Brookomore dropped the fireproof curtain
across her eyes. She glazed them.

" I think I shall tuck up my feet," she said, " and lie down."

" Just as there's a sunset coming on? "

" I'm tired. My head aches. My mind has been going incessantly all day. . . ."

Miss Collins showed her sympathy.

" Reading in the train would upset anyone," she observed. " I'm sure it would me."

" I was renewing my acquaintance with the classics."

" Before I came away mum made me get by heart a passage from *The Queen of Tartary* to recite to you the instant we landed, as a surprise. You know the great tirade! The Queen has taken the poison and leaves the Marquee on her confidante's arm. Inside, the banquet is in full swing. Now and again you can hear their hearty laughter. . . . Ha, ha, ha! Ha, ha, ha, ha! And the Queen turns to Melissa—and mum declares she shall never forget the impression Madam Dolce Naldi made as the Queen, although Miss Faucet, as Melissa, was exquisite in her fragility as a foil—and says: ' My hands are cold. It's as if my eyelids had weights upon them. . . . I hear a singing in my ears. I feel,' etc. And so on through the greater part of the medical dictionary."

" It's curious your mother did not select the triumphal speech. Act II, Scene 3: ' Everybody crowded round me, . . .' " Miss O'Brookomore remarked.

" I don't know. The only books I care for are those about Farms."

" My dear, when one speaks of Farms one forgets the animals. Little piggy-wiggs. . . ."

" I don't think that *that* would matter."

" Perhaps some day, when you marry a country squire, you will have a farm of your own."

" It isn't likely. Before leaving town I consulted a clairvoyant. There are indications, she said, that something *very disgraceful* will come about between January and July."

" Oh, Mabel! "

Miss Collins reached towards a bag of sweets.

" In the crystal she could see mum reading my letters . . . she could see her, she said, on all fours hunting about. . . ."

" Your poor mother."

" What's the good of grieving? "

" Mab dear, you're always nibbling! "

" To beguile the time."

" But so bad for you."

" Beware of a dazzlingly fair man, the woman said. Beware of him. And in the end, after many petty obstructions, which you will overcome, she said, you'll marry a raven! "

Miss O'Brookomore became attentive to the scenery.

To watch the trees slip past in the dusk was entrancing quite. In a meadow a shepherdess with one white wether stood up and waved her crook.

" Poor Palmer seems completely worn out."

The maid stirred slightly at her name.

" When Greek meets Greek, miss," she asked informingly, "can you tell me what they're supposed to do? "

" Since we're all English," Miss O'Brookomore replied, " I don't think it matters. . . ."

Miss Collins covered her face with a soiled *suède* glove.

" Another tunnel! "

" You should really rest, Mab. You'll arrive so tired."

" I'm that already. But I won't lean back—for fear of contracting something . . infectious."

" Some day, dear, I may arrange your sayings in a wreath. . . ."

" Our coachman once——"

" No, please—I'm altogether incurious."

" Although, even bolt upright, dear, I can sleep as easily as a *prima donna* upon a dais! Nothing wakes me."

Palmer raised an eye towards the waning moon.

" The evenings," she remarked, " turn quite bleak. Had I known, I'd not have come away without my bit of fur."

V

" AND then we almost ran. Anybody would have said
our husbands were behind. . . . And perhaps they
pitied us. But Miss O'Brookomore's so unpunctual
always; it's a marvel we ever catch a train."

He waved a hand.

" Those talents! That gift! Her mind! "

" At Marseilles we even missed the boat. Otherwise, very likely, we would have never met."

" M-a-b-e-l," Miss O'Brookomore called.

Miss Collins turned.

" Do you need me, dear? "

" Who is your handsome friend? "

" He's . . . Oh, Gerald! "

" Where did you pick him up? "

" He began by speaking of the tedium of water for
a sailor, and then——"

" I see! "

" Oh, Gerald, it's Count Pastorelli. . . ."

Miss O'Brookomore leaned back a little in her
deck-chair..

" Take my word for it," she said, " he's not so
pastoral as he sounds."

" And there's another! "

" You mean——? "

" A porpoise! "

Miss O'Brookomore crossed herself.

" I always do," she said, " when anyone points."

" Shall we take a little prowl? "

" Voluntarily."

" There's a person on board, someone perhaps
should speak to her, who sits all day staring at the sea

beneath a very vivid violet veil. And when the waves break over her she never even moves. . . ."

The Biographer watched sagaciously the sun touch the dark water into slow diamonds.

" One should blur," she observed, " the agony."

Miss Collins became evidently intellectual.

" Which would you prefer," she inquired, " a wedding or a funeral out at sea? "

" I'd prefer there was no unpacking."

" For the one emergency I've enough, of course, of white . . . and for the other, I dare say I could lean from the ship-side in a silver hat crowned with black Scotch roses."

" Were it mine, I'd give that hat to Palmer."

" Poor thing, every time the ship rolls she seems to hear something say: *The captain—his telescope.*"

" She will see the land very soon now with her naked eye."

Miss Collins slipped an arm about her friend.

" I look forward first to eleven o'clock," she said, " when the ship-boy goes round with bananas."

" Tell me, at Bovonorsip does every one speak so loud? "

Miss Collins clicked her tongue.

" Shall we go down upon the lower-deck, Gerald, and look through the cabin windows? There's the Negress you called a *Gaugin*. . . . All alone in her cabin it would be interesting to see what she does. . . ."

" Somehow I'd sooner save that poor veiled thing from getting wet."

But that " poor veiled thing " was enjoying herself, it appeared.

" . . . I don't object to it, really," she said. " I rather like the sea! . . . I'm Miss Arne. Mary Arne —the actress. Some people call me their Mary Ann, others think of me as Marianne."

" The tragedienne."

" Comedy is my province. I often say I'm the only Lady Teazle! "

" Then of course you've met Lizzie Elstree? "

" . . . I can recall her running about the green-room of the Garden Theatre in I should be afraid to say quite what. . . ."

" Well, I always hate to hustle."

Miss Collins nodded.

" There's the Count," she exclaimed. " He will keep bumping into me."

" I wonder who he can be."

" I believe he's a briefless barrister."

Miss O'Brookomore looked wary.

" How is one to tell? " she murmured. " He may *not* be so briefless . . . ! "

" I know nothing about the law," Miss Arne said. " Although when I played in *The Coronation of Lucy* there was a trial scene that lasted nearly forty minutes."

" You must be delighted now to rest."

"Rest! I'm on my way to Greece to study Lysistrata."

" But couldn't you have done it at home? "

" Not with the same results. As I told the silly critics, I mean to treat her as a character-part."

" I understand. When one traces a shadow it's mostly for the scenery."

" At Cape Sunium," Miss Collins said, " I shall lie like a starfish all day upon the sand."

" My dear, at Sunium there is no sand. It's all rocks."

" How do you know there are rocks? "

" Do you think I haven't seen old engravings? "

" Perhaps I might paddle."

" ' Oh! joy, joy! no more helmet, no more cheese nor onions! ' " Miss Arne soliloquised.

" I adore Aristophanes."

" Certainly, he has a flavour——"

Miss Arne stood up.

" What can that be over there? "
" Those slopes. . . ."
" These villas. . . ."
" And temples. . . ."
" It must be . . ."
" It is——"
Miss Collins commenced a feverish country dance.
" It's Athens! "

VI

" So far I've not observed one! "

" Of what? "

" A nose! Athens and heavenly noses. . . . Mum said I should."

Miss O'Brookomore threw upon her head a bewildering affair with a vampire-bat's-wing slanting behind.

" Patience," she murmured. " We haven't been here long enough."

" Quite long enough to find out the English chemist isn't English! "

" Why, aren't you up to the mark? "

" I was attempting to ward off freckles."

" Pretty Mrs. Wilna often used to say the utmost she ever did was to apply a little cold-cream *just* as she got into bed."

Miss Collins moved from one chair to another.

" Oh, come and look! Oh!"

" What ever is it? "

" There's such a shocking dispute in the Square! "

Beneath a bruised blue, almost a violet, sky lay the town. Very white and very clean.

On the pavement some youths, with arms entwined, seemed to be locked in the convulsions of a dance.

" Let us go down and sit in a café."

Miss O'Brookomore became evasive.

" I want you to repress yourself a little for a few days. Be more discreet."

" Because——"

" Professor and Mrs. Cowsend have the rooms next ours. . . ."

226

" Buz! Let them! "

" Also, the Arbanels are here on their honeymoon.
. . . You never saw such ghosts on their rambles."

" Who is Mr. Arbanel? "

" He's very blasé."

Miss Collins clasped her hands.

" I'd give almost anything to be blasé."

Miss O'Brookomore turned from her.

" Those Customs! " she lamented. " Everything
arrives so *crushed*."

" Are you going out to see what you can find? "

" I dare say I may look in at the library of the
University."

Miss Collins became contemplative.

" Who knows, away in the Underworld she may
be watching you. . . ."

" My poor puss, Athens must seem to you a trifle
dull."

" It isn't really. I could sit for hours on my balcony
and watch the passers-by. So many of them don't pass.
At least, not directly."

" You mean they stop? "

" Sometimes. But what does it matter?—when
one isn't a linguist."

" Palmer should be with you more."

" Palmer seems so squeamish."

The Biographer fetched a sigh.

" Indeed, the way she sprinkles naphthaline has
quite put out the violets."

" All except her own! "

" Her own? "

" Oh, Gerald. . . . Every week there is a dance,
dear, in the hotel."

Miss O'Brookomore shrugged her shoulders.

" Don't expect me to attend any of them," she said,
" that's all."

" Oh, darling, how can you be so Spartan! How? "

" You forget, dear, my dancing days are nearly done."

" Wait. . . . Wait. . . . *Wait* till you hear the throb-thrum-throb of a string band. . . . Oh, Gerald!"

" I should be sound asleep."

" Fiddlesticks! You'd fling a wrap about you and down you'd come."

" It's true."

" And you'd heighten your cheeks in such a hurry that everybody would suppose you'd been using jam."

" Believe me, I'd deal with the manager without the least compunction."

" You'd complain? "

" I'd demand to change my room."

" S-s-s-h! Here's Palmer."

" Ah, no more naphthaline, please."

" There's a packet for Miss Hill. . . ."

" Take it away. It's not for us."

" I expect it's for me! Collins, Colline, Collina *Hill*. I thought it was advisable not to give my own name at any of the shops. . . ."

" Collina! Have you been chatting with the Count?"

" As I went out he was stirring up the weather-glass in the front hall."

" I fear he takes you to be an heiress."

" But he's very well off as it is! Haven't you noticed? He doesn't tip. He *rewards*. Besides, dear, I could never marry a man who had corns on his feet, or who didn't say his prayers."

" How do you know he has corns? "

" Because he told me. He couldn't get up to the Acropolis, he said, on account of his corns. . . ."

" Isn't that a blessing? "

" Look, Gerald, I bought these tags to keep off flies."

" In Arcadia they will be just the thing."

"The Count was saying how rash it was for two docile women to go alone into such inaccessible places. . . ."

With pursed lips the Historian tuned her veil.

"Pooh!" she fiddled.

VII

" AND when papa's reverse of fortune did come . . . why, then, of course, I thought of *everything* . . . to be a maid, I thought. . . . To look up at the moon through the palings. . . . But somehow, no! I couldn't. . . ."

" . . . Shall we have our coffee in the lounge? "

" The night is wonderful," a woman with a thrilling voice declared.

" Evening here is really the nicest time! "

In an alcove, unable to contain her laughter, Miss Collins was teaching English versicles to the Count.

" The naked oak-tree in the deer-park stands
   Mocking the brooding moose."

" Dear? "
" *D-e-e-r!* "
" Oh, my dear! "
" *Hinds! . . . Deer!* "
" I adore you, dear."
" *Harts!* "
" Our two hearts! "
" Mabel! Miss O'Brookomore called."
" Oh, Gerald, what ever is it? "
" Come and thank Mrs. Cowsend. . . . She has consented to take you out occasionally when I'm engaged."

" I shall be delighted," Mrs. Cowsend said. " To-morrow we intend to pass the morning in the royal gardens."

" Unfortunately I'm not overfond of flowers.

Gardening in the rain was one of our punishments at home."

" But at the palace there are so few flowers. Scarcely any! It's bays a bit, and cypress a bit, and ilex a little, and laurel a lot, with here and there an oleander, perhaps, or a larch. . . . Nothing that could remind you!"

" The very sight of a wheelbarrow quite upsets me."

" Personally, I'm inclined to worship a wheelbarrow. It makes a change with the temples."

Miss O'Brookomore became introspective.

" To visit Greece with Professor Cowsend," she said, " would be *my* idea of happiness. . . ."

" My dear Miss O'Brookomore, I have found things in Somerset just as lovely as in the Vale of Tempe. And with none of the fatigue."

The Historian held up a map.

" Where we are going," she announced, " is dotted white."

" You must be very careful! . . . It's just the region——"

Miss O'Brookomore stiffened.

" Tell me everything," she begged.

" I dare say you've not encountered a sheep-dog here before? Some of them are so fierce. More like wolves."

" And dogs frequently fly at me!"

" Round Delphi they are quite dreadful. Parnassos, I assure you, is literally overrun. . . ."

" Dogs delight to lick me," Miss Collins said, " when they get the chance. . . ."

With a lorgnon Mrs. Cowsend drummed the map.

" At Megara," she said, " there is a calvary to commemorate one of the Seymoures. But of course Lady Maisie attracted attention by her peplum even in the town."

" I'm told the measles in Athens just now is very bad."

" Even so, I must say, I find the city dull. Mr. Cowsend, you see, is continually out gathering notes for lectures. Often he will leave the hotel as soon as it is light and pass the entire day poking about the Pnyx. . . . And the shops for me. . . . Well, on the whole, I don't think much of them."

" I would take a camp-stool sometimes and sit on the Pnyx as well."

" . . . When I did the other day he didn't seem to like it! And, in any case, he never tells me much. I approach Greece by way of the Renaissance, and I don't pretend to know anything about either."

Miss O'Brookomore bowed amicably.

" Mrs. Arbanel to-night is really an Eastern dream. . . ."

" Her husband, it seems, is incredibly inattentive to her, poor dear."

" It seems a little soon."

" There's a boy in the porch selling strings and strings of amber," the lady murmured as she ambled by.

" Miss O'Brookomore has just been saying you could scarcely be more Zara or Turkish if you tried."

" How suggestive that is of chains! "

Miss O'Brookomore protested.

" With you," she said, " I only see the beads."

" We were wedded at St. Margaret's almost a month ago! "

" I read of your little adventure in the *Morning Post*."

" I forget if you know Gilbert at all. . . ."

" I can hardly say I know him, but I think we sat together once upon the same settee."

" Would it be lately? "

Mrs. Cowsend smiled urbanely.

" Absence or surfeit," she observed, " it seems there's nothing between."

" Although it *is* my honeymoon I'm not at all exacting."

Miss O'Brookomore used her fan.

" It's been such a heavenly day! "

" I spent most of it in a wood, on the Marathon Road," Mrs. Arbanel said, " with *A Midsummer Night's Dream. . . .*"

" Hermia! Lysander! Oberon! Titania! Oh dear! " Miss Collins showed her culture.

" Bottom," she added.

" . . . I hate to sight-see. However, to-morrow, I'm told I must. Mr. Arbanel has engaged an open coach. . . . But, as I said to him, it would no longer be a coach. It would be a waggon. . . ."

" You should take a cab and drive to Eleusis. . . . On Sunday, I believe, it's the only thing to do."

Mrs. Arbanel looked bored.

" I've seen nothing here quite as delicate," she confessed, "as the Little Trianon in a shower of April rain."

Mrs. Cowsend twinkled.

" You should tell that to the Professor presently when he comes in."

" Where do the men tide through the evening? They invariably disappear."

" In the covered passage behind the hotel," Miss Collins said, " there's a Viennese beer hall and a picture palace. Oh, Gerald! "

" Mr. Cowsend after dinner usually goes to a café in the Rue d'Hèrmes and does dominoes."

" All alone! "

" Or with Professor Pappas—who's apt, on the whole, to be dull. When he was introduced he started off about the county of Warwick. Or the Countess of Warwick. And then he referred to Shakespeare."

Miss Arne turned.

" What is that about the stage? "

" Nothing," Miss Collins said.

" One of these days, Marianne, you should arrange a Lysistrata *matinée* upon the Acropolis."

" Boxes full. Stalls full. Gallery full. Pit full. *Standing-room only!* "

" Don't people stand at concerts? They promenade. . . .".

" I dare say."

" There is a girl in the corner over there watching you who'd make a rare Lampito. . . ."

" She is an Australian, poor thing, seeking her parents."

Miss O'Brookomore blinked.

" Well, she needn't start staring at me! "

" In certain lights," Miss Collins murmured, " she has a look of Edith Jackson, who was sacked from York Hill."

" Why, what had she done? "

" Oh, nothing very much."

" She must have done something."

" . . . She gave a dance in her bedroom—the *houla-houla!* But that wasn't *really* all. . . . Oh, good gracious! "

" To-morrow we shall have one here I expect in the hotel."

" Mr. Arbanel has composed a charming air expressly for it."

" My dear, how can one dance to his brain pictures? "

" Oh, listen! "

" When the wind breaks this way you can hear distinctly what they're saying in the café."

" Ta-lirra-lirra-lo-la-la.
La-lirra-lirra-lo-la-la!
Ta-lirra-lirra-lirra,
La-lirra-lirra-lirra,
Ta-lirra-lirra-lo-la-la! "

" It's politics! "
" It must be."
" Such optimism! "
" One does hope that Mr. Cowsend——"
Miss Collins drifted over to the Count.
" Deer—have you forgotten? . . ."
" Oh, the ' little dear '! "
" Mercy! "
" Another verse."
" Not now; I mustn't! "
" When shall I see you again? "
" To-morrow, I dare say, at the siesta hour—when
Miss O'Brookomore goes to her room for a snooze...."
He bent his head above her fingers.
" Good night, Miss Mabina. I kiss those charming
hands."
Miss Collins glanced at them.
" Mine? " she sighed.

VIII

SARDONIC, she stirred the salad: tumbling, jostling, pricking, poking it, parting the trembling leaves. Pursuing a rosy radish, or . . .

" Oh, Gerald, everyone is watching you! . . . " unearthing the glaring eyes of eggs.

" Why begin throwing it about? "

Orchestrating olives and tomatoes, breaking the violet beetroot. . . .

" Oh, Gerald! "

. . . tracking provoking peas—scattering paprinka, pouring tarragon, dashing *huile*.

" Yoicks, dear! "

" Athenæus, you know, maintains a lettuce is calming to Love! "

" Who ever mentioned love? I only said I liked him dreadfully."

Miss O'Brookomore leaned her chin upon her hand: she rested.

" Where *is* this Pastorelli? " she asked. " I mean the town."

" It's a little way outside of Orvieto. Not very far from Rome."

" Really? Rome. . . . "

" Avid thing! I believe you long to be there."

" I see no reason to complain."

" Think of the countless persons who've never come to Greece." Then finding Worcester Sauce—

" It doesn't seem fair! "

Miss Collins looked sage.

" Such," she remarked, " is life! "

" You haven't told me, Mab, about Pastorelli yet.

236

. . . There's a cathedral with frescoes there, you say.
Scuola di—*who?* A campo-santo. And what else? "

" There's the house, of course, where he was born.
It stands beside such a wicked-looking lake, and the
gardens sowed with statues. He showed me a photograph of his family seated in it. Oh, my gracious! "

" His family? "

" Just the natural blood ones. . . ."

" After *déjeuner* you should really write to your——"

" What's the good? . . . Mum's away in Edinburgh.
She says she must try to content herself with *Modern
Athens* as she doesn't suppose she shall ever see the
other. So papa—poor old gentleman—is left all alone
to look after my kiddy sister Daisy, who can neither
read nor write. Mum won't let her be educated, she
says, as it hasn't answered at all with me. And frequently, for a f-f-friend, she is asked to display her
ignorance."

" Her what? "

" How you said it: What! I love Napier *best*, dear,
always when he says, ' What.' W-h-a-t! What! Oh,
Gerald, I can't explain. . . . You'll never know——"

" I do know. It's like the crack of a cart-whip.
Exactly."

Miss Collins began eating crumbs at random.

" A whip? Oh, Gerald——"

" You seem to have entirely forgotten Napier since
you've become interested in the Count."

" After all, what is he but a Yorkshire pudding? "

" Still, he's your fiancé! "

" Do look at the man exactly opposite. Doesn't
he give you the impression rather of something torn
up by the roots? "

" He obviously has a little money, and she is spending it! "

Miss Collins whisked her eyes over the room.
Midway along Mrs. Arbanel appeared to be ab-

sorbed in a vivacious and seemingly vital conversation
with the *maitre d'hôtel*.

" I should love to seem so thoughtful! "

" I don't see Mrs. Cowsend, do you? "

" Breakfast was laid for four covers in her room."

" For four! "

" Or perhaps it was only three."

" Greece via the Renaissance would knock up most
of us."

" Why, even the Tartary tirade——"

" Remember you owe me that."

" The library at Bovon, you know, is full of that
sort of thing. . . . Although mum detests all serious
books. She likes them frothy. Whenever she goes
into York she's sure to come back with something
smart."

" Hasn't the eccentricity of living near York ever
occurred to your mother? "

"Oh, Gerald, it's dreadful for us all, dear, but what
can we do if nobody takes the house? "

" There must be some way of getting rid of it."

" Mum's in Edinburgh now to see what can be
done. She thinks some person perhaps pining for the
South——"

" One never knows! "

" I'll read you her letter, shall I? There's a message
too for you."

Miss O'Brookomore sipped listlessly her Château
Décélée.

" ' My adored angel,' she says, ' my darling child,
Mab. . . . If you knew how wretched I am without
you!' Oh! . . . ' Couldn't you have got a *quieter*
violet? . . .' She's interested too in Miss Arne! 'As
Juliet,' she says, ' she was astonishing! Though one
can't help feeling she has danced at the Empire. Crossing Princes Street I let fall the Ethiopian skin that I
got from Mrs. Mattocks.' And she asks me to be

photographed in your . . . something . . . 'hat and
Zouave jacket and a bunch of violets on one shoulder.'
(Then she says, as I told you:) ' I must try to content
myself with Modern Athens,' she says, ' as I don't
suppose I shall ever see the Other. . . . Who should
I come across at the Caledonian but Sukey and Booboo.
They *were* so glad to find me here, and on Sunday we
all went together to hear Father Brown. He spoke to
us so simply, so eloquently, so touchingly that I quite
. . . Never forget, my pet, that . . .

" ' He reminds me just a little of St. Anthony of
Padua. . . . What is all this about *an Italian?* Oh,
Girlie. If ever we let the Chase we must persuade papa
to travel. . . .

" ' Listening lately to the Y.M.C.A. singing " There
is a Green Hill," I felt I wanted to take a taxi and
drive straight to it. Mum's picnic days are nearly over
now. . . . Soon it's *she* who'll be the ruin. Those
that care enough for her will toil to her bedside, perhaps, with their baskets, as they would to some de-
cayed, romantic tower—the Lermers, poor Nell Flint,
dear Mrs. Day—and they will sprawl upon her *causeuse*
and trot out their ginger beer. Doctors will try to
restore her, patch her up . . .

" ' But mum won't let them. She will just roll over
on one side and show them . . .' "

" And the message? "

" I'm coming."

" ' . . . and show them, as Dolce Naldi did, they
arrive *too late.* The prospect of another damp winter
——' "

" The message! "

" ' Give my kind regards to Miss O'Brookomore.' "

" She writes curiously in the style of one of my
unknown correspondents."

" She's full of trivial sadness."

" Scotland should do her good."

" What would you do, Gerald, if you were to look round and there was somebody in a kilt? "

Miss O'Brookomore blinked.

" I don't suppose I should do anything," she said.

" Oh wouldn't you? "

" I *might* . . ."

" Try one. . . . I don't know what they are; at school we called them French Madonnas."

" They look fairly rich, anyway."

" Once I ate nineteen méringues. . . ."

" Pig! "

" You've to eat a peck of dirt before you die, Gerald."

" Not if I know it."

" Give me a bit of the brown."

" What are your father's initials, in case I should write to him? "

" C. It's for Charles! . . . Poor old gentleman."

" You should answer your mother yourself. Promise her a photograph."

" On the night they draw the lottery there's to be a subscription ball at the opera."

" What has that to do with it? "

" It's to be in fancy dress."

" I understand."

" I thought we could be photographed in our dresses."

" I see."

" Oh, Gerald, you could be a silver-tasselled Portia almost with what you have, and I a Maid of Orleans."

" You! "

" Don't be tiresome, darling. It's not as if we were going in *boys'* clothes! "

" Really, Mabel——"

" Of course, it's as you like! "

" So that's settled."

" Oh, Gerald, for my sake subscribe."

" I subscribe? I subscribe! I subscribe nothing."

" When the Shire-Hall at home was blown away I helped to collect for the restorations. . . ."

Miss O'Brookomore pinned up her veil.

" After the siesta what do you propose to do? "

" I'm going out to do some shopping. I should like to buy a small piece of old pottery for Mrs. Elk, of York. You know she collects jars. And then our head housemaid asked me to lay out a few shillings on ' some very Greek-looking thing,' she said. And I mustn't forget the footman. . . ."

" What did he want? "

" A knife."

" You seem to have commissions for all the servants."

"At home, you see, dear, I nearly always use the back stairs . . . They're so much more interesting than the front ones . . . Once Daisy saw a soldier on them . . . He was going up! And another time——"

Miss O'Brookomore yawned.

" Mercy," she said, " the siesta-hour's upon us! "

"No, there's really no resisting him. I'm sure there isn't. Who could? There's no resisting him at all— none. No. . . ."

Demurely she shed a shoe.

"I shouldn't care to be more in love than I am at present. No, indeed! Even if I could. . . ."

She sank slowly into bed.

"Oh, you silly creature!

"Love! O Lord!

"I shall never sleep. I don't see how I can. The die is cast! There's no telling, child, how it will end! . . .

". . . Via Tiber. . . . Countess P-a-s-t-o-r-e-l-l-i. Via Tiber. . . . 'O Tiber, Father Tiber, *to whom the Romans pray.*' Impossible! . . . If they did, it was a perfect scandal.

"And suppose he made me too? Oh, good gracious!"

By the bedside, mellowing among a number of vellum volumes, were the *Nine Prayers* of the Countess of Cochrane and Cray.

Who would do the burning?

That eighth one! What a clamour for a crown!

On the subject of jewels there wasn't much she didn't teach.

Two loose diamonds made a charming toc-toc sound.

At a dinner-party, now, who would work in first? She or Lady Cray? One would push past her probably, in any case—" the *Italian* woman!" . . . "*The Pasto* Countess thing!"

She played her eyes and flung out a hand towards a sugar-crystal-rose.

No; one couldn't exactly tell how it would end.
" My dear, I shouldn't care to say! . . ."
There were those Beer-Hall voices. . . . " Fal de
rol di do do, *di do do!* Fal de rol———"
Miss Collins turned her pillow.
" I suppose I've to lie and listen! . . . Oh, good
gracious! "

" ' I AM sure I always found her to be most industrious, clever, natty, and honest.' That was Mrs. Vernigan's. This is Miss Miser. And here is the Ex-Princess Thleeanouhee."

" Why bother Miss Palmer any more about it? I always say it's a lottery wherever one goes."

" Once," Mrs. Arbanel's maid declared, " I took a situation with a literary lady—the Scottish-Sappho. She wrote *Violet's Virtue*, or it might have been *The Virtue of Violet*."

" Anyway! "

" Oh, for the wings of a dove."

" Come along, Miss Clint, now. It's not so far."

Before them the Acropolis, half hidden by thin clouds, showed like a broken toy.

" Naturally, one sees it has its old associations. . . ."

" I dare say. But to my mind it doesn't look half the age of the Abbey church at home. Now, that does look worn if you like."

" Worn, my dear, don't speak of being worn! "

Clint sighed.

" Whenever I'm lonely or depressed," she said, " or valeting anyone who's just a little wee bit . . . Well! I know there's only one thing for me to do. I take a taxi and go and sit in the church of St. Bartholomew the Great. It has a *je ne sais quoi* about it somehow that comforts me."

" It would give some people the dismals, dear."

" Well, I always leave when I'm annoyed! "

" ' Quick with her needle, an early riser, I am sure—— ' "

" Give them back to me."

" ' I am sure no hours are too *long* for her.' "

" It's what I should call the portrait of a slave."

" Where is Elizabeth? "

" I'm here."

" And Mademoiselle? "

" Lagging along behind."

Miss Clint made a gesture towards the Erechtheum.

" Come along, girls! " she called.

" Oh! I never knew Lot had six wives. .. . . ."

" Can't you see she's always the same? "

" Our previous butler was a widower. He seemed inconsolable."

" Sooner or later, we each of us bear our cross! . . . Where I lived last you might gather one of those downy-puffy things and, blowing, say: ' First footman, second footman, third footman, fourth footman . . . .' And if there was any down over ' Pantry-boy, page. . . .' "

" With the Jamjanets, of course, it was hotel-life half the time. Eating, drinking and dressing made up *their* day."

" In Arcady, if you go, you'll find the food is vile."

" What I look forward to most is the Cyclops Castle at Tiryns. We've a dwarf in our family, you see."

" There's nothing more lucky, is there? "

"Oh well, my dear, perhaps it may come, some day." Clint turned.

" Come along, girls! "

" I shouldn't care to go with *them* on a walking tour. . . ."

" Mam'zelle Croizette, *chérie*, where ever have you been? "

" Looking for the Arbanel's bracelet."

" I'd forgotten it! ' The true-love-knot bangle he gave me when we became engaged.' "

Clint stood still.

"I don't know," she said, "but I believe I smell a rat."

"Fresh from the East, one is used to indelicate scents."

"Of course it's not for me to say. . . ."

"In a strange land, Miss Clint, we women should stand together."

"I noticed nothing until yesterday."

"And what did you notice then?"

."There's more than one trap set for Miss Collins."

"Lauk!"

"My gentleman's after her too."

"Oh, my poor strained nerves!"

"I suppose the bride's a bore."

"Of course she's neurasthenic and excitable and highly tuned. This morning, for instance, she sat and stormed at me because her white tennis shoes weren't white enough."

"Most young married women are ashamed of anything pale. . . . The Honourable Hester Dish on her wedding tour wore black all the time."

"Well, were there twenty traps laid for Miss Mabel she has too much gumption ever to go in."

"You astonish me! I'd have said now she would be very easily *épris*."

"Oh, mind the step!"

They had reached the Belvedere.

"I'd dearly like to carve my name on the leg of this seat."

"Without a fiancé's entwined, Miss Palmer, it looks almost as if——"

"*My* boy is in the Guards."

"Once I was engaged to a soldier."

"And you broke it off?"

"How he did bore me with his battles!"

Croizette peered down.

"Such a sunset," she remarked, "would have scared the ancients."

246

Palmer cleared her throat.

" I doubt it! . . ." she said. " When I went out into the world my dear mother told me a little about *them*. . . . There was the adventure of Titia Clarges. . . . She was one of those smart girls like the Midianites in Paris. Believe me, senility takes some scaring."

" Chatterbox! "

" What is the matter with Elizabeth? "

Elizabeth hid her face.

" There's a man," she said, " Miss Clint, carrying on in such a crazy way. . . . I think he means to draw us! "

" Let him ask permission."

" All this note-taking out of doors in my opinion really isn't nice. I'd as soon start hair-dressing in the street."

" It's on the cards you may. Professor Cowsend is to lecture in the Museum shortly from busts and coins and vases upon the Classic Coiffure. ' I shall expect you to attend,' Miss O'Brookomore said to me. ' It is never too l-l-late to learn! Campstools, flowers, unguents, pins and *peignoirs* provided. And we just sit down and do each other's hair."

" He'll not catch me there, I can promise him! "

" There'll be a prize."

" So I should hope! "

" The winner will have her expenses to any one of the islands—a day off."

" Who'd take an airing here from choice? "

" *Alone!* "

" Sprinkle ashes over me," Elizabeth murmured, " sooner! "

" Because Miss O'Brookomore's a bit of a bluestocking it doesn't signify that Dorinda, Lady Gaiheart's that way! Ours is quite another story. We're here to be nearer to Colonel Sweetish, who's at Malta. . . ."

" In your place, I'd not own it."

247

" How we do enjoy the saline breezes! ' Where's the wind? ' ' Which way's the wind? ' ' I don't know, your ladyship,' I reply, ' but it's as keen as mustard! ' "

Palmer examined her nails.

" My mistress isn't that sort," she said.

" What do you mean? "

" When I tapped at her door one night she didn't seem earthly. She came out to me with her pen in her hand, looking quite deranged—and old! My word! More like a mummy! "

" Worn out in intellectual excesses I dare say."

" *When she's with Miss Mabel she looks quite different.*"

" Were ever footsteps more out of tune! "

" An old dirge and a valse! "

Elizabeth giggled.

" Don't forget, Miss Palmer," she said, " you've promised to dance with me to-night when the band begins."

" Surely; only bear it, please, in mind, I never will dance gentleman."

" It doesn't matter. The chef said directly he'd finished he'd——"

" Finish me! "

" Whereabouts now were you born? "

" What makes you so inquisitive? "

" I could tell a London voice anywhere! Even in the dark."

" Hammersmith's my home."

" Hammersm—— "

The Captive Women stared before them.

It was a bright and windy evening, with a mist that almost hid the sea. Now and then across Hymettos at a hint of sun swept a few pale shadows.

Miss Clint scanned the great groups of sailing clouds.

" Come along, girls," she murmured. " If it comes on to rain and we in our *derniers cris* . . .! "

XI

" Night came with a big brown moon. . . . Ignatius knocked repeatedly on the door. At last a feeble voice —it was Haidèe's—cried: ' Come in! . . ' And I was led into the room by a Cowley Father. Oh, good gracious! "

" Go on. . . . His tired ecstasy makes me——"

" How's the poor head? " ·

" The dove did it good."

" I shouldn't have thought you had held it long enough."

" Quite long enough."

" Soon it'll grow weary of flying about the room."

" It sickens me so to watch it."

Miss Collins got up stealthily.

" Coo! "

" Don't, Mabel."

" It's looking at us both, dear, as much as to say . . ."

Miss O'Brookomore tittered.

" I believe all the time you're shamming."

" Oh, very well! "

" I'd do anything for you, Gerald."

" That's sweet. . . ."

" . . . It's exploring the ceiling now! "

" Open the window wide."

" Oh, listen! What tune is it? It's a slow-step of some sort."

The Biographer sat up slightly among her pillows.

" It sounds like the Incest-music," she murmured, " to some new opera."

" Oh, Gerald. . . . You do look bad. Upon my word you do."

" Really, Mabel, you have the tongue of a midwife, my dear."

" I'd run over to the pharmacy willingly if you thought. . . . It was they who invented the ' Eau de Parnasse.' It's made mostly out of sunflower seed. It's really *violets*."

" You'd stop to dance on the way! "

" Well? And if I did! "

" Just lately I've felt so nervous. I don't know why! "

" Accidents don't occur in a room full of people. Not often."

" It depends."

" Be good, Gerald. Now, there's a dear."

Miss O'Brookomore seemed touched.

" Run, twirl, dance, spin! " she said, " and come back in ten minutes."

" You're an angel."

" Carry me in your thoughts! "

" What good could *that* do you, Gerald? "

" Enjoy yourself—that's all."

In a black gauze gown with glorious garnitures, her hair tied up behind in a very Greek way, Miss Collins walked out into the hall where Miss Arne, to her surprise, was drilling a huge recruit.

" ' Good day, Lampito,' " she was saying, " ' dear friend from Lacedæmon. How well and handsome you look! What a rosy complexion! and how strong you seem; why, you could strangle a bull surely! ' "

The Australian girl grew rigid.

" ' Yes, indeed,' " she drawled, " ' I really think I could. 'Tis because I do gymnastics and practise the kick dance.' "

" There, of course, I think Lampito should throw up a leg. We'd better begin again."

Miss Collins paused.

"Haven't you got it pat by this time?" she inquired.

Miss Arne waved a fan with the names of some old adorers scribbled across the sticks.

"Art," she remarked, "doesn't like being jostled. How's your friend?"

"Gerald? She's pretty bad."

"Health is like a revue. It comes and goes. Even I —in the morning when I rise I feel fit enough—at least! . . . But by lunch-time I'm exhausted . . . and then in the evening I'm myself again! . . ."

"Oh, good gracious!"

The Australian girl sat down.

"Phew! . . . It's warm acting!" she observed.

"We might have an ice."

"Won't you have a Vermouth-Cobbler with me?"

"What's that?"

"It's just a drink."

"Is it refreshing?"

"As a liqueur," Miss Collins said, "there's nothing like *mint sauce*. You can't fancy what it's like alone."

The Colonial looked intriguing.

"Tell me about the stage," she implored, "or of the people on your fan."

"I've forgotten! I forget!"

"Who's *Wellbridge?*"

"Ah! Dublin was a gay place when *he* was viceroy there. . . ."

"Silent Stanley!"

"At the Garden Theatre he was Bassanio. . . ."

"Freddy Fortune?"

"Oh, my dear, he was the lover in Lady Twyford's last play. He's the paramour in all her pieces."

"Alice."

Miss Arne took back her fan.

"I rang," she said to the waiter. "It's for an ice."

Miss Collins turned towards the ball-room. People either were pushing their way in or struggling to get out.

The Count touched her arm.

"Could you spare me half-an-ear for half-a-minute?" he asked.

" I'd sooner dance, if you don't mind."

" Are you fond of dancing? "

" I love it. Every winter nearly we give a ball. At least Mrs. Collins does. . . . It's really for me and Daisy. . . . We begin about half-past five and go on till about eight. After that there's a wizard."

" Outside the snow would be falling. The land would be white."

" Naturally *we* supply the rabbits."

" Have you much shooting? "

" We get all Lord Linco s birds as they fly across." The Count sighed.

" With us," he said, " it's mostly hares and larks."

" I suppose you mean the Opera."

" Indeed no! "

" Are you in the country much? "

" Now and then. My mother, you see, is obliged to be a good deal in Orvieto. She has also an apartment in Rome."

Miss Collins was mystified.

" *Apartments?* " she asked.

" An apartment, a flat, a floor—it is the first floor."

" Oh, good gracious! "

" This is your very first season, isn't it? "

" I don't know. I shouldn't care to say! "

" Excuse me."

" I live like a buried diamond half the year."

" Enjoy yourself now."

" Ah, that's . . . easier said than done . . ."

" Your friend ought not to be too hard on you."

" Gerald isn't really hard . . . You wouldn't say

so if you knew her well . . . Once she bought a little
calf for some special binding, but let it grow up . . .
and now it's a cow! "

They swung slowly out into the throng.

" I know this dance well. It's *Lady Randolph and the
Old Shepherd!* "

" The old shepherd part is charming."

Miss Collins looked languid.

" Would you care to Cook me? " she asked.

" Cook you? "

" Show me round."

" Certainly. I should be delighted."

All Athens was responding to the dance. To Elizabeth, craning from the stairs, it seemed that the men
resembled big black pearls while the women diamond
drops—

" We might sit the rest out."

" Of course it's just as you like. . . ."

" There's such a moon! "

" I've just been reading to Gerald about the moon
—a big brown one! "

" Do you read a lot? "

" Lately, out of pure politeness, I've been dipping
into some of Gerald's spawn. But I never open a book
unless I'm obliged. And my sister's just the same.
Poor mite, she can't! . . . Oh, she's such a pickle!
She is really *too* obstreperous. . . . You never know
what she's up to! "

Mrs. Arbanel approached.

" What weapons can you muster," she asked,
" besides darts? "

" Darts? "

" Did you bring a gun? "

" Gerald has a gold revolver. ' *Honour* ' she calls it."

" Well, to-morrow I and a few other women are
going wild-duck shooting round Salamis, if you would
care to come."

" Oh, wouldn't I enjoy it! "

" We meet outside the church in the Rue d'Hermès at ten o'clock."

" Gerald is very particular about whom she meets."

" She can pick and choose. We're sure to be rather a band."

" I don't know what Gerald will say. . . ."

" I noticed there was a tray outside her door."

" We did all we could to tempt her. But she took her tea. And that was a mercy."

" It's nothing, I hope, serious? "

" She gets these turns. . . . I think it's due to diet. Lately she has complained so much of her extraordinarily vivid dreams. . . ."

Mrs. Arbanel smiled darkly.

" When I dream," she said, " I'm watching most."

" What—for instance? "

" How do I know? "

" Then don't expect me to say."

Mrs. Arbanel addressed the " Hippolytus Charioteer " upon the ceiling.

" At the Rotunda," she murmured, as she moved away, " please to turn. . . ."

" What could she mean? "

" I've not the least idea! "

" Be careful of her if you go! "

" She's a jealous fury. . . ."

" Her husband appears completely depressed."

" I fancy he wants me to dance."

" Don't! And never let him."

" Why not? "

"Little miss, when love springs under your nose! . . ."

" Love? . . ."

" Only dance with me! "

" No. I'm going back to Gerald. Were anything to happen to her while I'm off duty I should never forgive myself."

Miss O'Brookomore had lowered her lights.

" Is that you, Mabel? " she asked.

" How's the poor head? "

" I've been drowsing."

" I'm glad you could manage that."

" Isn't the band *awful?* "

" Boom, boom, boom. . . ."

" Did you have a nice time? "

" I've found out one or two things by going down."

" What things? "

" Oh, Gerald, his mother keeps Apartments! "

" There. What did I tell you? "

" She has an Apartment in Rome. And I suppose
it's a Boarding-house in the country. . . ."

" Well, to be sure! "

" After all, dear, Lady Frithelstock sells her fruit!"

" Even so! "

" And he has asked me, I think, to marry him."

" He's proposed? "

" Of course it's purely verbal . . ."

" What did he say? "

" First he asked to speak to me . . . and then he
said, 'Little miss,' he said, 'when Love springs
under your nose! . . .' That was his expression."

" A pretty one. But it has nothing to do with marriage. Oh, Mabel! "

" I long to be loved, Gerald."

" My dear."

" When he spoke of love it made me feel so important."

Miss O'Brookomore looked grim.

" You've yet to learn, I find, what frivolous things
men are. . . ."

" What has that got to do with it, Gerald? "

" Be patient. You are sure to find a better *parti*."

" A party? "

" A girl like you."

"And Mrs. Arbanel has invited us to join her at a shoot."

"In town?"

"At Salamís."

"It's so far off. . . ."

"Bring 'Honour,' she said."

"Honour's no use. It won't go off!"

"Oh, good gracious!"

"Besides, if I went I would lie on the Plage and watch you all."

"Gracious me, Gerald!"

"It's the dove again!"

"Unless I'm much mistaken, dear, that bird will stay in the room all night."

XII

A WARM, miraculous morning made the Athenian pavements split.

Before an Ikon in the little dark building of the Kapnikaræa Miss O'Brookomore knelt. And if she stopped long upon her knees most likely it was more that she found herself comfortable than anything else.

Miss Collins touched her arm.

" Oh, Gerald, we're all waiting for you," she said.

" I'm just coming."

" I shouldn't over care to be troubled by a conscience like that! "

The Biographer drew on a glove.

" After all," she inquired, " isn't heaven a sort of snobbism? A looking-up, a preference for the best hotel? "

" It's no good asking me, Gerald. It's like that button-hook of yours. . . ."

" We won't discuss that now."

" You don't imagine, do you, dear, I'd take your button-hook? I suppose you think I'd steal it! "

" Hush, Mabel! "

" I'm glad it isn't teaspoons. Although, of course, it's equally unpleasant."

Outside all was confusion, chatter, cracking of whips.

" *βρεκεκεκέξ κοάξ κοάξ!*" Miss Arne harangued the mob.

" I don't suppose I shall knock down much," the Australian girl declared. " And, frankly, I don't much care. I'm one of those girls who wouldn't harm a fly. . . ."

" Dear Miss Dawkins. You'd think she was an auctioneer! "

With a sword-stick Mrs. Cowsend gave a sudden lunge into the air.

" In case the birds fly near," she said, " I shall simply prod them——"

" Mind the man."

" . . . δεν ἐχω χρήματα."

" What does he say? "

" He says he has no money."

" Hasn't he any? "

" οὐχί! "

" Apparently not. . . ."

" Oh, isn't it dreadful, Gerald? "

" Some of these heads are really rather fine."

" That looks like the English Consul! "

Miss Dawkins pressed her heart.

" Every time I see anyone——" she said.

" Is your father tall? "

" As we drive I shall give you all his measurements."

Along a sympathetic, winding road skirting the Acropolis their carriages made their way.

" All these open-air theatres amuse me," Miss Arne said. " It is like old *café-chantant* days."

Seated between Mrs. Arbanel and Dorinda, Lady Gaiheart, her personality struggled.

" Thank you, I never touch tobacco," Lady Dorinda said. " A cigarette with me would create a thirst. . . ."

" Fortunately Miss Dawkins has a flask."

" At the Antiquarians in Priam Place just now they've some nice Phœnician bottles."

Miss Collins nestled herself winningly against her neighbour.

" They showed me the smartest set of tea-things," she said, " that I ever saw. It belonged to Iphigenia —in Tauris. Oh, such little tiny cups! Such little teeny spoons! Such a darling of a cream-jug. . . . And such

a sturdy little tea-pot! With the sweetest spout. . . .
Pout. And a little sugar-basin! And a little slop-bowl.
. . ."

"I suppose all destined for America!"

Mrs. Arbanel turned and threw a few kisses to
someone in the brake behind.

"Who's the sun-helmet?"

"It's a Mrs. Lily Gordon Lawson—she has that
big new villa on the Olympian Road. You know."

"They say Olympia for Love!"

"For love?"

"If people should come together there—it's all
up with them."

"My dear, to see Greece, it's what I came out
for!"

"Well, somewhere in me, far down," Miss Dawkins
declared, "I don't mind admitting, there's a field
with cows browsing."

"Have you been seeking them long?"

"Almost always."

"Just wandering!"

"Hotels, always hotels. *Yes!* And one does get
so tired of tavern life!"

"You must be very weary."

"After this I propose to do the I's . . . India,
Italy, Ireland, Iceland. . . ."

"When you've found them you'll be so bored."

Miss Dawkins raised to her lips her flask.

"What ever is in it?" Miss Collins asked.

Miss Dawkins fixed her.

"It's a digestive—cocktail," she said at last. "Or
a *Blue Brazilian*, as some people prefer to call it . . .
that is so."

Mrs. Arbanel gave a cry.

"The *sea*."

"Have you never seen it?"

"Mabel! . . ."

" What emerald or sapphire! " Miss Arne asked.
" Aren't you ravished? "

" I mean to bathe," Miss Collins announced.

" My dear, how can you ? "

" Oh, Gerald, just a dip! "

Dorinda, Lady Gaiheart, relaxed.

" Colonel Sweetish and Captain Muckmaisie, both
old and very dear friends of mine," her attitude
seemed to say, " are somewhere across that light. . . ."

" How many guns are there? "

" Not so many as there seem. Neither Mrs. Cowsend nor Lady Dorinda will be shots. They're only
going to pick up the birds."

Mrs. Cowsend chuckled.

" Like good retrievers," she said.

Mrs. Arbanel turned to throw an extra kiss.

" There's Mrs. Erso-Ennis and Mrs. Viviott," she
said.

" Those two! "

" And little Mrs. Lawson, who's really *très*
sport. . . ."

" She says she's sure she shall shoot someone! "

" Oh, she's clever, she's fascinating."

Miss Collins scowled.

" I should like her to start trying her tricks on me!"

" And then there're ourselves."

" I've no gun," Miss O'Brookomore said. " At
most I could throw a book. . . ."

" What have you brought with you? "

" I've my Wordsworth."

" Is he your poet? "

" I'm told I should read *Le Charme d'Athènes*,"
Mrs. Cowsend said. " But I always disliked that
series."

" I fancy there's a new one: *Notes on the Tedium of
Places*—comprising almost everywhere."

Miss Collins glanced at her guardian.

" It's extraordinary Gerald doesn't go dotty," she observed, " writing as she does. . . ."

" Does the *Life* progress? "

" It's enough to say it assumes proportions."

Lady Dorinda spread out her parasol.

" The Kettler cult seems the only shade we have to speak of! " she said. " Since . . . Eleusis."

Mrs. Cowsend freckled faintly.

" Were I to have a baby girl here," she said at random, " O'Brien would insist on calling her Athene; and it would be Olympia. Or Delphine. Or, if on the way there, Helen! . . ."

" I should have thought Violet, or *Violets*," Mrs. Arbanel suggested as the carriage stopped.

Across a vivid, a perfectly pirate sea, Salamis showed shimmering in the sun.

Miss Arne held out arms towards it.

" It's like a happy ending! " she breathed.

Boats were in readiness.

" Where's the wind? " the Countess sniffed.

" There's almost an autumnal feel, isn't there? "

The wild apple-trees along the shore stood tipped with gold.

" Perhaps we shall see Pan! "

Mrs. Arbanel shouldered her gun.

" To avoid accidents," she said, " we should drift about in line."

" My dear, I always fire sideways! "

Mrs. Viviott covered up her ears.

" Don't! " she said.

" Why not? "

" I never could bear the crack-of-a-gun business," she confessed.

" Then what ever made you come? " Miss Collins queried.

" Mainly for Mrs. Erso-Ennis—to look after her."

" ' And the sun went down and the stars came out far over the summer sea! '—eh, Gerald? "

Miss O'Brookomore looked blank.

" I hope you know we're sweeping straight south-west! " she murmured presently. . . ." I've an inkling there's Megara."

" It was above Megara the Seymoures———"

Overhead the sky was purely blue.

Miss Arne scanned it.

" What is that large bird? " she inquired.

" Where? "

Miss Dawkins picked up an imaginary guitar.

> " ' That which yonder flies,' " [she sang]
> " ' Wild goose is it?—Swan is it?
> Wild goose if it be—
> > Haréya tōtō,
> > Haréya tōtō,
> Wild goose if it be,
> It's name I soon shall say. . . .
> Wild swan if it be—better still!
> > Tōtō! ' "

" Enchanting! "

" I learnt it in Japan—that is so."

Miss Collins drooped.

" The water's so clear you can see everything that's going on."

" Couldn't we moor ourselves somewhere and anchor? "

" I could fancy I hear turtle doves," Lady Dorinda remarked.

" Oh, they're city! "

Miss Arne appeared to pray.

" I love Finsbury Circus for its Doves," she said. " And I adore the Aspens in Cadogan Square. . . ."

" Does the sea upset you? "

" Oh, Gerald! . . . She's certainly going to be queer."

" I'm fond of that garden too, behind Farm Street, with those bow-windows ſtaring out upon it. I could sit for ever huddled up in a black frock there exciting sympathy . . . liſtening to the prieſts' voices in the Farm."

Miss Collins jumped up.

" Don't, Mabel! You'll capsize the boat."

Mrs. Cowsend shuddered.

" I never could swim," she said.

" I truſt the gods would drop down ſtrings—a sort of parachute affair—drawing us through the water."

Mrs. Viviott addressed her friend.

" Were yours to give, Genevieve! . . ." she said.

" That's juſt *you*, Iris! "

Miss O'Brookomore fluttered her eyelids.

" Did you ever see such a rag of a sail? "

" It's black."

" O-h, there went a fish with wings! "

" With——"

" Where? "

" Oh, my dear——! "

Mrs. Arbanel turned her gun about and—fired.

XIII

" I SHALL never forget the hideous moment! "

" They're driving her round the town."

Lady Dorinda slowly wiped an eye.

" To the departed," she said, " short cuts are disrespectful."

" I know Athens pretty well," Mrs. Viviott declared. " And they're going a statesman's way! "

Miss Collins threw herself into an easy seat.

" Oh, it's awful, awful, awful! " she said. " It doesn't do to think. . . ."

The Room of the Minerva in the National Museum lay steeped in light.

" It's as though one held a Memorial service to her somehow," Miss O'Brookomore commented, " amidst all these busts and urns and friezes. . . ."

" For the Lysistrata that Nymph in the corner was to have inspired her gown. ' I shall play her in lavender and helio,' she said to me. And now, poor dear, where is she? "

" Oh, it's awful, it's hideous! " Miss Collins broke out . . . " To-day I feel turned forty! This has made an old woman of me. Oh, good gracious! "

In her silver hat crowned with black Scotch roses drawn down close across the eyes she might perhaps have been taken for more.

" Mr. Arbanel, poor man, seems almost to be broken. Vina's vulgar violence, he said, disgusts me more than I can ever say—and when her maid went to her door she said, ' Go away! I'm Proserpine.' "

" Oh. . . . If anyone had *told* me, Gerald, that I'd

become acquainted with a bride-murderess . . . I should never have believed it."

" What do they intend to do? "

" Decamp—if they're wise."

" When I saw her in her black dress, Gerald! "

" It was a pure accident—naturally, she said, when questioned."

" One tries to believe it was."

" She *would* wave her gun about so. I was in terrors all the time! "

" I suppose there was an inquest? " Miss Collins said.

" I really couldn't say. . . ."

" I should like to have been at it."

" One longs for the country now—to get away."

" We leave for Delphi directly," Miss O'Brookomore said.

" Kettling? "

" Well . . . more or less. . . . Poor Kitty, she went to Delphi to consult the Oracle and found it had gone. You can imagine her bitterness."

" I dare say she consoled herself with the fruit. . . . There's a garden on the way to Itea. . . . You never *saw* such apples! "

" I dare say that's gone too."

" Be careful in Olympia."

" What *does* one do in Olympia? Tell me, please! " Mrs. Viviott fetched a sigh.

" Oh, well," she said, " of course one sits, and sits, and sits, and *sits*, before the Praxiteles. . . . And then, if two people come together there I warn you they're sure to fall in love. . . ."

Miss O'Brookomore bowed.

" Here're more mourners! " she exclaimed.

" Oh, isn't it gruesome, Gerald? "

" We turned in here, dear," Mrs. Cowsend said. " I didn't feel I wanted to go on. . . ."

" That turquoise tinsel thing—*violet*, I should say
—the pall! "

The Historian seemed to touch it.

" It was her doom, poor dear. . . . On the voyage
out I've a recollection still of the way she sat on board
while the waves burst over her."

" At any rate she had the sad satisfaction of dying
in Greece."

" My dear, there was no time for reflections! "

Miss Collins covered her face.

" Was there no post-mortem? " she inquired.

Mrs. Cowsend showed distress.

" Have you been to look at the coiffures yet? " she
asked. " It's to-day my husband holds his classes, and
they're all in the Vase Room now."

" There's a room set aside somewhere for the
' Obscene,' " Miss Collins said. " Where is it? "

" My dear, how could one think of such a thing at
such a minute!"

" Only to distract us."

" The Professor's classes are more likely to do that."

" In Arcadia," Miss O'Brookomore declared, " I
intend to coil my hair like rams' horns."

Mrs. Viviott vibrated.

" My dear," she said, " I never vary. I *couldn't!* "

" In Arcadia you'll find the continual singing of
the cicadas require some excluding."

Lady Dorinda raised a hand.

" Were I the wife of a gunner," she protested,
" it would make no difference. I should always be
high! "

Miss Collins slipped an arm about her companion's
waist.

" Oh . . It's a Dance of the Hours, Gerald! "

" Dance of the Drumerdairies, my dear."

" Whose doing was it? "

Miss O'Brookomore appeared absorbed. . . . For

a moment Time hovered, wobbled, swerved. Miss Collins aged for her.

" It's lovely, Mabel," she said, " when—— Oh, Mabel! " she said.

Miss Collins started.

" This caps everything! " she exclaimed.

" Is there anything wrong, dear? "

" Mrs. Arbanel's actually dressing. . . ."

Mrs. Viviott glided forward.

" Geneviève! " she implored—" Geneviève *Erso-En-n-is!* "

Miss Collins caught at the Historian.

" Let us go, Gerald," she said, " before it happens again."

XIV

" It's nice to be in Delphi, Gerald! "

" After Athens," Miss O'Brookomore said, " it really is delightful."

" . . . We never saw the king and queen, dear."

" No more we did! "

" This morning I followed an empty river bed for miles and miles. . . ."

" To do justice to the walks," Miss O'Brookomore observed, " one would need to have legs as hard, pink and resisting as a ballerina."

" Aren't you going round to look at the Auriga as usual? "

" I hardly know. Possibly I may take a turn presently in the direction of Parnassos. . . ."

" There's a shrub in the garden, Gerald, all covered in mauve rosettes! "

" It's perhaps a Delphinium."

" Oh! I do think it sweet! "

" I wonder who's here beside ourselves."

" I noticed the names of Cyril Cloudcap and of Charlie Cumston in the Visitors' Book. . . ."

" That sounds English."

" They left yesterday for Olympia, and there was a Mrs. Clacton, Gerald."

" Has she gone too? "

" The Count said we weren't to be surprised if——"

" My dear, if Pastorelli turns up here we move on."

" Fussy, fidgety thing! "

" When he makes that sort of *clearing* noise . . . No! Really——"

" That's nothing, Gerald. Why I do it myself."

Miss O'Brookomore stared hard at the floor.

" I miss a carpet," she said.

" In my bedroom at home, Gerald, the carpet has big blue tulips on a yellow ground."

" Has the postman been? "

" He's been."

" Wasn't there anything? "

" There was a letter from mum. And another from Daisy."

" I thought she couldn't write."

" She sets her mark."

" Let me see."

" It's only a smear."

" Is the house disposed of—does your mother say? "

" I conclude it isn't. She says the greenfly this year has destroyed almost everything. Hardly anybody has been spared. At Patchpole Park the peaches just dried on the walls as though they were dates. And she's quite in despair about Daisy! She says she gets more hopeless hourly. She's taking her into York so as to have her ears pierced, poor mite. And papa, he's at Helstan with Napier—it's that new seaside——"

" Is the Count aware you're fidanzata? "

" I didn't tell him I wasn't quite free, and I don't think I will. I must write to Napier, I suppose, and break it off—I feel sorry for him, poor boy." ·

Miss O'Brookomore wandered to the window.

" It's going to be hot to-day."

" In the Gulf there's been rain in two places."

" Here we've the sun."

" What ever would the vines do, Gerald, without the olives to hold them up? "

" I can't think."

" They always say at home nothing can compare with the view from Mockbird Hill. On a clear day you can see to Ditchley."

T

Miss O'Brookomore shaded her eyes.

" There's an arrival," she said.

" Oh! "

" What is it? "

" He's here! "

" Oh! Mabel! "

" Oh! Gerald! "

" Oh! Mabel! "

" Oh! Gerald! "

Hand meeting hand, palm meeting palm (the vitality of the one rambling off into the other), they sought to find vent to their emotion.

X V

THE inn of the Pythian Apollo winked its lights.

Moving about the bare boards of her room, Miss O'Brookomore made her box. Now bending, now rising, now falling to her knees, it appeared from the road below as though she were imploring for forgiveness.

" For I am the old King's daughter,
The *youngest*, sir, said she!
The King he is my father,
And my name is Marjorie. . . .

Oh, my name is Marjorie, she said,
My father he is the King,
I am the youngest child he had,
And what will to-morrow bring?

What will to-morrow bring, she said,
Oh, what will to-morrow bring?
The King he is my father,
And what will to-morrow bring? "

" . . . Gerald, she always sings as she packs! Just making it up as she goes——"

" Why is she in such a hurry to be off? "

" I don't know. To-day she's been all veins and moods, whims and foibles."

" Induce her to remain."

" If only she would. . . . We haven't yet been up to the Cave of the Nymphs! "

" Ecco! "

" It's annoying to have to miss it."

" One night I sat upon the stairs
And heard him call my name!
I crept into the darkness
And covered my head for shame.

I covered my head for shame, she said,
Oh, I covered my head for shame!
The King he is my father,
And I covered my head for shame."

" Sometimes when she starts to sing she'll keep it
up for hours. It depends on what she's doing! "

" My sister Yoland she is dead,
And Ygrind is no more. . . .
They went away to Ireland,
And nobody knows where they are!

Nobody knows where they are at all,
No one seems able to say——"

" Will you come for a little stroll? "
" Where ever to? "
" Anywhere."
She raised her eyes towards Parnassos, whose cold
white heights glimmered amid the stars.
" Oh, it gets grimmish! "
" You shouldn't be afraid."
" Tell me," she asked, " would it be a Pension? "
" A Pension? "
" Those apartments of your mother's."
" What does it matter now? "
" Oh! . . . Perhaps I ought to aid poor Gerald! "
" Aiding harms the hands."
" Mine are spoilt already."
" I can't believe it."
" Mum pretends my hands are large because Time
hangs heavy upon them."

" Time in the country, they say, is apt to drag."

" Not if there's a farm. Who could be bored by watching the manners of some old surly bull, or a dog on the scent of things, or a dove paying visits? "

" Very likely! "

" You're blasé."

" Nothing of the sort."

" Poor little Geraldine, her weariness exceeds most things. She says the world's an ' 8.' "

" That's better than an ' o.' "

" The repetition palls."

" There is always a nuance."

" It's better to be an Indifferentist, she says. Not to care! But if anything ever goes wrong . . . It's impossible not to smile at her philosophy."

" You must be her comfort."

" I don't know what she'd do without me. Because the maid's a perfect fool. When we arrive anywhere usually it's I who improve the terms. . . . Gerald hates to bargain. She seems to think it sordid. So I do it for her. Oh, it's such fun! . . . Is it to be a back room or a front room, with a double bed or a single bed, or would the lady disdain a back bedroom without any balcony? Then Gerald asserts herself. ' The lady requires a balcony with an unobstructed horizon ' —and if there isn't such a thing, then we try elsewhere."

He stooped a little.

" It's the case of a courier," he said.

" I think we ought to turn."

" We will," he answered, " when the road bends. Remember, the world's an ' 8 '! "

XVI

" Will you talk to me about the Moon and Stars? . . .
Would it amuse you ? "

Miss O'Brookomore raised herself. . . . A young
man whom she had never seen until now stood before
her.

" I shall be delighted to talk to you about anything,"
she replied.

" When did you arrive? "

" My dear, we only got here yesterday."

There came a voice of protest.

" Oh, Gerald! It was the day before."

" What are your impressions of Olympia? "

" I love it, I think it sweet."

" Everybody says the same."

Miss OBrookomore breathed a sigh.

" I should like you to be my Literary Executor,"
she said.

He knelt down and took her hand.

" No, my dear Thing! " he answered. " I'm sorry
—but I simply can't. Simply I should love to, my dear
Thing! But it's impossible. . . ."

Miss Collins rose discreetly.

" Gerald—I think I shall leave you," she said.

XVII

" Who ever was it, Gerald? . . ."
Seated before a mirror, her shoulders gilded by the
evening sun, Miss O'Brookomore drew a net of
sapphire stones across her hair.

" Some god of the woods—no doubt! "

" That's only for a diary. . . . It doesn't do for
me. . . ."
" Things do happen so quickly! "
" Very likely it was Cyril Cloudcap. . . ."
" It may have been Charlie Cumston."
" Mer-cy! Gerald."
" How soon will you be ready? "
" I've no appetite, Gerald. While the Count's at
Delphi I don't seem to care."
" Foolish girl! "
" Oh! I do long to be married, Gerald. . . . It's
what I long to be most. Just married, dear."
" Not without your parents' consent."
" Nonsense, Gerald! "
" It's a caprice that will pass."
" Oh, Gerald, his love talk with me and what I
reply—it's a real duet! "
Miss O'Brookomore tucked a few mauve satin
flowers into her frock.
" Aren't they heavenly? " she inquired. " Especially
the purple ones. . . ."
" Oh, Gerald! "
" My poor puss——"
" People's lives, dearie, don't seem to be a bit their
own once they're in love."

" Love is a seed that needs watering from day to day. Otherwise it dies."

" With me it all accumulates."

" Don't let's miss the sunset—the later half."

" It's a sunset and a sobset, Gerald. Oh, it's so sad. . . ."

" In the end everything has to be paid for."

" Principally for that I'd sooner I didn't dine. It really isn't worth it, Gerald. . . ."

" No dinner? "

" Even gratis. Oh, Gerald! "

" We're sure to meet the Arbanels."

" I tapped at their door as I came along."

" I fear that was intrusive."

" Directly it dawned upon her it was me she flew forward brandishing a powder-puff."

" Her behaviour's getting Byzantine—more and more."

Miss Collins folded an arm about her friend.

" Why do you think it's Byzantine, Gerald? What ever makes you think it is? "

" On certain natures environment frequently reacts. I can recall the Queen of Snowland (when a guest at Windsor) frisking off one afternoon into the town in search of lodgings. She came to the very house where I was writing her life . . . and we met in the front hall."

" Oh, good gracious! "

" Similarly, I feel inclined to believe that Mrs. Arbanel in Egypt would be less vivid and more *Athenian* in her ways."

" Can a leopard change its spots, Gerald? "

" My dear, it can modify them."

" I'm surprised you lend her Palmer."

" I've only offered her, of course, until the faithless Clint can be replaced. Mrs. Arbanel hopes to secure someone locally."

" I shouldn't think there were many maids to be found locally, Gerald. I shouldn't think there was one. Not in Olympia."

" The deciphering of their characters, in any case, would require a skilful student," Miss O'Brookomore observed as Palmer came in.

Miss Collins rolled her eyes.

" Thank heaven! " she exclaimed.

" It didn't take you long! "

" I was as quick with her, miss, as I could be."

" We were prepared to hear some screams. . . ."

" Were I to be stabbed, Miss Mabel, I should endeavour to be considerate."

" Violets! "

" I suppose, poor thing, she is still very dazed? "

" She seemed lost in reverie, miss."

" I expect it's the air."

" She intends to ride to Sparta almost immediately, since Olympia, she hears, is nothing but cliques and coteries."

" It's their season now."

" There's a good deal of entertaining, miss, to-night. Dorinda, Lady Gaiheart, is to have a party for the Irish Archæological School. And Mrs. L. G. Lawson is bringing over some of her friends from the Villa Sophonisba."

Miss O'Brookomore began muffling a foot up in a silver-spangled shoe.

" Had I been told earlier I'd have gone into Corinth," she said.

" No doubt you'd have found Miss Dawkins there."

" My dear, she's in Olympia. She arrived this afternoon. I overheard her telling her father's chest-measurements to the boy that works the lift."

" And I dare say half-seas-over? "

" Poor thing."

" Oh, she's so common, Gerald! "

" I should like to be on a balcony, miss, for the Recognition."

" I dare say she'll be made to display her birthmarks first."

" There's no need, miss—if you'll pardon me—for birthmarks with a face like that."

" Brute! . . . You've pricked me. . . ."

The sound of the dinner-gong came dwindling up.

" Oh, the way they beat it! "

Miss O'Brookomore smothered a sigh.

" It might be the Ramadan! " she declared.

XVIII

O STARS! O perfumes! O night!

In the grey cedar crests, from the blue fir-trees of the Kronian hill, the owls flapped gabbling; among the fields of mournful olives the cicadas called; over the fragments of fallen marble, crushing the wild thyme, the fire-flies flashed; and on the verandah of the Hôtel de France, the scintillation of her diamonds harmonising equally with the heavens as with the earth, Dorinda, Lady Gaiheart was finishing a tale.

" He then walked off with her," she said, " in an appalling pair of old black slippers."

" He didn't run! "

" Why should he? Men seldom run away with girls. Not in these days."

Miss O'Brookomore looked relieved.

" I always think of Europa," she said.

" That comes from chattering so much about farms."

" With daughters of your own I was determined to consult you."

" I never bothered. They were just a nest of sisters, until one by one, alas, without requiring my advice, they deserted the family tree."

> " Her hour of love,
> How soon it passed!
> It passed ere Mary knew.

And that is the worst of all these rash marriages."

" I fear the Arbanels are already getting fidgety."

" She was crying so much at dinner, poor thing."

" He was telling me they propose to plant a bed of

violets, big white single ones, on the Acropolis, to
the glory of the delicate and individual artiste, *Arne*
—the ' only ' Lady Teazle of our time—in the presence of the *corps diplomatique* and the king and
queen."

" Tears ! "

" Toilettes ! "

" Speeches ! "

" I expect so ! "

Miss Dawkins dropped a sigh.

" Where's Troy ? " she said, wheeling round in her
chair.

" You surely don't think they're there ! "

Lady Dorinda looked reserved.

" I must rejoin my friends," she murmured. " In a
few minutes we're all going over to the ruins."

Miss O'Brookomore lifted up her eyes.

" I shall stay where I am for the new girl dancer,"
she devoutly mumbled.

" Is she one of the Sophonisba set ? "

" Mrs. Viviott found her . . . whirling to herself
among the Treasuries."

" At Tanagra," Miss Dawkins said, " she was
balancing herself, not long ago, in the village street.
I was obliged to interrupt her to ask if a smart fair
woman with an elderly, stoutish man had been seen
that way: S-s-s-s-h! she said. In the evening when the
peacocks dance . . ."

" I should be afraid of her ! "

" She is really wildly pretty."

" Those deep wonder-rings about her eyes are quite
unholy."

" At dinner Mrs. Viviott sat like a player with an
unsatisfactory hand at cards."

" I hate all ingratitude," Miss O'Brookomore
observed. " In Biography, of course, one sees so
much of it. . . ."

" Tell me! How is *it* getting on? "

" Gaps! Gaps! ! Gaps! ! ! "

" There are bound to be a few. "

" Did you ever meet Max Metal? " Miss Dawkins asked.

" No, never. "

" Or Nodo Vostry? "

" I don't remember him. "

" Or Harry Strai? "

" I'm sure I never did! "

" Why? . . ."

" In my opinion their books for girls are full of unsound advice. "

" I'm glad I can still sometimes drug my senses with a book, " Lady Dorinda exclaimed.

" Unluckily, racing round as I do, I very rarely find a chance. "

" You must have met with some adventures by the way. "

Miss Dawkins mixed herself a sombre liqueur.

" I had a good time in Smyrna, " she drowsily declared.

" Only there? "

" Oh, my dears, I'm weary of streets; so weary! "

" And have you never found any trace——? "

" At Palermo, once. . . . I was wandering in the Public Gardens before the hotel, amid blown bus tickets and autumn leaves, when I thought I saw them. Father, anyway. He was standing at an open window of an eau-de-Nil greenhouse. He looked very much younger—altered almost to be a boy. I stood and stared. He smiled. I believe I spoke. And then, before I was able to realise it, I was inside his dark front hall. . . ."

" Who was he? "

" I can only tell you he was a dear thing. I shall hope to meet him in heaven. "

Mrs. Arbanel swooped up lightly.

" I respond to the sound of the sea," she said, " and the tinkle of ice! "

" Let me make you a Cherry Cobbler."

" After interviewing a temporary-maid there's nothing I'd like *more!* "

" Are you satisfied? "

" Is one ever——"

" Still, if she understands hair! "

" That is all she seemed to follow."

" She'll do, I'm sure, for Sparta."

Miss O'Brookomore unfurled her fan.

" Frankly, I rather shrink from Sparta," she said.

" What is there to take one there? "

" I really forget—I believe there's a crouching Venus."

" What does Mr. Arbanel say? "

" He doesn't say anything. He leaves me to go alone."

" What? Isn't he going at all? "

" When the weather is milder he may."

" A man will have his comforts," Lady Dorinda affirmed.

" I long to hear about your new home."

" . . . Oh well. . . . It's quite a clever little house. . . . Five bedrooms. . . ."

" Modest."

" If you would care to see the plans——"

" My dear, there's no hurry," Miss Dawkins said. " Any-old-time will do."

Miss O'Brookomore turned her head stiffly towards the stars.

On all sides through the dusk, intermingling with faint nocturnal noises, rose up a sound of kisses.

She shivered as she felt something touch her own exceedingly sensitive skin.

" Where have you been, Mabel? " she asked.

" Writing letters. I've been describing the Temples
to mum."

" Writing letters," Mrs. Arbanel said. " I think it
must be an Olympic Game."

" Why, what? "

" Do you ask me for the rules? "

" How should I know—the rules? "

" They're really very simple. . . . You sit two at
a table. A young man, perhaps, and a chit of a girl.
With a piece of plate-glass in between. And then,
when you've drummed with your fingers and played
with your pen, you shuffle with your feet, and you
throw dying glances over the top."

Miss Collins challenged.

" . . . Prove it! " she said.

" Wild girl! You surely don't suppose I'm going
to prove it? "

" Why, I was sitting with a widow! "

Miss Dawkins speared herself a cherry.

" Oh, for a quiet corner! "

" First, Mrs. Lawson's guest is going to dance."

" Who, exactly, is she? "

" She's a pupil of Tasajara, Gerald."

Miss O'Brookomore's nose grew long.

" I never heard of her," she said.

" Oh, she's a study, Gerald."

" One sees so many artists here——"

" With a water-colour in the Academy. Some people
seem to think it permissible to look a little mad and
to behave as if they *really* were. . . ."

" I heard the flowers scream as I picked them! "
Mrs. Erso-Ennis was saying as she scattered a shower
of blossoms upon the floor.

" If it's to be Botticelli——" Miss O'Brookomore
complained.

Mrs. Erso-Ennis looked indignant.

"Botticelli! . . . I invented the whole thing just now."

" How could you! "

" It's the *Hesitation of Klytemneſtra*. The poor Queen, you see, cannot quite bring herself to kill the King, and while he sleeps she performs a suite of intereſting, *idyllic* poses over him with a knife."

" Better wait, Gerald," Miss Collins advised.

Mrs. Erso-Ennis flung a few laſt leaves of roses.

" Oh! Think of the earwigs! "

" In these old-fashioned places one should only wear short skirts."

" At the summer sales in Athens," Miss Dawkins seraphically said, " I picked up a regular siren's gown. . . . Looped up upon one side to reveal the knee."

" What you have now, if one may say so, is also very original."

" It doesn't fit. But it isn't meant to," Miss Dawkins replied.

Mrs. Erso-Ennis direﬆed her eyes to the room.

On a couch, deﬆined to be the royal bed, a young woman, evidently a prima donna, was caressing rapturously her little boy.

" My son," she was saying, " my opera . . . x! Opera . . . xx ! My Johannes . . . !! My *bébé!* . . ."

" She muﬅ be removed, I fear."

" And there're some horrid arrivals, too."

For those with ears fine enough Miss Collins caused an innocent bud to wail.

" Oh, Gerald," she said, " who do yóu think is here? "

" Not——! "

" He's in the bus, dearie! "

" My poor puss . . . You've turned quite pale."

" Oh, the shock to me, Gerald! . . ."

" You look so tired, dear . . . so sad and so worn out."

" It's because I'm dead beat, Gerald."

"Feel faint, at all?"

"No—but I've never felt like this before, Gerald.
. . . You little know how I feel—I could not have
believed it was possible."

XIX

" SIXTEEN of them," she counted, " and a diamond drop! "

" *Au revoir.* Until to-night."

" Oh, the rush! "

" You're ready? Packed——"

" All I dare. I could hardly bring away my big box —the one with the furs and flannels! . . ."

" You'll need your passport."

" It's lost."

" Lost! "

" Gerald muſt have burnt it, she says, among her papers. She's everlaſtingly burning things. She lights her fire in the evening juſt as she bolts her door. . . . And then she burns things, and dreams things, and pokes things, and mutters things—*l'heure exquise,* she calls it."

". . . Very likely."

" I've an idea it's rheumatics, poor soul. . . ."

" M-a-b-e-l! " Miss O'Brookomore called again.

" I muſt go to her. . . ."

" One kiss! "

" O-o-o-o-h! "

" Another! "

" Not till we get in the train."

" *Cara mia dolce!* "

" And thanks very much for the diamonds," Miss Collins replied.

Loitering up and down the hall among the tubs of orange-trees—now in full flower—Miss O'Brookomore was growing ruffled.

" It's charming! " she said. " It appears he's on our floor."

" Oh no, he's not, Gerald . . . He's on the floor
above. Right overhead, dearie."

Miss O'Brookomore looked away.

" There are people, I find, who have no heads,"
she ruefully remarked. " They've lost them."

" I don't know why you should dislike him, Gerald.
Because he doesn't you. He calls you the pretty
priestess. . . ."

The Biographer unbent a shade.

" Does he? " she inquired.

" Are you going for your walk? "

" I told Miss Dawkins we would help her to find
her parents."

" It's too late to go far, dearie."

" Nonsense! "

" How can she expect to find them, Gerald, sitting
all day with a Gin Daisy or a Brandy Flip? Tell me
that now! "

" Anyway we might take a turn round the garden.
. . . If they're here at all I expect they're in the
shrubbery."

It was the hour when, to a subtle string band, the
bustling waiters would be bringing tea.

" Oh, the Sophonisbas, Gerald!—some of them."

Their tired, art-stained faces turned towards a little
Saint with rose lips, eyes and crown, Mrs. Erso-Ennis
and Mrs. Viviott were overwhelming with attentions
the pupil of Tasajara.

" Mercy, Gerald! "

" Hein! "

" There's bound to be heart-burnings, Gerald."

" . . . I shouldn't wonder."

" And there's your God-of-the-Wood, dearie. . . ."

Miss O'Brookomore changed her course.

" Not before the windows! " she exclaimed.

" Olympia for love, Gerald."

" Olympia for tattle."

" Oh, Gerald! I mean to fling in my lot with a crowd of absolute strangers. . . ."

" What! "

" Love isn't logical, Gerald."

" Alas! "

" Oh! Gerald! "

" What has your friend a year? "

" How should I know, dearie? "

" It's important to know."

" It's better to be poor—I've often heard mum say—than to have a soft seat in hell."

" An Italian is very easily enamoured."

" I love his dark plastered hair, Gerald. I think it quite sweet."

" It isn't enough. . . ."

" He's like somebody from Marathon, Gerald! "

" You're young yet."

" Oh, Gerald, when he sang the Shepherd-Star-Song from *Tannhäuser* and gave that shake! . . . You can't think how much I was moved . . . How I responded. . . ."

" His *catches from Butterfly* would get on my nerves! "

" Had I nerves like you I couldn't rest without a passport."

" It's tiresome, I admit."

" It's that, dearie. . . ."

" Don't despond! "

" Suppose they detained you, Gerald ? "

" Why, we'd sing a duet together."

" Wait till there's a warrant! "

" A warrant? "

" Sometimes I think of the prison we saw in Patras, with the prisoners all thrusting their heads out between the bars."

" Don't, Mabel! "

" Oh, Gerald! It's a climax and a perfect semax, dear."

" We're not helping Miss Dawkins at all! "

" You go one way, Gerald. And I'll go another. . . ."

Miss O'Brookomore glanced behind her.

Already the sun-topped hills were lost in lilac towards the ground. It would soon be night.

" Very well," she murmured, letting fall a glove; " we will meet again at dinner."

X X

"MABEL! Mabel! Mabel! Mabel!
Mabel! Mabel! Mabel! Mabel!"

X X I

HOTEL CENTRAL,
CONSTITUTIONAL PLACE,
ATHENS.

Saturday.

DEAR GERALD,—I was married this morning and we leave to-morrow early for Corfu don't worry about me dear I'm alright O darling I'm the happiest girl in Greece I wore my little amber tricorne satin cap dear and Oio gave me the violets I shall get my trousseau bit by bit I suppose as we go along I had wanted rather badly to be married in the Kapnikaraea but it was a Registry after all good-bye now Gerald and take care of yourself dear do in haste yrs always affectionately

MABINA PASTORELLI.

P.S.—I laughed the whole time the priest who married us would keep whisking his skirt.

Mrs. Cowsend is here still Old ox.

Oio says if I write another word he'll pour all my ink away.

INCLINATIONS

PART II

" *Do you remember that picture of Jesus that poor Miss Turner used to show us?*" The Honeysuckle—D'ANNUNZIO

I

THE sunlight passing through the glass candlestick by the bedside shot out its rays towards her threefold and woke her with a start.

—Bovon! Home!

—The Countess gaped.

There was the fine old carpet stained with tulips, and the familiar text upon the lightly figured walls, and the dress bust in the corner behind the *causeuse* that cast its consoling outline so effectively at night, and the medicine chest above the rocking-chair, with the sage-chinoiseries on top, that would swing their heads in the affirmative almost for a glance—which responsiveness had been known to work like a spell upon certain sensitive natures in more instances than one.

The Countess sat up.

" Bianca! " she called.

By the wide " Elysium " bed stood a bassinet tricked in bows.

" Bianca, Borghese, Nancy, Sabina! "

From the doorway came a whirl of skirts—a croon —and Mrs. Collins entered.

" While the mother was asleep the granny came and stole the darling, and whipped down the corridor, out into the garden, and round and round the house."

The Countess held out her arms.

" Oh, my honey bear! "

" Don't, Mabel. You'll kill it."

" Oh, the interesting little pickle! Oh, the Roman rascal! . . . Poveretta! *Ah, Dio!* "

Mrs. Collins considered her daughter.

" . . . There's something I want to say to you,"
she said.

" Yes, what is it? "

" Everyone's inquiring for the Count—all the
Bovon busybodies."

" Kra, kra, Mrs. Rook."

" They're concerned he hasn't come! "

" It's the Vintage. Directly that's over he will."
Mrs. Collins beamed affectionately.

" In any case," she murmured, " I mean to give a
small dinner for you, and that, my dear, directly."

" Oh, good gracious! "

" I shall take you the rounds."

" Visits! "

" Rectory, Patchpole, Rising-Proudly."
The Countess lay back.

" I wish to offend the Warristons," she said, " and
Napier—and the gorgeous Mrs. Lampsacus. Oh, and
a whole pack besides! "

" Napier has asked for you repeatedly—almost
every day."
The Countess averted her face.

" I dare say," she said, " when he first heard of my
marriage he was frightfully, frightfully upset? "

" Not so very. For five minutes he seemed incon-
solably unhappy—and then he smiled! "

" Providentially! "

" Oh, my dear, you can't think how I've prayed
for you all this while."

" Of course it's Catholicism now with both of us."

" It must be so strange."

" The child was baptized in Santa Maria in Cos-
medin—she's been baptized twice, poor dear."

" For sake of ceremony? "

" At Santa Maria it was on account of *them*. It's
their parish. But afterwards I took her round quietly
and had it done in St. Peter's."

" You obtained your audience? "

" At the very last minute."

" Well! "

" Oh, well! I was prepared to do anything. Naturally! I'm sure! Oh, good gracious!"

" Was the child with you? "

" Oh, she waved her fat little wrinkled wrists—and smacked his Holiness—mother's Bianca did! My blessing! "

" As a family I gather you're inclined to be devout."

" Of course the dowager's goody. She never goes out without a string of nuns."

" Is there any reason for it! "

" I couldn't say. Often she'll kneel in the garden. Or on the stairs. Or in a shop. Or on a tram. Whenever she wants to she'll kneel! "

" She appears to be insatiable."

" It doesn't affect me. . . . On Sunday, as a rule, I've a box at the Argentina or a sofa stall at the Alcaza."

" Oio too? "

" Occasionally he comes."

" And when he doesn't! "

" There's always someone."

Mrs. Collins looked round.

" Wow! Here comes a big black doggie! "

" Daisy—my *dear!* . . ."

" Papa's waiting breakfast. He wants you to boil him an egg."

" Tell him I'll come."

" He's grumbling so. According to him, nobody cares at all whether he lives or dies. . . ."

Mrs. Collins raised a hand to her curls!

" Oh, poor granny! " she murmured as she withdrew.

Daisy subdued her ways.

" How did your little child sleep? " she asked.

" Well."

" Do you regret Rome? "

" It's a joy to have no mosquitoes! "

" That's not so bad as snakes. Suppose you had married an Indian."

" Thank goodness."

" Tell me about the Marriage State. Is it what you expected it to be? "

The Countess threw up her eyes.

" I didn't expect anything," she said.

" Let me look at your wedding-ring, Mabel, may I? Only for a minute."

" What do you want it for? "

" I won't eat it. "

" There's nothing very novel in a wedding-ring. Wait till you see my pearls? "

" Where are they ? "

" With my other jewels. . . ."

" I should like to borrow some."

" I dare say."

" Do you know of anyone likely to suit me? "

" A lover? "

" Nobody, Mab! . . ."

" I'm sorry."

" . . . Mabsey? "

" Oh, have *patience*."

" It's a pity the Bovon boys are so rabbity—they're for ever with their noses down a hole."

The Countess fluttered her eyelids.

" How are the dear ferrets? " she asked.

" All right."

" And the farm? "

" All right."

" Any changes? "

" Only in the house. Olga and Minnie have gone. Olga said she was glad to go. She said nothing would induce her to stop."

" Is Queen as queer as ever? "

" Queerer."

" Impossible."

" He and Mrs. Prixon don't get on. What Spicer endures at meals—talk about silence! And next week there'll be a fresh footman. It's funny the effect it always has upon me—it's something no one could explain! "

" In days gone by," the Countess said, " the pantry with a stranger in it was as dull as any drawing-room. . . ."

Daisy wriggled.

" Shall you ever forget the time Frank flew at you and clapped his hands? You were reaching for the pickled walnuts."

" Mercy! "

" And I was steadying the table for you as you got on it. Suddenly he . . . sprang."

The Countess looked vexed.

" Now you've scared the child."

" Oh, the poor wee sweetie! "

" Zito! Zito! Ah, Madonna!"

" I'll take her a turn in her little pram if she likes. Just the Aunt and the Niece together."

" Stay within call."

" We'll peep in the larder, shall we, Babs? There may be a bare birdie dangling there, and perhaps a little white corpse."

The Countess rang.

" Better wheel her under the yew-trees," she said, " out of the wind. And don't upset the pram! "

II

" WHEN the crow's-feet come
  And twirl about my eyes,
  And my lips turn pale . . .
  And my cheeks sink in,
  Oh, say, wilt thou love me then? "

Divorcing itself from the piano, the voice trailed
magnificently away, ignoring altogether the tragical
scepticism of the accompaniment.

The listeners looked shrewd.

Above the little party rose the Chase, dark and eerie
in the autumn sun.

" Wilt thou love me truly when my hair has flown,
  When my teeth have fallen
  And my hands are wan?
  Oh, say, wilt thou love me then?

  I will love you (said he) for ever and ever,
  For ever and ever and ever and ever,
  Amen."

" Bis. Bis."

" It's the air from *Cunigonde*," Mrs. Collins explained,
coming to the window.

" We were wondering what it was."

" In the death scene she introduces parts of it again
in her delirium."

Mr. Collins frowned ferociously.

" Hag! " he muttered.

" By-and-by I will rattle you some of the ballet-
music from *The Judgment of Paris*," the Countess said.

" Oh, the valse Paris sings—! He and the Three
Graces. —Da-da-da-di-da! "

" If only the Chase were rid of! " Mrs. Collins
complained.

" Has anyone been to view it? "

" Madame La Chose had the impudence to come. . . .
Queen came to me one morning with the news that
a lady with *an order* desired to see over the house. I
guessed by his tone there was something extraordinary,
and on going into the drawing-room there was Madame
La Chose."

" Did you show her round? "

" Oh, my dear . . . yes. We even went so far as to
fix some of the rooms."

" Mercy! "

" I must say I thought her rather charming."

" Would she care to take it? "

" Without the meadow she might. . . ."

" It shows her sense. Land nowadays is much too
impoverishing."

" Her idea is to revive *Basset.* . . ."

" York being mainly a military town it would
probably be a boon."

" In any case the decision, it seems, does not rest
with herself alone, and she has asked to come back
again."

" My dear, if she does . . .! " Mr. Collins said.

The Countess caressed her child.

" Mother, oh! . . . Poor mother, oh! Give a kiss
to mother, oh! She says she *won't!* Oh, good gracious! . . ."

" I'm unhappy about her nurse," Mrs. Collins said.
" A trustworthy person is everything."

The Countess crossed herself dejectedly.

" Oh, when I think of her nurses! . . ." she said.
" At first I had a Roman one for the child. She was a
regular contadina—La Marietta! La Mariuccia! But

she was so dirty! . . . A regular slut she was . . .
she wasn't even clean. And too *sans gêne*, by far. Bianca's
most impressionable. Nothing escapes her little eyes.
. . . So I sent her away and took a stranded Irish-
woman instead. Oh she was a terror. ' I always try to
please everybody,' she said, ' and I'm sorry I can't
you! ' But it was the tone of voice, dear, in which she
said it more than the actual words. . . . *Sapristi!*
However, one or two of them I liked. There was a
Swiss. . . . If she hadn't been so vague. One night,
my dear, she overturned the pram right in the middle
of the Corso! It might have killed the child. . . ."

" Are there no nice gardens that she could play
in? "

" There are. But it's a climb to get to them! "

" I'd an idea that Rome was flat. . . ."

Mr. Collins handled meditatively his cigar.

" What of the seven hills? "

" Ah, Charles! "

" Seven little hilly-willies! "

" I suppose the surrounding scenery is."

" You'd love Frascati. The land falls and rises, falls
and rises. Oh, it's ever so dear."

" I've a letter of yours from there."

" Did you keep the Greek ones? "

" I kept them all."

" I should like you to show me Gerald's."

Mrs. Collins looked away.

" Had I known the sort of woman she was! But
living as we do one never hears a thing."

" You had read her books."

" Ah, don't, Mabel."

" You liked her style."

" I'm told she's a noted Vampire."

" Who ever said so? "

" Some friend of hers—in Chelsea."

" What do Vampires do? "

" What don't they! "

" Of course she was always bizarre."

" Who could have foreseen her secret schemes?"
The Countess grew wan.

" Some of her literary secrets," she said, " were
simply disgusting."

" Dissolute! "

" She'd force them from printers'-devils."

" Mabel."

" Was her last remarkable? "

" . . . The Londonisms! The Cockney! The slang!"

" She was a little too fond of her freedoms. . . ."

" Boys with their tutors. Girls with their mothers."

" According to you, Charles," Mrs. Collins said
with umbrage, " I might be unwilling to chaperon the
girls instead of fretting my life out in a hole like
Bovon! "

Mr. Collins quelled the rising storm.

" There, Isabel," he said, with a glance towards
the house, " if I thought we'd be here another summer
I'd get new sun-blinds, dear . . . but what's the good?
Just leaving them as fixtures."

III

" QUEEN," Daisy said to him one day. " If a fair young gentleman with large blue eyes should call and ask for Mrs. Collins you're to say she has gone out. . . . But he'll find the Sisters in. The Aunt and the Niece will be in the Yew-tree walk. With the Mother."

" Very good, miss."

" And, Queen——! "

" Fie, miss."

" Bashful? "

" I'm surprised."

The Yew-tree walk, the cause of so much gloom, ran ring-like about the house, to meet again before the drawing-room windows above the main road, where a marble nymph with a worn flat face dispensed water, rather meanly, out of a cornucopia into a trough full of green scum.

On a garden swing near by the Countess was swaying fitfully to and fro.

" Units, tens, hundreds, thousands. . . . Tens of thousands. . . . Hundreds of thousands! *Units*——" she was murmuring cryptically to herself with half rapt looks.

" Shall I push you, Mabs? "

" No. Ta."

" To prevent the perspiration? . . ."

The Countess sighed.

" I'd sell my soul for an ice."

" A strawberry. . . ."

" Or vanilla."

" I told Queen we'd be in."

" Where's mum? "

" Upstairs. Trying on. It's the armpits again. . . ."

" Goodness! "

" Do you know the new snook, Mab? "

" Is there one? "

" A beauty."

" Not before Bianca."

" It's a pity the child's so young. . . ."

" Carissima! "

" Her little amours. Tell me about them. . . . Has she many? "

" She makes new conquests from day to day."

" Tell me things, Mabel."

" What things ? "

" All sorts of things."

" Really! "

" In Italy have they Brussels sprouts—like we have? "

" In Italy they've everything," the Countess replied.

" Can *he* speak English? "

" Fluently. Oh! . . ."

" Swear? "

" Certainly."

" A foreign husband wouldn't suit me—not if he stayed abroad."

" No? "

" Mabsey! "

" What is it ?"

" Nothing. In the afternoon the yew-trees turn quite blue."

" The quietness. . . . You can almost hear the clouds go by."

" Let's all lie down on the grass as if we were dead."

" It's too hot for rough games."

" I shouldn't wonder if it rained."

" Pitter-patter! "

" Every now and then she turns her great beseech-

ing eyes at me and whispers ' Aunt.' Aunt! she says,
come back with me to Rome. Come! And let me have
no nonsense now. Oh, Blanche, I reply . . . it's my
poverty, dear. But what can one do on a penny a
week? "

" Papa, poor-old-gentleman, was saying how you
should be going to school."

" To school ?"

" That was what he said."

" He can't force me to if I choose to remain un-
lettered."

" It's for the companionship there'd be."

" Never."

" School isn't so dreadful, Daisy."

" Nothing would induce me to go."

The Countess rocked drowsily.

" At York Hill," she said, " looking back on it all,
I seem to have enjoyed everything. Even the walks!
Oh. . . . Often we'd go round the city walls . . . or
along the Ouse perhaps out to Bishopsthorp and there
we'd take the ferry. All we screaming girls and gover-
nesses in mid-river. . . . Oh, good gracious! "

" I remember the letters you sent from there. And
the complaints that were in them! "

" And in the evening of course there'd be Prepara-
tion. . . . Oh—! That was always a time for mischief.
. . . One of us, Annie Oldport perhaps ('Any-Old-
Port' we used to call her), would give her next neighbour a squeeze, with orders to pass it on. How we did
thrill when little Evelyn Rise, one of the new kids,
took hold of the Principal herself. 'What are you
doing to me, Evelyn?' 'I'm pinching you, Mrs.
Whewell.' 'Are you indeed! Well, then——' And
she dealt her a blow on the ears before us all. . . .
Oh, Evelyn Rise! She was a little silly. . . . She
hadn't any brains at all."

" No brains, Mabsey? "

" No," the Countess crooned. " She hadn't any."

" There! Queen's beckoning. . . ."

" Imbecile."

" It may be him."

" Who, him? "

" Your husband."

" Hardly."

" Your Excellency. . . ."

" Here I am."

" There's a person at the gate."

" Open it then."

" I fear it's a trouble."

" Why, who is it? "

" A stranger."

" It's perhaps the Count."

" It looks to be like a woman."

" The Sisters have gone away, Queen. . . ."

" Does she refuse her name? "

" Quite."

" A foreigner? "

" And *so* suspicious."

" The Aunt's away from home. . . ."

" I've often heard of the Black Hand, your Excellence, and lately I've noticed chalk-marks on the gate."

" *Ah, Dio!* "

" Is there no gentleman, Queen? "

" No, miss."

" It may be Jocaster Gisman."

" What Gisman? "

" The accomplice of Bessie Bleek that suffocated seven little boys and girls and was tried and executed for doing so. . . ."

" Oh, heavens! "

" Jocasta got herself off at the last Assizes—there were extenuating circumstances the judge said—and so he forgave her."

" *Bô!* "

" Mercy! "

" My dear, it's me," Miss Dawkins said, peering through the fence.

" That is so," she added, with an impetuous bound.

" Oh, the child! "

" Her aversion—I should say it's a flea," Miss Dawkins commented, subsiding upon the swing.

The Countess pushed it.

" Of all the surprises! " she said.

" I refused to give my name because it makes me cry to say it. I break down. . . ."

" You've not found them then? "

" No, dear."

" I imagined you in the I's."

" I sail for India within a week."

" The cathedral cities bring you north? "

" York and—they rhyme together . . . the first few letters. And I cling to every straw."

" Courage."

" Call me Ola."

" Ola."

" When I was in the Holy City I saw you one day."

" When was it? "

" During Passion Week."

" Were you with friends? "

" I scarcely knew anybody. I had an introduction to Countess Roderigos Samurez Dalmatia, but as I didn't like the look of her I didn't make use of it."

" I've heard of her often," the Countess said, " through the Grittis."

" Besides a letter to Princess Anna di Portici. . . ."

" Her house is occupied at present by the Marquesa Refoscosca! "

" And a card for Monsignor Ferrol."

" Old *débauché.*"

" Well . . . and how's the pleasant husband? "

" Oio? He's in Orvieto still. It's the Vintage. . . ."
Miss Dawkins looked devout.

" In my opinion," she said, " Orvieto wine is superior to the best Castelli."

" You should have a dozen, dear, of our Old-Old-Old—the *Certosa*, if I knew where it would find you."

" I'm at the ' Wheat Sheaf.' "

" What? "

" Yes. I thought I'd repose myself there until I start."

" If you've made no other plans you'll just stay and rest with us until your ship sails."

" It's kind of you to ask me, but what will your kindred say? "

" My dear, they'll love to have you. And mum will tell you so herself. She's with the tailor now."

" It's the arm-pits! . . ."

" This is my little sister."

" And is that your babe? "

" Isn't she a darling! "

" Tell me, Contessa—have I changed since Greece?"

" I should say you're a little stouter."

" Ireland makes one sloppy."

" And I? . . ."

" My dear, you don't look fifteen."

" She's seventeen," Daisy said, " or thereabouts. And the child will soon be two."

" Were *I* to have a child I should be just like a lunatic," Miss Dawkins declared.

" With your tender heart I wonder you don't marry."

" Marriages are made in heaven, you know."

" Let me find you someone! "

" You, my dear. . . . I've a sprig of the real Chinduai charm-flower from the Malay. I've only to wear it! "

" Why don't you then? "

" Voyagers lose their illusions somehow. . . .
They lose them. . . ."

" Take off your hat and really rest! "

" Shall I? "

" Do."

" It's pretty peaceful here anyway," Miss Dawkins
said, with a sigh, her eyes riveted upon the cornucopia
of the niggardly nymph.

" Is it iron? " she inquired.

" What, the water? It's always rather brown. . . ."
Miss Dawkins pressed a hand to her hip.

" It looks like a stream of brandy," she said, going
off into a laugh.

IV

THE " intimate " dinner arranged by Mrs. Collins in honour of her daughter proved to be a large one.

A dinner of twenty at a table to hold eighteen.

As course succeeded course came the recurring pressure of a forward footman's knee.

Half asleep holding a shell-shaped spoon Miss Dawkins explored a sauce-boat as though it had been an Orient liner.

" Yes Mr. Collins."

" No Mr. Collins."

" Aha Mr. Collins."

(" *Thanks!*")

" Yes, God is Love, Mr. Collins, and I'm sure they couldn't help it! " she said at last.

" *Già! Già!* " the Countess struck in, allegro, across a bank of flowers.

" Well, here's health, old girl. The very best! "

" And success to you . . . and may the gods permit you to find them! "

" If you ask me, I think it silly to find people," the Countess's former inamorato declared. " I don't want to find anybody! . . ."

" No doubt you've tried clairvoyance? " the Member for Bovon asked.

" Indeed. And palmistry, and phrenology, and cards, and sand. . . ."

" Well? "

" Oh well . . ." Miss Dawkins said, " I was warned I'd marry a septuagenarian within the forbidden degrees and never know it! . . . Helios, Mene, Tetragrammaton! "

" Have you looked by the Rhine at all? "

" Where haven't I? "

" Courage! " the Countess crooned.

" I've a presentiment they're in India. Somehow I connect my mother's fair hair with Bombay. . . ."

Mr. Collins raised his glass.

" Then here's to Bombay! "

" Oh, nectar, Mr. Collins! Show me the cork—I always like to see the cork—! And my dear father was like me there. ' The cork, Ola,' he'd say. ' A bottle of wine is nothing without the cork.' "

" The Count! " Napier Fairmile with generosity proposed.

The Countess shrugged her shoulders.

" I'd a letter from Italy this morning," she said. " It appears in Rome all the roads are up."

" Up? "

" There's no getting by the Corso at all. Persons going to the Villa Borghese have to pass by the Via Babuino. Oh, good gracious! And my friend says the heat! It's a grill. Everyone is away still, of course, in villegiatura. But even so! At the Baths at Lucca she says she hears they're burning. . . ."

" Well, it was pretty warm, dear, in Greece," Miss Dawkins said. " The day of the accident I shall never forget how very hot it was! "

" At Salamis. . . ."

" Ah, don't."

" Was there ever such a misfortune? "

" There seems to have been some inexcusable carelessness."

" There are certain things we shall never know," the Countess murmured, " but I've sometimes thought that shot was aimed at me! "

Mrs. Collins shook her fan.

" The crazy people Mabel met in Greece! "

" Both Dorinda, Lady Gaiheart and Mrs. Arbanel

are parting from their husbands, so I understand."

" Poor Lady Dorinda! I fear she has fallen between two stools," the Member for Bovon said.

" And a piano. And a waste-paper basket, if reports are true," the Countess replied.

" Did you meet the Viviotts at all? "

" There was a Mrs. Viviott," Miss Dawkins said— " a nervy, pretty thing. She and a Mrs. Erso-Ennis. . . . Inseparable. And always quarrelling."

" They're reconciled again. And are gone to live at Birdingbury—quite near us—because it sounds Saxon..."

" Really, Viola? "

Mrs. Newhouse, *née* Neffal, nodded.

" Anything *fair!* " the Countess crooned. " Even a dancer."

" La Tasajara? I saw her one night. I believe it was at Astrea Fortri's house in Pall Mall. . . ."

" Such a little starved-soul ghost-face. Like a little thin-pale-pinched St. John," the Countess critically said.

" In the end she became indispensable to Miss O'Brookomore," Miss Dawkins stated.

" With Gerald? "

" Oh, that woman." Mrs. Collins shuddered.

" They tell me she's to chaperon an Eton boy straight to Tibet."

Miss Dawkins became abstracted.

" She evidently likes them young and fresh! " she observed.

The Countess started.

" What is it? " she asked.

" Come quickly! " her sister said. " The child's in her cups."

" Bianca is? "

" What have you been giving her? "

" It's only the little hiccoughs. . . ."

" Remember you weren't to come in till dessert."

"During the Stratford mulberries papa said I might. You've had them."

"Just look at her waist!"

"Now I'm here, mayn't I stop?"

"If you like to display your natural gifts," Mr. Collins murmured, "you may."

"You can't do much on an empty stomach."

"You can recite, I suppose," the Countess said.

"Recite? It's always an effort for me to recite. . . . I feel struck dumb in society."

"Remember Rome!" the Countess warned. "We've no use for shyness there."

"On his tombstone in the grass,
Record of him he was an ass,
He stretched out his neck and he flicked up his ears
And bid farewell to this valley of tears.

He lay himself down on a bed to die,
Right in a flower-bed himself he lay,
He stiffened his back and he whisked round his tail
And bid farewell to this earthly vale.

—On his tombstone in the grass,
Record of him he was an *Ass*."

"Charming!"

"How very, very, very, very vulgar!" the Countess frowned.

"Was it the devil, my dear?"

Mrs. Collins rose.

"Gentlemen," she murmured, "*à tout à l'heure!*"

"Let's all go into the garden, Mabsey."

"There's no moon."

"There are stars."

Miss Dawkins peered out.

"It's dark and like Gethsemane," she said.

[Chapter IV appears here as it stood in the edition of 1916.]

[Another, dated "Rome, April 1925," is now printed for the first time.]

IV

THE "intimate" dinner arranged by Mrs. Collins in honour of her elder daughter promised to be a large one. Covers for twenty guests, at a table to hold eighteen, insured nevertheless a touch of welcome snugness. In the crepuscular double drawing-room, commanding the eternal moors,* county society, as it assembled, exchanged cheery greetings. It was indeed to all intents the Doncaster Meeting lot.

Discanting away from homely topics, Sir Harry Ortop had just seen a fox, it seemed, crossing Cockaway Common, while Miss Rosalba Roggers had passed a traction-engine in the Rectory lane. "Horrid thing; but the Scarboro' road is really a disgrace," she pronounced, turning her attention to an angular beauty clad in sugary pink and a crown of birds' feathers.

Holding forth in a quizzical, hoarse-sweet voice, she was arraigning her husband with indescribable archness: "He always gets into his carriage first, and then half shuts the door on you!"

Momentous in his butlerhood, Queen, supported by an extra footman, announced each new advent with an air of serene detachment.

Mr. Napier Fairmile, Miss Nespole——

Entering on the heels of the former inamorato of the Countess sailed a mite of a woman enveloped fancifully in a fairy-hued cashmere shawl. The Cyclopean chatelaine of Cupingforth Castle, and one of the wealthiest women in the Riding, she was held, by local

* "Finely situated on the edge of the moors."—*Vide* Estate Agents' Announcements.

opinion, to be eccentric for preferring to live all alone, which may possibly have had its dangers for a person of her condition and sex; nevertheless, on occasion, to convince an intrusive stranger she had a male in the house, she would discharge a cartridge out of window, and knot her hair across her chin in front in a thick cascade to imitate *a beard*.

Lady Watercarriage, The Hon. Viola West-Wind, Captain Margaret-Baker——

Quite re-vitalised, performing her duties, Mrs. Collins circulated smilingly here and there. Throwing a veil of glamour upon each guest, she had introduced Miss Dawkins twice as " The Great Traveller."

" I ain't going back to Australia not yet awhile. That is so! " Miss Dawkins declared, recognising across the Rector's shoulder in the damp-stained mezzotints upon the walls some views of popular thoroughfares her foot had trodden—Trafalgar Square, the Place de la Concorde, the Piazza Colonna, the Puerta del Sol. " If I don't just spit at them! " she commented, idly opening and closing her fan.

The Farquhar of Farquhar, Mrs. Lampsacus of Gisborough Park——

Already a full quarter-of-an-hour late, they were yet not the last.

Masticating, chewing the air, Mr. Collins appeared to have become involved against his will in the esoteric confidences of a pair of expansive matrons: " In York I saw some very pretty . . . I enquired the price. . . . Would you believe . . . *Need* I say I bought them!"

Delivered from their effusive unbosoming by The Farquhar of Farquhar, Mr. Collins turned away.

Advancing like some marvellous automaton, The Farquhar, known as " Lulu " to all frequenters of the Turf, brought with him an atmosphere of one who had supplied a daughter, or at least a filly, to a Prince of the Blood. Excusing his wife Serafima (a woman for whom undergraduates had shot themselves), he inquired, with a leer, for " la petite Comtesse."

She was looking summery and semi-Southern in an imaginative gown in every shade of white.

" Precious darling! She's only eight months; it's a critical age," she was exclaiming; apropos, doubtless, of her child.

Chatting to a bottle-nosed dowager in garnets and goose-flesh, she appeared indeed even prettier than she was.

Descending on her, The Farquhar was circumvented by Miss Viola West-Wind, a young girl of the County with a little Tatler-tainted face. She was supplying blocks of tickets, it seemed, for *The League of Patriots* ball . . . "*Fancy dress! Everyone to go as animals.*"

Dr. Dee——

It was as much as to say dinner; but an announcement, breathed from Queen, was to fill Mrs. Collins with apprehension.

" There's been a little catastrophe, 'm."

" What, not . . . ? . . . ! . . . ? ? "

" To a cinder, 'm."

In the long low-ceiled dining-room, all in the robust mid-Victorian style, the failure of an *entrée* seemed a more or less trivial thing; in such an environment it is the haunch that matters, it is the loin that tells. . . .

" Even so," Mrs. Collins heard herself murmuring (almost callously) as she gained a chair on The Farquhar's arm—" Even so. The mornings begin to be frosty."

A random word wafting the talk naturally to the subject of foxes.

" Count Pastorelli is fond of hunting? "

But Mrs. Collins presumed a prudent deafness.

Adorned with foreign spring flowers, smart jonquils and early tulips, the table-arrangements left nothing to be desired.

" I could never go to Russia; I turn quite green in
the snow," Miss Dawkins was telling Sir Harry Ortop
of her Odyssey.

" I take it you've tried clairvoyance?" he asked.

" Indeed. And palmistry, and phrenology, and
cards, and sand. . . ."

" Well? "

" Oh well . . ." she replied, regarding a scar on his
third blue chin; " I was warned I'd marry a septuagenarian within the forbidden degrees and never know
it. . . . Helios, Mene, Tetragrammaton! "

" According to my experience, it's a mistake to find
people. I don't want to find anybody. . . ."

Miss Dawkins used her fan.

" I've a presentiment they're in India," she said.
" Somehow I connect my mother's fair hair with
Bombay. . . ."

Owing to the absence of a guest, it was agreeable
to find the Countess in juxtaposition. With the Member for Bovon on her right, her tongue tripped heed-
lessly from Mussolini to Miss Anne : " Poor soul,
she was interred in her lace, with a coin of Greece in
her mouth, and a flask of Chalkis wine, and a tambourine."

A version of the Salamis affair that was new to Miss
Dawkins.

" ——! " she cooed, lifting her eyes in protest to a painting of Mary Marchioness of Jamaica
and Miss Elizabeth Cockduck, of the school of Sir
Thomas Lawrence.

" . . . just as in the Golden Age; and the moon
that night was extra enormous," the Countess broke
off her tale, arrested by a wail of distress from the
direction of the nursery.

The notion that Daisy might be diverting herself
at Bianca's expense caused the Countess to rise.

" Precious darling! *C'est l'heure du berger* for the

child," she exclaimed, directing her steps towards the door.

Traversing the hall, she perceived Daisy in the morning-room examining the visitors' wraps; lifting the fabrics to her nose (much as might a savage), she appeared to be voluptuously revelling in the human odours they exhaled.

" Fie, girl! What are you up to?" her sister asked.

" The Farquhar of Farquhar's muffler, Mabel, has such a funny smell, something between honey and flowers and new goloshes."

" Oh! "

" And Lady Watercarriage's cloak! I don't know what it is, but it's almost overpowering."

" *Santo dio,*" the Countess breathed, lending an ear to the uproar above.

Daisy displayed indifference.

" She's overturned her little Tamara again, I suppose, that's all! ! ! !"

In the shadowy nursery, bafflingly lit by the dancing stars, some romantic fancy, it seemed, had disquieted the child.

On beholding both Mother and Aunt with a radiant light, she crowed, she smiled.

" Bianca . . . Mother's heaven." The Countess hovered.

" From the look in those endless eyes of hers I shouldn't wonder if she hadn't seen the Owl that lived in an Oak.

> There was an owl lived in an oak—
> Whiskey, waskey, weedle;
> And every word he ever spoke
> Was fiddle, faddle, feedle."

" Don't, Daisy! "

" Oh, she loves her little Buen Retiro (when it's dry); her own private corner in Bedfordshire."

X

" Let her be," the Countess answered, availing herself of the opportunity to deck with fresh white and red her constantly piquant face.

" Has anyone cast a doubt on your union, Mab, being legal ? " Daisy asked, surveying with the eyes of a retired bus-horse her sister's comfortable back.

" Don't ask silly questions, Daisy, if you don't want foolish answers," the Countess returned, following in the mirror her infant's yearning glance towards a bespangled negro doll, Topolobampa, Queen of the Sunset Isles.

" 'Cos I s'pose you know that's what Spicer's been tellin' George. . . ."

" George ? "

" The extra footman."

" Oh, good gracious ! "

" Naturally he'll repeat it. It seems he goes all over Yorkshire waiting, but his home-proper is the Capital. Hull, he says, is a dreadful place. No season, and with the morals of Sodom. And, fancy, Mabsey, his brother is the boy from Willinghorse and Wheelits. . . ."

" What ! "

" He aspires to the concert hall, he says, on account of his voice. So we made him sing and I must say his rendering of ' Early one morning before the sun was dawning ' won all our hearts."

The Countess shrugged.

" She wants, I think, to take Topolobampa to bed ! " she irrelevantly exclaimed.

" She'd rather take her old Aunt—eh, chubby ? "

" Madonna, what next ! "

" Her little body, Mab . . . it's as soft as satin ! Oh, it's terrible ! "

" —— . . . ? "

" How arch the puss looks in her little nainsook ! "

" Mind and don't tease her, Daisy," the Countess enjoined as she frisked away.

An odour of meat, wine and flowers hung erotically upon the dining-room air.

" I want my life to be purple—— Never less," Miss Dawkins was assuring the Member for Bovon.

Curtailing their colloquy, the Countess resumed her place.

At a delicate advantage with her newly-geraniumed lips, she was in a mood to enjoy herself.

" Look two to your right; who is she, Countess? " Miss Dawkins asked.

" An immense heiress! Miss Nespole of Cuping-forth."

" My dear, she's the most extraordinarily-looking woman that I ever set eyes on! " Miss Dawkins serenely stated.

Taking umbrage from her stare, Miss Nespole (with the eccentricity permitted to wealth) put out her tongue at her and drew it slowly in again.

" Oh, good gracious! " the Countess exclaimed, shooting a glance towards her father.

Listening to a description of Gleneagles from Lady Watercarriage, he appeared almost to have grown into his chair.

" And from there we went on to a ghastly hotel where *all the bedclothes are grey,*" the peeress fluted, fingering the pearls on her forward-falling shoulders.

The Countess raised a discreet glass of Perrier to her lips.

But as course succeeded course The Farquhar was moved to beg his hostess to allow her younger daughter to join them for the sugared kickshaws at dessert.

A lover of young girls and with a cult for them, he was believed to harbour Satanesque inclinations to-wards the Age of Candour.

" Just for a prune! " he insidiously pressed, brushing a napkin to the spreading branches of his moustache.

319

Miss Dawkins, meanwhile, was becoming blandly
Bacchic.

"Oh, thank you, Member for Bovon, sweetest of
men to me," she exclaimed, addressing him cham-
pagnishly across her friend.

It was towards the close of dessert, just as the ladies
were about to withdraw, that Daisy, clasping Bianca,
chose to present herself. "I brought Niece, too; I
thought it would widen her little sphere," she chir-
ruped, coming blithely forward into the room.

She had a coronet-brooch on a well trussed-out
blouse, and a strip of deep green velvet tied sparkishly
below the middle.

Cautioned by her sister's eye, she turned towards
the Rector, who was engaging to loan a stallion to a
parishioner. "A thing I seldom do," he murmured,
bestowing a frigid smile on the infant papist.

Refusing to wet her lips in some curaçoa, Daisy
approached The Farquhar. Appreciating notice, his
jolly ogle was a welcome stimulus.

A blood-orange? Grapes? . . . Preserve-of-ginger?
She answered him whimsically by a little leap of the
tongue.

"She's an amusette, Mrs. Collins, your wee girl;
a sweet piece; ah, these golden blondes! . . . these
golden blondes!"

"But why is that?" Mrs. Collins inattentively
answered, watching her grandchild circulate, as might
a fruit, from guest to guest along the table.

Flattered by The Farquhar's interest, Daisy was
demonstrating already her social acumen.

"I've seen statues . . . often. Oh it's terrible!" she
rapported, shooting back her hair.

"Little deviless! Where?" the Farquhar queried,
stealing a surreptitious arm about her middle.

"Often on lawns, and in gardens, too; oh it's terrible!"

" . . . Indeed," he murmured, alarmed by an ear-piercing shriek, attesting to Bianca's aversion to the Rector.

It was a warning, it seemed, to adjourn. Laughing hectically as she rose, Miss Dawkins had lost her bearings.

" Where ever was I last old October? " she exclaimed, waving the long lyric feathers of her fan in Sir Harry Ortop's face. " I'll own I forget. . . ."

V

"Yes, dear, and so I'm really off—! And there were so many things I had wanted to say to you. But somehow I've not found time."

"Stay another week," the Countess begged.

"Call me Ola."

"Ola."

"Your father's a regular rake, darling."

"What are you looking for?"

Miss Dawkins gazed with lethargy about the room. Above the mantelpiece were engravings of Salammbô in Matho's tent and Monna Vanna in Prinzivalle's, known collectively as *The Fair Trespassers*, and published by the Fine Art Society " as the Act directs."

"The Isol," she said.

"I love your box, Ola."

"It's not distinguished."

"The labels it has on it!"

"Driving to and from a place in carnival time the students take it away."

"I envy you your independence."

"I'd rather roost."

"Domesticity tires one so. Every time I enter the nursery now it's a strain. To-day was the climax. I've had many years' experience, Mrs. Occles said to me, as a nurse, and I'll have no meddling. Very well, I said to her, you can go! Oh, good gracious! Then at the door, dear, I turned back and I added, Am I the child's mother or are you? That, she said, is no affair of mine! But as a rule I'm accustomed to see the father!! What do you mean by the father? I said. But she wouldn't say."

322

Miss Dawkins passed her parasol beneath the bed.

" My button boots——! "

" A child has so many little wants, nurse, I said. . . .
It should have proper attention. . . . *I* know what
a child wants, she said (so rudely), and when it wants
it. . . . And there was Bianca looking at her with her
little eyes. . . ."

" Still, I wish the Count would come! "

"I hope he's not false to me," the Countess quavered.

" Foreigners usually are, dear. They deceive their
wives. . . ."

" If I thought he was unworthy. . .?"

" You're sure, of course, it's binding ?"

" Binding? "

" No loopholes? "

The Countess tittered.

" None," she said.

" Knowing the world as I know it," Miss Dawkins
sighed. " Ah, well. . . ."

" There . . . the carriage is at the door."

" I'm ready."

" Have you a magazine or anything for the train? "

" I've a novel only—*Three Lilies and a Moustache.*"

" I like a love story," the Countess confessed, " so
long as it isn't drivel."

" Here is Daisy to say good-bye."

" Where's Niece? "

" In France! " the Countess crooned.

" Isn't the child here? "

" Come and kiss me," Miss Dawkins invited.

" I've such news! "

" What is it? "

" The Chase is let at last."

" Goodness! "

" Madame La Chose is in the library now with a
professional witness."

" Well? "

" And they've taken the house. I was listening. . . .
Madame La Chose said she was prepared to put her
hand to an agreement for a ninety-nine years' lease
without the farm. And it's to be pulled down immediately. . . . Oh, the rats ! "

" Who's the witness? "

" General Lover."

" My dear father once struck me for listening at a
door," Miss Dawkins observed.

" And as a reference she gives La Belle Zula. She says
her diamonds *alone* are worth the half of Yorkshire."

" Mum must be overjoyed."

" She is."

" One place or another ! " Miss Dawkins drawled.
" Once the glamour's gone."

" Oh, Ola ! "

" I maintain there's little in it.'

" I long to go about ! " Daisy murmured, pirouetting vainly before the glass.

" Jesu ! "

" What openings have I here? "

" There's time enough yet," the Countess assured.
" One sister should help another."

" When you're eligible we'll see."

" If I'm not eligible now I don't know who is ! "
Miss Dawkins drew on nervously a glove.

" You've my address in Australia, Viscountess, all
right? "

" Belleview—isn't it? Lake George? . . ."

" That's it, old girl."

" I shan't forget."

"Ihopethesea'llbelevel, dear. I can't endure it rough."

" Write soon."

Miss Dawkins nodded.

" It depends on the Master Potter now. But if I
ever should find my beloved ones in the East I'll be
sure to let you know."

VI

" How would Phryne Street appeal to you, Isabel? "
Mr. Collins asked his wife as they sat one morning at
breakfast.

" H-m, Charles! . . ."

" Maxilla Gardens then? "

" H-m! . . ."

" Or Gardingore Gate? "

" I want to live in Lisbon," Mrs. Collins said.

Mr. Collins cast aside the paper.

" Where to bend our footsteps to is a problem and
a tragedy," he muttered.

" 'Vieto," Daisy suggested in an insinuating voice.

" What would one do dumped down in Orvieto? "
Mrs. Collins asked. " It would be as bad as Bovon."

" At 'Vieto it's all arcades, and right on top of a hill!
You've to take a lift to get to it. It's the funicular for
all. . . ."

" If it's to be Italy I'd sooner it was Rome."

Daisy showed fervour.

" Mab was telling me of the preserves they sell
there. All speared on little sticks. At the street corners,
she says, the sugar-plums sparkle in the sun just as if
they were jewels. . . . I should like to see them. . . .
And to taste them too," she added.

" Papa has written to Mrs. Whewell already, alas,"
Mrs. Collins said, " to inquire whether she has a vacancy
at all at York Hill."

" If I studied anywhere it would be abroad."

" Master your native tongue at any rate to begin
with," Mr. Collins advised.

" I don't care a jot for distinctions! "

" At your age," Mrs. Collins asserted, " I had a diploma."

" For what? "

" As a nurse."

" Nursing's different."

" I assure you it's very disagreeable. Often it's by no means pleasant."

" Why? "

" What I never could bear about nursing," Mrs. Collins reminiscently said, " was sponging the paint off the face of a corpse."

" I would leave it."

" Even a hospital nurse can go too far. . . ."

" Where's Mabel? "

" I heard her romping with Bianca as I passed her door."

" She doesn't bother herself much of a morning about the time," Mr. Collins complained.

" It's on account of prayers, Charles. Until they're over she naturally doesn't care to come down."

Daisy sipped her tea.

" She did her best to convert me the other day," she said. " With one of her hatpins."

" What? "

" . . . An old bead affair. Such a common thing. Not worth sixpence."

" Mab did? "

" And she has her eye on Queen! "

" I fear the tap-room at the Mitre is as near as *he'll* ever get to Rome," Mr. Collins remarked.

" S-s-s-h, Charles. Here he is! "

" Is the Signora stirring yet, Queen? " Daisy asked.

" She has just received her letters."

" Is there anything for me? "

" No, Miss Daisy. There is not."

" I was only wondering——"

Mrs. Collins raised a hand.

" Hark! "

" O-o-o-o-o-o-h! "

" It's her ladyship's cry."

" You'd think Great Pan was dead again—at least."

" Very likely it's her husband's handwriting that affects her," Daisy said. " Or it may be only a parcel! She's expecting, on approval, I know, some fancy-work pyjamas."

" O-o-o-o-o-o-h! "

" Breakfast! " Mrs. Collins carolled.

" He's coming. He'll be here to-day," the Countess announced, elated. " Oio will! "

" Positively? "

" So he says. Oh. . . . And in the night I was dreaming so vividly of a runaway hearse. . . . As it galloped by me one of the mourners gave me *such* a look. I can see it now."

" Was it anybody, Mabsey? "

" How anybody? "

" Likely to suit me."

" A husband! "

" Mabsey! "

" It was a young woman. . . . Poor soul!" the Countess replied.

" What does he say? "

" I'll read you out some of his letter. But it isn't all for you."

" Is it in Italian, Mabel? "

" It's half and half."

" Well? "

" ' My dear dearly,' he begins—he always calls me *dearly!*—' My own, own, little wife. My Mabina——' And then he simply says he's coming. ' *Spero di venire Sabato verso la sera.* . . .' And he sends his filial love, with a kiss, to the English mother—à la mamma Inglese. . . ."

" Ah? "

" Yes. . . . And he intends to take her back with him to Italy, where he has prepared for her benefit a violet and rose salotto. . . ."

" Bless the boy! "

" And then there's a piece of scandal. Oh, good gracious! . . . He says poor Citta Zocchia isn't to wait on the Queen any more! She's done it *this* time. . . . And Dona Formosa de Bergère is to be married in Naples—*Naples!* Oh! Mercy!—to a certain Signor Popi! . . ."

" At what o'clock will he be here? "

" *Verso la sera!* "

" What time would that be? "

" Towards night."

" How vague these husbands are."

" He'll be here for dinner, I dare say," Daisy said.

" We must try to consult his tastes."

" Simple, nourishing things," the Countess said, " he likes. He has a passion for curry."

Mrs. Collins concealed her anxiety.

" In Rome, for example, Mab," she asked, " what do they have when they dine? "

" It depends."

" Besides curry . . ."

" Oh, well, perhaps some little round, pink, sweet potatoes they'll have, and some plain stewed rice. Or, again, very likely it'll be a piece of cold pickled pork. With olive oil and onions. . . . Whatever's seasonable they'll have. . . . And on Friday, of course, it's *fish.*"

" You'll need to tell all this presently to Mrs. Prixon," Mrs. Collins said. " And don't forget one thing. . . . You've to replace that Mrs. Occles."

The Countess sighed.

" If I can't be suited with a Bovon girl or a York young thing I shall have an ayah and get the baby used to things. . . ."

Daisy raised a finger.

" There's her little howl! "

" Poor mite. She can't bear to be left alone with a
strange Scotch woman. When Bianca takes an aversion! . . . She's a peculiar child in many ways."

" Let me dress her to-day, Mabsey, may I—just for
once? "

" What ever for? "

" Leave her to me. I'll turn her out what's what! "

" Goodness! "

" I've my secrets. . . ."

" I dare say."

" I can build her quite a presence. . . ."

" Mercy! "

" With a proper projection you wouldn't know the
child."

" I must fly to her."

" And do, dear, finish your toilet," Mrs. Collins
beseeched.

" I trust her husband will confiscate all her trailing,
bedraggled negligeys," Mr. Collins said. " Slovenly,
nasty things! "

Daisy rippled.

" I wouldn't build upon it," she replied. " Her
husband often doesn't get up himself in the morning
at all."

" Not? "

" He lies a-bed until all hours. He's a regular slug-
gard. The shadows will be falling sometimes, she says,
and daylight almost gone, and you'll find him still between the sheets."

" Fortunately Madame La Chose will be routing us
out of this before very long."

" Eh, Is-a-bel! "

Mrs. Collins glowed.

" And what heavenly happiness," she remarked,
" to have no housekeeping—ever any more! "

" Let's all dance to-night."

" My madcap fairy ! "

" Her husband dances quite wonderfully, she says."

" Who would there be to play ? "

" Victoria owns a concertina."

" That's no good."

" And William has a banjo. . . . According to him, the banjo is the king of instruments."

" Nonsense. I shouldn't think it was."

" Oh! Mumsey ! . . ."

" We might perhaps call in the Bovon string quartet," Mrs. Collins said. " Just for a serenade."

" Oh! what ever has happened to Niece ? "

" If she's peevish, poor mite," the Countess said, returning, " it's on account of the little mulligrubs. . . ."

" You can't expect a child of her years to be reasonable," Mrs. Collins commented. " It wouldn't be natural."

" Let me have her," Daisy begged.

" Don't, Daisy ! "

" What the child likes best is a reel of cotton. She'll play with that when she wouldn't play with me. . . ."

" *Pucci ! Pucci !* " Mrs. Collins ventured.

" *Ecco la nonna ! La buona cara nonna.* . . . Ah, *santo Dio !* "

" When I say *cui* to her, somehow she doesn't seem to like it ! "

Daisy wagged her tongue.

" Lat-lat ! "

" How can you be so gross ! "

" Let me lull her. Shall I ? "

" She's never quiet for you."

" Wait till she hears the story of Blowzalinda and the Fairy Bee."

" Oh, it's beyond the child. . . . She wouldn't know. Buz-z-z! "

" Isabel ! "

" Yes, dear? "

" Cook requires her orders."

" Where is she? "

" Behind the screen."

" Help me, Mabel," Mrs. Collins said.

" *Gigi! Ribu!* Oh, the clim pickle! "

" Give her to me, Mabsey."

" Yum. Yum."

" Give her to me."

" She lifts her little hand up to her little nose and then she presses it."

" It's one of her little sarcasms, I expect."

" She finds the world *so* weird."

" Still it's good to know she has such an aunt. A good aunt, she says, is an untold blessing."

" Help me! " Mrs. Collins implored.

" How? "

" Curry—and then? . . ."

The Countess turned her head.

" He can't endure a rabbit," she remarked.

" My dear, no one proposes it! "

" Once the child and I were driving on the Via Appia Nuova when we saw a bunny peeping out of a tomb. Oh, such a darling! So I stopped the carriage and told Luigi, the footman, to run and dispatch it if he possibly could. He brought it back to me. . . . And a few hours afterwards it was bubbling away into a fine chicken broth. Oio had it all. . . . But hardly had it passed his lips when he was seized with the most violent spasms. Whereupon he turned round and accused me of attempting to do what certain Renaissance wives are supposed to have sometimes done. Oh! He was so cross. He was as cross as cross. . . . So don't let's have rabbit."

" Polpettino, perhaps? "

" In olive oil; garnished ' Mussolini-wise.' "

" And then? "

331

"Oh, then, what he really adores, what he simply can't resist, is a fritter."

"Cheese?"

"Any kind. And he loves a savoury! Zuccata, he likes. Zuccata, Zuccatini. . . . And he's fond of a soufflé too, so long as it isn't *led*."

"Not to anticipate, my dear . . ."

"Then——"

"Olive oil!"

"And then——"

"Then," Mrs. Collins' voice rose as if inspired, "then Côtelettes—à la Milanaise. . . ."

CAPRICE
1917

TO
STEPHEN HAMMERTON

Τίς δ'ἀγροιῶτίς τοι θέλγει νόον,
οὐκ ἐπωταμένα τὰ βράκε᾽᾽ελκην ἐπὶ τῶν σφύρων.—*Sappho.*

I

THE clangour of bells grew insistent. In uncontrollable hilarity pealed S. Mary, contrasting clearly with the subdued carillon of S. Mark. From all sides, seldom in unison, resounded bells. S. Elizabeth and S. Sebastian, in Flower Street, seemed in loud dispute, while S. Ann " on the Hill," all hollow, cracked, consumptive, fretful, did nothing but complain. Near by S. Nicaise, half paralysed and impotent, feebly shook. Then, triumphant, in a hurricane of sound, S. Irene hushed them all.

It was Sunday again.

Up and up, and still up, the winding ways of the city the straggling townsfolk toiled.

Now and again a pilgrim perhaps would pause in the narrow lane behind the Deanery to rest.

Opening a black lacquer fan and setting the window of her bedroom wide, Miss Sarah Sinquier peered out.

The lane, very frequently, would prove interesting of an afternoon.

Across it, the Cathedral rose up before her with wizardry against the evening sky.

Miss Sinquier raised her eyes towards the twin grey spires, threw up her arms, and yawned.

From a pinnacle a devil with limbs entwined about some struggling crowned-coiffed prey grimaced.

" For I yearn for those kisses you gave me once
   On the steps by Bakerloo! "

Miss Sinquier crooned caressingly, craning further out.

Under the little old lime trees by the Cathedral door lounged Lady Caroline Dempsey's Catholic footman.

Miss Sinquier considered him.

In her mind's eye she saw the impression her own conversion would make in the parochial world.

" Canon Sinquier's only daughter has gone over to Rome. . . ." Or, " Canon Sinquier's daughter has taken the veil." Or, "Miss Sinquier, having suffered untold persecution at the hands of her family, has been received into the Convent of the Holy Dove."

Her eyes strayed leisurely from the powdered head and weeping shoulder-knots of Lady Caroline Dempsey's Catholic footman. The lack of movement was oppressive.

Why was not Miss Worrall in her customary collapse being borne senseless to her Gate in the Sacristan's arms? And why to-night were they not chaunting the Psalms?

Darting out her tongue, Miss Sinquier withdrew her head and resumed her book.

" Pouf! "

She shook her fan.

The room would soon be dark.

From the grey-toned walls, scriptural, a *Sasso Sassi* frowned.

" In all these fruitful years," she read, " the only time he is recorded to have smiled was when a great rat ran in and out among some statues. . . . *He* was the Ideal Hamlet. Morose of countenance, and cynical by nature, his outbursts, at times, would completely freeze the company."

Miss Sinquier passed her finger-tips lightly across her hair.

" Somehow it makes no difference," she murmured, turning towards a glass. To feign Ophelia—no matter what!

She pulled about her a lace Manilla shawl.

It was as though it were Andalusia whenever she wrapped it on.

"*Dona Rosarda!*"

"*Fernan Perez? What do you want?*"

"*Ravishing Rosarda, I need you.*"

"*I am the wife of Don José Cuchillo—the Moor.*"

"*Dona Rosarda Castilda Cuchillo, I love you.*"

"*Sh—! My husband will be back directly.*"

Stretched at ease before a pier-glass, Miss Sinquier grew enthralled.

An hour sped by.

The room was almost dark.

Don José would wish his revenge.

"*Rosarda.*"

"*Fernando?*"

"*Ah-h!*"

Miss Sinquier got up.

She must compose herself for dinner—wash off the blood.

Poor Fernan!

She glanced about her, a trifle Spanish still.

From a clothes-peg something hanging seemed to implore.

"To see me? Why, bless you. Yes!"

With an impetuous, pretty gesture she flung it upon a couch.

"How do I like America?"

"I adore it . . . You see . . . I've lost my heart here—! Tell them so—oh! especially to the men. . . . Whereabouts was I born? In Westmorland; yes. *In England, Sir!* Inquisitive? Why not at all. I was born in the sleepy peaceful town of Applethorp (three p's), in the inmost heart—right in the very middle," Miss. Sinquier murmured, tucking a few wild flowers under her chin, "of the *Close.*"

" SALLY," her father said, " I could not make out where
you sat at Vespers, child, to-night."

In the old-world Deanery drawing-room, coffee
and liqueurs—a Sunday indulgence—had been brought
in.

Miss Sinquier set down her cup.

Behind her, through the open windows, a riot of light
leaves and creepers was swaying restively to and fro.

" I imagine the *Font* hid me," she answered with a
little laugh.

Canon Sinquier considered with an absent air an
abundant-looking moon, then turned towards his wife.

" To-morrow, Mary," he said, " there's poor Mrs.
Cushman again."

At her cylinder-desk, between two flickering candles,
Mrs. Sinquier, while her coffee grew cold, was opening her heart to a friend.

" Do, Mike, keep still," she begged.

" Still? "

" Don't fidget. Don't talk."

" Or dare to breathe," her daughter added, taking
up a Sunday journal and approaching nearer the light.

" ' At the Olive Theatre,' " she read, " ' Mrs.
Starcross will produce a new comedy, in the coming
autumn, which promises to be of the highest interest.' "

Her eyes kindled.

" O God! "

" ' At the Kehama, Yvonde Yalta will be seen
shortly in a Japanese piece, with singing mandarins,
geishas, and old samurai—' "

" Dear Lord! "

" ' Mr. and Mrs. Mary are said to be contemplating management again.' "

" Heavens above! "

" ' For the revival of *She Stoops to*——' "

Crescendo, across the mist-clad Close broke a sorrowful, sated voice.

" You can fasten the window, Sarah," Canon Sinquier said.

" It's Miss Biggs! "

" Who could have taught her? How? " the Canon wondered.

Mrs. Sinquier laid down her pen.

" I dread her intimate dinner! " she said.

" Is it to be intimate? "

" Isn't she always? ' Come round and see me soon, Miss Sarah, *there's* a dear, and let's be intimate!' "

" Really, Sally! "

" Sally can take off anyone."

" It's vulgar, dear, to mimic."

" Vulgar? "

" It isn't nice."

" Many people do."

" Only mountebanks."

" I'd bear a good deal to be on the stage."

Canon Sinquier closed his eyes.

" Recite, dear, something; soothe me," he said.

" Of course, if you wish it."

" Soothe me, Sally! "

" Something to obliterate the sermon? "

Miss Sinquier looked down at her feet. She had on black babouches all over little pearls with filigree butterflies that trembled above her toes.

" Since first I beheld you, Adele,
 While dancing the celinda,
 I have remained faithful to the thought of you;
 My freedom has departed from me,

339

I care no longer for all other negresses;
I have no heart left for them;—
You have such grace and cunning;—
You are like the Congo serpent."

Miss Sinquier paused.
" You need the proper movements . . . " she explained. " One ought *really* to shake one's shanks! "
" Being a day of rest, my dear, we will dispense
with it."

" I love you too much, my beautiful one—
I am not able to help it.
My heart has become just like a grasshopper,—
It does nothing but leap.
I have never met any woman
Who has so beautiful a form as yours.
Your eyes flash flame;
Your body has enchained me captive.

Ah, you are like the rattlesnake
Who knows how to charm the little bird,
And who has a mouth ever ready for it
To serve it for a tomb.
I have never known any negress
Who could walk with such grace as you can,
Or who could make such beautiful gestures;
Your body is a beautiful doll.

When I cannot see you, Adele,
I feel myself ready to die;
My life becomes like a candle
Which has almost burned itself out.
I cannot then find anything in the world
Which is able to give me pleasure:

I could well go down to the river
And throw myself in so that I might cease to suffer.

Tell me if you have a man,
And I will make an ouanga charm for him;
I will make him turn into a phantom,
If you will only take me for your husband.
I will not go to see you when you are cross:
Other women are mere trash to me;
I will make you very happy
And I will give you a beautiful Madras handker-
chief."

" Thank you, thank you, Sally."
" It is from *Ozias Midwinter*."
Mrs. Sinquier shuddered.
" Those scandalous topsies that entrap our mission-
aries! " she said.
" In Oshkosh——"
" Don't, Mike. The horrors that go on in certain
places, I'm sure no one would believe."
Miss Sinquier caressed lightly the Canon's cheek.
" Soothed? " she asked.
" . . . Fairly."
" When I think of those coloured coons," Mrs.
Sinquier went on, " at the Palace fête last year! Roam-
ing all night in the Close. . . . And when I went to
look out next day there stood an old mulattress holding
up the baker's boy in the lane."
" There, Mary! "
" Tired, dear? "
" Sunday's always a strain."
" For you, alas! it's bound to be."
" There were the Catechetical Classes to-day."
" Very soon now Sally will learn to relieve you."
Miss Sinquier threw up her eyes.
" I? " she wondered.

"Next Sunday; it's time you should begin."

"Between now and *that*," Miss Sinquier reflected, shortly afterwards, on her way upstairs, "I shall almost certainly be in town."

"O London—City of Love!" she warbled softly as she locked her door.

III

In the gazebo at the extremity of the garden, by the new parterre, Miss Sinquier, in a morning wrapper, was waiting for the post.

Through the trellis chinks, semi-circular, showed the Close, with its plentiful, seasoned timber and sedate, tall houses, a stimulating sequence, architecturally, of whitewash, stone and brick.

Miss Sinquier stirred impatiently.

Wretch!—to deliver at the Palace before the Deanery, when the Deanery was as near!

" Shower down over there, O Lord, ten thousand fearsome bills," extemporaneously she prayed, " and spare them not at all. Amen."

Hierarchic hands shot upwards.

Dull skies.

She waited.

Through the Palace gates, at length, the fellow lurched, sorting as he came.

" Dolt! "

Her eyes devoured his bag.

Coiled round and round like some sleek snake her future slumbered in it.

Husband; lovers . . . little lives, perhaps—yet to be . . . besides voyages, bouquets, diamonds, chocolates, duels, casinos! . . .

She shivered.

" Anything for me, Hodge, to-day," she inquired, " by chance? "

" A fine morning, miss."

" Unusually."

It had come . . .

343

That large mauve envelope, with the wild hand-writing and the haunting scent was from *her*.

As she whisked away her heart throbbed fast. Through the light spring foliage she could see her father, with folded hands, pacing meditatively to and fro before the front of the house.

" Humbug! " she murmured, darting down a gravel path towards the tradesmen's door.

Regaining her room, she promptly undid the seal.

> " Panvale Priory, Shaftesbury Avenue,
> " London, W.

" Mrs. Albert Bromley presents her compliments to Miss S. Sinquier and will be pleased to offer her her experience and advice on Thursday morning next at the hour Miss Sinquier names.

" *P.S.* Mrs. Bromley already feels a parent's sympathetic interest in Miss Sinquier. Is she dark or fair?... Does she shape for Lady Macbeth or is she a Lady Teazle? "

" Both! " Miss Sinquier gurgled, turning a deft somersault before the glass.

To keep the appointment, without being rushed, she would be obliged to set out, essentially baggage-less, to-night—a few requisites merely, looped together and concealed beneath her dress, would be the utmost she could manage.

" A lump here and a lump there! " she breathed, " and I can unburden myself in the train."

" Okh! "

She peeped within her purse.

. . . And there was Godmother's chain that she would sell!

It should bring grist; perhaps close on a thousand pounds. Misericordia: to be compelled to part with it!

Opening a levant-covered box, she drew out a long flat tray.

Adorable pearls!

How clearly now they brought her Godmother to mind . . . a little old body . . . with improbable cherry-cheeks and excrescent upper lip, with always the miniatures of her three deceased husbands clinging about one arm. . . . " Aren't they pleasant? " she would say proudly every now and then. . . . What talks they had had; and sometimes of an evening through the mauve moonlight they would strut together.

Ah! She had been almost ugly then; clumsy, gawky, *gauche* . . .

Now that she was leaving Applethorp, for ever perhaps, how dormant impressions revived!

The Saunders' Fifeshire bull, one New Year's night, ravaging the Close, driven frantic by the pealings of the bells. The time poor Dixon got drowned—at a Flower Show, a curate's eyes—a German governess's walk—a mould of calves'-foot jelly she had let fall in the Cathedral once, on her way somewhere——

She replaced ruefully her pearls.

What else?

Her artist fingers hovered.

Mere bridesmaid's rubbish; such frightful frippery.

She turned her thoughts to the room.

Over the bed, an antique bush-knife of barbaric shape, supposed to have been *Abraham's*, was quite a collector's piece.

It might be offered to some museum perhaps. The Nation ought to have it . . .

She sighed shortly.

And downstairs in the butler's room there were possessions of hers, besides. What of those Apostle spoons, and the two-pronged forks, and the chased tureen?

Leonard frequently had said it took the best part of a day to polish her plate alone.

345

And to go away and leave it all!

" O God, help me, Dear," she prayed. " This little once, O Lord! For Thou knowest my rights . . ."

She waited.

Why did not an angel with a basket of silver appear?

" Oh, well . . ."

Gripper, no doubt, would suspect something odd if she asked for her things " to play with " for an hour. . . .

A more satisfactory scheme would be to swoop into the pantry, on her way to the station, and to take them away for herself.

She had only to say, " Make haste with them crevets," for Gripper to go off in a huff, and Leonard, should he be there, would be almost sure to follow.

Men were so touchy.

Hush!

Her mother's voice came drifting from below.

" Kate! Kate! Kate! Kate! "

She listened.

" Have the chintz curtains in the white room folded," she could hear her say, " and remember what I said about the carpet . . ."

Dear soul!

Miss Sinquier sniffed.

Was it a tear?

Dear soul! Dear souls! . . .

" Never mind," she murmured, " they shall have *sofas* in their box on the night of my debut . . ."

She consoled herself with the thought.

I V

"Make haste now with them crevets!"

"For shame, miss. I shall go straight to the Dean!"

"Cr-r-r-evets!" Miss Sinquier called.

Clad in full black, with a dark felt *chapeau de résistance* and a long Lancastrian shawl, she felt herself no mean match for any man.

"C-r-r-r," she growled, throwing back her shawl.

After all, were not the things her own?

She laughed gaily.

"If dear Mrs. Bromley could see me," she beamed, tucking dexterously away an apostolic spoon.

"'St. Matthew—St. Mark—St. Luke—St. John—
These sprang into bed with their breeches on.'"

At a friendly frolic once a Candidate for Orders had waltzed her about to that.

She recalled Fräulein's erudite query still:

"Pray, why did they not take off all like the others?"

And the young man's significant reasons and elaborate suppositions, and Fräulein's creamy tone as she said she *quite* understood.

Miss Sinquier turned a key.

S-s-s-st!

"Butter fingers."

In a moment she must run.

Terrible to forgo her great tureen . . .

She poked it. What magnitude to be sure!

Impossible to tow it along.

Under the circumstances, why not take something less cumbersome instead?

There were the Caroline sauce-boats, or the best Anne teapot, hardly if ever in use.

Her ideas raced on.

And who could resist those gorgeous grapes, for the train?

Together with their dish . . .

" Tudor, ' Harry '! " she breathed.

From the corridor came a hum of voices.

Flinging her wrap about her, Miss Sinquier slipped quietly out by way of a small room, where the Canon preserved his lawn.

Outside, the moon was already up—a full moon, high and white, a wisp of cloud stretched across it like a blindfold face.

Oh Fame, dear!

She put up her face.

Across the garden the Cathedral loomed out of a mist as white as milk.

The damp, she reasoned, alone would justify her flight!

She shivered.

How sombre it looked in the lane.

There were roughs there frequently too.

" Villains . . ."

She felt fearfully her pearls.

After all, the initial step in any career was usually reckoned the worst.

Some day, at the King's, or the Canary, or the Olive, in the warmth of a stage dressing-room, she would be amused, perhaps, and say:

" I left my father's roof, sir, one sweet spring night —without so much as a word! "

V

Raindrops were falling although the sky was visibly brightening as Miss Sinquier, tired, and a little uncertain, passed through the main exit of Euston terminus.

She wavered a moment upon the curb.

On a hoarding, as if to welcome her, a dramatic poster of Fan Fisher unexpectedly warmed her heart; it was almost like being met . . .

There stood Fan, at concert pitch, as Masha Olgaruski in *The Spy*.

Miss Sinquier tingled.

A thing like that was enough to give one wings for a week.

She set off briskly, already largely braced.

Before meeting Mrs. Bromley on the morrow much would have to be done.

There was the difficulty of lodgment to consider.

Whenever she had been in the metropolis before she had stayed at *Millars* in Eric Street, overlooking Percy Place; because Mr. Millar had formerly been employed at the Deanery, and had, moreover, married their cook. . . .

But before going anywhere she must acquire a trunk.

Even Church dignitaries had been known to be refused accommodation on arriving at a strange hotel with nothing but themselves.

She threw a glance upwards towards a clock.

It was early yet!

All the wonderful day stretched before her, and in the evening she would take a ticket perhaps for some light vaudeville or new revue.

She studied the pleasure announcements on the motor-buses as they swayed along.

Stella Starcross—The Lady from the Sea—This evening, Betty Buttermilk and Co.—Rose Tournesol —Mr. and Mrs. Mary's Season: The Carmelite—The Shop Boy—Clemenza di Tito. To-night!

Miss Sinquier blinked.

Meanwhile the family teapot was becoming a bore.

Until the shops should open up it might be well to take a taxi and rest in the Park for an hour.

The weather was clearing fast; the day showed signs of heat.

She hailed a passing cab.

" Hyde Park," she murmured, climbing slowly in.

She thrilled.

Upon the floor and over the cushions of the cab were sprinkled fresh confetti—turquoise, pink and violet, gold and green.

She took up some.

As a mascot, she reflected, it would be equivalent to a cinqfoil of clover, or a tuft of edelweiss, or a twist of hangman's rope.

VI

FROM the big hotel in the vicinity of the Marble Arch, to the consulting rooms in Shaftesbury Avenue of Mrs. Albert Bromley, it appeared, on inquiry, that the distance might easily be accomplished in less than forty minutes.

Miss Sinquier, nevertheless, decided to allow herself more.

Garmented charmingly in a cornflower-blue frock with a black gauze turban trimmed with a forest of tinted leaves, she lingered, uplifted by her appearance, before the glass.

The sober turban, no doubt, would suggest to Mrs. Bromley Macbeth—the forest-scene, and the blue, she murmured, " might be anything."

It occurred to her as she left her room that Mr. Bromley might quite conceivably be there to assist his wife.

" Odious if he is," she decided, passing gaily out into the street.

It was just the morning for a walk. A pale silvery light spread over Oxford Street, while above the shop fronts the sun flashed down upon a sea of brass-tipped masts, from whence trade flags trembled in a vagrant breeze. Rejoicing in her independence, and in the exhilarating brightness of the day, Miss Sinquier sailed along. The ordeal of a first meeting with a distinguished dramatic expert diminished at every step. She could conjecture with assurance, almost, upon their ultimate mutual understanding. But before expressing any opinion, Mrs. Bromley, no doubt, would require to test her voice; perhaps, also, expect her to dance and declaim.

Miss Sinquier thrust out her lips.

" Not before Albert! Or at any rate not yet . . ."
she muttered.

She wondered what she knew.

There was the thing from *Rizzio*. The Mistress of
the Robes' lament upon her vanished youth, on dis-
covering a mirror unexpectedly, one morning, at
Holyrood, outside Queen Mary's door.

Diamond, Lady Drummond, bearing the Queen a
cap, raps, smiles, listens . . . smiles, raps again, puts out
her leg and rustles . . . giggles, ventures to drop a ring,
effusive facial play and sundry tentative noises, when,
catching sight of her reflection, she starts back with:

" O obnoxious old age! O hideous horror! O
youthful years all gone! O childhood spent! Decrepi-
tude at hand . . . Infirmities drawing near. . . ."

Interrupted by Mary's hearty laugh.

" Yes," Miss Sinquier decided, crossing into Regent
Street, " should Mrs. Bromley bid me declaim, I'll do
Diamond."

Her eyes brightened.

How prettily the street swerved.

As a rule, great thoroughfares were free from tricks.

She sauntered.

" A picture-palace."

And just beyond were the playhouses themselves.
Theatreland!

Shaftesbury Avenue with its slightly foreign aspect
stretched before her.

With a springing foot she turned up it.

Oh, those fragile glass façades with the players'
names suspended!

There was the new Merrymount Theatre with its
roguish Amorini supporting torches and smiling down
over gay flower-boxes on to the passers-by.

And beyond, where the burgeoning trees began,
must be Panvale Priory itself.

Miss Sinquier surveyed it.

It looked to be public offices. . . .

On the mat, dressed in a violet riband, with its paw in the air, lay a great sly, black, joyous cat.

" Toms! "

She scratched it.

Could it be Mrs. Bromley's?

In the threshold, here and there, were small brass plates, that brought to mind somehow memorial tablets to departed virtue at home.

Miss Sinquier studied the inscriptions.

Ah, there showed hers!

" M-m-m! " she murmured, commencing to climb.

Under the skylight a caged bird was singing shrilly.

As much to listen as to brush something to her cheeks, Miss Sinquier paused.

If a microscopic mirror could be relied upon she had seldom looked so well.

Scrambling up the remaining stairs with alacrity, she knocked.

A maid with her head wreathed in curl-papers answered the door, surveying the visitor first through a muslin blind.

Miss Sinquier pulled out a card.

" Is Mrs. Bromley in? " she asked.

The woman gazed at her feet.

" Mrs. Bromley's gone! " she replied.

" I suppose she won't be long? "

" She's in Elysium."

" At the——? "

" Poor Mrs. Bromley's dead."

" Mrs. Bromley *dead* . . .? "

" Poor Mrs. Bromley died last night."

Miss Sinquier staggered.

" Impossible! "

" Perhaps you'd care to come in and sit down? "

Miss Sinquier hesitated.

" No, no, not if . . . *is?* Oh! " she stammered.

" She was taken quite of a sudden."

" One can hardly yet believe it? "

" She'll be a loss to her world, alas, poor Betty Bromley will!"

Miss Sinquier swallowed.

" I should like to attend the funeral," she said.

" There's no funeral."

" No funeral? "

" No invitations, that is."

Miss Sinquier turned away.

The very ground under her seemed to slide . . .

Mrs. Bromley dead!

Why, the ink of her friendly note seemed scarcely dry!

On the pavement once more she halted to collect herself.

Who was there left at all?

At Croydon there was a conservatoire, of course—

She felt a little guilty at the rapidity of the idea.

Wool-gathering, she breasted the traffic in St. Martin's Lane.

She would turn over the situation presently more easily in the Park.

Instinctively, she stopped to examine a portrait of Yvonde Yalta in the open vestibule of the Dream.

She devoured it: Really . . . ? Really? She resembled more some Girton guy than a great coquette.

All down the street indeed, at the theatre doors, were studies of artists, scenes from current plays.

By the time she found herself back in Piccadilly Circus again Miss Sinquier was nearly fainting from inanition.

She peered around.

In Regent Street, she reflected, almost certainly, there must be some nice tea-shop, some cool creamery . . .

How did this do?

" The Café Royal! "

Miss Sinquier fluttered in.

By the door, the tables all proved to be taken.

Such a noise!

Everyone seemed to be chattering, smoking, lunching, casting dice, or playing dominoes.

She advanced slowly through a veil of opal mist, feeling her way from side to side with her parasol.

It was like penetrating deeper and deeper into a bath.

She put out her hand in a swimming, groping gesture, twirling as she did so, accidentally, an old gentleman's moustache.

Thank heaven! There, by that pillar, was a vacant place.

She sank down on to the edge of a crowded couch, as in a dream.

The tall mirrors that graced the walls told her she was tired.

" Bring me some China tea," she murmured to a passing waiter, " and a bun with currants in it."

She leaned back.

The realisation of her absolute loneliness overcame her suddenly.

Poor Mrs. Bromley, poor kindly little soul!

The tears sprang to her eyes.

It would have been a relief to have blotted her face against some neighbouring blouse or waistcoat and to have had a hearty cry.

" Excuse me, may I ask you to be so good——"

Just before her on the table was a stand for matches.

With a mournful glance she slid the apparatus from her in the direction of an adolescent of a sympathetic, somewhat sentimental, appearance, who, despite emphatic whiskers, had the air of a wildly pretty girl.

To have cherished such a one as a brother! Miss Sinquier reflected, as the waiter brought her tea.

While consuming it she studied the young man's chiselled profile from the corners of her eyes.

Supporting his chin upon the crook of a cane, he was listening, as if enthralled, to a large florid man, who, the centre of a small rapt group, was relating in a high-pitched, musical voice, how " Poor dear Chaliapin one day had asked for Kvass and was given Bass. And that reminds me," the speaker said, giving the table an impressive thump, " of the time when Anna Held—let go."

Miss Sinquier glowed.

Here were stage folk, artists, singers . . . that white thin girl in the shaggy hat opposite was without doubt a temperament akin.

She felt drawn to speak.

" Can you tell me how I should go to Croydon? " she asked.

The words came slowly, sadly almost . . .

" To Croydon? "

" You can't go to Croydon."

" Why not? "

The young man of the whiskers looked amused.

" When we all go to Spain to visit Velasquez——"

" Goya——! "

" Velasquez! "

" Goya! Goya! Goya! "

" . . . We'll set you on your way."

" Goose! "

" One goes to Croydon best by Underground," the pale-looking girl remarked.

Miss Sinquier winced.

" Underground! "

Her lip quivered.

" Is there anything the matter? "

" Only——"

Folding her arms upon the table she sank despairingly forward and burst into tears.

" Poor Mrs. Bromley! " she sobbed.

" In the name of *Fortune* . . ." The pale young woman wondered.

" What has Serephine said? What has Mrs. Sixsmith done? "

" Monstrous tease! "

The stout man wagged a finger.

" Wicked! " he commented.

The lady addressed kindled.

" I merely advised her to go Underground. By tube."

" O God." Miss Sinquier shook.

" It's hysteria. Poor thing, you can see she's overwrought."

" Give her a *fine; un bon petit cognac.*"

" Waiter! "

" Garçon."

" Never mind, Precious," the fat man crooned. " You shall ride in a comfy taxi-cab with me."

" No; indeed she shan't," Mrs. Sixsmith snapped. " You may rely on me, Ernest, for that! "

Rejecting the proffered spirits with a gesture, Miss Sinquier controlled her grief.

" It's not *often* I'm so silly," she said.

" There, there! "

" Excuse this exhibition. . . ."

Mrs. Sixsmith squeezed her hand.

" My poor child," she said, " I fear you've had a shock."

" It's over now."

" I'm so glad."

" You've been very good."

" Not at all. You interest me."

" Why? "

" Why? Why? . . . I'm sure I can't say *why!* But directly I saw you . . ."

" It's simply wonderful."

" You marched in here for all the world like some great coquette."

" You mean the Father Christmas at the door? "

" Tell me what had happened."

In a few words Miss Sinquier recounted her tale.

" My dear," Mrs. Sixsmith said, " I shouldn't think of it again. I expect this Mrs. Bromley was nothing but an old procuress."

" A procuress? "

" A stage procuress."

" How dreadful it sounds."

" Have you no artistic connections in town *at all?*"

" Not really . . ."

" Then here, close at hand . . . sitting with you and me," she informally presented, " is Mr. Ernest Stubbs, whose wild wanderings in the Gog-magog hills in sight of Cambridge, orchestrally described, recently thrilled us all. Next to him—tuning his locks and twisting his cane—you'll notice Mr. Harold Weathercock, an exponent of calf-love parts at the Dream. And, beyond, blackening her nose with a cigarette, sprawls the most resigned of women—Miss Whipsina Peters, a daughter of the famous flagellist —and a coryphée herself."

Miss Peters nodded listlessly.

" Toodle-doo," she murmured.

" As a coryphée, I suppose her diamonds are a sight? "

" A sight!" Mrs. Sixsmith closed her eyes. "They're all laid up in lavender, I fear."

" In lavender? "

" Pledged."

" Oh, poor soul!"

" Just now you spoke of a necklace of your own . . . a pearl rope, or something, that you wish to sell."

" Unhappily I'm obliged."

" I've a notion I might be of service in the matter."

" How? "

" Through an old banker-friend of mine—Sir Oliver Dawtry. Down Hatton Garden way and throughout the City he has enormous interests. And I should say *he* could place your pearls—if anyone could! "

" Do you think he'd be bothered? "

" That I'll undertake. "

" Does he live in town? "

" In a sense: he has a large house in the Poultry. "

" Of course I should be willing to show him my pearls. "

" Sir Oliver is offering me a little dinner to-night. And I should be happy for you to join us. "

" Oh? . . . I think I scarcely dare! "

" Rubbish! One must be bolder than that if one means to get on! "

" Tell me where you dine. "

" At Angrezini's. It's a little restaurant . . . with a nigger band. And we sing between the courses. "

" Will Mr. Sixsmith be there? "

" My dear, Mr. Sixsmith and I don't live together any more. "

" Forgive me. "

" That's all right . . . "

Miss Sinquier's eyes grew dim.

" Used he to act? " she asked.

" *Act!* "

" I seem to have heard of him. "

Mrs. Sixsmith looked away.

"Are you coming, Serephine?" her neighbour asked.

" Are you all off? "

The florid man nodded impressively.

" Yes . . . we're going now . . ." he said.

" What are Whipsina's plans? "

Miss Peters leaned closely forward over several pairs of knees.

" I shall stay where I am," she murmured, " and perhaps take a nap. There's sure to be a tremendous exodus directly."

Miss Sinquier rose. " I've some shopping," she said, " to do."

" Until this evening, then."

" At what o'clock? "

" At eight."

" On arrival, am I to ask for you? "

" Better ask for Sir Oliver—one never knows . . . And I might perhaps happen to be late."

" But you won't be? You mustn't . . ."

" I will explain whatever's needful by telephone to Sir Oliver now. And during dinner," Mrs. Sixsmith bubbled, " while the old gentleman picks a quail, we will see what we can do! "

" How can I express my thanks . . .? "

" The question of commission," Mrs. Sixsmith murmured with a slight smile, " we will discuss more fully later on."

VII

SUBJECTIVE. On a rack in the loom. Powerless one-self to grasp the design. Operated on by others. At the mercy of chance fingers, unskilled fingers, tender fingers; nails of all sorts. Unable to progress alone. Finding fulfilment through friction and because of friction. Stung into sentiency gradually, bit by bit—a toe at a time.

After all there was a *zest* in it; and who should blame the raw material should an accident occur by the way . . .

Careless of an intriguing world about her, Miss Sinquier left her hotel, just so as to arrive at Angrezini's last.

"For Thou knowest well my safety is in *Thee*," she murmured to herself mazily as her taxi skirted the Park.

Having disposed of her Anne teapot for close on seventy pounds, she was looking more radiant than ever in a frail Byzantine tunic that had cost her fifty guineas.

"Thy Sally's safety," she repeated, absently scanning the Park.

Through the shadowy palings it slipped away, abundantly dotted with lovers. Some were plighting themselves on little chairs, others preferred the green ground: and beyond them, behind the whispering trees, the sky gleamed pale and luminous as church glass.

Glory to have a lover too, she reflected, and to stroll leisurely-united through the evening streets, between an avenue of sparkling lamps . . .

Her thoughts turned back to the young man in the Café Royal.

"Of all the bonny loves!" she breathed, as her taxi stopped.

"Angrezini!"

A sturdy negro helped her out.

"For Thou knowest very well——" her lips moved faintly.

The swinging doors whirled her in.

She found herself directly in a small bemirrored room with a hatch on one side of it, in which an old woman in a voluminous cap was serenely knitting.

Behind her dangled furs and wraps that scintillated or made pools of heavy shade as they caught or missed the light.

Relinquishing her own strip of tulle, Miss Sinquier turned about her.

Through a glass door she could make out Mrs. Sixsmith herself, seated in a cosy red-walled sitting-room beyond.

She was looking staid as a porcelain goddess in a garment of trailing white with a minute griffin-eared dog peeping out its sheeny paws and head wakefully from beneath her train.

At sight of her guest Mrs. Sixsmith smiled and rose.

"Sir Oliver hasn't yet come!" she said, imprinting on Miss Sinquier's youthful cheek a salute of *hospitality*.

"He hasn't? And I made sure I should be last."

Mrs. Sixsmith consulted the time.

"From the Bank to the Poultry, and from the Poultry on . . . just consider," she calculated, subsiding leisurely with Miss Sinquier upon a spindle-legged settee.

"You telephoned?"

"I told him all your story."

"Well?"

" He has promised me to do his utmost."

" He will? "

" You should have heard us. This Mrs. Bromley, he pretends . . . Oh, well . . . one must not be too harsh on the dead."

" Poor little woman."

" Let me admire your frock."

" You like it? "

" I never saw anything so waggish."

" No, no, *please*——! "

" Tell me where they are! "

" What? "

" I'm looking for your pearls."

" They're in my hair."

" Show me."

" I'll miss them terribly."

" Incline! "

" How? "

" More."

" I can't! "

" They're very nice. But bear in mind one thing ——"

" Yes? "

Mrs. Sixsmith slipped an encircling arm about Miss Sinquier's waist.

" Always remember," she said, " to a City man, twelve hundred sounds less than a thousand. Just as a year, to you and me, sounds more than eighteen months! "

" I'll not forget."

" Here is Sir Oliver now."

Through the swing doors an elderly man with a ruddy, rather apoplectic face, and close-set opaque eyes, precipitantly advanced.

" Ladies! "

" ' Ladies ' indeed, Sir Oliver."

" As if——"

" Monster."

" Excuse me, Serephine."

" Your pardon rests with Miss Sinquier," Mrs. Sixsmith said with melodious inflections as she showed the way towards the restaurant. " Address your petitions to her."

In the crescent-shaped, cedar-walled, cedar-beamed room, a table at a confidential angle had been reserved.

" There's a big gathering here to-night," Sir Oliver observed, glancing round him, a " board-room " mask clinging to him still.

Miss Sinquier looked intellectual.

" I find it hot! " she said.

" You do."

" I find London really very hot. . . . It's after the north, I suppose. In the north it's always much cooler."

" Are you from the north? "

" Yes, indeed she is," Mrs. Sixsmith chimed in. " And so am *I*," she said. " Two north-country girls!" she added gaily.

Sir Oliver spread sentimentally his feet.

" The swans at Blenheim; the peacocks at Warwick! " he sighed.

" What do you mean, Sir Oliver? "

" Intimate souvenirs . . ."

" I should say so. . . . Swans and peacocks! I wonder you're prepared to admit it."

" Admit it? "

" Outside of *Confessions*, Sir Oliver."

Miss Sinquier raised a hurried hand to her glass.

" No, no, no, no, no, no wine! " she exclaimed. " Something milky . . ."

" Fiddlesticks! Our first little dinner."

" Oh, Sir Oliver!"

" And not, I trust, our last! "

" I enjoy it so much—going out."

364

Mrs. Sixsmith slapped her little dog smartly upon
the eyes with her fan.

" Couch-toi," she admonished.

" What can fret her? "

" She fancies she sees Paúl."

" Worthless fellow! " Sir Oliver snapped.

" I was his rib, Sir Oliver."

" Forget it."

" I can't forget it."

" J-j-j——"

" Only this afternoon I ran right into him—it was
juſt outside the Café Royal . . ."

" Scamp."

" He looked superb. Oh, so smart; spats, speckled
trousers, the reſt all deep indigo. Rather Russian."

" Who? "

" My aċtor-husband, Paul. There. One has only to
speak his name for Juno to jerk her tail."

" With whom is he at present? "

" With Sydney Iphis."

" We went laſt night to see Mrs. Starcross," Sir
Oliver said.

" She's no draw."

" I long to see her," Miss Sinquier breathed.

" I underſtand, my dear young lady, you've an itch
for the footlights yourself."

Miss Sinquier began eating crumbs at random.

" God knows! " she declared.

" C'eſt une âme d'élite, Sir Oliver."

" You've no experience at all? "

" None."

Sir Oliver refused a dish.

" We old ones . . ." he lamented. " Once upon a
time, I was in closer touch with the ſtage."

" Even so, Sir Oliver, you ſtill retain your footing."

" Footing, f-f-f——; among the whole demned
lot, who persiſts ſtill but, perhaps, the Marys? "

" Take the Marys. A word to them; just think what a boon! "

" Nothing so easy."

Miss Sinquier clasped her hands.

" One has heard of them often, of course."

" Mr. and Mrs. Mary have won repute throughout the realm," Mrs. Sixsmith impressively said, wondering (as middlewoman) what commission she should ask.

" Mrs. Mary, I dare say, is no longer what she was!"

" Mrs. Mary, *aujourd'hui*, is a trifle, perhaps, full-blown, but she's most magnetic still. And a warmer, quicker heart never beat in any breast."

" In her heyday, Sir Oliver—but you wouldn't have seen her, of course."

The baronet's eyes grew extinct.

" In my younger days," he said, " she was come-liness itself . . . full of fun. I well recall her as the ' wife ' in *Macbeth;* I assure you she was positively roguish."

" Being fairly on now in years," Miss Sinquier reflected, " she naturally wouldn't fill very juvenile parts—which would be a blessing."

" She too often does."

" She used to make Paul ill——" Mrs. Sixsmith began, but stopped discreetly. " Oh, listen," she murmured, glancing up towards the nigger band and insouciantly commencing to hum.

" What is it . . .? "

" It's the *Belle of Benares*—

" ' My other females all yellow, fair or black,
       To thy charms shall prostrate fall,
       As every kind of elephant does
       To the white elephant Buitenack.
       And thou alone shall have from me,
       Jimminy, Gomminy, whee, whee, whee,
       The Gomminy, Jimminy, whee.' "

" Serephine, you're eating nothing at all."

" I shall wait for the *pâtisserie*, Sir Oliver."

" Disgraceful."

" Father Francis forbids me meat; it's a little novena he makes me do.

" ' The great Jaw-waw that rules our land,
    And pearly Indian sea,
    Has not such *ab-solute* command
    As thou hast over me,
    With a Jimminy, Gomminy, Gomminy,
    Jimminy, Jimminy, Gomminy, whee.' "

" Apropos of pearls ·. . ." Sir Oliver addressed Miss Sinquier, " I look forward to the privilege before long of inspecting your own."

" They're on her head, Sir Oliver! "

Sir Oliver started as a plate was passed unexpectedly over him from behind.

" Before approaching some City firm, it's possible Lady Dawtry might welcome an opportunity of acquiring this poor child's jewels for herself," Mrs. Sixsmith said.

" Lady Dawtry! "

" Why not? "

" Lady Dawtry seldom wears ornaments; often I wish she would."

" I wonder you don't *insist*."

Sir Oliver fetched a sigh.

" Many's the time," he said, " I've asked her to be a little more spectacular—but she won't."

" How women do vary! " Mrs. Sixsmith covertly smiled.

" To be sure."

" My poor old friend . . .? "

Sir Oliver turned away.

" I notice Miss Peters here to-night," he said.

" Whipsina? "

" With two young men."

" *Un trio n'excite pas de soupçons*, they say."

" They do . . ."

" Have you a programme for presently, Sir Oliver?"

" I've a box at the Kehama."

Miss Sinquier looked tragic.

" It'll have begun! " she said.

" At a variety, the later the better as a rule."

" I never like to miss *any* part."

" My dear, you'll miss very little; besides it's too close to linger over dinner long."

" Toc, toc; I don't find it so," Sir Oliver demurred.

Mrs. Sixsmith plied her fan.

" I feel very much like sitting, *à la* Chaste Suzanne, in the nearest ice-pail! " she declared.

VIII

MARY LODGE, or Maryland, as it was more familiarly known, stood quite at the end of Gardingore Gate, facing the Park.

Half-way down the row, on the Knightsbridge side, you caught a glimpse of it set well back in its strip of garden with a curtain of rustling aspen-trees before the door.

Erected towards the close of the eighteenth century as a retreat for a fallen minister, it had, on his demise, become the residence of a minor member of the reigning Royal House, from whose executors, it had, in due course, passed into the hands of the first histrionic couple in the land.

A gravel sweep leading between a pair of grotesquely attenuated sphinxes conducted, via a fountain, to the plain, sober façade in the Grecian style.

Moving demurely up this approach some few minutes prior to the hour telegraphically specified by the mistress of the house, Miss Sinquier, clad in a light summer dress, with a bow like a great gold butterfly under her chin, pulled the bell of Mary Lodge.

Some day Others would be standing at her own front gate, their hearts a-hammer . . .

A trim manservant answered the door.

" Is Mrs. Mary . . .? "

" Please to come this way."

Miss Sinquier followed him in.

The entrance hall bare but for a porphyry sarcophagus containing visiting cards, and a few stiff chairs, clung obviously to royal tradition still.

To right and left of the broad stairway two colossal battle-pictures, by Uccello, were narrowly divided by a pedestalled recess in which a frowning bust of Mrs. Mary as Medusa was enshrined.

Miss Sinquier, following closely, was shown into a compartment whose windows faced the Park.

"Mrs. Mary has not yet risen from lunch," the man said as he went away. "But she won't be many minutes."

Selecting herself a chair with a back suited to the occasion, Miss Sinquier prepared to wait.

It was an irregularly planned, rather lofty room, connected by a wide arch with other rooms beyond. From the painted boiseries hung glowing Eastern carpets, on which warriors astride fleet-legged fantastic horses were seen to pursue wild animals, that fled helter-skelter through transparent thickets of may. A number of fragile French chairs formed a broken ring about a Louis XVI bed—all fretted, massive pillars of twisted, gilded wood—converted now to be a seat. Persian and Pesaro pottery conserving "eternal" grasses, fans of feathers, strange sea-shells, bits of Blue-John, blocks of malachite, morsels of coral, images of jade littered the *guéridons* and *étagères*. A portrait of Mrs. Mary, by Watts, was suspended above the chimney-place, from whence came the momentous ticking of a clock.

"The old girl's lair, no doubt!" Miss Sinquier reflected, lifting her eyes towards a carved mythological ceiling describing the Zodiac and the Milky Way.

Tongue protruding, face upturned, it was something to mortify her for ever that Mrs. Mary, entering quietly, should so get her unawares.

"Look on your left."

"Oh?"

"And you'll see it; in trine of Mars. The Seventh House. The House of *Marriage*. The House of Happiness."

" Oh! Mrs. Mary! "

" You're fond of astrology? "

" I know very little about the heavenly bodies."

" Ah! *Don't* be too impatient there."

Miss Sinquier stared.

Mrs. Mary was large and robust, with commanding features and an upright carriage. She had a Redfern gown of " navy " blue stuff infinitely laced. One white long hand, curved and jewelled, clung as if paralysed above her breast.

Seating herself majestically, with a glance of invitation to Miss Sinquier to do the same, the eminent actress appraised her visitor slowly with a cold, dry eye.

" And so you're his ' little mouse '! . . ."

" Whose? "

" Sir Oliver's ' second Siddons.' "

" Indeed—— "

" Well, and what is your forte? "

" My forte, Mrs. Mary? "

" Comedy? Tragedy? "

" Either. Both come easy."

" You've no bent? "

" So long as the part is good."

" ' Sarah '! Are you of Jewish stock?—Sarahs sometimes are! "

" Oh dear no."

" Tell me something of the home circle. Have you brothers, sisters? "

" Neither."

" Is your heart free? "

" Quite."

" The Boards, I believe, are new to you? "

" Absolutely."

" Kindly stand."

" I'm five full feet."

" Say, ' Abyssinia.' "

" Abyssinia! "

" As I guessed . . ."

" I was never there."

" Now say ' Joan.' "

" Joan! "

" You're Comedy, my dear. Distinctly! And now sit down."

Miss Sinquier gasped.

" You know with us it's Repertoire, I suppose? "

" Of course."

" In parts such as one would cast Jane Jacks you should score."

" Is she giving up? "

" Unfortunately she's obliged. She's just had another babelet, poor dear."

" What were her parts? "

" In *Bashful Miss Bardine* the governess was one of them."

" Oh! "

" And in *Lara* she was the orphan. That part should suit you well," Mrs. Mary murmured, rising and taking from a cabinet a bundle of printed sheets.

" Is it rags? "

" Rags? "

" May she . . . is she allowed Evening dress? "

" Never mind about her dress. Let me hear how you'd deliver her lines," Mrs. Mary tartly said, placing in Miss Sinquier's hands a brochure of the play.

" I should like to know my cue."

" A twitter of birds is all. You are now in Lord and Lady Lara's garden—near Nice. Begin."

" *How full the hedges are of roses!* "

" Speak up."

" *How full the hedges are of roses! What perfume to be sure.*"

" And don't do that."

" The directions are: ' *she stoops.*' "

" Continue! "

" What's next? "

" A start."

" *Oh! Sir Harry!* "

" Proceed."

Miss Sinquier lodged a complaint.

" How can I when I don't know the plot? "

" What does it matter—the plot? "

" Besides, I feel up to something stronger."

Mrs. Mary caressed the backs of her books.

" Then take the slave in *Arsinoe* and I'll read out the queen."

" These little legs, Mrs. Mary, would look queerly in tights."

" Think less of your costume, dear, do; and learn to do what you're told. Begin! "

" Arsinoe opens."

" Arsi——? So she does. You should understand we're in Egypt, in the halls of Ptolemy Philadelphus, on the banks of the River Nile. I will begin.

Cease . . . Cease your song. Arisba! Lotos! THANKS.
And for thy pains accept this ivory pin . . .
Shall it be said in many-gated Thebes
That Arsinoe's mean?
The desert wind . . .
Hark to't!
Methinks 'twill blow all night;.
Lashing the lebbek trees anent Great Cheops' Pyre;
Tracing sombre shadows o'er its stony walls.
Within the wombats wail
Tearing the scarabs from Prince Kamphé's tomb.
His end was sudden . . . strangely so;
Osiris stalks our land. Kamphé and little Ti (his daugh-
    ter—wife)
Both dead within a week. Ah me, I fear
Some priestly treachery; but see! What crouching shape
    is this? . . . Peace, fool! "

"*I did not speak . . . Oh, Queen.*"
"*ENOUGH. Thou weariest me.*"
"*I go!*"
"*Yet stay! Where is thy Lord?*"
"*Alas! I do not know.*"
"*Then get ye gone—from hence!*"
"*I shall obey.*"

"*. . .* Wail it!" Mrs. Mary rested.
"Wail what, Mrs. Mary?"
"Let me hear that *bey*: O-bey. Sound your menace."
"I shall o-bey."
"*O beating heart*," Mrs. Mary paced stormily the
room, "*Tumultuous throbbing breast. Alas! how art thou
laden? . . .*"
She turned.
"Slave!"
"Me, Mrs. Mary?"
"Come on. Come on."
"Slave's off."
"Pst, girl. Then take *the Duke!*"
"*Fairest——*"
"*High Horus! . . . What! Back from Ethiopia and
the Nubian Army! Is't indeed Ismenias . . .?*"
"*Listen.*"
"*Hast deserted Ptolemy?*"
"*Fairest——*"
"*O Gods of Egypt——*"
"Some one wants you, Mrs. Mary."
"Wants me?"
"Your chauffeur, I think."
"The car, M'm," a servant announced.
"Ah!" she broke off. "An engagement, I fear.
But come and see me again. Come one day to the
theatre. Our stage-door is in Sloop Street, an *impasse*
off the Strand." And Mrs. Mary, gathering up her
skirts, nodded and withdrew.

IX

" Black her great boots! Not I," Miss Sinquier said
to herself as she turned her back on Mary Lodge to
wend her way westward across the Park.

She was to meet Mrs. Sixsmith at a certain club on
Hay Hill towards dusk to learn whether any tempting
offer had been submitted Sir Oliver for her pearls.

" If I chose I suppose I could keep them," she
murmured incoherently to herself as she crossed the
Row.

It was an airless afternoon.

Under the small formal trees sheltering the path
she clapped her sunshade to, and slackened speed.

The rhododendrons, in vivid clumps of new and
subtle colours brushing the ground, were in their
pride. Above, the sky showed purely blue. She walked
on a little way towards Stanhope Gate, when, overcome by the odoriferous fragrance of heliotropes and
xenias, she sank serenely to a bench.

Far off by the Serpentine a woman was preaching
from a tree to a small audience gathered beneath.
How primeval she looked as her arms shot out in
argument, a discarded cock's-feather boa looped to
an upper bough dangling like some dark python in the
air above.

Miss Sinquier sat on until the shadows fell.

She found her friend on reaching Hay Hill in the
midst of muffins and tea.

" I gave you up. I thought you lost," Mrs. Sixsmith
exclaimed, hitching higher her veil with fingers super-
manicured, covered in oxydised metal rings.

" I was dozing in the Park."

" Dreamy kid."

" On my back neck I've such a freckle."

" Did you see Mammy Mary? "

" I did."

" Well? "

" Nothing; she offered me Miss Jacks' leavings."

" Not good enough."

" What of Sir Oliver? "

" I hardly know how to tell you."

" Has he——? "

Mrs. Sixsmith nodded.

" He has had an offer of two thousand pounds,"
she triumphantly said, " for the pearls alone."

" Two thousand pounds! "

" Call it three o's."

" Okh! "

" Consider what commercial credit that means. . . ."

" I shall play Juliet."

" Juliet? "

" I shall have a season."

" Let me take the theatre for you."

" Is it a dream? "

" I will find you actors—great artists."

" Oh, God! "

" And, moreover, I have hopes for the silver too.
Sir Oliver is enchanted with the spoons—the Barnabas
spoon especially. He said he had never seen a finer.
Such a beautiful little Barny, such a rapture of a little
sinner as it is, in every way."

Miss Sinquier's eyes shone.

" I'll have that boy."

" What—what boy? "

" Harold Weathercock."

" You desire him? "

" To be my Romeo, of course."

" It depends if the Dream will release him."

" It must! It shall! "

" I'll peep in on him and sound him, if you like."

" We'll go together."

" Very well."

" Do you know where he lives? "

" In Foreign-Colony Street. He and a friend of his, Noel Nice, share a studio there. Not to paint in, alas! It's to wash."

" What? "

" They've made a little laundry of it. And when they're not acting actually, they wash. Oh! sometimes when Mr. Nice spits across his iron and says Pah! it makes one ill."

" Have they any connection? "

Mrs. Sixsmith bent her eyes to her dress.

" Mr. Sixsmith often sent them things . . . little things," she said. " His linen was his pride. You might annex him, perhaps. He's played Mercutio before."

" Is he handsome? "

" Paul? He's more interesting than handsome. *Unusual*, if you know . . ."

" What *did* you do to separate? "

" I believe I bit him."

" You did! "

" He ran at me with the fire-dogs first."

" I suppose you annoyed him? "

" The cur! "

" Something tells me you're fond of him still."

From her reticule Mrs. Sixsmith took a small note-book and made an entry therein.

" . . . The divine Shakespeare! " she sighed.

" I mean to make a hit with him."

" Listen to me."

" Well? "

" My advice to you is, hire a playhouse—the Cobbler's End, for example—for three round months at a reasonable rent, with a right, should you wish, to sub-let."

" It's so far off."

" Define ' far off.' "

" Blackfriars Bridge."

" I've no doubt by paying a fortune you could find a more central position if you care to wait. The Bolivar Theatre, possibly——; or the Cone . . . At the Cone there's a joy-plank from the auditorium to the stage, so that, should you want to ever, you can come right out into the stalls."

" I want my season at once," Miss Sinquier said.

Mrs. Sixsmith toyed with her rings.

" What do you say," she asked, " to making an informal début (before ' royal ' auspices!) at the Esmé Fisher ' Farewell ' coming off next week? "

" Why not! "

" Some of the stage's brightest ornaments have consented to appear."

" I'd like particulars."

" I'll send a note to the secretary, Miss Willing-horse, straight away," Mrs. Sixsmith murmured, gathering up her constant Juno beneath her arm, and looking about her for some ink.

" Send it later, from the Café Royal."

" I can't go any more to the Café Royal," Mrs. Sixsmith said. " I owe money there . . . To all the waiters."

" Wait till after we've seen the Washingtons."

" The Washingtons? Who are they? "

" Don't you know? "

" Besides, I've a small headache," Mrs. Sixsmith said, selecting herself a quill.

" What can I do to relieve it? " Miss Sinquier wondered, taking up a newspaper as her friend commenced to write.

Heading the agony list some initials caught her eye.

" S——h S——r. Come back. All shall be forgiven," she read.

" I can't epistolise while you make those *unearthly* noises," Mrs. Sixsmith complained.

" I didn't mean to."

" Where are we going to dine? "

" Where is there wonderful to go? "

" How about a grill? "

" I don't mind."

" The Piccadilly? We're both about got up for it." Miss Sinquier rolled her eyes.

" The Grill-room at the Piccadilly isn't going to cure a headache," she remarked.

X

To watch Diana rise blurred above a damp chemise
from a fifth-floor laundry garden in Foreign-Colony
Street, Soho, had brought all Chelsea (and part of
Paris) to study illusive atmospherical effects from the
dizzy drying-ground of those versatile young men
Harold Weathercock and Noel Nice.

Like a necropolis at the Resurrection, or some moody
vision of Blake, would it appear under the evanescent
rays of the moon.

Nighties, as evening fell, would go off into proud
Praxiteles-torsos of Nymphs or Muses: pants and
ready-mades, at a hint of air, would pirouette and
execute a phantom ballet from Don John.

Beyond the clothes-lines was a Pagoda, set up in an
extravagant mood, containing a gilded Buddha—a
thorn and a symbol of unrighteousness to a convent
of Ursulines whose recreation yard was underneath.

Here, at a certain hour when the Mother Superior
was wont to walk round and round her preserves, a
young, bewhiskered man frequently would come
bearing ceremonial offerings of rice or linen newly
washed, and falling flat before the shrine would roll
himself about and beat the ground as if in mortal
anguish of his sins before her fascinated eye. Here,
too, from time to time, festivities would take place—
sauteries (to a piano-organ), or convivial *petits soupers*
after the play.

An iron ladder connected the roof with the work-
rooms and living-rooms below.

Ascending this by the light of the stars, Mrs. Sixsmith and the *New Juliet*, gay from a certain grill,

audaciously advanced, their playful screams rendered inaudible by the sounds of a tricksome waltz wafted down to them from the piano-organ above.

Items of linen nestling close to a line overhead showed palely against the night like roosting doves.

" Help . . . Oh! she's falling," Mrs. Sixsmith screamed. " Are you there, Mr. Nice? "

" Give me your hand," Miss Sinquier begged.

" Should she rick her spine . . ."

" Whew-ps! " Miss Sinquier exclaimed, scrambling to the top.

London, beyond the frail filigree cross on the Ursulines' bleached wall, blazed with light. From the Old Boar and Castle over the way came a perfect flood of it. And all along the curved river-line from Westminster to St. Paul's glittered lamps, lamps, lamps.

Folding an arm about her friend's " wasp " waist, Mrs. Sixsmith whirled her deftly round to a wild street air:

" I like your ways,
I like your style,
You are my darling——"

she hummed as the organ stopped.

" Come to finish the evening? "

A small, thick-set, grizzled man with dark æsthetic eyes and a pinkish nose, the result maybe of continuously tinting it for music-hall purposes, addressed the breathless ladies in a broad, inquiring voice.

" Is that *you*, Mr. Smee? " Mrs. Sixsmith asked, surprised.

" Call me ' Shawn.' "

" We've only come on business."

" Don't! You make me laf."

" Then—do it," Mrs. Sixsmith serenely said, resting her left knee against an empty beer keg

" They're not back from the theatre yet."

" Turn for us till they come."

Mr. Smee dashed from a crimpled brow a wisp of drooping hair.

" By your leave, ladies," he said, " I'll just slip across to the Old Boar and Castle and sample a snack at the bar."

" Don't run off, Mr. Smee. You really mustn't. On tiles, they say, one usually meets with *cats*."

" Oh, my word."

Mrs. Sixsmith placed a hand to her hip in the style of an early John.

" How long is it—say—since we met? " she inquired. " Not since my wedding, I do believe."

" What's become of those kiddy bridesmaids you had? " Mr. Smee warily asked.

" Gerty Gale and Joy Patterson?—I'm sure I don't know."

" Oh, my word! "

" Well, how goes the world with *you*, Mr. Smee? "

" So-so. I've been away on tour. Mildred Milson and Co. Oh! my Lord—it was. No sooner did we get to Buxton—down in Derbyshire—than Miss Milson fell sick and had to be left behind."

" What was wrong with her? "

" Exposure . . . On Bank Holiday some of the company hired a three-horse char-à-banc and drove from Buxton over to Castleton Caves—my hat. What hills!—and from there we went to take a squint at Chatsworth, where Miss Milson came over queer."

" And how does Mrs. Smee? "

" So-so."

" One never sees her now."

" There she sits all day, reading Russian novels. Talk of gloom! "

" Really? "

" Oh, it is! "

" Well . . . I'm fond of thoughtful, theosophical

reading, too, Mr. Smee," Mrs. Sixsmith said. "Madame Blavatsky and Mrs. Annie Besant are both favourites with me."

Mr. Smee jerked an eloquent thumb.

" Who have you brought along? "

" She's a special pal of mine."

" Married? "

" Mon Dieu," Mrs. Sixsmith doubtfully said. " Je crois que c'est une Pucelle."

" Never! " Mr. Smee, completely mystified, hazarded.

" Fie donc. Comme c'est méchant."

" Wee, wee."

Mrs. Sixsmith tittered.

" She's going into management very soon."

" Swank? "

" We seek a Romeo, Mr. Smee."

" Now, now! . . . "

" Don't look like that, Mr. Smee—nobody's asking you," Mrs. Sixsmith murmured.

Mr. Smee scratched reflectively his head.

" Who is it you're after? " he asked.

" We fancied Mr. Weathercock might suit."

" God has given him looks, but no brains," Mr. Smee emphatically declared. " No more brains than a cow in a field."

" His is indeed a charming face," Mrs. Sixsmith sighed. " And as to his brains, Mr. Smee—why, come! "

" Who's to create the countess? " he asked.

" Lady Capulet? It's not determined yet."

" Why not canvass the wife? "

" Has she been in Shakespeare before? "

" From the time she could toddle; in *A Midsummer-Night's Dream*, when not quite two, she was the Bug with gilded wings."

" Pet! "

" Sure . . ."

Mrs. Sixsmith clasped prayerfully her hands.

" And in Mr. Smee," she said, " I see the makings of a fine Friar Lawrence! "

" How's that? "

" With a few choice *concetti*."

" Faith! "

" I see the lonely cell, the chianti-flask, the crucifix . . ."

" Gosh! "

" I see Verona . . . the torrid sky . . . the town ascending, up, up, up. I hear the panting nurse. She knocks. Your priest's eyes glisten. She enters, blouse-a-gape—a thorough coster. You raise your cowl . . . Chianti? She shakes her head. Benedictine? No! no! A little Chartreuse, then? Certainly not! Nothing . . . You squeeze her waist. Her cries ' go through ' Lady Capulet and her daughter in the distant city on their way to mass. Romeo enters. So! " Mrs. Sixsmith broke off as Mr. Weathercock and a curly-headed lad, followed by a swathed woman and a whey-faced child, showed themselves upon the stairs.

Mrs. Sixsmith sought Miss Sinquier's arm.

" Listen to me, my darling! " she said.

" Well? "

" Write."

" What? "

" Write."

" Why? "

" Because I fear we intrude."

"Intrude?" Harold Weathercock exclaimed, coming up. " I assure you it's a treat . . ."

Mrs. Sixsmith threw a sidelong, intriguing glance across her shoulder.

" Who's the cure in plaits? " she demanded.

" It's Little Mary Mant—she's seeing her sister home."

" Oh! . . . Is that Ita? " Mrs. Sixsmith murmured, stepping forward to embrace Miss " Ita Iris " of the Dream.

Miss Sinquier swooped.

" I'm having a season, she, without further preamble, began. " And I want to persuade you to join——"

" Principal? "

" Yes."

" I should like to play for you," Mr. Weathercock said.

" Harold! "

Miss Mant addressed him softly.

" Well? "

" Honey husband . . ."

" Hook it! "

" Give me a cigarette."

" Mary! " her sister called.

" Quick! 'cos of Ita."

" Mary Mant."

Miss Mant tossed disdainfully an ultra-large and pasty-faced head.

" Why must you insult me, Ita? " she bitterly asked. " You *know* I'm Miss Iris."

" I know you're Miss Mant."

" No, I'm not."

" Yes, you are."

" No, I'm *not*."

" I tell you, you are! "

" Liar! "

" M-A-N-T! "

" Oh, stow it," Mr. Smee said. " Put it by."

" I'm Réné Iris."

" Réné Rats."

Mrs. Sixsmith looked detached.

" Is that a wash-tub? " she asked.

" Certainly."

" What's that odd thing floating, like the ghost of a child unborn? "

" It belongs to Mrs. Mary."

" There's a rumour—she refuses a fortune to show herself in Revue."

" With her hearse-horse tread . . ."

" Sh—— Harold worships her."

" Oh, no."

" He sees things in her that we don't, perhaps."

" To some ideas," Mrs. Sixsmith said, " I suppose she's very blooming still . . ."

"If it wasn't for her figure, which is really a disgrace." Miss Iris smiled.

She had a tired mouth, contrasting vividly with the artificial freshness of her teeth.

" When I reach my zenith," she declared, " it's Farewell."

" Shall you assist at poor Esmé Fisher's? "

" A couple of songs—that's all."

Mrs. Sixsmith looked away.

" Naturally," Miss Sinquier was saying, " one can't expect instantly to be a draw. More than—perhaps—just a little! "

"With a man who understands in the Box Office . . ."

" Some one with a big nose and a strong will, eh? "

Mr. Nice lifted a rusty iron and wiped it across his leg.

" In my opinion," he said, " to associate oneself with a sanctified classic is a huge mistake. And why start a season on the tragic tack? "

" Because——"

" Suppose it's a frost? "

" Oh!"

" Suppose your venture fails. Suppose the thing's a drizzle."

" What then? "

"There's a light comedy of mine that should suit you."

" Of yours! "

" Appelled *Sweet Maggie Maguire*."

" Tell me why she was sweet, Mr. Nice," Mrs. Six-smith begged.

" Why she was sweet? I really don't know."

" Was she sentimental? . . . "

" She was an invalid. A bed-ridden beauty . . . and, of course, the hero's a Doctor."

" Oh! my word! "

" Is there anyone at home? " A tired voice came thrilling up from below.

" Who comes? "

Mrs. Sixsmith started.

" It sounds to me like my husband," she said, with an involuntary nervous movement of the hands.

" I forgot," Mr. Weathercock said. " He mentioned he might blow in."

" Oh! "

" I'd take to my heels! " Miss Iris advised.

Mrs. Sixsmith stood transfixed.

The moonlight fell full on her, making her feature look drawn and haggard.

X I

LIKE wildfire the rumour ran. The King had knighted
—he had knighted—by what accident?—Mr. Mary,
in lieu of Mr. Fisher, at Mr. Fisher's own farewell. In
the annals of the stage such an occurrence was unheard
of, unique.

The excitement in the green-room was intense.

" M-m! He is not de first to zell 'is birs-r-rite for a
mess of porridge! " Yvonde Yalta, the playgoers'
darling, remarked as she poised with an extravagant
play of arms, a black glittering bandeau on her short
flaxen hair.

" A mess of pottage! " some one near her said.

" You correct me? Ah, sanx! I am so grateful, so—
so grateful," the charming creature murmured as she
sailed away.

From the auditorium came a suppressed titter.

The curtain had risen some few minutes since on
Mlle. Fanfette and Monsieur Coquelet de Chausse-
pierre of the Théâtre Sans Rancune in the comedietta,
Sydney, or There's No Resisting Him.

" It's extraordinary I've never seen a man knighted,"
a show-girl twittered, " and I've seen a good deal
. . ."

" How do they do them? "

" Like this," a sparkling brunette answered, bestowing a sly pat on the interlocutress with the back
of a brush.

" Of all the common——! "

" Ladies! Ladies! "

" Who was in front at the time? "

" I was! " Mrs. Sixsmith said, who had just peeped
in to exchange a few words with her friend.

" You were? "

" I was selling sweets in the vestibule and saw it all.
Really! If I live to be an old woman I shan't forget it.
Mr. Mary—*Sir Maurice*—was in the lobby chatting
with Sylvester Fry of the *Dispatch*, when the Royal
party arrived. The King instantly noticed him and
sent one of his suite, quite unpremeditatedly, it seemed,
to summon him, and in a trice . . . Oh! . . . and I
never saw the Queen look so charming. She has a gold
dress turning to white through the most exquisite
gradations . . ."

Mrs. Sixsmith was overcome.

" A-wheel," Miss Sinquier's dresser disrespectfully
said, " how was the poor man to tell? Both the bligh-
ters—God forgive me—are equally on their last legs."

Miss Sinquier shivered.

" Is it a good house? " she inquired.

" Splendid! Outside they're flying five ' full '
boards . . . There's not a single vacant place. Poor
Sydney Iphis gave half a guinea for a seat in the
slips."

" Are you here all alone? "

" I'm with Sir Oliver Dawtry," Mrs. Sixsmith
replied, " except when I'm running about! . . . Can
I sell anyone anything? " she inquired, raising sonor-
ously her voice. " Vanilla! Caramel! Chocolate! . . .
Comfits!" she warbled.

" What have you netted? "

" Eighteenpence only, so far;—from such an angel!"

" Comfits, did you say? " a round-faced, piquant
little woman asked.

" Despite disguise! If it isn't Arthurine Smee! "

The actress displayed astonishment.

Nature had thrown up upon her lip and cheek two
big blonde moles that procured for her physiognomy,

somehow or other, an unusual degree of expression.

" My husband has been waiting to hear from you," she said, " as agent to this *Miss Sin*——, the new star with the naughty name, and from all I could make out I understand it would be likely to be a *Double Engagement*."

" This is Miss Sinquier," Mrs. Sixsmith exclaimed. Miss Sinquier blinked.

" Have you done it much? " she asked.

" Often."

" Where? "

" Everywhere."

" For example? "

" I may say I've played Pauline and Portia and Puck . . ."

" Mother-to-Juliet I fear's the best I've to offer."

Mrs. Smee consulted enigmatically the nearest mole in reach of her tongue.

" Were I to play her in ' good preservation,' " she inquired, " I suppose there'd be no objection? "

" Why, none! "

" Just a girlish touch . . ."

" Mrs. Smee defies time," Mrs. Sixsmith remarked.

" My dear, I once was thought to be a very pretty woman. . . . All I can do now is to urge my remains."

Miss Sinquier raised a forefinger.

Voices shivering in altercation issued loudly from a private dressing-room next door.

" What's up? "

" Oh, dear! Oh, dear! " the wardrobe-mistress, entering, said. " Sir Maurice and Mr. Fisher are passing sharp words with a couple of pitchforks."

" What! "

" The ' Farm-players ' sent them over from the Bolivar for their Pig-sty scene—and now poor Mr. Mary, *Sir M'riss*, and Mr. Fisher are fighting it out, and Mrs. Mary, *her ladyship*, has joined the struggle."

" Murder! " called a voice.

" Glory be to God."

Mrs. Sixsmith rolled her eyes.

" Da! " she gasped, as Lady Mary, a trifle dazed
but decked in smiles, came bustling in.

" Oh, Men! Men! Men! " she exclaimed, going off
into a hearty laugh. " Rough angelic brutes! . . ."

She was radiant.

She had a gown of shot brocade, a high lace ruff
and a silver girdle of old German work that had an
ivory missal falling from it.

" Quarrelsome, quarrelling kings," she stuttered,
drifting towards a toilet-table—the very one before
which Miss Sinquier was making her face.

On all sides from every lip rose up a chorus of
congratulations.

" Viva, Lady Mary! "

Touched, responsive, with a gesture springing
immediately from the heart, the consummate Victorian
extended impulsive happy hands.

" God bless you, dears," she said.

" Three cheers for Lady Mary! "

The illustrious woman quashed a tear.

" Am I white behind? " she asked.

" Allow me, milady," the wardrobe-mistress
wheezed.

" I fancy I heard a rip! . . ."

" There must have been quite a scrimmage."

From the orchestra a melodious throb-thrum-
hrob told a " curtain."

" Lady Mary—*you*, Mum," a call-boy chirped.

" Me? "

" Five minutes."

Lady Mary showed distress.

" For goodness sake, my dear," she addressed Miss
Sinquier, "do leave yourself alone. I want the glass."

But Miss Sinquier seemed engrossed.

At her elbow a slip of a " Joy-baby " was holding forth with animation to Mrs. Sixsmith and Mrs. Smee.

" That was one of my dreams," she was saying, " and last night again I had another—in spite of a night-light, too! It began by a ring formed of crags and boulders enclosing a troop of deer—oh, such a herd of them—delicate, distinguished animals with little pom-pom horns, and some had poodles' tails. Sitting behind a rhododendron bush was an old gentleman on a white horse; he never moved a muscle. Suddenly I became aware of a pack of dogs . . . And then, before my very eyes, one of the dogs transformed itself into a giraffe . . ."

" You must have been out to supper."

" It's true I had. Oh, it was a merry meal."

" Who gave it? "

" Dore Davis did: to meet her betrothed—Sir Francis Four."

" What's he like? "

" Don't ask me. It makes one tired to look at him."

" Was it a party? "

" Nothing but literary-people with their Beatrices . . . My dear *the scum!* Half-way through supper Dore got her revolver out and began shooting the glass drops off her chandelier."

" I should like to see her trousseau," Mrs. Sixsmith sighed.

" It isn't up to much. Anything good she sells—on account of bailiffs."

" Pooh! She should treat them all *en reine.*"

Mrs. Smee looked wise.

" Always be civil with bailiffs," she said; " never ruffle them! If you queen a sheriff's officer remember there's no getting rid of him. He clings on—like a poor relation."

" Oh, well," Mrs. Sixsmith replied, " I always treat

the worms *en reine;* not," she added wittily, "that I ever have . . ."

Miss Sinquier twirled herself finally about.

"There," she murmured, "I'm going out into the wings."

"When's your call?"

"After Lady Mary."

For her unofficial first appearance she was resolved to woo the world with a dance—a dance all fearless somersaults and quivering *battements;* a young Hungarian meanwhile recording her movements sensitively upon a violin.

She was looking well in an obedient little ballet skirt that made action a delight. Her hair, piled high in a towering toupee, had a white flower in it.

"Down a step and through an arch." A pierrette who passed her in the corridor directed her to the stage.

It was Miss Ita Iris of the Dream.

Miss Sinquier tingled.

How often on the cold flags of the great church at home had she asked the way before!

"O Lord," she prayed now, "let me conquer. Let me! Amen."

She was in the wings.

Above her, stars sparkled lavishly in a darkling sky, controlled by a bare-armed mechanic who was endeavouring, it seemed, to deliver himself of a moon; craning from a ladder at the risk of his life, he pushed it gently with a big soft hand.

Miss Sinquier turned her eyes to the stage.

The round of applause accorded Lady Mary on her entry was gradually dying away.

From her shelter Miss Sinquier could observe her, in opulent silhouette, perfectly at her ease.

She stood waiting for the last huzzas to subside with bowed head and folded hands—like some great sinner—looking reverently up through her eyelashes at the blue silk hangings of the Royal box.

By degrees all clatter ceased.

Approaching the footlights with a wistful smile, the favourite woman scanned the stalls.

" Now most of you here this afternoon," she intimately began, " I will venture to say, never heard of Judy Jacock. I grant you, certainly, there's nothing very singular in that; for her life, which was a strangely frail one, essentially was obscure. Judy herself was *obscure* . . . And so that is why I say you can't have ever heard of her! . . . Because she was totally unknown. . . . Ah, poor wee waif! alas, she's dead now. Judy's among the angels . . . and the beautiful little elegy which, with your consent, I intend forthwith to submit, is written around her, around little Judy, and around her old Father, her ' *Da* '—James, who was a waiter. And while he was away waiting one day—he used to wipe the plates on the seat of his breeches!—his little Judy died. Ah, poor old James. Poor Sir James. But let the poet," she broke off suddenly, confused, " take up the tale himself, or, rather —to be more specific!—*herself*. For the lines that follow, which are *inédits*, are from the seductive and charming pen of Lady Violet Sleepwell."

Lady Mary coughed, winked archly an eye, and began quite carelessly as if it were Swinburne:

" I never *knew* James Jacock's child . . .
    I knew he *had* a child!
    The daintiest little fairy that ever a father knew.
    She was all contentment . . ."

Miss Sinquier looked away.

To her surprise, lurking behind a property torso of " a Faun," her pigtails roped with beads of scarlet glass, was Miss May Mant.

" Tell me what you are up to? " she asked.

" Sh——! Don't warn Ita! "

" Why should I? "

" I dodged her. Beautifully."

" What for? "

" If she thought I was going on the stage, she'd be simply wild."

" Are you? "

" I intend tacking on in the Pope's Procession."

" That won't be just yet."

" Oh, isn't it wonderful? "

" What? "

" Being here."

" It's rather pleasant."

" Can you feel the boards? "

" A little."

" They go *right* through me. Through my shoes, up my legs, and at my heart they sting."

" Kiss me."

" I love you."

" Pet."

" Do I look interesting? "

" Ever so."

" Would you take me for a Cardinal's comfort? "
Lady Mary lifted up her voice:

" Come, Judy, the angel said,
And took her from her little bed,
And through the air they quickly sped
Until they reached God's throne;
So, there, they dressed her all in white,
They say she was a perfect sight,
Celestial was her mien! "

" Lady Violet Sleepwell admires Ita."

" Indeed."

" She's a victim to chloral."

" Rose-coiffed stood J.
   Amid the choir,
   Celestial-singing ! "

The august artiste glowed.
" Ita thinks she drinks."
" I shouldn't wonder," Miss Sinquier replied, covering her face with her hands.

Through her fingers she could contemplate her accompanist's lanky figure as he stood in the opposite wing busily powdering his nose.

The moment, it seemed, had come.

Yet not quite—the public, who loved tradition, was determined on obtaining an encore.

Lady Mary was prepared to acquiesce.

Curtseying from side to side and wafting kisses to the gods, she announced:

" The Death of Hortense; by *Desire*."

XII

The Source Theatre.

DEAR MOTHER,—I saw your notice in a newspaper
not very long ago, and this morning I came across it
again in the *Dispatch*. Really I don't know what there
can be to " forgive," and as to " coming back! "—
I have undertaken the management of this theatre,
where rehearsals of *Romeo and Juliet* have already begun.
This is the little house where Audrey Anderson made
her début, and where Avize Mendoza made such a hit.
You could imagine nothing cosier or more intimate
if you tried. Father would be charmed (tell him, for,
of course, he sometimes speaks of me in the long *triste*
evenings as he smokes a pipe) with the foyer, which
has a mural design in marquetry, showing Adam and
Eve in the Garden of Eden, sunning themselves by
the side of a well. They say the theatre contains a well
beneath the stage, which is why it's known as the Source.
I have left, I'm glad to say, the hotel, which was getting
dreadfully on my nerves, for a dressing-room here,
where I pass the nights now: an arrangement that
suits me, as I like to be on the spot. A sister of Ita Iris
of the Dream Theatre keeps me company, so that I'm
not a bit solitary. We understand each other to perfection, and I find her helpful to me in many ways.
She is such an affectionate child, and I do not think I
shall regret it. I've decided to have half my teeth taken
out by a man in Knightsbridge—some trial to me, I
fear; but, alas, we've all to carry our cross! I seem to
have nothing but debts. Clothes, *as well* as scenery,
would ruin anyone.

I'm allotting a little box to you and father for the opening night, unless you would prefer two stalls?

The other afternoon I " offered my services " and obtained three curtains at a gala matinée; I wish you could have been at it!

Your devoted Daughter.

I went to the oratory on Sunday; it was nothing but a blaze of candles.

Remember me to Leonard and Gripper—also Kate.

XIII

An absence of ventilation made the room an oven and discouraged sleep. Through the width of skylight, in inert recumbence, she could follow wonderingly the frail pristine tints of dawn. Flushed, rose-barred, it spread above her with fantastic drifting clouds masking the morning stars.

From a neighbouring church a clock struck five.

Miss Sinquier sighed; she had not closed her eyes the whole night through.

" One needs a blind," she mused, " and a pane——"

She looked about her for something to throw.

Cinquecento Italian things—a chest, a crucifix, a huge guitar, a grim carved catafalque all purple sticks and violet legs (Juliet's) crowded the floor.

" A mess of glass . . . and cut my feet . . ." she murmured, gathering about her a *négligé* of oxydised knitted stuff and sauntering out towards the footlights in quest of air.

Notwithstanding the thermometer, she could hear Miss May Mant breathing nasally from behind her door.

The stage was almost dark.

" Verona," set in autumn trees, looked fast asleep. Here and there a campanile shot up, in high relief, backed by a scenic hill, or an umbrella-pine. On a column in the " Market Place " crouched a brazen lion.

An acrobatic impulse took her at the sight of it.

> " Sono pazza per te
> *Si!* Sono pazza, pazza, pazza . . .
> Pazza per amore,"

she warbled, leaping lightly over the footlights into the stalls.

The auditorium, steeped in darkness, felt extinguished, chill.

Making a circuit of the boxes, she found her way up a stairway into the promenade.

Busts of players, busts of poets, busts of peris, interspersed by tall mirrors in gilt-bordered mouldings, smiled on her good-day.

Sinking to a low, sprucely-cushioned seat, she breathed a sigh of content.

Rid of the perpetual frictions of the inevitable *personnel*, she could possess the theatre, for a little while, in quietude to herself.

In the long window boxes, tufts of white daisies inclining to the air brought back to mind a certain meadow, known as *Basings*, a pet haunt with her at home.

At the pond end, in a small coppice, doves cried " Coucoussou-coucoussou " all the day long.

Here, soon a year ago, while weaving herself a garland (she was playing at being Europa with the Saunders' Fifeshire bull; flourishing flowers at it; tempting it with waving poppies; defying it to bear her away from the surrounding stagnance), the realisation of her dramatic gift first discovered itself.

And then, her thoughts tripped on, *he* came, the Rev. George—" just as I was wondering to whom to apply "—and drew all Applethorp to St. Ann-on-the-Hill by the persuasive magnetism of his voice; largely due—so he said—to " scientific production." To the *Bromley Breath!* He never could adequately thank Elizabeth, Mrs. Albert Bromley, for all she had done. No; because words failed . . . Her Institute, for him, would be always " top-o'-the-tree," and when asked, by her, " What tree ? " he had answered with a cryptic look: " She trains them for the stage."

Dear heart! How much he seemed to love 'it. He had known by their green-room names all the leading stars, and could tell, on occasion, little anecdotes of each.

It was he who narrated how Mrs. Mary (as she was then), on the first night of *Gulnara, Queen of the Lattermonians*, got caught in the passenger-lift on the way from her dressing-room to the stage and was obliged to allow her understudy to replace her, which with the utmost *éclat* she did, while Mrs. Mary, who could overhear the salvos from her prison, was driven quite distraught at a triumph that, but for the irony of things, would most certainly have been hers.

Miss Sinquier sighed.

" Which reminds me," she murmured, fixing her eyes upon the storied ceiling, " that I've no one at all, should anything happen to me."

She lay back and considered the inchoate imagery painted in gouache above her.

Hydropic loves with arms outstretched in invitation, ladies in hectic hats and billowing silks, courtiers, lap-dogs, peacocks, etc., all intermingled in the pleasantest way.

As she gazed a great peace fell upon her. Her eyelids closed.

.   .   .   .

" Breakfast! "

Miss May Mant woke her with a start.

" Oh ! "

" I laid it to-day in the stalls. "

" Extraordinary child."

" Crumbs in the boxes, I've noticed, encourage mice. . . . They must come from the spring, I think, under the stage."

" One ought to set a trap! "

" Poor creatures . . . they enjoy a good play, I expect, as much as we do," Miss Mant murmured,

setting down the kettle she was holding and lowering
her cheek graciously for a kiss.

" Well? "

" You were asleep."

" Was I horrid? "

" You looked too perfectly orchidaceous."

" Orchidaceous? "

" Like the little women of Outa-Maro."

Miss Sinquier sat up.

" What is there for breakfast? " she asked.

" Do you like porridge? "

" Oh, Réné! "

Miss Mant raised a bare shoulder and crushed it to
an ear.

" Really," she remarked, " I'm at a loss to know
what to give you, Sally; I sometimes ask myself what
Juliet took . . ."

" Why, potions."

" *Ita* takes tea luke with a lemon; and it makes her
so cross."

" Disgusting."

" A la Russe."

" Is she still away? "

" Yes . . . She writes from a toy bungalow, she
says, with the sea at the very door and a small ship-
wreck lying on the beach."

" What of Paris? "

" I'm Page to him, you said so! "

" With her consent."

" Oh, Ita hates the stage. She's only *on it* of course
to make a match . . . she could have been an Irish
countess had she pleased, only she said it wasn't smart
enough, and it sounded too Sicilian."

" Everyone can't be Roman."

" . . . Oh, she's such a minx! In her letter she writes,
' I don't doubt you'll soon grow tired of the Sally-Sin
Theatre and of dancing attendance on the Fair Sink.' "

" Cat."

" And her Manting ways just to annoy. Mant, Mant, Mant! She does it to humiliate. Whenever the Tirds are in earshot she's sure to begin."

" The Tirds? "

" Llewellyn and Lydia. Lydia Tird has an understanding with my big brother. Poor lad! Just before I left home he took the name of Isadore: Isadore Iris. Oh, when Ita heard! Bill Mant she said and made Llewellyn laugh."

" Oh! "

" And now that Mrs. Sixsmith ' Mants ' me almost as much as Ita."

" Why do you dislike her so much? "

" Cadging creature! "

" Réné? "

" Limpet."

" Réné? "

" Parasite."

" Réné——! "

" Scavenger."

" *Basta!* "

" I know all about her."

" What do you know? "

" If I tell you, I'll have to tell you in French."

" Then tell me in French."

" Elle fait les cornes à son mari! "

" What next? "

" She's *divorcée!* "

" Poor soul."

" Out at *Bois St. Jean*—St. John's Wood—she has a villa."

Miss Sinquier got up.

" Anyway," she murmured.

" Oh, Sally . . ."

" Well? "

" You do love me? "

" Why, *of course.*"

" Let's go presently to a Turkish bath—after rehearsal."

" Not to-day."

" . . . Just for a ' Liver Pack '? "

" No."

" Why not? "

" Because . . . and when you're out, don't, dear, forget a mousetrap! "

XIV

To bring together certain of the dramatic critics (such high arbiters of the stage as Sylvester Fry of the *Dispatch*, Lupin Petrol of *Now*, Amethyst Valer of *Fashion*, Berinthia of *Woodfalls*, the terrible, the embittered Berinthia who was also Angela) cards had been sent out from Foreign-Colony Street, in the comprehensive name of Sir Oliver Dawtry, the famous banker and financier, inviting them to meet the new lessee of the Source.

It was one of those sultry summer nights of electricity and tension, when nerves are apt to explode at almost nothing. Beyond the iron Calvary on the Ursulines' great wall, London flared with lights.

Perched upon a parapet in brilliant solitude, her identity unsuspected by the throng, Miss Sinquier, swathed in black mousseline and nursing a sheaf of calla lilies, surveyed the scene with inexpressive eyes.

" And there was the wind bellowing and we witches wailing: and no Macbeth! " a young man with a voice like cheap scent was saying to a sympathetic journalist for whatever it might be worth. . . .

Miss Sinquier craned her head.

Where were the two " Washingtons "? or the little Iris girl?

By the Buddha shrine, festively decked with lamps, couples were pirouetting to a nigger band, while in the vicinity of the buffet a masked adept was holding a clairaudience of a nature only to be guessed at from afar. An agile negro melody, wild rag-time with passages of almost Wesleyan hymnishness—reminiscent of Georgia gospel-missions; the eighteenth century in the Dutch East Indies—charmed and soothed the ear.

Miss Sinquier jigged her foot.

At their cell windows, as if riveted by the lights and commotion, leaned a few pale nuns.

Poor things!

The call of the world could seldom wholly be quenched!

She started as a fan of seabirds' feathers skimmed her arm.

" Sylvester's come," Mrs. Sixsmith in passing said.

" Oh! "

" Aren't you scared? "

" Scared? "

" You know, he always belittles people. Sylvester traduces everyone; he even crabs his daughter; he damns all he sees."

" Boom! "

" How he got up those narrow stairs is a mystery to me." Mrs. Sixsmith smiled.

Miss Sinquier raised her face towards the bustling stars. An elfish horse-shoe moon, felicitously bright, struck her as auspicious.

" One should bow to it," she said.

" Idolatry! "

" There! look what nodding does."

A blanche bacchante with a top-knot of leaves venturesomely approached.

" I'm Amethyst," she murmured.

" Indeed? "

" Of *Fashion*. You are Miss Sinquier, I take it, whose costumes for Romeo—Renaissance, and ergo à *la mode!*—I so long to hear about."

Miss Sinquier dimpled.

" The frocks," she said, " some of them, will be simply killing."

" I want your first."

" Loose white."

" I suppose, *coiffé de sphinx avec un tortis de perles?* "
Miss Sinquier shook her head.

" No ' Juliet-cap ' of spurious pearls for me," she said.

" You dare to abolish it? "

" I do."

" You excite me."

" Unless the bloom is off the peach, Juliet needs
no nets."

Miss Valer lowered discreetly her voice.

" And your Romeo? " she queried. " He must make
love angelically? "

" He does."

" I admire enormously his friend."

" Mr. Nice? "

" He has such perfect sloth. I love his lazaroni-ness,
his Riva-degli-Schiavoni-ness . . . He's very, very
handsome. But, of course, it cannot last! "

" No? "

" Like an open rose. Have you no sympathy yourself? "

" None."

" That's a pity. An actress . . . she needs a lover:
a sort of husbandina, as it were . . . I always say
Passion tells: *L'amour!* "

Miss Sinquier threw a glance towards Mrs. Sixsmith, who stood listlessly flirting her fan.

" I'm going to the buffet, child," she said.

" Then I think I'll join you."

And drawing her friend's arm within her own, Miss
Sinquier moved away.

" She must belong to more than one weekly! " she
reflected.

" You didn't mention your Old Mechlin scarf, or
your fox-trimmed nightie," Mrs. Sixsmith murmured,
dexterously evading the psychic freedoms of the
masked adept.

" Have you no shame, Paul?" she asked.

" Paul! "

Miss Sinquier wondered.

" Mephisto! I know his parlour tricks . . . though it would only be just, perhaps, to say he did foresee our separation some time before it occurred."

" Oh, how extraordinary."

" Once as I was making ready to pay some calls, in order to frighten me, he caused the hare's foot on my toilet-table to leave its carton sheath and go skipping about the room."

" What ever did you do? "

" My dear, I was disgusted. It really seemed as if the whole of Womanhood was outraged. So, to *punish* him—for revenge—instead of going to a number of houses that day, I went to only one."

" There wouldn't be time? "

" I shall always blame myself . . ."

" Why? "

But a lanthorn falling in flames just then above them put an end to the conversation.

" That's the second I've seen drop," Miss May Mant exclaimed, darting up.

" What have you been up to? "

" Having my bumps examined."

" What! "

" By the masked professor . . . Oh, the things he said; only fancy, he told me I'd cause the death of one both near and dear! Ita's near . . . but she certainly isn't dear—odious cat."

" He must have thought you curiously credulous," Miss Sinquier murmured, turning her head aside.

To her annoyance she perceived the scholarly representative of the *Dispatch*—a man of prodigious size —leaning solidly on a gold-headed cane while appraising her to Sir Oliver Dawtry, from her bebandeaued head to her jewelly shoes.

" She reminds me just a little of some one *de l'Évangile!*" she could hear the great critic say.

" Sylvester! "

" Oh? "

" Should he speak," Mrs. Sixsmith murmured, wincing at the summer lightning that flickered every now and then, " don't forget the mediæval nightie or the Mechlin lace! Five long yards—a cloud . . ."

Miss Sinquier buried her lips in her flowers.

Through the barred windows of the convent opposite certain novices appeared to be enjoying a small saltation among themselves.

Up and down the corridor·to the yearning melody of the minstrel players they twirled, clinging to one another in an ecstasy of delight.

Her fine eyes looked beautiful as, raising them fraught with soul, they met the veteran critic's own.

XV

" O, DEAR God, help me. Hear me, Jesu. Hear me
and forgive me and be offended not if what I ask is
vain . . . soften all hostile hearts and let them love
me—adore me!—O Heaven, help me to please.
Vouchsafe at each *finale* countless curtains; and in the
' Potion Scene,' O Lord, pull me through . . ."

Unwilling to genuflect in the presence of her maid,
who would interpret any unwontedness of gesture as
first-night symptoms of fear, Miss Sinquier lifted her
face towards the bluish light of day that filtered
obliquely through the long glass-plating above.

" There's a cat on the skylight, Smith," was what
she said as her maid with a telegram recalled her
wandering gaze to earth.

It was a telegram from her father.

" Missed conveyance York," she read. " Bishop-
thorpe to-night archiepiscopal blessings."

" Ah, well . . ." she professionally philosophised,
" there'll be *deadheads* besides, I've no doubt."

" Any answer, miss? "

" Go, Smith, to the box office, and say G 2 and 3
(orchestra) have been returned; there's no answer," she
added, moving towards the brightly lit dressing-room
beyond.

Ensconced in an easy chair, before a folding mirror
that, rich in reflections, encompassed her screen-like
about, sat Mrs. Sixsmith pensively polishing her nails.

Miss Sinquier bit her lip.

" I thought——" she began.

" Sh——! Be Juliet now. We're in Verona," Mrs.
Sixsmith exclaimed. " *Fuori* the doors."

410

" Fancy finding *you*."

" Me? "

" What are you doing in *my Italy?* "

Mrs. Sixsmith threw a glance at herself in the glass. " I'm a girl friend," she said; " a Venetian acquaint- ance: someone *Julie* met while paddling in the Adriatic —in fact, *cara cuore*, I'm a daughter of the Doge. Yes; I'm one of the Dolfin-Trons."

" Don't be ridiculous."

" I'm Catarina Dolfin-Tron."

" Kitty Tron! "

" Your own true Kate."

" When are you going round? "

" Let me finish my hands. My manicurist has left me with such claws. . . . Poor little soul! When she came to my wedding-finger she just twiddled her rasp and broke out crying. ' To be filing people's nails,' she said, ' while my husband is filing a petition! ' "

" Wonderful that she could."

" This city has its sadness. Your maid, Smith, while you were in the other room, said, ' Oh, marm, what you must have endured; *one Smith* was enough for me.' "

" Poor Kate! "

" Ah, Julie . . ." Mrs. Sixsmith sighed, when the opening of the door gently was followed by the entry of Mrs. Smee.

" Am I disturbing you? " she asked.

" No, come in."

" I want to tell you my husband isn't himself."

" He's ill? "

" He's not himself."

" In what way? "

" It's a hard thing for a wife to confess. But for a première he's nearly always in wine."

" Is he . . . *much?* "

" I never knew him like it! "

411

Mrs. Sixsmith examined her nails.

" So violent? " she ventured.

" He's more confused, dear, than violent," Mrs.
Smee explained. " He seems to think we're doing
The Tempest; Romeo's tanned breast he takes for
Ferdinand's. ' Mind, Ferdy boy,' I heard him say, ' and
keep the —— out.' Whereupon, his mind wandered
to the Russian plays I love, and he ran through some
of Irina's lines from *The Three Sisters.* ' My soul,' you
know she says, ' my soul is like an expensive piano
which is locked and the key lost.' Ah, there's for you;
Shakespeare never wrote that. He couldn't. Even by
making piano, spinet. O Russia! Russia! land of
Tchekhov, land of Andrief, of Solugub, of Korelenko,
of Artzibashef—Maria Capulet salutes thee! And then
my man was moved to sing. His love, she was in
Otaheite . . . But as soon as he saw me he was back
at *The Tempest* again, calling me Caliban, Countess,
and I don't know what."

" Oh, how disgraceful!"

" After the performance I'll pop home—Home!—
in a drosky and shut him out."

" Meanwhile? "

" He'll pass for a Friar. The Moujik! "

" Still . . ."

" He'll probably be priceless; the masses always
love the man who can make them laugh."

Miss Sinquier moved restlessly towards the door
and looked out.

All was activity.

Plants for the balcony set, of a rambling, twining
nature, together with a quantity of small wicker cages
labelled " Atmospherics," and containing bats, owls,
lizards, etc., were in course of being prepared.

The manageress knit her brows.

" Miss Marquis," she called, " instead of teasing
the animals, I suggest you complete your toilet."

412

" . . . She'd better look sharp! "

Mrs. Smee consulted her notes.

" She reminds me more of a nurse-maid than a nurse," she murmured. " Not what *I* should have chosen for Juliet at all."

" Perhaps not."

" Miss Marquis has no stage presence. And such a poor physique—she's too mean."

" Anyway, Sally's got fine men. I never saw finer fellows. Even the Apothecary! Fancy taking the fatal dose from a lad like that; he makes me want to live."

Mrs. Smee purred.

" To have interesting workmates is everything," she said. " Hughie Huntress, as Producer, seemed quite stunned at the subtle material at his disposal. . . . In fact, he realised from the first, he told me, he *couldn't* ' produce ' all of it."

Mrs. Sixsmith lowered her voice.

" Where did Sally find her Balthasar?" she asked, " and where did she secure her Tybalt? "

" My dear Mrs. Sixsmith, I'm not in the management's secrets, remember, so much as you! "

" Or who put her in the way of Sampson and Gregory? And *where* did she get her Benvolio? "

" Through an agent, I don't doubt."

Mrs. Sixsmith threw a sidelong probing glance in the direction of the door. Already in her heart she felt herself losing her hold. Had the time inevitably come to make out the score?

Through the open door came a squeal.

" Sally, the owls! "

" Leave them, Réné," Miss Sinquier ordered.

" *Dearest*, what diddlies; one has a look of old Sir Oliver! " Miss Mant declared, coming forward into the room.

Clad in a pair of striped " culottes," she had assumed,

notwithstanding sororal remonstrance, the conspicuous livery of Paris.

" I just looked in to thank you, darling," she began, " for all your sweetness and goodness . . . Oh, Sally, when I saw the playbill with my name on it (right in among the gentlemen!) I thought I should have died. Who could have guessed ever it would be a breeches part? "

" Turn round."

" Such jealous murmurings already as there are; a-citizen-of-Verona, an envious super without a line, whispered, as I went by, that my legs in these tissue tights had a look of forced asparagus."

" Nonsense."

" Of course: I knew that, Sally. But devil take me. How I'll hate going back into virginals again; these trousers spoil you for skirts."

" Sprite."

" And I'd a trifling triumph too, darling, which I chose to ignore: just as I was leaving my dressing-room, Jack Whorwood, all dressed up for Tybalt, accosted me with a fatuous, easy smile. ' I want your picture, Miss Iris, with your name on it,' he said. ' Do you?' I said. ' I do,' he said. ' Then I fear you'll have to,' I said. Oh, he was cross! But all the while, Sally, he was speaking I could feel the wolf . . ."

" Better be careful," Mrs. Sixsmith snapped.

" As if I'd cater to his blue besoins! "

" Réné, Réné? "

" Although I snubbed him," Miss Iris murmured, stooping to examine upon the toilet-table a berib-boned aeroplane filled with sweets, " he looked *too* charming! "

Mrs. Smee chafed gently her hands.

" I must return to my Friar," she said.

" He is saying the grossest, the wickedest things! "

" Mr. Smee's sallies at times are not for young ears,"

Mrs. Smee loftily observed. " His witticisms," she added, " aren't for everyone."

" My friend, Miss Tird, who came to watch me dress, was quite upset by his cochonneries! "

" Although your little friend appears scarcely to be nine, she seems *dazed* by her sex and power," Mrs. Smee unfavourably commented.

" I'll have to go, I suppose," Miss Sinquier sighed, " and see how matters stand."

" Prenez garde: for when making up he mostly makes a palette of his hand," Mrs. Sixsmith said. " I happen to know—because one day he caught hold of me."

Mrs. Smee protruded her tongue and drew it slowly in.

" Hist! " she exclaimed.

Along the corridor the call-boy was going his rounds.

" First act beginners," chirped he.

Miss Sinquier quivered.

" . . . Soften all hostile hearts and let them love me . . ." she prayed.

XVI

THE sound of rain-drops falling vigorously upon the glass roof awoke her. A few wind-tossed, fan-shaped leaves tinged with heƈtic autumnal colours spotted marvellously the skylight without, half-screening the pale and monotonous sky beyond.

With a yawn she sat up amid her pillows, cushioning her chin on her knees.

After last night's proceedings the room was a bower of gardenia, heliotrope, and tuberose, whose allied odours during slumber had bewildered juſt a little her head.

Flinging back the bed-clothes, she discovered as she did so a note.

" Sally," she read, " should you be conscious before I return, I'm only gone to market, cordially yours R. Iris. Such mixed verdiƈts! I've arranged the early papers on your dressing-table. I could find no reference to me. This morning there were rat-marks again, and part of a mangled bat."

" Oh, those ' atmospherics' ! " Miss Sinquier complained, finding somnolently her way into the inner room.

Here all was Italy—even the gauze-winged aeroplane filled with sweets had an air of a silver water-fly from some serene trans-Alpine garden.

Dropping to a fine *cassone* she perused with contraƈted brows a small sheaf of notices, the giſt of which bore faint pencilled lines below.

" Her aƈting is a revelation."

" We found her very refreshing."

" There has been nothing like it for years."

416

" Go to the Source."

" An unfeminine Juliet."

" A decadent Juliet."

" . . . The Romeo kiss—you take your broadest fan."

" The kiss in Romeo takes only fifteen minutes . . . ' Some ' kiss! "

" The Romeo kiss will be the talk of the town."

" A distinctive revival."

" I sat at the back of the pit-stalls and trembled."

" Kiss—— "

" The last word in kisses."

" Tio, Tio, Io! Io! jug—jug! "

" Shakespeare as a Cloak."

" A smart Juliet."

" An immoral Juliet."

" Before a house packed to suffocation—— "

" Among those present at the Source last night were"—she looked—" were, Queen Henriette Marie, Duchess of Norwich, Dismalia Duchess of Meath-and-Mann, Lady Di Flattery, Lord and Lady New-blood, Mr. and Lady Caroline Crofts, Sir Gottlieb and Lady Gretel Teuton-Haven, ex-King Bomba, ex-King Kacatogan, ex-Queen of Snowland, ex-Prince Marphise, Hon. Mrs. Mordecai, Lady Wimbush, Lord and Lady Drumliemore, Sir John and Lady Journeyman, Lord and Lady Lonely, Lady Harrier, Feodorowna Lady Meadowbank, Lady Lucy Lacy, Duchess of Netherland and Lady Diana Haviours, Miss Azra, Miss Christine Cross, Sir Francis and Lady Four, Madame Kotzebue, Comtesse Yvonde de Tot, Mlle. de Tot, Duque de Quaranta, Marquesa Pitti-Riffa and Sir Siegfried Seitz."

So . . . she sneezed, all was well!

A success: undoubtedly.

" O God! How quite . . . *delicious!* " she mur-mured, snatching up a cinquecento cope transformed to be a dressing-gown, and faring forth for an airing upon the stage.

At that hour there wasn't a soul.

The darkened auditorium looked wan and eerie, the boxes caves.

The churchyard scene with its unassuming crosses, accentuating the regal sepulchre of the Capulets (and there for that), showed grimly.

" Wisht! " she exclaimed, as a lizard ran over her foot.

Frisking along the footlights, it disappeared down a dark trap-hole.

Had Réné been setting more traps? Upon a mysterious mound by a jam jar full of flowers was a hunk of cheese.

She stood a moment fascinated.

Then bracing herself, head level, hands on hips, she executed a few athletic figures to shake off sleep.

Suddenly there was a cry, a cry that was heard outside the theatre walls, blending half-harmoniously with the London streets.

XVII

THE rich trot of funeral horses died imperceptibly away.

Looking out somewhat furtively from beneath her veil, Mrs. Sixsmith could observe only a few farmers conversing together beneath the immemorial yews of S. Irene.

It was over.

There was nothing left to do but to throw a last glance at the wreaths.

" From the artists and staff of the Source Theatre as a trifling proof of their esteem "—such the large lyre crushing her own " Resurgam." And there also was the Marys' with their motto: " All men and women are merely players. They have their exits and their entrances." And the " Heureuse! " tribute by the sexton's tools—she craned—was Yvonde de Yalta's, it appeared.

" Yvonde de Yalta! "

Mrs. Sixsmith gulped.

" You grieve? "

Canon Sinquier stood beside her.

" I——" she stammered.

" So many tributes," he said.

" Indeed, sir, the flowers are extremely handsome."

" So many crowns and crosses, harps and garlands."

" One has to die for friends to rally! "

" Were you in her company? "

" I, Canon? . . . I never was on the stage in my life! "

" No? "

" My husband never would listen to it: he holds with Newman."

" . . . I don't recollect."

" Besides, I'm no use at acting at all."

" You knew my poor daughter well? "

" I was her protégée . . . that is . . . it was *I* who tried to protect her," Mrs. Sixsmith replied.

" My dear madam."

" Oh, Canon, why was her tomb not in Westminster where so many of her profession are? I was reading somewhere only the other day there are more *actresses* buried there than kings! "

" It may be so."

" Here . . . she is so isolated . . . so lost. Sally loved town."

" Tell me," he begged, " something of her end."

" Indeed, sir——"

" You're too weary? "

" Oh, I *hate* a funeral, Canon! Listening to their Jeremiads."

" You shall take my arm."

" Her father was her cult, Canon. . . . In that she resembled much the irresistible Venetian—*Catarina Dolfin-Tron*."

" Sally seldom wrote."

" Her time, you should remember, was hardly her own."

" Tell me something," he insisted, " of her broken brilliance."

" Only by keening her could I hope to do that."

" One would need to be a Bion. Or a Moschus . . ."

" We laid her, star-like, in the dress-circle—out on Juliet's bier . . . Mr. and Mrs. Smee and her dresser watched . . . Berinthia . . . Sylvester . . . came. I cannot lose from mind how one of the scene-shifters said to me, ' How bonny she looked on the bloody balcony.' "

" My poor darling."

" On the evening of her dissolution, I regret to say, there was a most unseemly fracas in the foyer—some crazy wretch demanding back her money, having booked her place in advance; every one of the staff in tears and too unstrung to heed her. Had it been a box, Canon; or even a stall! But she only paid four shillings."

" Was there anything on my poor child's mind distressing her at all? "

" Not that I'm aware of."

" No little affair . . . ? "

" No . . ."

" Nothing? "

" Your girl was never loose, Canon. She was straight. Sally was straight . . . at least," Mrs. Sixsmith added (with a slight shrug) . . . " to the best of my knowledge, she was! "

" In a life of opportunity . . ."

" Ah, sh——, sir, sh——! "

" Had my daughter debts? "

" Indeed she had . . . she owed me money. Much money. But I won't refer to that . . . Sally owed me one thousand pounds."

" She owed you a thousand pounds? "

" She was infinitely involved."

" Upon what could she spend so much? "

" Her clothes," Mrs. Sixsmith replied with a nervous titter, " for one thing, were exquisite. All from the atelier of the divine Katinka King . . ."

" King? "

" She *knew!* Puss! The white mantilla for the balcony scene alone cost her close on three hundred pounds."

" And where, may I ask, is it now? "

" It disappeared," Mrs. Sixsmith answered, a quick red shooting over her face, " in the general confusion. I hear," she murmured with a little laugh, " they even filched the till! "

" What of the little *ingénue* she took to live with her? "

" May Mant? Her sister is sending her to school—if (that is) she can get her to go! "

" It was her inadvertence, I take it, that caused my daughter's death."

" Indeed, sir, yes. But for her—she had been setting traps! She and a girl called Tird! a charming couple!"

" Oh? "

" Your daughter and she used frequently to take their meals in the boxes, which made, of course, for mice. There was a well, you know, below the stage."

" So she wrote her mother."

Mrs. Sixsmith fumbled in the depths of a beaded pouch.

" There was a letter found in one of her jacket-pockets, Canon," she said. " Perhaps you might care to have it."

" A letter? From whom? "

" A young coster of Covent Garden, who saw your daughter at a stage-farewell."

" Be so good, dear lady, as to inform me of its contents."

" It's quite illiterate," Mrs. Sixsmith murmured, putting back her veil and glancing humorously towards the grave.

" DEAR MISS,

" I seed you at the Fisher Mat. on Friday last and you took my heart a treat. I'm only a young Gallery boy—wot's in the flower trade. But I knows wot I knows—And you're It. Oh Miss! I does want to see you act in Juliet in your own butey-ful ouse, if only you ad a seat as you could spare just for me and a pal o' mine as is alright. I send you some red cars sweet and scenty fresh from Covent Market, your true-gone

" BILL.

" Hoping for tickets."

" Poor lad. Sally would have obliged him, I feel sure," Canon Sinquier said.

" Alas, what ephemeral creatures, Canon, we are!"

" We are in His hands."

" She knew that. Sally's faith never forsook her . . . Oh, Canon, some day perhaps I may come to you to direct me. I'm so soul-sick."

" Is there no one in London to advise you? "

" Nobody at all."

" Indeed? You astonish me."

" I'm perfectly tired of London, Canon! "

" Your husband, no doubt, has his occupation there."

" My husband and I are estranged . . ."

" You've no child? "

" Alas, Canon! I often think . . . sometimes . . . I would like to adopt one. A little country buttercup! Really . . . a dog, even the best of mannered—isn't very *comme il faut*."

" You seek a boy? "

" Mer-cy *no!* Nothing of the sort . . . You quite mistake my meaning."

" Your meaning, madam, was obscure."

" I imply a girl . . . a blonde! And she'd share with me, sir, every facility, every advantage. Her education should be my care."

" What is your age? "

" From thirteen——"

" An orphan? "

" Preferably."

" I will discuss the affair presently with my wife," Canon Sinquier said, turning in meditation his steps towards the wicket-gate.

" Before leaving your charming city, Canon, I should like beyond everything to visit the episcopal Palace: Sally used often to speak of the art-treasures there."

" Art-treasures? "

" Old pictures! "

" Are you an amateur of old pictures? "

" Indeed I am. My husband once—Paul—he paid a perfect fortune for a Dutch painting; and will you believe me, Canon! It was only of the back view of a horse."

" A Cuyp? "

" A Circus—with straw-knots in its tail. It used to hang in Mr. Sixsmith's study; and there it always was! Frankly," she added, brushing a black kid glove to her face, " I used sometimes to wish it would kick."

" If you're remaining here any length of time, there are some portraits at the Deanery that are considered to be of interest, I believe."

" Portraits! "

" Old ecclesiastical ones."

" Oh, Canon? "

" Perhaps you would come quietly to dinner. At which of our inns are you? "

" I'm at the ' Antelope.' "

" I know that my girl would have wished our house to be open to you. You were her friend. Her champion. . . ."

" Dear Canon—don't . . . don't: you mustn't! She's at peace. Nothing can fret her. Nothing shall fret her . . . ever now. And, you know, as a manageress, she was liable to vast vexations."

" My poor pet."

" She's *hors de combat:* free from a calculating and dishonest world; ah, Canon! "

" We shall expect you, then, dear Sally's friend, to dinner this evening at eight," Canon Sinquier murmured as he walked away.

Mrs. Sixsmith put up a large chiffon sunshade and hovered staccato before the dwindling spires and ogee dome of S. Irene.

424

It was one of the finest days imaginable. The sun shone triumphantly in the midst of a cloudless sky.

She would loiter awhile among the bougainvillæas and dark, spreading laurels of the Cathedral green, trespassing obtusely now and then into quiet gardens, through tall wrought-iron gates.

New visions and possibilities rare rose in her mind.

With Sally still, she could do a lot. Through her she would be received with honours into the courtly circles of the Close.

Those fine palatial houses, she reflected, must be full of wealth . . . old Caroline plate and gorgeous green Limoges: Sally indeed had proved it! The day she had opened her heart in the Café Royal she had spoken of a massive tureen *too heavy even to hold*.

Mrs. Sixsmith's eyes grew big.

Her lost friend's father wished for anecdotes, anecdotes of her " broken brilliance"; he should have them. She saw herself indulging him with " Salliana," wrapped in a white mantilla of old Mechlin lace.

An invitation from Canon and Mrs. Sinquier should be adroitly played for to-night: " And once in the house! . . ." she schemed, starting, as a peacock, symbol of S. Irene, stretched from a bougainvillæa-shrouded wall its sapphire neck at her as if to peck.

Her thoughts raced on.

On a near hill beyond the river reach the sombre little church of S. Ann changed to a thing of fancy against a yellowing sky.

From all sides, seldom in unison, pealed forth bells. In fine religious gaiety struck S. Mary, contrasting clearly with the bumble-dumble of S. Mark. S. Elizabeth and S. Sebastian in Flower Street seemed in high dispute, while across the sunset water S. Ann-on-the-Hill did nothing but complain. Near by S. Nicaise, half-paralysed and impotent, scarcely shook. Then triumphant, in a hurricane of sound, S. Irene hushed the lot.

Mrs. Sixsmith fetched a long, calm breath.

It was already the hour he had said.

" And my experience tells me," she murmured, as she took her way towards the Deanery, " that with opportunity and time he may hope to succeed to Sir Oliver."